GRAECO~ROMAN AREA
in time of
Constantine

BY FRANK G. SLAUGHTER

Constantine

The Purple Quest

A Savage Place

Upon This Rock

Devil's Harvest

Tomorrow's Miracle

David: Warrior and King

The Curse of Jezebel

Epidemic!

Pilgrims in Paradise

The Land and the Promise

Lorena

The Crown and the Cross

The Thorn of Arimathea

Daybreak

The Mapmaker

Sword and Scalpel

The Warrior

The Scarlet Cord

Flight from Natchez

The Healer

Apalachee Gold

The Song of Ruth

Storm Haven

The Galileans

East Side General

Fort Everglades

The Road to Bithynia

The Stubborn Heart

Immortal Magyar

Divine Mistress

Sangaree

Medicine for Moderns

The Golden Isle

The New Science of Surgery

In a Dark Garden

A Touch of Glory

Battle Surgeon

Air Surgeon

Spencer Brade, M.D.

That None Should Die

UNDER PENNAME C. V. TERRY

Buccaneer Surgeon

The Deadly Lady of
   Madagascar

Darien Venture

The Golden Ones

CONSTANTINE

Constantine

THE MIRACLE OF
THE FLAMING CROSS

by
Frank G. Slaughter

DOUBLEDAY & COMPANY, INC.
GARDEN CITY, NEW YORK

FOR MY WIFE, JANE
*to whom my first novel was dedicated
forty-five books ago*

ROMAN EMPERORS, A.D. 275–337

TACITUS	A.D. 275–276
PROBUS	A.D. 276–282
CARUS, CARINUS, NUMERIAN	A.D. 282–284
DIOCLETIAN	A.D. 284–305
MAXIMIAN (Co-Emperor)	A.D. 286–305
GALERIUS, CONSTANTIUS CHLORUS	A.D. 305–306
GALERIUS, SEVERUS, MAXENTIUS, LICINIUS, MAXIMIN DAIA, CONSTANTINE	A.D. 306–323
CONSTANTINE, THE GREAT	A.D. 323–337

THE HOUSE OF CONSTANTINE

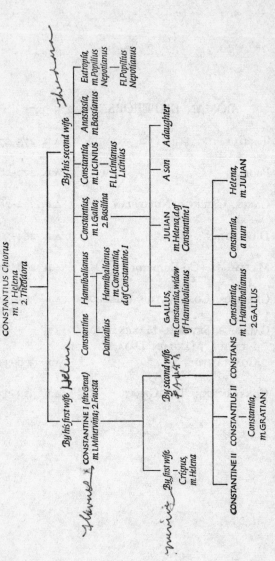

From *A Manual of Ancient History*, by George Rawlinson, Harper & Brothers, New York, 1869.

CONSTANTINE

1

I<small>T WAS A DAY</small> to turn a boy's thoughts away from the school-room—where he had spent the morning at the feet of his tutor, old Lucullus—and the packet of scrolls slung over his shoulder by a strap looped around his wrist. As he walked along in the warm spring sunlight, kicking up the dust of the street in little puffs with his sandals, the thoughts of Flavius Valerius Constantinus—known to his friends as Constantine, the Greek variant of his name—was far away from Naissus* and the Dalmatian uplands where he had been born and had spent his childhood. In his imagination, he was hotly pursuing a band of fleeing Visigoths, leading his *turma* of thirty-two mounted fighting men in a slashing attack that sent the enemy reeling back and opened a breach in their lines which the legions, doggedly advancing on foot behind him, could turn into a mortal wound.

Just now changing from boy to youth, Constantine moved with the coltish grace that came from limbs growing faster than the body to which they were attached. He never thought of himself as any-thing but the leader of the *turma*, except perhaps in larger actions when he would command an entire regiment, or *ala*, made up of twelve *turmae* in a single formation. For after all, was he not the son of Emperor Diocletian's most famous general, Constantius Chlorus? And of royal birth as well through descent from the Em-peror Claudius Gothicus, who had defeated a south-driving Gothic horde a few years before Constantine was born, sending them reeling in retreat up the Vardar Valley, until finally he was able to pin them down before this very city of Naissus and destroy them?

From a low rise in the homeward road, Constantine paused to

---

* Nis

look down upon the scene of the great battle that had ended the campaign, freeing Thessalonica from siege and rescuing Greece, Rhodes, Cyprus and the whole Ionian coast from the heavy hand of the ruthless Teutonic invader. He stood proudly erect for, in his imagination, he was now Emperor Claudius himself, receiving reports of the fighting from the tribunes commanding the legions and sending couriers back with orders that spelled final doom for the invaders.

The city of Naissus and the Dalmatian uplands around it were the only world Constantine knew intimately. But his vivid capacity for fancy left him free to roam the whole range of the Roman Empire, stretching from Hadrian's Wall across Britain in the Northwest to the lands of Persia beyond the Euphrates in the East, as well as from the Danube in the North to the cataracts of the Nile far to the South in Egypt.

Most often Constantine placed himself at the eastern center of the Empire, the palace of the Emperor Diocletian at Nicomedia in the beautiful province of Bithynia, whose shores were washed by the warm waters of the Euxine—or Black—Sea. But sometimes he was at Mediolanum—or Milan—in northern Italy, where the Co-Emperor Maximian held his court and ruled the Empire's western half. For as the descendant of an Emperor, he fully expected one day to wear the purple cloak of an Augustus and rule from one of the two capitals—if not both.

To the east, Constantine could see a familiar dark irregular line on the horizon marking the Haemus mountain range where his father and his great-uncle Marios had taken him on a hunting trip the spring before. A former companion-in-arms of Emperor Diocletian, Constantius ranked high among the Roman generals and was presently governor of a province in Dalmatia, the rugged seacoast area lying between the Danube bastions of Pannonia and Greece to the south. Busy with the affairs of government, Constantius rarely had a chance to visit Naissus anymore, however, and the boy sensed that this was somehow connected with the fact that his mother, Helena, was only a *concubina*—though legally married to his father.

Fiercely he reminded himself once again that, though not of noble birth, his mother's family was important in Drepanum, the Bithynian city that was the family seat—as well as in the capital city of

Nicomedia not far away. And he knew that his great-uncle Marios, though little older than Helena, had served ably in the army with his father, until crippled by a sword thrust while fighting the Persians on the banks of the river Tigris.

A more inquiring mind might have wondered why he and his mother lived here in Naissus instead of with his father at the capital of the district. But it was enough for Constantine that the city had been the site of the famous victory of his imperial ancestor, that it was a pleasant place near where two rivers joined to form a tributary flowing north to the Danube and the frontier with the Germanic tribes; and that Constantius had promised to let him begin his military training soon.

A flash of sunlight reflected from the copper plates forming its roof called Constantine's attention to a small temple not far from the center of the town, where two highways crossed. Once the temple had been dedicated to Asklepios, the Greek god of healing, but lately had been used as a meeting place by that strange sect known as Christians.

He knew his mother sympathized with these often persecuted people. He had been intrigued, too, by the stories his fellow schoolmates told of strange and horrible rites in which, it was said, blood was drunk by the participants and the most depraved of orgies occurred. But when he and several other boys had crept into the temple one day, after finding the door ajar, they had seen nothing more terrifying than a faded wall painting of a man crucified upon a rude wooden cross, above which had been painted a strange emblem Constantine had never seen before. After that he had dismissed the Christians without another thought, for Mithras and the Emperor were the soldiers' gods. And when the time came for him to think of such things, he had no doubt that he would follow the traditions of the Roman army.

Constantine remembered noticing two horsemen approaching Naissus from the east just before his attention had been attracted by the roof of the temple. When he looked more closely now, he saw that they were nearing the center of the town and hurried down the hill, thinking they might be couriers of the Imperial Post by which mail and important passengers were carried throughout the Empire.

Sometimes, especially when trouble flared on the frontier, he and

the other schoolboys would linger after classes at the yard of the
inn beside the crossroads, eager to hear the stories told by the dust-
covered couriers, as they hurriedly ate their meat, bread and wine
while waiting for a change of mount. But except for the upstart
Carausius, who had seized the province of Britain while Diocletian
and Maximian had been busy with rebellion elsewhere, and an occasional sporadic outburst from the peasant rebels of Gaul called the
Bagaudae, the frontiers of the Empire were quiet at the moment.

As he walked along the familiar street in the warm sunshine,
Constantine once again let his thoughts race with his *turma,* as he
led them in a charge. Then a clod of dirt struck his shoulder and
he whirled to find himself facing a group of jeering boys, led by
an older and larger one. They had obviously been waiting to hem
him in where the wall of the butcher shop at his back cut off
escape and, engrossed in fancy, he had let them catch him unawares.

II

*"Nothus—*bastard." The largest of the boys spat the word at Constantine, his broad peasant face with its small piggish eyes con-
tracted in a sneer.

"Let me pass, Trophimus!" Constantine ignored the epithet, as his
eyes moved from one to another of his captors in a quick scanning
glance before coming to rest once again upon the largest boy. In
that rapid appraisal he was able to decide that Trophimus was the
aggressor—as he had been on numerous other occasions—and that
with him defeated the others would not be likely to intervene.

"I'm not alone now," the larger boy boasted. "We are four against
one."

"Tell us the story of your ancestor, the Emperor Claudius," another of the boys taunted, but Constantine ignored him, his eyes
never leaving the one called Trophimus.

Absorbed in the drama in which they were engaged, none of the
boys noticed the approach of the two horsemen Constantine had
seen entering the town. When the shorter of the two started to
spur his horse forward to break up the incipient fight, however, his

companion reached out a restraining hand to hold him back. The second man was taller and broader of shoulder than the first and, though the riding cloak he wore as protection against dust hid his uniform and his rank, soldierly bearing and the habit of command were evident in the way he sat his horse and the carriage of his body.

"Nay, Marios," he said softly. "Let us see how the boy handles himself."

"Against such odds?"

"He will know worse."

Constantine spoke again, interrupting any further words the two travelers might have spoken. "You are four and I am but one," he pointed out to those who threatened him. "I will challenge each of you to single combat, one at a time, beginning with this tub of lard before me."

The youth called Trophimus flushed at the taunt but still hesitated, not certain whether the others would follow him. Then realizing that they were waiting for him to make the first move, his right hand darted to his belt and came up clenching the handle of a knife. It was not a dagger but a short blade with a wooden handle, such as butchers used to trim off the lean meat beside the spine of a beef or a hog. But against an unarmed boy, it was a dangerous weapon, nevertheless.

Now it was the second of the travelers who started to spur forward, but the swift ruthlessness of Constantine's action in the face of the threatening knife took care of the situation long before he could intervene. And when the rider saw that the boy was quite able to fend for himself, he reined in his horse again, though watching closely and ready to act, if any of the group chose to attack.

As the blade of the knife flashed in the sunlight, Constantine moved, covering the short distance separating him from the youth called Trophimus in two swift steps. At the same moment, he swung the packet of scrolls he had carried over his shoulder by the end of the heavy strap holding them together. He was careful to keep clear of the knife, but his would-be attacker had been so startled by the speed with which his intended prey suddenly became the hunter that he had no time to use the weapon.

Swung at the end of the strap—as barbarians swung the spike-studded iron balls attached to chains, called *matteae,* for close fighting—the packet of scrolls struck the boy called Trophimus on the wrist, sending the knife spinning through the air. Following up his advantage, Constantine slammed into his opponent with the full weight of his body behind an outthrust shoulder, spinning Trophimus around and sending him crashing to the ground.

"Who's next?" Constantine taunted the others as, howling with pain, Trophimus scuttled crablike for the open door of the butcher shop, which belonged to his father.

"You, Siscal" he addressed the boy who had gibed about his relationship with Emperor Claudius Gothicus. "How is it that you are among such as these, when I counted you as my friend?"

"Trophimus said we would only make fun of you," the boy mumbled. "None of us knew he had a knife."

Constantine was stooping to pick up the knife, when a fat man, his jowls beetling with rage, charged through the door of the butcher shop with a meat cleaver in his hand.

"Caught redhanded!" he shouted. "I'll teach you to attack others with knives."

Before Constantine could protest his innocence, the shorter of the two onlookers spurred his horse forward, drawing a long dagger such as travelers often wore for protection against thieves.

"Drop the cleaver!" the man ordered and, when the butcher did not immediately obey, pricked his beefy neck with the dagger, bringing a howl of pain and rage, but also the release of the cleaver.

"That boy attacked my son, sir," the butcher bellowed. "See? He still has the knife in his hand."

"It was your son who drew the knife." The second man spoke quietly and Constantine turned to look at him for the first time, a sudden look of happiness glowing in his eyes.

"That is a lie!" The butcher spluttered. "He still has the—"

"Do you give the lie to Caesar Constantius?" The man with the dagger gave the butcher another prick.

"Cae—" The butcher goggled at the second rider and, his knees suddenly turning to water, sagged to the ground. "But noble—"

"Hand him the knife, Flavius." Constantius addressed his son in the same quiet voice. "And also his cleaver."

Constantine picked up the cleaver and gave the two implements to the butcher, but the man's fingers were trembling so much that he was barely able to hold them.

"Whose initials are carved in the wood of the handles?" Constantius demanded of the butcher.

The man looked down at the wooden handles and the red tide of anger surged once again into his face, replacing the pallor of fear. "They are mine," he mumbled. "But—"

"Your son drew the knife—one of your butcher tools, I presume—on my son," Constantius said contemptuously.

"Your son!" The butcher looked as if he were going to faint. "But they say—"

"Whoever *they* are, you can now set them aright," Constantius said curtly. "Flavius Valerius Constantinus is my son, born in holy wedlock."

He swung down from his horse in a single lithe movement and flung back his riding cloak, revealing the purple of an officer of high rank. A murmur of awe went up from the small knot of spectators, but he ignored them and, tossing the reins of his horse to his companion, gave Constantine a quick grip of affection upon the arm.

"I trust you usually put your scrolls to better use," he said with a smile. "Though perhaps I've been overlooking a valuable weapon for my troops."

"I never used them this way before." Constantine's pride in his handsome father shone in his eyes. "Master Lucullus will probably cane me tomorrow, but it was worth it." He turned to the other man. "May I lead father's horse, Uncle Marios?"

"Of course." Marios tossed him the reins, which he caught expertly.

"Can you stay with us long this time, Father?" Constantine asked as they left the center of town.

"Only for the night, I'm afraid, but I have important news. Is your mother at home?"

"She will be soon, if she isn't already. She sometimes goes at this time of day to pray in the temple over there." Constantine nodded toward the small structure with the copper roof. "Only they call it a church now."

"Do I gather that you don't approve?"

Constantine shrugged. "Christians are good people: Mother likes them. But Mithras is the soldier's god and the Emperor requires the worship of Jupiter."

"So he does," Constantius agreed soberly. "Perhaps it is still too early for you to make a choice. There will be enough time later, when you are a soldier yourself."

Constantine forgot about any question of religion in the excitement of another subject, his own military career. Since he was a small boy, playing with a wooden sword carved for him by his great-uncle Marios, who had been his father's aide until the wound had ended his military career, there had never been any question about his following in his father's steps as a Roman officer. And though he had confided his very secret ambition to no one else, he had never doubted for a moment that he would one day become Augustus—Emperor—as his illustrious ancestor Claudius Gothicus had been.

"Are you really a Caesar, Father?" Constantine asked.

"Yes. I was invested with the purple four days ago in Nicomedia, by Emperor Diocletian himself."

"I wish I could have been there! It must have been a sight to see!"

"It was. Galerius and I stood side by side while the Emperor gave us our purple cloaks and named each of us Filius Augusti—adoptive sons of Diocletian himself."

"Why General Galerius? Everyone knows you would be the choice of the legions to command all the forces of the Empire, if it were left up to the soldiers themselves."

"Diocletian will rue the day he let Galerius Valerius Maximianus get a foot in the door," Marios said dourly. "It was bad enough when he gave half of the Empire to Maximian. Now he must needs divide it into four parts for his generals to squabble over, when your father could have held everything together himself."

Constantine was fairly bursting with questions, but they had reached the small villa where he and his mother lived with only a pair of servants. Helena came to the door to greet them and when he saw the light in the eyes of his tall and beautiful mother at the sight of his father and the way Constantius went to take her in his arms for the kiss of greeting, some of the vague feeling of apprehension that had disturbed the boy during the brief conversation with his father began to fade.

Even here at Naissus, a good week's journey on horseback from Diocletian's eastern capital of Nicomedia in Bithynia—and, it seemed to the boy, half the world away from storied Rome—news came quickly. Constantine was quite familiar with the plan of succession devised by Diocletian, when he had become Augustus a little over six years earlier.

The shrewd peasant brain of Diocletian had seen that a division of both power and responsibility was necessary if he were to maintain peace from the district of the often rebellious Picts in northern Britain to the domain of the equally militant Sassanid kings in Persia. Characteristically his solution had been simple. By sharing rule of the Empire's western half with another general named Maximian—who took the surname Herculius to please the soldier's god that was also patron deity of Rome—Diocletian hoped to remove the temptation of ambition which had caused so much turmoil over the past century. But he had strengthened the ambitious plan by retaining final control, as Senior Augustus, while at the same time taking a completely unheard-of further step in announcing his intention to rule only for twenty years and forcing his Co-Emperor Maximian to agree to relinquish the title of Augustus at the end of a similar period. Completing the plan, Diocletian had also promised to name, well before the end of his twenty-year reign, the two Caesars who would eventually succeed to the title of Augustus. The Emperor had been as good as his word, too, by designating Constantius and Galerius Caesars and, as Filii Augusti, Emperors-to-be.

III

On other occasions when Constantius had visited them—farther and farther apart of late though they had been—the small villa had been filled with merriment and laughter while they lingered in the *triclinium,* or dining chamber, for wine and sweet cakes after dinner. Tonight, things were different and his mother and father treated each other a little like two people forced to fence with naked blades when neither wished to hurt the other. Finally, after a long silence when no one seemed willing to speak, Constantine could stand the strained atmosphere no longer.

"Where will you reign as Caesar, Father?" he asked. "Here in Illyricum?"

"No, Son. I have been given the Prefecture of Gaul."

"The land of the barbarians!" Helena cried.

"Gaul is no longer populated by barbarians, Helena," Constantius protested. "After all, Julius Caesar conquered it more than three hundred years ago in the days of the Republic."

"The only trouble was that Caesar was bewitched by a Queen of Egypt named Cleopatra and let the Gauls get out from under his thumb," Marios said. "No one has quite been able to hold them in since."

"My palace will be at Augusta Treverorum—they call it Treves* in Gaul," Constantius explained. "But my main concern will be farther west. The rebel emperor, Carausius, has been boasting that he will soon rule Gaul as well as Britain."

"Lucullus told us about him," Constantine said eagerly. "I'll wager he won't last long when you start after him, Father."

"That is my hope." Constantius reached out to ruffle the boy's dark hair. "I take it you know the story then?"

"Lucullus says Carausius betrayed the Emperor's trust after he was put in charge of the Classis Britannia."

"Carausius did take the fleet that guards the Fretum Gallicum —the channel between Britain and Gaul—and use it to set himself up as emperor," Constantius agreed.

"But why did Emperor Diocletian wait so long to put down a usurper, when you could do it in a few months?" Constantine asked.

"They claim Britain is too far away," Marios said, "but the real truth is so many of the generals are jealous of your father that they persuaded the Emperor to keep him governor of a province, instead of giving him a prefecture to rule, as the descendant of an emperor deserves."

"Nay," Constantius demurred mildly. "It was only a little over twenty years ago that Claudius Gothicus defeated the Teutons on the plains before this very city, after they had overrun the country

* Trier

as far south as Macedonia and Greece and even taken Cyprus and
Crete. The Danube frontier had to be secured first and then the
Rhine frontier had to be brought under control. Now that Maximian
has the Rhine firmly in hand, we can turn our attention elsewhere."

"Must there always be war, and suffering?" Helena had barely
spoken during the spirited discussion, except to make the comment
about the barbarians.

"We cannot let them push us out of Roman territory," Marios
protested.

"Why not, when it originally belonged to them? We could all dwell
together in peace, if we would only respect each other's rights."

"What sort of talk is this from the wife of a Caesar and a Filius
Augusti?" Marios stopped suddenly. "I mean—"

"You're right, Helena." Constantine had the strange feeling that
his father was speaking so his Uncle Marios would not say any
more, though he had no idea what might have been revealed. "Soc-
rates and Plato knew the answer to maintaining peace more than
five hundred years ago, but we are human and, I am afraid, unable
to save ourselves most of the time."

"The Christians believe the Son of God gave up his life as a
ransom for anyone who wishes to earn the right to eternal life
by believing in him," Helena said.

"I must confess that I find their beliefs attractive," Constantius
admitted. "Though they are not much different from the principles
that govern those of us who worship Mithras. But I am not sure
they would be satisfactory as a means of governing an empire."

"Are you a Christian, Helena?" Marios demanded.

"No, but I could easily be."

"Don't," Marios advised. "Galerius hates them. Now that Diocletian has made him a Caesar, I look for him to start persecuting the
followers of the Jewish rabbi any day."

"But why?" Helena protested.

"Politics! What else? With a new court to establish and people
fawning over him, Galerius will have to raise taxes. Nothing takes
people's minds off such things like a good scapegoat—and the
blacker the better."

"But why persecute people who are harmless? I've never heard a single word in the teachings of Jesus that urges one person to hurt another."

"Marios is not saying exactly what he means, Helena," Constantius said quietly. "Diocletian believes dividing the Empire into four prefectures, with a strong ruler in each, will prevent war and bloodshed between those who rule in each region. Perhaps it will, at least as long as he is alive. But Maximian is weak and he has an ambitious son in Maxentius—"

A snort of disgust from Marios interrupted him. "You mean a serpent hiding in the grass waiting to strike, don't you?"

"Not every man is fortunate in having such a fine son as Helena has given me," Constantius agreed, rumpling Constantine's hair once again. "As for Galerius, he no doubt expects to rule the whole Empire after Diocletian abdicates and that means destroying me, by whatever means he can find."

"I'll wager it was Galerius who persuaded the Emperor to send you to Gaul," Marios said. "He knows that nothing is more difficult than conducting a military operation across a stormy body of water like the channel between Gaul and Britain. And if the Rhine garrisons have to be depleted for the expedition against Carausius, the Franks will surely strike southward again."

"Then it is true that more than military reasons are behind your being sent to Gaul and Britain, Constantius?" Helena asked.

"I told you there was no point in trying to deceive her, or the boy." Marios turned and spoke directly to Constantine. "That's why your task is so important, Flavius."

Constantine—only his immediate family ever called him by his given name of Flavius—looked blank. "What your Uncle Marios is telling you in his own blunt way," his father explained, "is that you are going to Nicomedia with him tomorrow to begin your military training."

The boy was stunned by the news for even his rosiest imaginings had not taken him to Nicomedia until he was several years older.

"And that everyone will try to find fault in you because your father will one day become an Augustus," Marios added.

"Will he be safe?" Helena asked quickly.

"Diocletian has given me his promise that my son's rights will be guarded," Constantius assured her. "I insisted upon that before I agreed to his going to Nicomedia. Naturally he will receive no more favor than the other young officers training there."

IV

It was well after midnight when Constantine awakened. He'd had trouble going to sleep, excited by the news that he was about to become an officer-cadet, starting the upward climb which he confidently expected would eventually win him the purple cloak of a Caesar, or even an Augustus.

In the hour or more while he lay awake, Constantine had come to a number of decisions. First, he must work hard at Nicomedia, so he would be commissioned as a tribune and given a command. Next he must earn the respect of Emperor Diocletian, for everyone knew that when the aging ruler abdicated, the present Caesars would become Augusti and in turn would appoint Caesars to succeed themselves. Sobered by these thoughts and his own responsibilities, he finally drifted off to sleep and had not even awakened when Marios had come to his own couch in the same room—the villa not being very large.

His uncle's snoring must have awakened him, he decided now, and feeling thirsty he got up from the couch and padded across the garden barefooted to the kitchen, where the servants always kept a crock of water filled from the nearby well. The house was dark, though the rising moon illuminated faintly the garden around which it was built in the shape of a rectangle with one side open. From long experience Constantine was able to find his way to the kitchen and drink deeply from the crock without having to light another candle from the one that burned all night in the *triclinium*, so there would be a flame in the morning with which to light fires.

His thirst satisfied, he was returning to the sleeping quarters by way of the *atrium*, the large room at the front of the house, when the murmur of voices brought him up short. He recognized the tones of his father and his mother and was turning to creep unobserved to his room by the route he had used to reach the kitchen, when his father's voice rose suddenly and he was able to distinguish the words.

"I can still give it all up, dearest," Constantius was saying to Helena. "Diocletian wrote the decree of divorcement himself, but I insisted on coming here with it before I made a final decision."

"When will the marriage to Theodora take place?"

"When I reach Milan. Maximian and his court are there."

The names were not strange to Constantine. Theodora, the stepdaughter of the Emperor Maximian, was said to possess great beauty. She was still unmarried, however, and what Constantine had overheard could only mean that his father was divorcing his *concubina* to make way for a marriage more favorable to the promotion of his own career, now that he was Caesar and Filius Augusti, with the prospect of one day becoming Augustus. Shaken by his father's words, Constantine felt a flood of anger and pain surge through him—anger that Constantius would even consider divorcing his mother for political reasons, and pain that the man he had idolized above all others should turn out to be moved by the same impulses that governed most men.

"You must not even think of refusing to go through with the marriage," Helena said and Constantine wondered how she could speak so calmly when their whole world was being destroyed.

"But it is not right that I should put you away, as if you were a dancing girl hired for the night," Constantius protested.

"We must think of your career more than my feelings, and Flavius' future most of all," Helena said quietly. "What would happen if you refused to accept the decree of divorcement and marry Theodora?"

"Rome has no place for a Caesar who rebels against the Augustus who named him."

"Then neither you nor I have any choice."

"My heart will be broken. Even the thought of divorcing you causes me pain."

"But can either of us sacrifice less for our son?"

There was a long silence, broken only by his mother's quiet sobbing and his father's murmuring voice as he sought to comfort her. Numbed beyond all feeling and fighting against the urge to hate the father who until a few moments ago had been his only god, Constantine crept back to his couch. He was still awake almost an hour later when his father came to the room but shut his eyes tightly, less Constantius realize that he was not asleep. And when his father's hand touched his dark hair in a tender caress he could hardly keep from striking it away.

In the morning Constantine managed to avoid both his father and mother until it was time to say goodbye to Constantius. No one had mentioned the decree of divorcement to him and, as he stood in the yard of the villa while a servant was bringing his father's horse from the stable, he remained stony-faced and silent.

"Your Uncle Marios will go with you to Nicomedia, Flavius," Constantius said, as he mounted his horse. "He will be within call if you need him."

"Take care, Caesar." Marios' voice was husky with emotion. "May Mithras guide your steps."

"And the God of the Christians," Helena added. "I hear there are many of them in Britain."

"With two gods to look after me, I shall hardly need to take an army across the channel." Constantius smiled as he urged his horse forward and reached down to ruffle Constantine's dark hair. "Guard your mother well, my son," he said, his voice husky. "When you are a great soldier, perhaps you can come to Gaul and Britain to be with me."

"I—" Constantine started to blurt out that he never wanted to see his father again but Constantius, moved deeply by the parting, abruptly guided his horse away and was out in the roadway in front of the house before the boy could finish the sentence. Helena, however, noticed his strained manner.

"Is something wrong, Son?" she asked quickly.

"N-no." He looked away quickly, fighting tears of anger and disappointment.

"Last night you seemed so happy over your father's coming, but this morning you didn't even tell him goodbye."

"Are you happy that he has divorced you?" the boy burst out.

Marios was limping across the yard toward the door, but turned so sharply at Constantine's words that his wounded leg almost gave way. "Who told you such foolishness?" he demanded.

"It is the truth, not foolishness!" Constantine's voice broke. "Or did he deceive you too, as he deceived my mother?"

"Silence, boy!"

"Please, Uncle Marios," Helena said. "Let us all go inside where we can talk about this."

Marios opened the door for Helena and followed her inside, leaving Constantine to close it. "Come sit by me, Flavius," she said, going to the couch upon which she and Constantius had been sitting the night before. "There is much we must talk over."

He shook his head. "I'd rather stand."

"Now what is all this about?" Marios eased himself into a chair, grimacing from the pain in his leg. "Have you been snooping into your father's affairs, boy?"

"You woke me up last night with your snoring," Constantine said spitefully. "I went to get a drink of water, not knowing anyone else was awake, and heard my father and mother talking in here."

"You mean you eavesdropped?"

"I—I guess I was so stunned that I couldn't move." Constantine turned quickly to his mother. "Is it true that Emperor Diocletian has given my father a decree of divorcement so he can marry Lady Theodora?"

"What you heard is true," Helena confirmed. "I signed the decree this morning, giving my agreement to the divorce."

"But why? Last night I heard father say it's you he loves."

Helena looked away quickly and when he saw her shoulders jerk in a sob, Constantine knelt and put his arm around her. She buried her face against his tunic and he felt the warm dampness of her tears against his skin through the thin fabric.

"All of us thought it would be better if you didn't know the truth for a little while." Marios' voice was kindly now. "But someone was bound to tell you and perhaps it is best that you learn it now, from those who love you."

Helena dried her eyes on Constantine's sleeve. "You must never believe anything except that I am the most fortunate of women, Flavius," she said firmly. "I have had your father's love and I have had you. Those who would rule are rarely able to marry for love, so I am happy that my birth did not make me a piece to be moved about, as in a game or at a throw of the dice."

"But why did Father divorce you?"

"A strong general is needed in the West, with the authority of a

Caesar to expel the usurper Carausius from Britain and rule the Prefecture of Gaul," Marios explained. "If Diocletian sent a man of your father's ability there without some assurance to Maximian that he is not to be supplanted as Augustus, Maximian would try to hamper your father in every way he can. But by having Constantius marry Theodora, Maximian is appeased and your father can prosecute the war without hindrance. If your mother had been the usual *concubina*, there would have been no difficulty at all; many nobles have them. But your parents were legally married in Drepanum. I witnessed the ceremony myself. So the Emperor was forced to draw up a decree of divorcement."

"Your father refused to sign it until he had talked to me," Helena said, "but I love him enough not to stand in the way of his becoming Augustus and what that would mean for everyone, especially you."

"Was it his idea for me to go to Nicomedia now?" Constantine asked.

"You can thank Galerius for that," Marios told him. "With your father allied to the House of Maximian by marriage, our new Caesar feared that too much power would be concentrated in the West. He got around that by persuading Diocletian to make Constantius send you to Nicomedia for your military training."

"Then Flavius will be little more than a hostage!" It was Helena's turn to be disturbed now. "I didn't realize that."

"Constantius wanted it that way," Marios assured her. "Diocletian has always considered him almost a son, and Flavius here is so much like his father that the Emperor is sure to notice the resemblance, as well as the boy's good qualities. Galerius is smart but this time I think he outfoxed himself. Unless I miss my guess, Flavius will be Diocletian's favorite in less than a year."

2

I T WAS MIDAFTERNOON of a lovely spring day when Marios and Constantine rounded a low bluff on the road from Drepanum —where they had left Helena with her family—to the Western Roman capital of Nicomedia and reined in their horses for a moment. A scene of rare beauty met their eyes, with rolling hills in the foreground, green-clad with vineyard, pasture and field, set against the backdrop of the mountains in the distance.

The land sloped down to the Gulf of Nicomedia, a rather narrow arm of the largely landlocked Sea of Marmara that connected the Mediterranean with the Euxine, or Black Sea. From the hills, streams tumbled toward the gulf through grassy valleys, broken here and there by rocky outcrops. But the land was generally fertile, and rustling bamboos, bays, junipers and rough oaks lined the valleys in their lower courses, while higher up were groves of gaunt-looking pines surrounded by fields of yellow flowering broom, heath and bracken.

Constantine caught his breath in a gasp of admiration as a sleek galley rounded a point below them and came into their range of vision. Its oars kicked up a spray, which the sun turned instantly into the colors of the rainbow, and the broad white sail on its tall mast rippled with the change of course, as the crew scrambled to change the angle presented by the canvas to the wind and make it taut again.

In school he had read about the adventures long ago of a doughty band of Greek mariners led by one of their heroes called Jason. These daring sailors, the story said, had penetrated the waters upon which he was gazing now, fighting off a savage people who sought to turn them back as they pushed ever onward in search of gold.

For in ancient times rugged miners had dug the precious ore from
the hills overlooking the Euxine Sea, washing the rare metal from
base earth in flowing mountain streams and collecting it upon sheep-
skins which, when spread to dry, gained for themselves the name of
Golden Fleece.

"This is such a beautiful land." Marios' voice broke into Constantine's thoughts. "I often wonder why I ever left it for the life of a
soldier. So I could wind up half a man?"

"But think what you would have missed, Uncle Marios." In a new
tunic, with his sturdy legs bare, Constantine already gave promise
of the handsome figure he would make in the uniform of a Roman officer before he was very much older. "Britain! Gaul! Syria
Palaestina! Egypt! You have seen the whole world, but this is farther than I have ever been from home in my whole life."

"You'll find most of it the same. Roman camps differ little, no
matter where they're pitched. And the flies in Britain can sting just
as sharply as those in Egypt."

"Why did the Emperor choose Nicomedia as his capital, instead
of Rome?"

"Rome is dead, as far as being a center of empire is concerned.
The real frontier now is with Persia in the East."

"But the Senate is still there."

"And a good place for them, too," Marios said. "In Rome the
pompous fools who still think they have a say in ruling the Empire
can debate as long as they wish with no way to put their decisions into effect. Diocletian rules with an iron hand, even over
Maximian, and from here the legions can move quickly either by
land or by sea to put down any revolt."

"Then is Rome doomed?"

"Hardly, though I would not be sad to see it wither away. The
Empire needs a symbol to represent it in the minds of the subjects
who pay taxes to support it. Rome will always be that, and by
staging a triumph there occasionally in honor of his victories any
emperor can keep it thus. You can be sure Diocletian understands
this and Maximian too, as well as your father."

"What about Caesar Galerius?"

"Galerius is a pompous ass, but he is married to Diocletian's daughter, so his position is secure. My advice to you is to stay out of his way."

"Why?"

"You are remarkably like your father, Flavius, and Constantius is beloved by every man who wears the short sword. Seeing you will remind Galerius that if there should be a contest for control when Diocletian and Maximian step down, your father could win without even trying."

"Do you think both Emperors will really abdicate at the end of twenty years?"

"Diocletian will keep his word; I never knew him to break it. Maximian is younger and probably wants to stay in power. Besides his son, Maxentius, is training at Nicomedia and probably aspires to wear purple one day, so there's likely to be trouble."

They were approaching the capital now and the shores of the gulf, at whose head it stood, were lined with villas and country houses, surrounded by elaborate gardens. Many piers extended out into the water with here and there an elaborate pleasure barge, roofed over with a canopy and large enough for an entire family to live upon, moored beside them. The main channel appeared to be silting up, however, for the galley they had seen moving upstream was now being moored to a pier well below the main part of the city itself.

Located on rolling ground, the main architectural feature of Diocletian's capital, as far as Constantine could see, was the sprawling bulk of the imperial palace. Across a low vale from it on a rounded elevation stood a much more beautiful structure, though built of wood. It appeared to be a temple, but when they passed close by it Constantine saw no statue of a god to identify the deity to whose worship it was dedicated.

"Only the Christians would dare build one of their churches almost on the Emperor's doorstep," Marios said.

"They must be very strong in Nicomedia."

"There have been Christian churches in Bithynia since a few years after the death of their god."

"The god, or his son? Mother says they worship both."

Marios shrugged. "What can you expect from people who argue

among themselves over whether their god is one person or three?
But I'll say this much for the Nazarene's followers among the legions. They are steadfast and dependable, and not afraid to die."

II

Constantine's eyes danced with eagerness and excitement as they
rode through the busy streets of Nicomedia. On every side he could
see new buildings going up, magnificent temples to the favorite
Roman gods, Jove, Hercules and Apollo, as well as additions to
stadium and amphitheater—all signs of a prosperous and rapidly
growing Roman city.

Workmen in short tunics of cloth reaching to their knees carried
burdens through the streets to their shops. Lucullus, Constantine's
tutor in Naissus, had said that these men were highly organized
into guilds and corporations, some of them so influential that even
the Emperor had to deal with them in carrying on the affairs of
government, and over almost every shop he could distinguish the
emblem of the guild to which its owner belonged.

Merchants and members of the nobility wore longer tunics as a
rule than the artisans, but only very occasionally did he see a ceremonial toga, such as he had heard was still frequently worn in
Rome. The workmen were usually barefoot or wore sandals with
wooden soles, but those who could afford the price affected leather
boots reaching sometimes to the calf. Occasionally he saw a high
government official robed in silken tunic and embroidered dalmatic
—a strip of rich cloth draped about his neck—moving through the
streets preceded by his lictors. These bore proudly the bundled
rods and axes that were their official emblem, while a slave held
over his master's head a richly colored umbrella as protection
against the hot rays of the sun.

Once the two riders were forced to pull their horses aside to
allow the passage of a large wagon drawn by oxen. Constantine
was surprised to see people looking out of windows cut into the
sides, but Marios told him there was even space in some vehicles
such as this for people to sleep while on long journeys from city to
city along the highways traveled by the Imperial Post. Signs hang-

ing from the shops along the streets indicated the crafts practiced
by those inside: veterinary surgeons, sheep shearers, barbers, seam-
stresses, tailors, attendants for the bath, teachers of rhetoric, solici-
tors, scribes with their scrolls and waxed tablets, and skilled workers in marble and tile. Sellers of fruit displayed upon their stands
such delicacies as roast apples, apricots and sweet melons, almonds,
walnuts, figs from Syria, dates, peaches and cherries. And vege-
table peddlers cried their stores of carrots, artichokes, asparagus
and many other delicacies.

The massive bulk of Diocletian's palace had restricted Constantine's view until now. When they rounded it on the way to the barracks, where the legions were quartered, he saw that a number of
new and splendid buildings had been erected beyond it against the
background of a wooded hill, including an amphitheater for the
games which were such an important part of Roman life. Behind
the palace too were the quarters of the garrison, including the elite
troops of the Imperial Guard.

A similar organization was stationed, Constantine knew, in
Rome, the famed Praetorians, who had acted as kingmakers on
more than one occasion, assassinating emperors who did not please
them and raising up others instead. But with the capital of the
Senior Augustus now in the East, the influence of the Praetorians
in Rome had waned markedly.

At the gate of the military compound Marios reined in his horse.
"It was your father's wish that I go no farther," he told Constantine. "But I will see that Diocletian learns you are here. His chamberlain, Plotinus, is an old friend of mine." He smiled briefly. "After
all, we Illyrians have to support each other. Too many toadies from
Rome are trying to gain influence here in the East."

"I shall walk carefully, Uncle Marios," Constantine promised,
"and none of you will be ashamed of me."

"I'm sure of that," Marios told him. "Ask inside for Centurion
Dacius and don't be fooled by his manner; he would give his life
for your father. Obey him to the letter, no matter how hard the
tasks he puts upon you, and you will one day be worthy of the
title of Caesar."

"Augustus," Constantine corrected him gravely.

Marios looked deeply into the boy's eyes for a long moment,

then, pleased by what he saw, smiled. "I shall be very much surprised if you don't one day bear the title! But you will have to earn it. As the son of a Caesar, you will be barred from the normal paths of advancement beyond perhaps the rank of tribune as long as Diocletian is alive. And afterwards, your life may even be in grave danger."

As he watched the erect military figure of his great-uncle disappear down the street leading away from the palace, Constantine felt a deeper loneliness than he had ever known before. For a moment the urge to retrace the road they had followed from Drepanum, where his mother's love would confidently protect him as it had all through his childhood, was so great that he had to resist forcibly the impulse to spur the horse away from the forbidding walls of the army barracks. But the impulse lasted only a moment; then, lifting the reins, he urged the horse through the gate.

III

Just inside the compound a sentry leaned upon his spear talking to another soldier, but he paid no attention to Constantine until the youth started through the gate. Then the spear was lowered in a quick movement so close to the horse's nose that the animal reared up and would have thrown his rider, had he not tightened the reins and pressed his knees quickly against the saddle. Constantine's first impulse was a quick rush of anger that almost made him leap from the back of the horse to that of the sentry. But recognizing that the soldier's act was a deliberate exercise by a petty official of the small amount of authority granted him, he checked the impulse in time. Besides, in the week since he'd watched his father ride away from Naissus, he'd learned that much was expected from the son of a Caesar, most of all self-control.

"Where are you going, peasant?" the sentry demanded. "These are the quarters of the Imperial Guard and forbidden to anyone without authority."

"I seek Centurion Dacius."

"For what reason?"

"I bear a message for him." Constantine removed from the

breast of his tunic the small parchment roll upon which Constantius had written a brief letter to the Master-at-Arms charged with training officer cadets for the Imperial Guard.

"Let me see it." The sentry reached out to take the scroll but Constantine drew it back, turning it slowly until the heavy waxed seal securing the end of the parchment to the roll came into view.

"The seal of Constantius Caesar!" The soldier who had been talking to the sentry snapped suddenly to a position of attention and spoke from the side of his mouth to his companion. "Some day your impudence will cost you your head, Marcus."

The butt of the sentry's spear slammed against the ground at the sight of the seal and the weapon no longer barred Constantine's passage. "You will find the centurion in the second building on your right," he said, his body as rigid as the wooden shaft of the spear.

Centurion Dacius was seated behind a table in a room at the end of the long barracks building. His skin was burned to a leathery hue by the sun and wind, his hair was an iron gray, and his craggy face was scarred from the wounds of a hundred campaigns. When Constantine stood before him, the boy felt his very soul was being probed and appraised by the penetrating gray eyes of the Master-at-Arms. He met the scrutiny silently, however, and finally Dacius unrolled the scroll and began to read it slowly, his lips moving silently as they formed the words. Letters were not the grizzled officer's strong point, Constantine decided, and felt an immediate kinship of spirit, for neither were they his.

"So you are Constantius' get," Dacius said at last. "He and I fought together in many a campaign, but now that he is a Caesar, I suppose you expect me to prostrate myself before you and crown you with the plumed helmet of a tribune."

"My father sent me here to learn to be a soldier. I want nothing I cannot earn for myself."

"Spoken like Constantius' son," Dacius approved. "But still not quite the truth. You were sent here because Caesar Galerius persuaded the Emperor that a hostage is needed to keep Constantius from proclaiming himself an Augustus as soon as he gets to Treves in Gaul. The legions already know your father is the greatest soldier in the service of the Empire."

"I hope to be his equal, sir."

Dacius studied him again for a long moment without speaking. "You may be. We shall see. Flavius Valerius Severus commands the Imperial Guard, and the cadets, at the moment. You will find him fair, but he is a close friend of Galerius, who is also the Emperor's son-in-law, so you'll get no favors here." A wintry smile showed briefly on his weatherbeaten face. "But a true son of Constantius Chlorus should not need them. How did you come to Nicomedia?"

"On horseback."

"Then at least you can ride. Did you use the Imperial Post? The seal on this scroll would have entitled you to it."

"I—we rode our own horses."

"I'll have your mount sent to the stables of your Uncle Marios," Dacius told him. "The Persian curved sword that crippled him cost Rome a fine officer, but very likely did him a favor. No soldier ever got rich, unless he was a general."

He shouted an order and a slave wearing a short tunic of rough homespun appeared in the doorway.

"Find Cadet Flavius Valerius Constantinus a cubicle, a sleeping pallet, and some gear," Dacius ordered, and turned again to Constantine. "Your training will begin tomorrow; the exercises are finished for the day." The wintry smile appeared again momentarily. "May Jupiter give you luck. My guess is that you'll need it."

IV

The *cubicula* assigned to Constantine was barely large enough to contain a sleeping pallet—which could be rolled up in the daytime, enlarging the living space somewhat—and the military gear the slave shortly brought him. Pegs had been set into the walls upon which to hang the gear and a closet at one side afforded room for the clothing he had brought. A basin of earthenware stood upon a table in the corner, and beside it a bucket in which water could be carried from a nearby fountain filled by a pipe connected to the aqueduct bringing water into Nicomedia from a lake in the hills.

Constantine had no illusions about the program upon which he was embarking. At the age of seventeen, strong and healthy Roman youths undertook an obligation for military service which they bore —with time out, in periods of peace—until they were sixty. The last fifteen years of service were usually devoted to garrison duty, though not always in the neighborhood of their homes. Campaigns in the north were largely carried out in summer, so a soldier was often at home during the cold weather and obliged to fend for himself.

As an officer candidate, or cadet, Constantine could look forward to a somewhat less rigorous life than the common soldier, if he won his commission at the end of the training period. Once commissioned, he would have his own servant and sleep in a tent during campaigns, while the common soldier merely rolled up under a shelter of boughs, if he were lucky, in the heavy cloak that was both outer garment by day and blanket by night. But commissioned or not, he would share the food of the legions, unless he was fortunate enough to have private funds for purchasing something better. And even though an officer, he could not escape the rigors of a campaign and the dangers of battle.

Since he had learned to walk, Constantine had followed the routine prescribed by custom for young Romans, with emphasis upon running, jumping, climbing, and swimming. In Naissus, these activities had largely been pursued in friendly competition with his fellows, both in school and out. But now that he was enrolled for actual military training, he knew the program would be far more rigorous.

His initial military equipment was much less, however, than the some seventy-five pounds of weight carried by a soldier on the march, consisting of weapons, axe, spade, shield, armor, helmet, scythe, cooking pot, rations for a week or longer, and two stout palisades, or sharpened staves. The latter not only formed part of the framework upon which the pack was carried but were also used in building breastworks and other fortifications, as well as setting up a wall of wood around a night's encampment.

As a cadet, his equipment consisted of a pair of rough tunics for training and a supply of loin cloths and cotton shirts as undergarments, leaving his own clothing for wear otherwise. Heavy sandals with wooden soles were provided as foot gear, while a round helmet sufficed to ward off blows on the head during sham battles. A small training shield, the inevitable short and rather dull sword, and a stout staff—which would later be replaced by a spear, when he became more skilled in its use—completed the list.

He was wondering how long it would be before the evening meal, when a somewhat stocky young man of, Constantine estimated, perhaps twenty-five stepped through the open doorway into the room without announcement, a custom which he was to learn prevailed throughout the barracks. The newcomer wore the insignia of a decurion and his tunic was of a beautifully woven rich material, much more colorful than the usual garb of a young officer of that rank.

"I am Crocus, from Noviomagus," he announced.

"In Gaul?" Constantine exclaimed.

"My father is king of a province bordering on the Rhine frontier." Crocus grinned. "Did you expect a Gaul to have horns and a tail, like the Christian devil?"

"I'm sorry." Constantine was attracted to Crocus at once for there was an easy naturalness about him that seemed to invite friendship. "My name is Flavius Valerius Constantinus."

"So Dacius told me. I'm sure half of those who aspire to high place in the army and the Empire are named either Flavius or Valerius, so you have a head start."

"Are you a cadet?" Constantine asked.

Crocus shook his head. "Few of the officers commanding even the Gallic legions are from Gaul. My father sent me here for training, but when Dacius discovered I am part horse, he persuaded General Severus to make me the instructor in riding and cavalry tactics. Four of us will share the services of a slave here in the barracks, but I only get the same consideration as the cadets because my father is a king and our mounted troops the best in the Empire."

"You spoke of four. Who are the others?"

"A couple of Caesar cubs: Maxentius, the son of Emperor Maximian, and Maximin Daia, a nephew of Caesar Galerius from somewhere in the East." Crocus' eyes widened suddenly and he clapped his hand to his mouth with such a look of comical horror that Constantine burst out laughing.

"I'm a cub too," he admitted.

"But with the best blood in your veins of any of them, you can be sure of that. By the way, how old are you?" *18*

"Twenty," Constantine said, adding a good two years to his real age.

"So?" Crocus raised his eyebrows. "I would not have thought you quite that old. But the other two are older, so you'll have to fight for your rights." He gave Constantine a quizzical glance. "Or do you know that already?"

"I know why I'm here, if that's what you mean."

From outside came the sound of a trumpet. "There's the call to the evening meal," Crocus said. "I'll show you where we eat."

Most of the remainder of the building was open space, with no interior walls, as the *cubiculae* boasted. Every two paces, rows of pegs had been driven into holes drilled into the wall. From them hung military and other gear and beneath each cluster of pegs was a pallet, neatly rolled up and secured with heavy cords.

"The petty officers of the Imperial Guard sleep here," Crocus explained. "The two private *cubiculae* there at the end of the barracks are for the tribunes; their quarters are somewhat larger than ours. The men of the guard itself sleep in another building adjoining this and the eating place is between us, since everyone fares the same."

They passed along a roofed walkway to another structure, from which came the aroma of cooked food. When Crocus pushed open the door, a blast of sound greeted them, made up of human voices apparently shouting at each other to be heard over the constant roar of conversation and the clatter of utensils. Undisturbed by the noise and exchanging greetings and insults along the way—for he seemed to be quite popular—Crocus moved down the room toward a table in the corner where two other young men were already eating.

One, introduced by Crocus as Maxentius, was tall and thin, with a languid and foppish manner that repelled Constantine at the first glance. The other was Maximin Daia, a sturdy dark-skinned young man, who looked to be in his early twenties. Daia seemed surly, an attribute which Constantine was to learn characterized him much of the time, while the elegant Maxentius was much too languid to show enthusiasm for anything except the wine he drank steadily.

The food was good, though rough: a thick soup eaten from wooden bowls, followed by goat flesh with boiled lentils and hard cakes of bread. The wine had been thinned with water but was still of a good flavor, for the hill country along the southern shore of the Sea of Marmara and the Gulf of Nicomedia was famous for its vineyards.

Maximin Daia ate like a pig, snuffling and slobbering over his meat and wine, but no one seemed to pay any attention to him. When the meal was finished, he pushed himself away from the table and wiped his greasy mouth with a brawny, hair-covered forearm.

"What did you say your name was?" He spoke directly to Constantine for the first time.

"Constantine."

"After Constantius Chlorus?"

A sudden silence fell over the four tables in the corner and Constantine realized that the occupants were watching him now, waiting for his answer.

"He is my father."

"A bastard!" Daia snorted contemptuously. "By what right are you here with us?"

Constantine's first impulse was to lay one of the knives they had used in eating against the stocky young man's throat. But he was beginning to learn how to control his normally hot temper, and deliberately forced himself to relax.

"My mother is Helena of Drepanum."

"A *concubina?*"

"A legal wife, divorced from my father not a week ago in Naissus by decree of Emperor Diocletian."

"Why did he divorce her?" Maximin demanded. "I suppose she—"

"Constantius was divorced so he could marry my stepsister, Theodora." Maxentius yawned. "Really, Daia, I think you get more and more like a pig every day, a stupid, ignorant pig."

Maximin Daia was not offended; apparently the two were close enough comrades to trade insults without anger. "So Constantius left his whelp to spy for him while he is in Gaul and Britain," he said. "Just be careful where you do your spying, little Constantine, or you'll wind up with a javelin through your belly."

3

THE NEXT MORNING Constantine embarked upon a period of the hardest work he had ever done. At sunrise, while the night fog from the gulf still largely shrouded the city, the soldiers in training, officers and legionnaires alike, were routed out by a trumpet and led in a fast run across the country by Dacius himself. It was hard-going, with obstacles to be surmounted, fences to be leaped, and brawling streams, icy cold after their descent from the mountains, to be splashed through.

The pace never let up, in spite of the centurion's age. When they reached the barracks once again, Constantine was gasping for breath but was pleased to see that none of the others, particularly the stocky Daia and the languid Maxentius, fared any better than he—thanks to the hours he had spent running across the hillsides and along the river banks at Naissus, in preparation for the day when he would begin the rigorous period of training.

In the barracks after the run they had time only to splash their faces and bodies with water, the soldiers at a long trough that ran down the side of the building, and the officer candidates at the copper basins in their *cubiculae.* Then they trooped through to the *triclinium*—if so large a hall could be called simply a chamber for dining—and wolfed down a hearty morning meal, since noonday would bring only a husk of bread, some cheese and perhaps a little fruit.

After breakfast came interminable hours of marching and countermarching, as they learned to move in a unit without obstructing each other. Then followed practice in javelin throwing and in handling the *francisca,* the terrible battle-axe which the Franks had introduced into warfare and from which their name had been derived. This lethal weapon—thrown by men skilled in its use, or wielded simply as a battle-axe—had at first almost decimated the close files of the Roman legions in the early Gallic campaigns. Largely because of it, the legions now fought in a much more open formation and their shields, or *scutae,* had been modified into a half cylindrical pattern, so the blades would glance off them.

Another period of instruction followed in the use of *pilum* and *gladius.* The first was a throwing and thrusting spear taller than the man who wielded it; the latter, a sword about as long as a man's forearm and hand with a broad and heavy blade. Thrown or thrust by a strong man, the *pilum* could penetrate the stoutest armor, while in close fighting, the blade of the *gladius* could sever an arm or a leg.

For instruction in the military arts, Constantine was placed at first among the *velites,* made up largely of youths not yet seasoned enough to fight in the front lines of the legions, a place reserved for the superb human fighting machines called the *hastati.* The troops were further divided for purposes of maneuvering into maniples, with twelve files and ten ranks—in all one hundred and twenty men to the unit—with a battlewise centurion, or sometimes two, commanding each of them.

In the classical battle formation, as evolved to perhaps its highest point of efficiency in the time of Julius Caesar, one maniple of each classification—*hastati* in front, the seasoned troops called *principes* second, and a third line made up half of *triarii,* veteran reserves fighting their last campaigns, and young *velites* who could profit by the presence of such experienced warriors—functioned as a unit, the cohort, or battalion, amounting to four hundred and twenty men. Ten such cohorts could make up an army, though normally twenty were used, combined with nine hundred cavalry into a self-sustained unit of about ten thousand men.

Each army had been commanded originally by a consul responsible to the Senate, but now a general responsible to one of the two Emperors, or one of the two Caesars, headed each such unit. Under the top commander were six tribunes, usually young men of noble birth, but the active direction of the army's manifold activities unit by unit still rested upon the famous centurions, who were literally the backbone of the Roman army's officer corps.

Several times a week, the trainees were given instructions in horseback riding and fighting from a mounted position under the close supervision of Crocus who, like most of his countrymen was a skilled horseman. Constantine had always loved riding and enjoyed these periods most of all, particularly as his friendship with the Gallic prince ripened.

In training, the riders were grouped in *turmae* of thirty-two men in eight ranks, since it was a basic tenet of the Roman theory of warfare that a group of men fighting together as a unit was many times more effective than the total number of its members fighting individually. Observing Constantine's aptitude for cavalry leadership, Crocus and Dacius soon gave him command of his own training *turma*, and before long his group was outdistancing the others, when they engaged in speedy gallops across country or maneuvered in formation.

The months were so filled with activity that they sped swiftly by. Regular letters came from Helena and occasionally Constantine was able to leave the barracks for dinner with his Uncle Marios and his family at their lovely villa on the outskirts of the city, overlooking the clear blue waters of the gulf. Once, toward the end of the first year, a letter came from his father telling him that Dacius had sent a good report of his training. But of the things Constantine wished most to hear, the activities of the Franks in Gaul and the status of the expedition being prepared to put down the rebellious Britanni, his father said almost nothing.

For a while Constantine had dared to hope that when his training period was finished he might be assigned to join Constantius in the West for the campaign in Britain. But by now he was well enough versed in political matters at the Emperor's court to know that such a thing would not be likely to occur.

Like himself Constantine's barracks companions were tired at the end of the day's training, and thus they did not cause him much trouble. Maximin Daia remained surly, which seemed to be his nature, while Maxentius had little interest in anything except wine and the girls he sought in the taverns of the town, when he could slip away from the barracks undetected. Constantine rarely saw the Emperor and then only from a distance during military reviews. General Severus, under whose command the training maniples per-

formed their daily functions, congratulated him once on the progress he was making and spoke warmly of Constantius.

So a year passed and by its end Constantine—who showed all
the natural instincts of a fine soldier and particularly a cavalryman
—was the equal and generally the superior of the other young officer candidates.

The months of vigorous training had changed him from a youth
into a handsome young man. He was taller than average and his
shoulders broader, while his strength had increased immeasurably
under the rigorous training. Nor had the intellectual side of his
maturing been neglected, for the cadets were assigned as pupils
in rhetoric to Lucas Caelius Lactantius, one of the foremost teachers
of the Empire, who had been brought to Nicomedia by Diocletian
in order to assist with the instruction of the young men of the imperial household.

Lactantius insisted that Constantine improve his Greek, which
had been largely neglected, but progress here was rather slow for
he was not primarily a student. He was introduced by his tutor,
however, to much of the great literature of Rome, so his mind was
broadened and stimulated while his body was being hardened and
sharpened as an instrument of war.

For weeks they had been preparing for a huge military show to
be held in connection with the Festival of the Augustalia, a holiday
devoted to the worship of the deified emperors which had begun
with Augustus many years before. The day of the Augustalia
dawned bright and clear and household troops were aroused as
usual by a blast upon the *cornu* of the sentry assigned for that
purpose. Breakfast was eaten in the half light of early dawn, but
the morning run was dispensed with in order to allow time for
polishing gear and arraying themselves in the uniforms which had
been issued for the occasion.

Constantine had been assigned to lead one of two *turmae* of cavalry in a demonstration before the throne of the Emperor, which
had been set up at one side of the great stadium. The other commander was Prince Crocus, the Gallic instructor, and for weeks
the two groups had practiced until each man was at the peak of
his skill.

The opening exercise of the military review was carried out by

the household troops, marching and countermarching in full armor
and weapons. The display brought cheers from the members of the
court and the townspeople, who were crowded around the entire
field except the small area from which the troops maneuvered. Constantine had been looking forward to this opportunity to impress
the Emperor with his ability, but when he looked across the field,
he saw that the stocky erect figure occupying the central throne
this morning was not Diocletian. Dacius, who was acting as
seneschal for the affair, gave him the answer.

"Caesar Galerius rode in from Sirmium* yesterday, especially for
the Augustalia," he said. "Diocletian is always glad to delegate a
reviewing chore to someone else."

Court rumor said that Galerius exerted a strong influence upon
the Emperor through his command of a large contingent of the
Roman army and his position as Diocletian's son-in-law. But the
Caesar of the East had been occupied for most of the year with
frontier affairs on the Danube and this was the first time Constantine had been given an opportunity to see him.

As the foot soldiers marched off the field at the end of their
drill, a blast on the *cornu* of the trumpeter announced the beginning of Constantine's own part of the day's review. He was already
in the saddle and when he brought his upraised sword down and
spurred his horse into motion, the members of his *turma* followed
in formation at full gallop across the field and past the reviewing
stand.

For the exercise the *equites*, most of them youths from important
provinces of the Empire, were protected by the classic helmet of
Spanish steel with reinforcing bars across the crown in the pattern
of a cross, hinged cheek pieces extending down below the corners
of the mouth, and a small bar across the front as a visor. For body
protection, in case a sword failed to find its target on the small
round shield each carried on his left arm, they also wore scale
armor, because of its lightness and flexibility.

As his *turma* swept past the reviewing stand, Constantine was
able to get a good view of Galerius Caesar. It was a warm day
and the cloak of imperial purple had been put aside, revealing

* Mitrovica

broad shoulders beneath highly polished ceremonial body armor of
silver. The plumed helmet too had been put aside and Constantine saw that Galerius' short-cropped hair was flecked with gray,
the face beneath it broad, with a powerful-looking nose, prominent
cheekbones and deep-set eyes with all the warmth of a hooded
serpent.

When the notes of the *cornu* floated across the field once again,
Constantine set his mount into motion, as did those behind him,
shouting aloud in his exuberance of spirit. The distance between
the two lines of mounted men lessened rapidly as they charged
toward each other, but neither commander gave an order until,
with hardly ten paces separating the two lines of mounted men,
each struck the butt of his sword against the small round shield on
his left arm simultaneously in the agreed-upon signal.

At the metallic command, both lines turned slightly at full gallop,
passing through each other's ranks so closely that Constantine felt
the breath of Crocus' charger on his cheek and saw the fire of
excitement in his friend's eyes, as each struck the other on the small
shield with the blade of his sword. The whole troop did the same
and the clash of metal against metal was like a single stroke upon
a brazen gong ringing out across the field.

At a second blast from the *cornu*, the two ranks wheeled to race
through again, this time with such a clang of metal against metal
that they could hear the echoes returning from the hills around the
training field, as they re-formed into the traditional solid mass of
the *turmae* and swept across the field to come to a dirt-plowing
stop before the throne upon which Galerius sat.

A roar of applause came from the massed rank of the spectators
at this demonstration of equestrian and military skill. Expecting
some sign of appreciation or approval from Galerius, Constantine
was startled by the cold look of hostility in the older man's eyes
in the instant before Crocus gave the command to withdraw and
the two *turmae* of horse trotted off the field to where the soldiery
were massed, watching the spectacular exhibition. There Constantine swung down from his horse and handed the reins to one of
the troopers, while Crocus came over to pound him happily on the
back with a huge fist.

"Well ridden, my friend!" he cried. "No Goth or Frank could have done better."

"That is praise indeed. And you deserve likewise."

In their exuberance of spirit over the success of the exhibition, neither of the young men had noticed a runner leave the area near the throne and cross the field to where Dacius stood a little distance away. Still happily discussing the success of the exercise, they waited for the military review to end, so they could return to the barracks and dress for the social side of the Augustalia, an afternoon and evening of feasting and ogling the young ladies of the court and the town.

"Constantine! Crocus!" Dacius called. "Come here."

Both of them hurried over to where the centurion was standing. Constantine saw that his craggy face was concerned.

"Is anything wrong?" he asked.

"You did well—perhaps too well. Caesar Galerius has ordered a further exhibition by the leaders of the two ranks who just took part in the exercises."

"What kind of an exhibition?"

"Fighting from horseback."

"But why?"

"Perhaps he likes the sight of blood. You'll be hard put to keep from spilling some; he has also ordered the use of battle lances."

II

Constantine looked at Crocus and saw the same bewilderment in the eyes of the young Frank that he felt himself. The lance used by the *equites* in battle was a lighter and longer version of the *pilum*, the heavy spear with which the legions had conquered most of the known world, and only a little less important a weapon than the sword. Almost a third of the metal point of the lance was sharpened so it could penetrate armor, and the wooden socket to which the head was attached occupied another third of the shaft, serving not only as a place to grasp the weapon but also as a guard for the hand. It was a murderous weapon in skilled hands and, armed as the two were with only scale armor, swords and the

small round shields of the *equites,* it would be difficult indeed to
conduct even a sham battle on horseback without one or both of
them being wounded or killed.

It was Dacius who noted an inequality in their weapons, just
as Constantine was mounting. For the exercise that morning he had
used a training sword, a short weapon manufactured of an inferior
steel and poorly tempered. Crocus, however, was wearing his personal sword, a fine weapon of Spanish steel, longer and much more
able to take the clash of metal upon metal as they banged each
other's shields in mock attack.

"Here, Constantine." Dacius unbuckled his own sword and tossed
it to the younger rider. "Wear this."

While Constantine buckled on the longer weapon, Dacius moved
close to the horse and spoke in a low voice. "Crocus is your friend
but these Gauls are easily excited in battle and he is an experienced fighter. Guard yourself and keep your shield close to your
body, or he will tear it from your arm on the first pass."

Constantine nodded and swung into the saddle. Crocus' mount
was prancing a few paces away, eager to be off, and they galloped
across the field to the space before the reviewing stand. There,
the two saluted with upheld lances, then turned and trotted until
perhaps a hundred paces separated them. When the *cornu* signaled
the beginning of the mock battle, each urged his mount forward
and closed the distance between them at a gallop.

In the classic pattern such passages-at-arms were supposed to
follow, the first few passes were carried out with the lance held
level, as each man sought to strike the body of his opponent and
either kill or unhorse him. But, in a sham battle such as this, each
was supposed to aim for the shield of the other instead, hoping
to strike it such a blow that the bearer would be unhorsed and
forced to fight from the ground, placing him at a considerable disadvantage. Constantine therefore gripped his lance tightly in his
right hand and held the shield before him with his left, making it
an easy target for the weapon of his opponent, as they raced toward each other.

Only when he saw the feverish light in Crocus' eyes as he leaned
forward in his saddle, every muscle tensed, did Constantine realize
that the Gallic nobleman intended to give the supposedly sham en-

counter all the appearance of a real fight. The point of Crocus'
lance was hardly a length of the weapon's shaft away by then and,
when it suddenly veered toward him, Constantine saw that Crocus
intended to pass the shaft between his body and the shield, using
the tremendous leverage thus gained to twist his opponent from
the saddle and send him crashing to the ground.

Remembering Dacius' instructions, Constantine swung his body
away from the point of the lance and in the same movement pulled
the shield in close to his body. The jarring impact as the metal
point of Crocus' lance struck and glanced off the shield, shook him
from teeth to toes, but he managed to stay in the saddle. The
sudden maneuver disturbed his own aim, however, and the point
of his lance barely touched Crocus' shield, as the two horses passed
each other almost directly in front of the reviewing stand.

Constantine's quick action in shifting his body and pulling his
shield against it saved him from being thrown. But the sudden
change of position made it difficult for Crocus to control his own
lance. Glancing from the shield, it struck downward, and Constantine felt the point drive home into the body of his mount just
behind the saddle, followed immediately by the jarring impact of
steel against bone deep within the horse's body.

The wound was lethal and, as the forelegs of the dying horse
buckled, Constantine was forced to use the shaft of his spear like
a pole, and vault from the saddle before he was pinned under the
body of his mount. He landed a short distance from the stricken
animal, but still in possession of his weapons and his shield. Crocus,
meanwhile, had managed to pull his own lance from the body of
Constantine's dying horse, though almost unseated in the action.

As the Gallic prince wheeled his charger about a hundred paces
away, Constantine glanced toward Galerius sitting upon the throne
with his trumpeter standing beside him. He expected to hear the
blast of the *cornu* that would end the now decidedly uneven exhibition, but the sound did not come. And with a start he realized
that Galerius intended to let it go on to whatever might be its
termination.

Turning quickly, Constantine saw Crocus bearing down upon him
again, his lance extended for another blow. With the full momentum of horse and rider now behind Crocus' lance, Constantine could

see little chance of escaping without a severe wound, or even death. Fortunately he remembered just in time the trick by which the foot-soldier *hoplites* of Alexander the Great had managed to defeat the swift slashing attack of Persian cavalry.

Crocus was almost upon him, when he knelt suddenly, and dropped the butt of his lance to the ground, elevating the point. It struck his opponent's shield solidly, driving the butt of the weapon into the earth, and literally lifting Crocus from the saddle by the force of his own momentum. Catapulted end over end, Crocus struck the ground almost at Constantine's feet, the lance torn from his grasp and the shield, split in half by the point of Constantine's own weapon, dangling from his arm. The sudden unhorsing quite knocked the wind out of Crocus and for a moment he lay stunned and helpless on the field. Drawing his own sword Constantine crossed the short space separating the two and stood with the point touching the throat of the Gallic nobleman.

Vaguely Constantine heard a burst of sound behind him, as the crowd urged him on to the kill. A red haze of violent anger—at Crocus for letting himself be so carried away by enthusiasm that he had almost turned a sham battle into a total encounter and at Caesar Galerius for not halting the conflict—obscured his vision momentarily. The hand holding the sword at Crocus' throat even tightened a little and he saw a drop of blood appear where the point pricked the skin. He knew from the ˙sudden light of fear in Crocus' eyes that his friend realized how powerful was the urge to drive the sword point down, ending the contest, as the crowd was screaming for him to do. But the temptation lasted only a second; then sheathing his sword Constantine reached down and helped Crocus to his feet. A roar of disappointment came from the crowd but he ignored them, as he did Galerius, who should have stopped the sham battle before it turned into a near-fatal encounter.

Crocus was more hurt by the fall than Constantine realized. When he swayed and would have fallen, the younger man drew the arm of his recent opponent across his shoulders and with Constantine supporting and Crocus limping along, they marched across the field with the jeers of the bloodthirsty crowd in their ears. Meanwhile Dacius had sent horse handlers to catch Crocus' mount and cut the throat of Constantine's dying horse before dragging it from the field. As soon as the area before the throne was cleared, a blast of the trumpet signaled the beginning of the next event.

At another time Constantine would have been interested in seeing it, for a group of Illyrian legionnaires were demonstrating the use of *martiobarbuli,* the pairs of leaden balls joined together that were a traditional weapon among the Dalmatian troops. Boys started throwing the odd weapons as soon as they were strong enough to lift them. And by the time they were old enough for military service, they were able to use the leaden balls swinging at the end of a short chain as extremely lethal weapons, fully capable of bringing down a man.

Dacius met them at the edge of the field and together they led Crocus to a litter where he could lie down. The face of the Gallic prince was drawn with pain, as the centurion's gnarled hands moved swiftly over his body with surprising skill, but he bore the examination unflinchingly.

"I'm sure there are no broken bones," Dacius said, finally. "But it will be many a day before you can sit a horse comfortably again."

"Ordinarily a man on his feet has no chance against a skilled cavalryman, yet you made a fool of me, a veteran of the wars." Crocus looked up at Constantine and managed to smile wryly. "I'm still not sure just what happened."

"It was an old Greek trick. If you hadn't been overconfident, it would never have worked."

Crocus shook his head. "Not confidence—vanity. I told myself I would gain favor with Galerius by humbling the son of Caesar Constantius publicly, and you very rightly put me in my place. Will you forgive me for even having such a thought?"

"I almost spitted you with Dacius' sword," Constantine reminded him. "We were both wrong, so we really came out even."

"Unless I miss my guess, you have both lost today," Dacius said, and there was no levity in his tone. "If I had Galerius here, I would cheerfully cut his throat."

A messenger appeared just then at Dacius' side. "Caesar orders Cadet Constantinus to appear before him at once," he said. "I am to escort him to the palace."

Dacius put his hand on Constantine's arm. "You could be in more danger now than you were out there on the field," he warned. "Let Galerius do the talking and, above all, don't argue with him."

III

The messenger guided Constantine to a luxurious suite inside the palace where an aide was working on some maps behind a table and two scribes were busy in the corner, copying military documents on rolls of parchment. No one offered him a place to sit, so he stood and watched. Presently Galerius came striding into the room, followed by General Severus, who commanded the Emperor's household troops.

The Caesar of the East tossed his purple cloak on a couch and Constantine saw that he was appareled in the formal regalia of a high-ranking Roman officer. His sandals were laced with thongs which had been covered with gold leaf and his white silken tunic was pleated as only the highly trained slaves called *plicatae* were able to do. A silver breastplate and helmet, the latter complete with the towering formal plume of Phoenician purple that distinguished generals in the Roman army, completed the picture.

"You over there," Galerius spoke to Constantine as he might have spoken to a slave, and nodded to the half-open door leading to another room. "In here."

Severus followed Galerius through the door and, as he passed, Constantine was surprised by his quick nod of reassurance. Galerius went immediately to a cushioned couch and threw himself upon it, shouting for a slave to bring him wine. He extended no invitation to either Constantine or Severus to join him and only after draining a silver goblet at a gulp, did he speak again.

"So you are Constantius' son," he said. "How old are you?"

"Nineteen, sir," said Constantine.

"Why didn't you kill the Alemanni just now?"

"He is my friend. Besides, it was not a fight to the death."

"The crowd wanted it, and he tried to kill you."

"I understood that we were to engage simply in a demonstration of fighting from horseback."

"At which you are not very good," Galerius said contemptuously. "Any cavalryman in my army could have cut you down."

"I have not had much training yet in that kind of combat, sir." Constantine kept his voice even, though the taunt stung.

"I suppose you expect to be given a high place in the army because you are Constantius' bastard."

Constantine remembered Dacius' warning and made no denial. He was not quite certain why Galerius was goading him, though he was beginning to suspect. But he was determined not to give the older man an excuse to subject him to the kind of punishment he'd seen meted out to soldiers, and even officers, for the most trivial of offenses. The dreaded scourging with the whip of many tails, some tipped with small iron balls, could turn the deeper layers of a man's flesh into a pulp without breaking his skin, crippling him for life.

"I hope one day to earn a responsible place in the army, sir," he said. "But through my own efforts, not because I am the son of a Caesar."

"Where is your mother?" Galerius asked.

"At Drepanum, with her family."

"I remember her well, when she was a barmaid in Bithynia." Again Constantine forced himself to be calm, certain now that Galerius was seeking to goad him into a retort that would constitute an excuse for punishment.

"What sort of a son are you?" Galerius sneered. "Don't you even resent your father's deserting your mother?"

"She is well cared for, sir," Constantine said evenly. "We both understood it to be the will of the Emperor Diocletian that my father divorce her and marry the daughter of Maximian Augustus."

He had deliberately added the last half of the sentence as a reminder to the other man that he was under imperial protection on the order of Diocletian himself. And he saw that the thrust went home, for Galerius' eyes narrowed and he checked himself with an effort. Severus made no comment, but a quick smile of approval showed momentarily on his face and Constantine was heartened by the knowledge that he had at least one friend in high places.

"Away with you then," Galerius ordered sharply. "And tell my aide outside to come in."

The day's drill was over when Constantine got back to the parade ground and the crowd was already filing out. When he entered Dacius' office at the end of the many-windowed barracks building, he was surprised to find his Uncle Marios there.

"I was at the exhibition drill this morning," Marios told him. "The messenger escorted you from the field about the same time that Galerius left the reviewing stand, so I thought there might be a connection. I came here to learn what happened from Dacius."

"And found me as much in the dark as he is," Dacius admitted. "By all the rules of sham battle, Galerius' trumpeter should have ended the affair when your mount was killed. What did he say to you?"

"He demanded to know why I didn't kill Crocus."

"Galerius knows that if Crocus were killed during a spectacle here at Nicomedia, his father's people would almost certainly start a blood feud with your father's armies in Gaul—" Dacius broke off and whistled softly to himself. "By the winged heels of Mercury himself, that must be the answer."

"Of course it is," Marios agreed. "Even the troops know Constantius is by far the best general in the Empire and Galerius lives in constant fear that he will not become Senior Augustus when Diocletian abdicates."

"Or that Diocletian will realize how incompetent he is and not give up the purple," Dacius agreed.

"I-I'm not sure I understand all this," Constantine admitted.

"Crocus is an experienced fighter," Dacius explained, "and the odds were in his favor. If he had killed you during what was called an exhibition, Constantius' troops could have held Crocus' tribe responsible and the auxiliaries in Gaul might have been driven to rebellion. On the other hand, if you had killed Crocus, the Gallic tribes would have blamed your father. Either way Galerius felt sure he could win by letting the sham battle become something more serious, hoping Crocus would get excited—as he did—or that you would be so angry that you would fight back to the death."

"I almost did."

"We can be thankful that it all turned out so well," Marios said fervently.

"I'm glad it's over," Dacius agreed.

But it wasn't over, as Constantine learned when he came into the barracks a few days later and found Crocus packing his equipment and belongings.

"Where are you going?" he asked.

"Home—to Gaul."

"Did your father send for you?"

"No. Caesar Galerius expelled me from the army."

"On what grounds?"

"He is Caesar. What grounds does he need?"

"Weren't you even given a reason?"

"Dacius says it's because I failed to kill you the other day—or because you failed to kill me. Either way I don't understand."

"It's very simple," Constantine said and went on to tell him of his interview with Galerius.

"So that's it." Crocus grinned wryly. "You and I are being moved around like pieces on a board in a game. And neither has much to say about what square we land on."

"Why don't you appeal to the Emperor?"

"Dacius agrees it would do no good. No, friend Constantine. My career in the Roman army is finished and I'm happy—in a way." Crocus even managed to grin. "I'm certainly glad you didn't kill me, even with this happening. And I could never have forgiven myself for killing you."

"But what are you going to do?"

"Go home and flog my father's serfs, I suppose, to prove that I am a man of some importance."

"My father is Caesar of the West," Constantine said, "and I'm sure he needs all the trained cavalry officers he can get to put down the Picts and the Caledonians in Britain. I will give you a letter to him, and if you're not commander of the auxiliary cavalry in the whole Prefecture of Gaul, Britain and Spain by the time I get there, I shall flog you myself."

4

T HE END of the first year of training brought promotions for most of the cadets, though the rank they were given was only that of a decurion, who normally commanded ten men. Maxentius, being the son of an Augustus, and Maximin Daia, as the nephew and protégé of Caesar Galerius, could look forward to rapid promotion, but Constantine knew he could expect nothing from Galerius. And, since he rarely caught a glimpse of the Emperor, he sometimes doubted whether Diocletian even knew he existed.

As a decurion of the training maniples, Constantine was allowed much more freedom than while a cadet. And since Drepanum was not far away, he was able to visit his mother occasionally. Helena was comfortably established in the town, where she had many relatives, and was well supplied with funds sent regularly by his father from his capital at Treves in Gaul. It was from his mother that Constantine learned of the birth of a half brother, his father's son by Theodora, the stepdaughter of the Emperor Maximian. And when he was told that this son bore the same name as he, any hope of succeeding to his father's position as Caesar, and perhaps as Augustus, was dealt a body blow.

He was thoughtful and even resentful as he rode back to Nicomedia in the afternoon. But upon his return to the barracks he had no time to mope, for Dacius greeted him with news that the decurion in charge of a detail guarding the imperial gardens had fallen ill and ordered him to take the other man's place.

The gardens of the palace were beautiful, with terraced banks of flowers and shrubs and the musical rush of water from a succession of fountains, each at a lower level than the one above.

Constantine disposed his men in the posts they were to walk and having finished this chore paused at the end of the tour beside a quiet pool, where the moon penetrated through the branches of the trees to cast a dappled pattern of shadows and light upon the water. Lost in gloom, he turned quickly when he heard a movement almost at his elbow and his hand dropped to the hilt of his sword.

"An officer who is not alert doesn't live very long," a heavy voice said. Recognizing Emperor Diocletian, Constantine came rigidly to attention.

"My men are walking their posts, Dominus." He gave Rome's Emperor the title of an oriental monarch, which he was known to prefer to that of Imperator. "I just finished inspecting them."

"And being young, your mind turned to other things?"

"Yes, Dominus."

"What is your name, Decurion?"

"Flavius Valerius Constantinus."

"Constantius' son?"

"Yes, Dominus."

"I knew your mother well, when Constantius was courting her. She was very beautiful."

"For a barmaid?" From the depths of his frustration over the news he had heard at Drepanum, Constantine spoke bitterly and impetuously.

"Your mother's parents operated an inn on the Imperial Post Road, a legitimate business which they conducted honestly," Diocletian said sharply. Then he added in a tone less harsh, "But I suppose some here have accused you of being *nothus* because she was a *concubina*."

"Yes, Dominus."

"Give the next one who does it the lie then, on my authority. I drank wine at your father's wedding; you are legitimate."

"But he divorced my mother."

"On my orders, for the good of the Empire."

"And now he and the Lady Theodora have a son, also named Constantine."

"So that's why you're gloomy?" Diocletian put his hand on

Constantine's arm in a friendly gesture. "Come sit with me here on a bench beside the pool and I will explain a few things to you."

"Those who rule must learn early to put aside their own feelings in most things," Diocletian said, when they were seated. "I know how much your father loves your mother and I respect him for it, but he is also a soldier and required to obey my orders. By the way, Dacius reports that you are the best of the whole lot of cubs this year."

Constantine was too stunned to answer as the calm heavy voice continued, "You have noble blood in your veins, too, young Constantinus. Some might even say you are more fit to rule here than I."

"I have no such thought—"

"Then you're not as ambitious as I would expect you to be. Nevertheless I must warn you not to expect to be either Caesar or Augustus as long as I rule Rome. Do you know why?"

"Because I am unworthy."

"On the contrary. You are more worthy, I am sure, than many who have ruled Rome and many others who will. For nearly a hundred years the Empire has been torn by the ambitions of its generals and their sons to be emperors. The Emperor before me, Numerian, was one of the kindest and best men I ever knew, but he was murdered by his chief minister, Arrius Aper, who wished the title of Augustus for himself. I had no desire for it, but the soldiers chose me."

"It was an inspired choice, Dominus."

"At least I gave no bribes. I also swore to step down when my twenty years are ended, to let your father and Galerius take the place of myself and Maximian. And when they name the Caesars to succeed them, I hope they are as fortunate as I have been in the men who serve me." He changed the subject. "I am going to assign Maxentius and Maximin Daia to duty with the legions. Where would you like to serve?"

"In Gaul, at the siege of Gesoriacum."

"I'm afraid that cannot be."

"Then it's true that I am being held as a hostage for my father's loyalty?" Constantine was immediately aghast at his own temerity in thus addressing the most powerful man in the world, but Diocletian appeared not to take offense.

"I would trust your father with my life and, I am beginning to suspect, you also," he said. "But Galerius insists that you remain in the East. Daia goes to the Euphrates frontier; he will gain experience quickly there. Maxentius will be assigned to the Prefecture of Italy. He seems to prefer luxury and debauchery to his duty as an officer and will find plenty in Rome to keep him from ambitions that might roil the waters elsewhere. Besides, trouble is beginning to build up in Africa, so he will have an opportunity to gain experience there."

"He is brave and daring—"

"A little too daring for my liking," Diocletian said dryly. "As for you, I plan to keep you near me as an officer of the Imperial Guard. Dacius says you not only are a fine soldier but also have a wise head on your shoulders, and I must say that you proved it in the affair of the Gallic prince, Crocus."

"But you weren't even there that day, Dominus. I didn't think you knew anything about it."

Diocletian chuckled. "An emperor needs eyes and ears that do not show, if he would remain in power. Of course Prince Crocus could not continue as a cavalry instructor after being unhorsed and defeated by one of his own students. But Constantius took your word for his ability and he is now one of your father's best commanders."

"I'm glad, for Crocus."

"You will be transferred to a post as a centurion in my household troops immediately," Diocletian told him. "And if you are everything I think you are, your rank will soon be higher."

Overwelmed, Constantine had trouble finding words. "I— It is more than I deserve, sire."

"Then prove that you deserve it, and that you are as wise as Dacius says you are, by answering a question for me," Diocletian said crisply. "With four great armies to maintain and borders to guard, more money must always be found to pay the prices charged by the merchants. The emperors who went before me steadily debased the precious metal in our coin but that only made matters worse. What do you think would be the effect of an edict setting all prices and wages at their present levels?"

It was not an easy question and Constantine couldn't be sure whether Diocletian was really asking his advice, which seemed unlikely, or simply testing his powers of reason. Having grown up in Naissus close to the fertile earth of Illyricum, he had absorbed from it and from his parents some of the sturdy individuality which characterized alike the peasant and the nobility of that region, so his first instinct was to oppose the Emperor's projected scheme. Yet he realized that by agreeing with Diocletian, he might strengthen his own position at court and hasten his elevation into the military hierarchy that ranked just below the Emperor himself in the affairs of the Empire. Not for a moment, however, did he yield to the latter temptation.

"I can see the advantage of fixing the amount of precious metal in the coinage, Dominus," he said. "But I don't think setting prices and wages will be effective."

"Why? I'm only trying to bring order out of what is now a chaos of rising prices and wages."

"Then do it by fixing the amount of gold and silver in the coins at a higher level than is in them now and making the change permanent. Those who work will then be better paid for their labor and will not demand more. And those who sell will get more for their goods and thus will not be tempted to raise prices."

"How can you say that? All merchants are greedy."

"It is because they're greedy that I believe your plan will fail, Dominus," Constantine said earnestly, warming to his subject. "If you set the price of everything, merchants will hold goods off the market until they become scarce, then sell them under the table for more than the price set by the government."

"And risk flogging, or death?"

"Men will risk anything for money. We hardly have enough soldiers now to keep back the barbarians on our frontiers. How will you defend them when your armies are busy arresting merchants, who make more profit than they are entitled to, or artisans who refuse to work for the wages you set?"

"How would fixing the value of the coinage prevent all those evils?"

"Not all merchants sell the same thing for the same price now," Constantine pointed out. "Someone is always willing to decrease his profit in order to sell more. If left alone, the price of goods will come to a fair level, so long as no one can claim that all money does not have the same value."

"You realize, don't you, that by opposing me, you may be risking the favor I have promised to show you?" Diocletian's tone was harsh.

"Yes, Dominus. But if I agreed with you merely to gain your favor and afterwards my advice turned out to be wrong, you would think even less of me."

"Do you consider me fair enough not to hold a grudge, if you are proven right?"

"Your will governs all our lives, Dominus. If I don't trust in your justice, I can trust in nothing."

Diocletian studied him for a long moment before rising from the bench. "If you prove me wrong in this, young man," he said very soberly, "you may also prove me wrong in my belief that no Filius Augusti should succeed his father. I think Dacius was right about your having a wise head on your shoulders, though we shall have to see who is the wiser."

II

For whatever reason, Diocletian did not immediately put into effect the decree he had discussed with Constantine, but the promise of a position in the Imperial Guard was fulfilled immediately. The following day, the same orders that dispatched Maxentius to Italy and Maximin Daia to the Euphrates also named Flavius Valerius Constantinus a centurion assigned henceforth to duty in the palace.

At the first opportunity, about a week later, Constantine rode to Drepanum to tell his mother of his new honor. He found her in the garden of the small villa, with a slender girl who was, he judged, about sixteen. She was quite pretty, with delicate features, light hair and bright intelligent eyes.

"This is Minervina," Helena introduced the girl. "My son, Centurion Flavius Constantinus."

The girl acknowledged the introduction graciously but when she would have left, Helena insisted that she remain. "You will want to hear about the goings on at the palace, my dear," she said. "An officer of the Imperial Guard should know all the gossip."

"So my surprise is not a surprise." Constantine smiled wryly. "How did you know?"

"Marios sent word to me of your promotion at the same time that he sent a letter to your father at Gesoriacum."

"Has the seige already begun?"

"Yes." Helena looked at him keenly. "Are you very much disappointed that you will not be there?"

Constantine shrugged. "It makes no difference now. Emperor Diocletian told me I can never become either Caesar or Augustus."

"And you are accepting the verdict, without fighting back? That doesn't sound like the great-grandson of Claudius Gothicus."

After the formal protocol of the palace at Nicomedia, Constantine found it pleasant to linger in the garden and particularly to admire the fragile loveliness of Minervina. When Helena left them together while she supervised the preparation of the evening meal, he learned that the girl was the daughter of a merchant of Drepanum and a distant relative of his mother's family. She was bright, too, and much better informed about the affairs of the Empire than the young women who were constantly seeking to attract his attention in Nicomedia. More fluent in Greek than he, she had read the great sagas of that romantic and highly vocal people.

"Where did you learn all these things?" Constantine asked admiringly.

"My tutor is Theognis of Nicaea, a great scholar. He is as much at home in Greek as he is in Latin."

"It's a pity I didn't have him when I was a boy," Constantine admitted. "Old Lucullus knew only Latin and not too much of that. Fortunately a soldier has little need of education, except in the arts of war."

"When you're Emperor, you can hire a Greek minstrel to sing to you of Homer and Odysseus, or a Latin poet to recount the voyages of Aeneas."

"Are you a seeress, who looks into the future? Or perhaps a priestess serving an oracle?"

"I am a Christian," she said quietly. "We are forbidden to worship any god except our own, and any graven image."

"But it is dangerous to be a Christian." He was serious now, for he had taken an instantaneous liking to this lovely young girl, more of a liking, he admitted, than for any young woman he had ever known.

"We have been persecuted before," she said with the same calmness. "The Lord Christ has always protected us."

"What about those who were crucified, or burned as torches by Nero?"

"They dwell with Jesus in Heaven."

"How do you know that?"

"He told us so himself in the Holy Scriptures when he said, 'God so loved the world that he sent his only begotten Son, that whosoever believeth in him should not perish but have everlasting life.' That's why evil people who seek to destroy our faith always fail."

"Diocletian is beginning to listen to Galerius and some others who want to destroy the Christians."

"Then he must destroy his own wife, Prisca, and his daughter, Valeria."

"Who says they are Christians?"

"I cannot tell you."

"Because you have no proof?"

"No. Because one day you may have to order soldiers to kill us."

"I don't make war on women and children," he said stiffly. "Or on old men. Your secret is quite safe with me."

"What secret?" Helena had come into the garden in time to hear the last word.

"Did you know Minervina is a Christian?"

"Of course. It's one reason why she is good and kind, and why I love her."

"And why she may be put to death one day," Constantine said harshly. "Don't tell me you have been following their barbarous practices, Mother—eating flesh and drinking blood?"

"What fool's prattle have you been listening to?" Helena said

scornfully. "Christians are good people who help each other and
serve their god. Tomorrow is their Sabbath; come listen to them
and learn the truth."

"They subvert the authority of the Emperor and the gods of
Rome. Do you expect an officer of the Empire to listen to such
gabble?"

"Come with Minervina and me tomorrow and discover the
truth," Helena dared him. "Even a centurion of the Imperial Guard
can learn from a scholar like Theognis of Nicaea. Uncle Marios
keeps a tunic and cloak here to change into after riding from
Nicomedia. You're not too far from the same size and nobody need
recognize your rank."

Constantine had no wish to spend his brief holiday listening to
the caterwauling of priests. But the two women had backed him
into a corner and he had either to agree or to spend the rest of the
holiday knowing that each time he looked at either of them he
could read their thoughts. Besides, in some way he didn't yet
understand, it had become important for him to gain the favor of
a slip of a girl he had never seen until a few hours before.

III

The meeting place of the Christians in Drepanum was an un-
impressive building that appeared to have been used as a store. It
had none of the magnificence of the temples of Jupiter, patron
deity of Rome, with which Constantine was familiar, or even the
considerably more austere shrines of Mithras, at which many of
the soldiers worshiped.

The room was filled with benches in orderly rows, most of them
already occupied by worshipers. At one end was a simple altar,
actually little more than a table covered by a cloth upon which
had been placed a plate, also covered with an embroidered linen
cloth, a goblet and a flagon of wine. Behind the table was a cross
of hammered silver, easily the most expensive object in the room,
with a single candle burning before it.

Nor were the worshipers any different from those he would have
seen in a Roman temple, Constantine decided. A number of them

he recognized from previous visits to Drepanum as townspeople. Others wore the somewhat ruder garments of serfs from the surrounding countryside who tilled the soil belonging to the land-owners. The three took their seats near the back of the room and shortly afterwards the priest Minervina had called Theognis of Nicaea came in through a door at the rear of the building. He was a tall man with the delicately chiseled features of a Greek scholar and mystic, surmounted by a high forehead and graying hair.

The priest's white robe was ornamented only by a dalmatic of rich cloth, draped about his neck. Upon it was embroidered in gold a strange pattern which appeared to be made up of the Greek letters *i-ch-th-u-s* but in an odd arrangement that spelled no word with which Constantine was familiar. The letters were of varying height, those in the center being taller than those at the end, and the whole formed somewhat the outline of a fish.

Constantine was about to ask Helena the meaning of the strange acrostic, when he noticed at the foot of the hammered cross of silver a highly polished board into whose surface had been burned in Greek with some hot instrument: *IESOUS CHRISTOS THEOU UIOS SOTER.* And even with his somewhat limited knowledge of Greek, he recognized the words, "Jesus Christ, Son of God, Saviour," as the source of the acrostic.

A small reading stand or pulpit stood beside the altar. After going to it, the priest raised his arms and began to speak the words of a prayer in which the worshipers joined. It was a strangely beautiful and simple invocation which Constantine had never heard before:

"Our Father which art in heaven,
  Hallowed be thy name.
  Thy kingdom come.
  Thy will be done,
  As in heaven, so in earth.
  Give us day by day our daily bread.
  And forgive us our sins;
  For we also forgive every one that is indebted to us.
  And lead us not into temptation;
  But deliver us from evil. Amen."

"The prayer was given us by Jesus himself when he was on earth," Minervina whispered to Constantine. One phrase in particular—"Thy kingdom come"—had struck his ears, for it seemed to imply that the Christians were begging their god to set up a kingdom on earth, an act which would constitute treason against Rome, punishable by death. Before he could ask Minervina about it, however, the priest spoke again.

"I shall read to you," he announced, "from the sermon our Lord Jesus Christ spoke from the mountain in Galilee, as it is set down for our guidance in the Holy Scriptures:

> "Blessed are the poor in spirit, for
> theirs is the kingdom of heaven.
> Blessed are they who mourn, for they
> shall be comforted.
> Blessed are the meek, for they shall
> inherit the earth.
> Blessed are they who hunger and thirst
> after righteousness, for they shall be filled.
> Blessed are the merciful, for they shall
> obtain mercy.
> Blessed are the pure in heart, for they
> shall see God.
> Blessed are the peacemakers, for they
> shall be called the children of God.
> Blessed are they who are persecuted for
> righteousness' sake, for theirs is the kingdom
> of heaven.
> Blessed are you when men shall revile you,
> and persecute you, and shall say all manner of
> evil against you falsely, for my sake.
> Rejoice and be exceedingly glad, for great
> is your reward in heaven, for so did they persecute
> the prophets who were before you."

Theognis put down the scroll from which he had been reading and began to speak. His words were simple, as were those he had been reading. Briefly, yet eloquently, he told the story of a god who, though all-powerful, had loved mankind enough to send his only son to show them the way to eternal life. He spoke of the ministry of the man called Jesus Christ in far-off Syria Palaestina, how the people had thirsted for the truth he brought them, and how they had drunk deeply of his wisdom. He told how the authorities, both religious and civil, had opposed this simple teacher from an obscure town called Nazareth, and how, finally, they had brought him to trial on trumped-up charges of treason by claiming that he was the leader of a revolution against Rome. By swearing false evidence against him they had led the Roman governor of the province, Pontius Pilate, to condemn Jesus of Nazareth to the most shameful of deaths, upon a cross outside the city of Jerusalem, known to Constantine by its Roman name of Aelia Capitolina.

Finally, Theognis told a beautiful story of how devoted women came to the sepulcher where Jesus' body had been placed, ready to anoint it for the final rites, only to find the tomb empty. His voice ringing now with the hope that Jesus' resurrection from the dead had brought to all who followed him, he told of the Nazarene's appearances to his followers, who were called apostles. And particularly of one man called Saul of Tarsus, who, though at first a persecutor of the Christians, was renamed Paul when he was called by Jesus to spread the good news abroad, and who had become a veritable torch of truth.

"Jesus speaks in the hearts of all of us every day," Theognis said in closing his discourse. "If we but listen and give ourselves to him, we too shall know the gladness of the Apostle Paul when at last he was shown the purpose God intended for him. And sure then of our own purpose, whatever may befall us, we are filled always with the Holy Spirit with which we shall triumph over death, even as was promised us by our Lord and Saviour Jesus Christ."

The sermon was finished, but there was still another part of the service of worship, something called a sacrament, which Theognis announced as the Agape. Constantine wondered whether the dreadful rites of which he had heard, the drinking of blood and the eating of flesh, would come now. But the ceremony was simple and beautiful, marked by breaking bread and eating it in memory of the man the Christians believed to be the son of their god. And by the drinking of wine as, Theognis said, Jesus had drunk it during a farewell supper with his disciples in Jerusalem on the night before he had suffered the terrible death reserved usually for escaped criminals, soldiers who defected and the basest of traitors.

Constantine did not partake, nor did his mother, but Minervina joined those who knelt together before the altar to eat and to drink. After the service of worship, many people crowded around to speak to Helena and Minervina and finally the priest himself came over to where they were standing. Theognis did not appear quite so tall without his imposing robe, but the light in his eyes was friendly and the grip he gave Constantine's forearm when they were introduced was firm and strong.

"Congratulations upon your appointment as an officer of the Imperial Guard," he said. "It is said in Nicomedia that the Emperor favors you and that you will rise fast."

When Constantine's face showed his surprise, he added with a smile, "I possess no power of divination. It happens that your great-uncle Marios is an old friend, though he is not yet one of us. So is your tutor, Lactantius. Tell me, what did you think of the service this morning?"

"It was very interesting, and new to me."

"But not so different in many ways from the worship of the soldier's god, Mithras—is that what you are thinking?"

"H-how did you know?"

Theognis laughed. "Not by any devilish powers, you can be sure. You see, I once followed Mithras and was torn between him and Christ for many months, until I saw a man go through the rite of the *taurobolium*."

Constantine had witnessed several times the rite of which Theognis spoke. An expensive ceremony, it was thought to earn the highest favor of the soldier's god for the supplicant, who began the ritual by descending into a pit over which a grating was set. A young bull was then held securely over the grating and its throat slashed by a priest, deluging the man kneeling in the pit below with blood and—symbolically according to the ritual—purifying him in the service of Mithras and allowing him to rise from the pit a new and consecrated man.

"I asked myself what could any man gain from the blood of a young bull, when the son of God had given up his life as a sacrifice for all who followed him and named him their Lord and Saviour," Theognis continued. "And I realized then that neither Mithras, Jupiter nor any other could offer me the gift of eternal life that comes from Christ Jesus."

"Are you trying to convert me, sir?" Constantine asked.

Theognis shook his head. "From what your mother and Marios tell me, you think for yourself and are not swayed easily. I'm sure you will one day see the light, Centurion Constantine, but I suspect it will be only when Jesus Christ wills for you to see it."

Constantine was thoughtful as he rode the short distance back to Nicomedia and his duties in the palace. But his thoughts were not nearly so much of the service he had witnessed in Drepanum, or even the eloquent words of the priest-scholar, as they were of a slender girl with hair that was like a pale aureole around her lovely features in the sunlight. And already he was wondering how long it would be before he could find an excuse to leave his duties in the palace and visit Drepanum once again.

5

5

T HE THREE YEARS spent at Nicomedia while attaining his majority were in many ways a period of frustration for Constantine. For although he was honored by being in the Emperor's own household, he would gladly have exchanged all of it for a chance to participate in the exciting events going on in the West, under his father's able and vigorous direction.

Gesoriacum,* the major seaport of Gaul facing Britain, had fallen when Constantius, emulating the example of Alexander the Great in the siege of Tyre, had built a great mole that put the harbor within range of his machines of war. With the fall of the port to Rome, the usurper Augustus, Carausius, lost the base from which his fleet had ravaged shipping in the Fretum Gallicum and held the Alemanni tribes of the north in partial subjection. And with Gesoriacum in his hands, Constantius had been able to prepare a fleet for the invasion of Britain.

The main thrust was to have been launched directly against the British coast across the channel but, as a diversionary tactic, Constantius sent a squadron under command of the Prefect Asclepiodotus from the mouth of the river Seine. This smaller fleet succeeded beyond all expectations when, under the cover of a thick fog, they were able to enter one of the main rivers of Britain and ascend to the town of Londinium.† Meanwhile, Carausius had been murdered by his second-in-command, Allectus, and the latter, caught unprepared near Londinium, was quickly defeated by the forces under Asclepiodotus. As a result, Constantius made his major land-

* Boulogne
† London

ing almost without opposition and Britain fell without any battle of consequence.

It was about this time that Diocletian, in conjunction with the Co-Emperor Maximian, issued the edicts he had discussed with Constantine that evening in the palace garden. Under them, all prices of goods and services in the Empire were fixed at the time the edict went into effect, as well as the wages of every working person. The proportion of precious metal in the coinage was also set at a fixed proportion but its effect was not enough to counteract the evils resulting from the former actions, and the result was, literally, pandemonium.

Merchants held back goods, selling them secretly at higher prices when the supply became scarce. Men refused to work for the wages offered and those who hired workers were forced to pay extra wages secretly. Inevitably the populace became largely a nation of lawbreakers and a period of internal turbulence followed.

Constantine was finding a source of happiness during this time in visiting Drepanum and Minervina, who was blossoming into an extremely beautiful young woman. In addition, news from the South suddenly stirred once again his hopes of seeing actual military action.

In Africa and Egypt, what had long been an uneasy peace suddenly erupted into war when a group of five Moorish nations left their normal haunts in the desert and invaded the peaceful and rich provinces along the Nile. At the same time, a rude and savage people called the Blemmyes, who dwelt in the wild region between the mouth of the Nile and the Red Sea, also chose this moment to rebel against Roman rule.

Nor was the rebellion limited to Egypt. Farther westward along the North African coast, a Moor named Julian assumed the purple and proclaimed himself Augustus at Carthage. And at Alexandria, an Egyptian named Achilles claimed the same exalted position. Thus Maximian was forced to move from Italy across the narrow space of water separating the island of Sicily from Carthage on the African shore while Diocletian prepared to lead a second army into Egypt.

News from Constantius' headquarters at Treves had included an almost yearly announcement of the birth of another child to him and Theodora. A second boy, following the first, who had been called Constantine, was named Hannibalianus and a third was called Constantius. Helena naturally became anxious to have grandchildren of her own, in order to preserve the line of her son and, shortly before he departed with the Emperor for the expedition into Egypt, Constantine legally took Minervina, with whom he was very much in love, as his *concubina*—any other form of marriage between them being forbidden by the fact that he was of noble birth while she was not.

He spent a pleasant week of leave in the quiet village of Drepanum with his mother and his new bride, then rode back to Nicomedia to lead a cohort of the Emperor's personal guard on the expedition to Egypt, this time proudly wearing the insignia of Tribunus Primi Ordinarius.

II

It was a few weeks later that the galley bearing the Emperor Diocletian and the immediate members of his court, including Constantine, nudged to a mooring place at the great mole forming part of the harbor of Caesarea on the coast of Syria Palaestina. Dacius had managed to get himself assigned to the expeditionary force and, having fought in this area years earlier, was fairly familiar with its history. The port city, he told Constantine, had been built almost three hundred years earlier by a Jewish king called Herod, known as "the Great" to distinguish him from subsequent rulers bearing the same name.

Caesarea proved to be as magnificent a city as Nicomedia, with a great amphitheater and a palace-citadel where Diocletian took up his headquarters while they waited for auxiliary troops from nearby districts to augment the forces being prepared for the move southward against Alexandria. Constantine was eating dinner early one evening on a balcony of the palace looking westward toward a range of hills shutting the coastal plain away from a mountain—whose most striking characteristic was a towering snow-clad peak, colored a vivid pink now by the dying rays of the sun—when a visitor was announced. He looked up from his eating to see a slender man in his early thirties, wearing the simple robe of rough material he'd come to associate with Christian priests.

"Noble Tribune." The newcomer bowed. "My name is Eusebius Pamphilus."

"A Christian, and a priest?"

"Yes."

"What brings you here, sir?" Constantine gestured toward a chair. "I'm sure you know I am not of your faith."

"But you are the son of Caesar Constantius?"

"Yes."

"And known to my friend Theognis of Nicaea?"

"I have met the priest Theognis. But how did you know about that?"

"We were students together at the school of Pamphilus, the Presbyter of Caesarea."

"Presbyter?" Constantine frowned. "The word is not familiar."

"In our church it means a leader," Eusebius explained. "Pamphilus operated a school for priests here at Caesarea and I am custodian of his library."

"Why did you come to see me?"

"Yesterday the Emperor made a sacrifice in the Temple of Apollo. The High Priest examined the entrails of the animal, seeking an omen of the coming campaign in Egypt, and promised a victory—"

"But in words that leave a way out if things go wrong," Constantine reminded him.

"The priest also advised the Emperor to slaughter the inhabitants of Alexandria until their blood touches the knees of his horse."

"Surely you don't ask clemency for rebels who massacre Roman soldiers."

"No," Eusebius said. "The Apostle Paul taught us to pray for kings and for all who are in authority over us. Rebels must be punished, of course, or there will be anarchy and all will eventually suffer. But Alexandria was one of the earliest centers of our faith outside Palestine and many Christians live there. I know from reports received here that they are not in revolt, but if there is widespread slaughter after your victory, they will suffer, though innocent."

"I remember hearing Theognis speak of this man Paul," Constantine said. "You Christians seem to put much dependence in him."

"He was our greatest teacher after Jesus himself. The letters he wrote to the young churches he established are part of our Scriptures. I am sure you would find them interesting."

"Perhaps, when I have the time. But why come to me about the Christians in Alexandria? I am only a tribune, with little real authority."

"You are the son of a Caesar and will one day rule—"

"You're wrong there." Constantine did not hide his irritation. "Emperor Diocletian has no intention of letting Caesars appoint their sons to succeed them."

"But Caesar Galerius has already given his nephew great authority in the East. It is said here in Syria Palaestina that when Caesar Galerius becomes Augustus, Maximin Daia will be Caesar of this area and also of Egypt, so why shouldn't your father appoint you in the West?"

"You were speaking of Egypt." Constantine changed the subject abruptly. "What is it you want me to do?"

"The Emperor listens closely to you. If you were to ask that innocent people in Alexandria be spared, your request would carry much weight."

"And also give Caesar Galerius the opportunity he has been seeking to damage me with the Emperor," Constantine pointed out. "Don't you know that if it were left to him, he would destroy all you Christians?"

"I do know it," Eusebius said soberly. "From all appearances we shall soon be persecuted again, as we were in the time of Nero, so I would save as many as I can. You see, Tribune Constantinus, persecutions come and go with the rulers who begin them, but the Church of Christ is eternal and never-ending. Even if everyone in Alexandria is put to the sword, we will go on with the tasks Jesus set for us, when he was taken up into heaven after his resurrection. I ask only that, if the occasion arises, you do what you can to spare the innocent of Alexandria, whether Christian or pagan—the same thing your father has done in Gaul and Britain."

"I will do what I can," Constantine promised. "But don't expect much. The Emperor puts much store on pronouncements by soothsayers and oracles. If he has been told by them to make the streets of Alexandria flow with blood until it touches the knees of his horse, then I suspect he will do it."

III

Constantine's first view of Alexandria was exciting, coming as it did at night when the fires of the great lighthouse called the Pharos had already been lit and the mirrors behind them at the top of the great column of white stone reflected the rays of the fiery beacon far out to sea. Nowhere in the world, he knew, was there anything even remotely able to vie with the Pharos either in height or in grandeur. But his military instinct also reminded him that the great column was a considerable hazard to the Roman attack upon the city, since observers posted upon it constantly spied upon every activity in the Roman camp.

Seen the next morning, the city itself was only a low white mass on the horizon. But as the advancing troops grew near its defenses, he was able to make out the huge curving breakwater called the *Diabathra* that helped to form the protected harbor and upon which stood the royal palace and a magnificent Temple of Isis. Prior to the arrival of the army a Roman fleet had taken up its assigned position outside the harbor, blockading the entrance and exit of ships. But so fertile was the delta around the Nile's mouth and so great the warehouses in which grain and other foods were stored for shipment to ports all over the world, that the population was not likely to suffer from hunger for a considerable period.

One of Diocletian's first acts in the siege of Alexandria was to cut off the aqueduct that brought the waters of the Nile into every section of the great city. But since it was largely surrounded by water, Alexandria suffered but little from this deprivation.

Constantine had studied the classic Roman methods of siege during his years of training; now he was seeing them in operation for the first time. The initial step was the construction of an earthwork and stockade just beyond bowshot length, encircling the entire city except for the section fronting upon the water that was closed by ships engaged in the blockade. The normal second stage, after the erection of the earthwork, was mining, in which the attackers drove a tunnel beneath the walls of the place being attacked. The progress of a mining operation, however, could be followed easily by the defenders, simply by placing a shield against the ground and listening with an ear pressed to its round side, the sounds from beneath the earth being tremendously magnified in this way. And once the direction and progress of a tunnel had been determined, the defenders need only wait until it reached a point where they could dig a vertical shaft into it and scald the workers to death by pouring in boiling water.

Mining was not effective with Alexandria, since tunnels filled rapidly with ground water and even trenches soon turned into ditches, if dug to any effective depth. It was therefore necessary to use a large number of the great siege machines, which, though effective, also exposed those serving them to enemy attack. The result was a steady flow of casualties from the front line of attack to the rear where the injured were cared for by the surgeons, their wounds being washed with water and wine and bound with bandages of linen cloth.

Of the siege machines, the *ballista*, the *onager* and the *catapulta* —the three most commonly used—worked in much the same way. For a propulsive force, each utilized thick strands of cord twisted by means of windlasses until they exerted a powerful strain upon a wooden arm which, in turn, carried the projectile and, at the moment of release, flung it into the air.

The *onager*—named for the wild ass because of its kick when discharged—had only a single skein of rope activating the beam. When in use, the rope was first twisted by means of winches and gears, after which the beam was pulled down against it and the projectile attached before being released. Being mounted on wheels, the *onager* could be moved about fairly rapidly, and it was a favorite weapon for harrying troops.

The *ballista*, on the other hand, was a considerably larger machine, capable of heaving a stone roughly a third of a man's weight for a distance of as much as five hundred paces. And the *catapulta*, a device that used two tightly twisted ropes attached to wooden arms to drive a tough cord like a bowstring and project a heavy arrow or spear for roughly the same distance, could achieve enough force to penetrate even the heaviest armor.

The main Roman camp was established well behind the encircling fortification. It was in the customary form of a square, with streets crossing at right angles in the center where Emperor Diocletian's headquarters was located. No matter where such camps were formed, the pattern was always the same, not only in the arrangements to shelter the soldiers, but also in the location of supply tents, the headquarters of the various units and the like. Thus, in case of a sudden attack by night, a legionnaire could rise from his sleep and, almost without opening his eyes, locate his weapons and quickly reach his place in formation.

Slogging through the mud before Alexandria, Constantine's spirits were not particularly cheered by news that Maximian had reconquered the rebellious province of Mauritania far to the west in a lightning campaign launched from Italy against the African coast. Or that Maxentius, acting as his father's agent, was reported to have put much of the rebellious province to the torch, including a large part of Carthage. In doing so the ex-cadet earned himself a reputation of reckless daring and cold cruelty for which the Roman Senate had honored him with a triumph upon his return to that city, where he was his father's second-in-command, as well as Commander of the famed Praetorian Guard.

With missiles raining upon it night and day even Alexandria could not hold out forever against the might of Rome. After some eight months of continuous siege, during which disease felled a considerable part of the population—as well as no small number of the attackers—the governor of the city at last capitulated and begged for mercy. Mindful of the prediction made by the priest, who had forecast the future by examining the entrails of the sacrifice made to Apollo in Caesarea, Diocletian showed no mercy to the prostrate city. The legions marching ahead of him as he entered Alexandria triumphantly cut down thousands of inhabitants indiscriminately, until the streets did indeed run red with blood, as had been prophesied.

Hardened to suffering though he had become during the months of the siege and inclined to feel little sympathy for a people who had brought disaster upon themselves by their stubbornness, Constantine was nevertheless sobered by the needless carnage. He could do nothing, however, for Diocletian himself had ordered the Egyptian blood-bath. As the ranking officer in the elite Imperial Guard, he was just behind the Emperor when they rode into the city, from whose streets already rose a sickening sweet smell of blood so potent that the horses were nervous and had to be held under strict rein.

Ahead of him Constantine saw Diocletian's horse shy away from the body of a woman lying in the street with blood still pouring from her slashed throat and he spurred his own mount ahead, in case his help was needed. Before he could reach Diocletian, however, the jittery horse slipped, going down to its knees in the middle of the pool of blood. The Emperor would have been thrown to the stone pavement and no doubt severely injured, if Constantine had not managed to seize his arm just as the horse went down. Inspired by a sudden thought as he steadied Diocletian while the animal scrambled to its feet, Constantine shouted: "The prophecy of Apollo has been fulfilled! Look there at the knees of the Emperor's mount! They are red with blood."

An instant of stunned silence followed Constantine's announcement of the seemingly miraculous fulfillment of the prediction by the High Priest of Apollo at Caesarea. Diocletian hesitated, the instinct to destroy a people who had dared to resist him for eight months struggling against the innate superstitiousness of his nature. Then he leaned forward to look at the forelegs of the horse and saw that they were indeed covered with blood.

"No more killing!" he ordered. "The prophecy has been fulfilled! No more killing lest we offend the god."

"Carry the order to the troops ahead," Constantine ordered the decurion who had been riding beside him. "No more killing on pain of punishment by the Emperor."

"Forgive me for touching your divine person without leave, Dominus," he said, as the decurion spurred his horse forward, shouting the order to the line of troops as he passed. "I feared your mount would go down."

"You no doubt saved my life twice, Tribune Constantine," Diocletian said gratefully. "Once when you held me up and again when you kept me from incurring the displeasure of Apollo by going against his will. I would never have realized the prophecy had been fulfilled, if you had not recognized it. The people of Alexandria may yet raise a monument to your name, as Cleopatra did the obelisks in the square ahead in memory of Julius Caesar."

Constantine was not surprised, when the wealth captured in Alexandria was distributed, to find his own share larger than that of any Roman officer, save the Emperor himself. Nor did the great booty gained in Egypt come too soon for the Empire in general, since, even before the city fell, official dispatches brought word that the Persian king, Narses, taking advantage of Diocletian's preoccupation with Egypt, had attacked across the border of Augusta Euphratensia and was moving eastward toward Antioch.

Orders went immediately from Diocletian to Galerius, directing the Caesar of the East to prepare an army against the Emperor's return to Antioch, since it seemed that another campaign must now be fought upon the Persian frontier. Fortunately the Egyptian campaign was quickly consummated after the fall of Alexandria and emissaries soon began to arrive from cities farther up the Nile, assuring Diocletian of their allegiance.

During the long siege, a considerable section of the province of upper Egypt had joined with the black savages of Ethiopia and the Blemmyes—a barbaric tribe but little removed from the monkeys who swarmed in the trees of their land—to cause considerable trouble. When Busiris, one of the most ancient of Egyptian centers, and Coptos, through which for more than a thousand years had poured much of the Egyptian trade with India by way of the Red Sea, failed to send substantial payments as a token of allegiance, Diocletian decided to level them to the ground and Constantine was assigned the task of carrying out the order.

As he was preparing to ride out on the mission, an Imperial Courier brought him a letter from Drepanum. Written by his mother, it contained the news that, almost coincident with the fall of Alexandria, he had become the father of an infant son. And since there was already another Constantine—the son of his father and Theodora—Minervina and Helena had decided to call the baby Crispus, a family name on the mother's side.

Thus at the age of twenty-two, Flavius Valerius Constantinus was not only a father, an eventuality he had been quite too busy during the last months even to consider, but also seemed to have reached a point in his military career beyond which he could hardly expect to go. For the step from tribune to general was a great one and, even though he enjoyed the favor of Diocletian, he knew Galerius would never approve an elevation in rank for one he considered a potential military and political rival.

6

U PON HIS RETURN to Alexandria at the end of the brief campaign to humble Busiris and Coptos, Constantine found another letter from his mother. Written hardly a week after the one notifying him of his son's birth, it contained the tragic news that Minervina, never very strong, had not survived the aftermath of childbirth, succumbing to a fever a few days after the birth of the baby. The letter had arrived almost a month before but had been held in Alexandria, pending his return from the military expedition upriver.

The shock of Minervina's death was diluted somewhat by the fact that Constantine had not seen her for a full ten months. His only memory now was of a frail, fair-haired girl who was quiet and unassuming. Her features seemed to have blurred in his mind. And as for a child from the seed of his own loins, he found it quite impossible even to envision what the baby would look like. Fortunately he could be sure that Helena would care for Crispus as if he were her own son.

Constantine had barely finished the letter from Helena when he was summoned into the presence of the Emperor. He had not even had time to remove his clothing, dust-stained from the long ride, and soak himself in the bath to which he had been looking forward for days, but he knew better than to keep the Emperor waiting. Diocletian was in uniform, striding up and down in the building he had made his headquarters with a look of anger and annoyance on his face.

"What of your mission?" he demanded before Constantine could speak.

"Your orders were carried out, Dominus. Busiris and Coptos have been leveled to the ground."

"Perhaps these cursed Egyptians will think twice before they decide again not to pay Rome's taxes." Diocletian gave a snort of satisfaction, then paused to survey Constantine from head to foot. "You lost no time in answering my summons, I see."

"The message said you wanted to see me at once."

"Good! I'm glad to find somebody who obeys my orders." The Emperor's face softened. "It has come to my attention that you suffered a loss in your family recently."

"My wife died in childbirth at Drepanum. The letter was here when I returned."

"And the child?"

"My mother says he is strong and healthy."

"As he should be, with the blood of Claudius Gothicus and Constantius Chlorus in his veins, to say nothing of yours. Do you need to return to Drepanum?"

"No, Dominus. My mother will care for the child."

"Good! How soon can you start for Damascus and the Persian frontier in command of five hundred horse?"

It was the sort of question Constantine had come to expect from his years of close association with Diocletian and he had the answer. "Whenever the troops are ready, Dominus. Is there trouble in Damascus?"

"The whole Euphrates frontier has erupted! Narses of Persia has driven King Tiridates out of Armenia!"

Constantine needed no further explanation for Diocletian's anger. For centuries one of the most unstable frontiers of the Roman Empire had been along the river Euphrates, where the Persian kings were ever ready to take advantage of any difficulty requiring the presence of the legions elsewhere. While Julius Caesar had been carrying out his spectacular campaigns in Gaul over three centuries earlier, Crassus, who was serving that year as Consul, had sought a quick victory over the Persians in order to counteract the rapidly increasing popularity of Caesar. Moving eastward from Syria, he had attacked them at Carrhae, but was forced to retreat by their superior cavalry. While conducting an orderly withdrawal, Crassus had been tricked into a conference of war by the enemy and treacherously slain and, leaderless, his army had been almost completely destroyed on the plains around Carrhae in one of Rome's most humiliating defeats.

Again and again Rome had sought to stabilize the eastern frontier, but every few decades new fighting had broken out and the border had shifted east or west, depending upon the fortunes of war. During the reign of the Emperor Valerian, several decades before the accession of Diocletian, Armenia, a country lying north of Mesopotamia and touching the extreme eastern end of the Euxine Sea, had been snatched away by the Persians. And only through the bravery of followers of the assassinated Armenian King Chasroes had his infant son, Tiridates, been saved.

Brought up as a Roman, Tiridates had returned to Armenia after a victorious campaign against the Persians and had proved a very popular and capable ruler, stabilizing the northeastern corner of the Euphrates frontier. But with that bastion now fallen to the Persians, Constantine did not need to be told that it must be restored as quickly as possible, before the Scythians from the vast steppes farther to the north, and perhaps even the yellow men of the East, came pouring through the passes of the Caucasus to menace the fertile plains and valleys of Syria.

"Was King Tiridates killed?" Constantine asked. Though he had never met the Armenian king, he knew of his fine reputation.

"Not according to the reports that come here, but I haven't been getting a clear picture of the situation. There is even a rumor that Galerius is already moving the army I ordered him to raise to the eastern frontier."

"Leaving the Danube undefended?" Constantine exclaimed, aghast.

"Not even my son-in-law would be such a fool and expect to keep his purple cloak," Diocletian said dryly. "I am told that he left enough veterans to secure the forts along the Danube, so I hardly think the Goths will dare cross the river. But I shall move to Antioch as soon as we can get enough transport together, so as to be closer to the eastern front."

"What do you wish me to do, Dominus?"

"Find the battle line, if there is one, and back up Galerius' foot soldiers and auxiliaries with the five hundred horse I am entrusting to your command. But don't forget what happened to Crassus. The Persians are skilled cavalrymen."

"I remember."

"Evaluate the situation on the Euphrates frontier as soon as you arrive," Diocletian added, "and send me a private report."

The purpose of the mission was clear now; Constantine was really being sent to the Euphrates frontier to spy upon Galerius. Nor did he doubt that Galerius too would understand, as soon as he appeared with five hundred cavalry.

"Dacius will be your second-in-command," Diocletian told him. "He has fought through the area of Syria Palaestina and Mesopotamia, so he knows the lay of the land."

Constantine did not go at once to his quarters and the bath already drawn there. Instead, he sought out Dacius, to leave instructions for preparing the *ala,* or wing, of cavalry with which he would ride to the Euphrates frontier far to the northeast. There was an air of assuredness and purpose about him now that he had not possessed before leaving Alexandria. Dacius nodded approvingly when he finished the instructions.

"Somewhere between here and Busiris or Coptos, you became a man," he said. "I'm sorry about Minervina. She was a lovely child."

"It has been less than a year since I saw her last, yet I find it hard to remember exactly what she looked like."

"Does that trouble you?"

"I loved her very much, or thought I did. Now I cannot help wondering how permanent the love of men and women can be."

"Time has a habit of dulling memories, both good and bad," Dacius assured him. "And lucky for us that it does. Were you much disturbed when you ordered the men to destroy defenseless cities at Busiris and Coptos?"

"I still am," Constantine admitted. "It seemed so needless, when those people could have been left alive to help bring prosperity to the Empire."

"Peace is important too. Often it can be bought only in blood."

"I suppose so. But there should be a better way."

"Not while generals are ambitious enough to take chances," Dacius said cryptically.

"So Galerius did move against the Persians without consulting the Emperor?"

Dacius nodded. "Knowing Galerius, it must have seemed like too good an opportunity to let pass. After all, Maximian conquered Mauritania in a few months and in Britain your father has made steady progress, while Diocletian and the rest of us were holed up here outside Alexandria for nearly a year. When the Persians turned Tiridates out and started to bend the Euphrates frontier westward again, Diocletian ordered Galerius to prepare an army at Antioch. But Galerius saw a chance to win fame for himself, while the people are still complaining because Diocletian spent so much money in this Egyptian campaign."

"What chance does Galerius have of winning a quick victory?"

"Every chance, if he uses his head. After all, he is certain to have taken King Tiridates with him and, as soon as he starts retaking Armenia, the people of that kingdom will rally to his banners. That means a lot of auxiliary troops to swell the size of his army, so the Persians will have to send forces northward to hold Armenia, weakening their lines in Mesopotamia. With any kind of luck, Galerius should be able to turn their northern flank and, with his back to the desert, Narses could be forced to sue for peace, with Galerius getting all the glory."

"Do you think he is foolish enough to consider setting himself up as Emperor in Diocletian's place?"

"Not yet. But he's looking ahead to the time when Diocletian abdicates at the end of twenty years and forces Maximian to do the same. Your father may still be pinned down in Britain and Gaul then and Galerius could claim the whole Empire, with himself as sole Augustus, and you one of the first casualties."

Constantine smiled. "Sometimes I wonder why I listen to these wild tales of yours—"

"Because you know they're true. Empires are built, and maintained, by intrigues like the one Galerius is engaged in now. Fortunately for you, he is dull, even for a general, and you can easily outthink him."

"How?"

"That will have to be decided when we get to the frontier and see what is happening. But the gods obviously favor you."

"When did you decide that?"

"The day you bested Crocus and won the first round against Galerius. Some people were meant to be rulers, Constantine; it shows early in life. I believe you are one of them and only hope I live to see myself proved a prophet."

Constantine gave the grizzled centurion an affectionate punch on the shoulder. "When the time comes, if it ever does, you shall ride in triumph beside me, old friend," he promised. "But we'd better make an early start tomorrow, or fate will leave us behind."

II

Alexandria was over a week behind the five hundred when they crossed the Jordan River near the city of Jericho and took a road leading somewhat northeastward toward the ancient city of Amman, now called Philadelphia. Dacius had traveled this way before and assured Constantine that it was a shorter route to Damascus than another road which followed the winding course of the narrow, muddy stream.

All of them were glad to get back into an area where the hills were covered with green, for it had been rough going indeed since, near a town called Raphia, they had left the ancient "Way of the Sea" that followed the coast northward. From Raphia they had traveled some of the roughest and most desolate country Constantine had ever seen to the city of Hebron and on to the settlement of Engedi, overlooking the leaden blue surface of the strange sea which, Dacius said, knew no life because of the saltiness of its waters.

Great springs burst from the earth near Engedi, turning it into an oasis. But northward, as they followed the coast of the Dead Sea, the terrain had been marked by the same endless undulations of rock, broken into gorges and chasms like a piece of parchment crumpled in one's fist. The green irrigated fields around Jericho had been a welcome relief and now, with the route climbing steadily beyond the river, the character of the land became more like Illyricum, Constantine's homeland, as the road led past thickets of cedar, tere-

binth, arbutus, silver poplar, laurustinus, acacia, pistachio and ole-
ander.

Flocks of birds rose into flight, stirred from their feeding by the
passage of so many mounted men. And from the jungle along the
river bank they heard occasionally the roar of a lion, the growl of a
bear and the shrill cry of a wild boar. Several times they flushed an
odd-looking animal that Dacius called a *jerboa*, with hind legs fully
as long as its body and an even longer tail, enabling it to cover
ground in a series of startling leaps that created the illusion of flight.

Since they frequently crossed streams pouring down from the
plateau above, there was plenty of fresh water for the horses. Once
they paused to rest upon a height from which Dacius pointed out,
far to the north, the sparkling blue waters of a lake which he said
was called the Sea of Tiberius or Galilee. Beyond it, farther to the
north, was a mountain range capped with snow, which Constantine
remembered seeing from another direction when they had landed
at Caesarea. Dacius, who had fought through this region in an earlier campaign against the Persians, named the peak Mount Her-
mon and the area of rich pastureland, heavily forested hills, and the
prosperous people part of an ancient district called Gilead.

"It was to this region," he told Constantine, "that King David of
Israel fled nearly a thousand years ago, when he was driven out of
Jerusalem by Absalom, his oldest son."

"Where did you learn all this?" Constantine asked.

"It's no tale, if that's what you're thinking," Dacius assured him
with a grin. "A Jewish general named Josephus fought with our
armies under Titus, when they put down the great Jewish rebellion
in this country a little over two hundred years ago. Josephus wrote
a history of his people; you'll find it well worth reading."

"Why did this Absalom you spoke of rise against his father?"

"David was one of Israel's greatest kings, but when he grew old,
Absalom became impatient to succeed him. He was the darling
of the people and very vain, so some of the notables thought they
could gain power for themselves by setting him up as king in his
father's place."

"It has happened many times, before and since."

"And will keep on happening, unless men change in their hearts,"

Dacius agreed. "David and Joab, his chief general, needed time to get an army together and David didn't want Jerusalem destroyed in a battle between him and Absalom, so he left the capital. Even when Absalom pursued his father across the Jordan, David still ordered that the young prince not be killed, but Joab took care of that. Absalom wore his hair very long and as he was fleeing during the battle, it became caught in a tree, leaving him hanging. Joab saw him and pierced his heart with several darts."

"It was no more than he deserved for seeking to destroy his father."

"No doubt," Dacius agreed. "But the Jews have another explanation. They claim it was all the will of their god, so another son named Solomon could inherit the kingdom and build a temple to him in Jerusalem."

"Is this the same god whose son was supposed to have been crucified?"

Dacius gave him a quick, probing glance. "Where did you hear about Jesus of Nazareth?"

"Minervina was a Christian, and my mother leans toward them. In Drepanum I once went to a Christian church."

"When you write your mother again, tell her to keep her feelings about the Christians secret," Dacius advised. "Things are not going so well with these new edicts of Diocletian's setting prices and wages and the amount of gold and silver in the coins. I hear that some of the chamberlains charged with enforcing them are seeking to throw the blame on the Christians, claiming they use spells and evil spirits to stir up the people."

"I told the Emperor more than two years ago it wouldn't work," Constantine said.

"Then let us hope it is the Christians he blames and not you. The man called Jesus of Nazareth taught in this part of the world and had many followers, particularly around the Sea of Galilee north of here. It was a rebellion of Galileans in Jerusalem that cost him his life on the cross."

"But the Christians say he came to save the world and gave his life for those who believe in him."

Dacius gave a snort of disgust. "Then why didn't he save his

own people? Some forty years after he died, they rebelled against
Rome and had to be treated as you just finished treating Busiris
and Coptos."

III

At Philadelphia—or Amman—Constantine and his troop of horsemen made camp in the caravansary, a resting place for travelers
on the outskirts of the city. Several of the troopers were from
Philadelphia and Dacius gave them leave to spend the night with
their families. Constantine was surprised to see one of them talking
to Dacius hardly an hour after he had left the camp. Shortly the
two men came over to where Constantine's tent had been pitched
by his servant.

"Josiah here has brought a strange story," the centurion reported.
"His father is a merchant and heard it from a caravan driver who
arrived this morning to trade in the marketplace."

"What is it?"

"The caravan master says he heard that a Roman army under
Caesar Galerius is moving eastward from Antioch to attack the
Persians."

"That's hardly news. The Emperor knew it before we left Egypt."

"But the man says Galerius took the road to Carrhae, instead
of farther north through Armenia."

"Carrhae! Why would he risk that route?"

"For the same reason Crassus risked it several hundred years
ago—the hope of covering himself with glory with a sudden blow
at the center of the Persian frontier, while Narses is occupied in
keeping the Armenians under the sword."

"What chance does he have of succeeding?"

"It's a foolhardy move. But then fools sometimes win where wise
men lose."

"Bring the caravan master to me," Constantine ordered the
trooper called Josiah. "And Dacius, have the leaders of each *turma*
procure as much grain and rations as their mounts can carry besides themselves."

"In preparation for a forced march?"

"What else?"

Dacius didn't answer, but called for his orderly to bring the maps he always carried on the march in a cylindrical container behind his saddle. When they arrived, he spread one of them out.

"We are here," he said, pointing to Philadelphia. "Damascus lies almost directly north, about two days of hard riding. We can probably gain more information about what Galerius is doing there and have a report ready to go to the Emperor. It should reach him by the time he gets to Antioch and, if Galerius really lets himself be caught in the desert, a new Caesar of the East will have to be appointed."

Constantine bent over the map and studied it for a moment. "Why not bypass Damascus and strike directly northeastward for Circesium, where the frontier crosses the Euphrates? We should save several days that way."

"No matter how fast you travel, Galerius will claim you arrived too late to help in any victory he may win," Dacius reminded him. "And if he has walked into a trap, aren't we likely to be caught in it too?"

"Are you asking me or testing me, old fox?"

"Some of both," Dacius admitted with a grin.

"If Caesar Galerius is winning, I shall tell the Emperor we arrived too late to be of any help. And if he is losing, the army will need all the help it can get."

"Including a new general?"

Constantine shrugged. "Who can tell? The important thing now is to avoid another Carrhae."

Josiah arrived just then with the caravan master, a dark-skinned man with the proud face and hawk nose of the Bedawin traders, who were able to follow the ancient paths across desert wastes which their ancestors had traveled for centuries with their caravans. Constantine greeted him courteously and, with Josiah interpreting, launched immediately into a stream of questions.

"Did you see this Roman army of which you spoke?" he asked.

"Not with my own eyes, noble Tribune," the caravan master answered. "But I had word of it at Sura from one I trust. He had just come from Batnae and saw the army with his own eyes."

"Batnae is on the main route from Antioch to Carrhae and

Resaina." Dacius put a stubby forefinger on the map. "Galerius must intend to cross the headwaters of the river Aboras and go on to Nisibis on the frontier. If he reaches there while the forces of Narses are still bottled up to the north in Armenia, he can then strike southeastward by way of Singara to Ninus on the river Tigris."

"Putting an arrow into the very heart of the Persian kingdom," Constantine agreed. "It's a daring move and only a brave man would make it."

"Or a fool."

"Galerius is not that. You should know it as well as I, Dacius."

"Let us say then that ambition may have made a fool of him." Dacius pointed to an area on the map between Antioch and the broad western curve of the Euphrates. "From the hill country around Carrhae to the river Euphrates is a sandy desert, completely barren, without even a tree or a spring of fresh water to supply troops marching across it. Until you've made such a march, you can't realize how thirsty a man can get, but it's a hundred times worse coming back, in retreat. Then a legion must hold its ranks, closing up whenever someone falls by the wayside and not stopping to succour them. For once the ranks break, enemy cavalry can sweep in and cut an entire legion to pieces in a matter of moments."

"You paint a dreary picture," Constantine said. "But if Galerius succeeds in dividing the forces of Narses, the Roman frontier will extend farther eastward than it has ever been before." Then he added in a voice so low that only Dacius could hear him, "And a third Caesar will be needed to govern so vast a realm."

"Crassus wagered ten legions on just such a turn of the dice, and lost," Dacius reminded him. "What are your orders for tomorrow? Do we ride northward to Damascus, or into the desert?"

"What is the shortest route to Circesium, where the frontier with Persia crosses the river Euphrates?" Constantine asked the caravan master.

Josiah spoke rapidly to the dark-skinned man and listened intently to his answer, then turned to Constantine. "He says his people do not use maps such as this, sir," he reported. "The lore of

the caravan trails is handed down from father to son; in the desert,
the guide selects a star and follows it."

"Does he know a more direct route to Circesium than by way
of Damascus?" Constantine insisted. "If he does, tell him I will pay
him well to guide us there."

Again there was a brief colloquy, at the end of which Josiah
reported: "He knows of a caravan route to the neighborhood of
Circesium that is little used, sir. The way is rough, though pass-
able, and will cut several days off the longer journey. But he would
have to be paid for the caravan he has just brought here, since it
will go no farther."

"Isn't your father a merchant?" Constantine asked Josiah.

"Yes, noble Tribune."

"Tell him to buy the caravan from this man and resell it later
for what he can get. He will be paid the difference with a draft
on the Imperial Treasury."

"It shall be done, sir." Josiah did not quibble, but departed with
the caravan master.

Constantine watched silently while Dacius rolled up the maps
and put them back in their container. He was waiting for the old
centurion's verdict on his proposed action, but when Dacius spoke,
his words were more of a soliloquy.

"So the young eagle spreads its wings," he said with a smile,
then added: "We shall soon see how sharp are its claws."

7

Days of hard riding lay behind Constantine and his command when they drew rein on the west bank of the Euphrates, not far from where the great river angled sharply northward toward the Taurus mountain range. At this point they were a good day's ride west of their original destination of Circesium, where the eastern Roman frontier crossed the Euphrates.

The decision to turn northward had been made on the basis of disturbing rumors concerning a Roman disaster, which they had heard at an oasis on one of the ancient caravan routes by which the people of the Tigris-Euphrates basin had communicated with what for centuries had been called Canaan, but was now the Roman province of Syria Palaestina. Across the broad flood of the Euphrates they could see the walls of the Roman fortress guarding the area, but it appeared to be strangely deserted.

"What do you make of it?" More and more as the days passed the younger officer had assumed the habit of command—with the full approval of the grizzled centurion, who had been the first to realize that the fledgling was now fully able to leave the nest.

"Either they have evacuated the fortress," Dacius said, "or they expect to be besieged."

"We'll cross and see which it is. Send three *turmae* over to hold the east bank and scout the countryside."

So close had horses and riders become in the weeks since they had left Egypt that the crossing was accomplished almost without command. Constantine went over with the first of the men and, when all were across, ordered the trumpeter to marshal the troop into formation in a single column. Then, with the eagles of Rome at the head of the column and their banners proudly flying in the afternoon breeze, they approached the fortifications guarding the river crossing. They were still a good arrow range from it, however, when Constantine ordered the column to halt and rode up almost to the gates of the palisaded area that was typical of a Roman frontier fortress. He was accompanied only by his two standard bearers and, at his nod, the trumpeter blew a blast.

"Flavius Valerius Constantinus, Tribunus Primi Ordinarius, on a mission for the Emperor, asks admission to the fortress," he announced.

Nothing happened for a moment, then the gate of the fortification was pushed open and a stocky centurion in full uniform, followed by two legionaries bearing banners similar to those Constantine had displayed, strode through it. He came to a position of attention in the open space before the gate and gave the clenched-fist salute of the Roman soldier, which Constantine meticulously returned.

"Lucius Catullus, Centurion of the 14th Cohort, commanding the garrison," he announced. "Enter with your men, Tribune Constantinus. The stables are empty, but there is grain and fodder for your horses."

When the *ala* was inside the fortress, Constantine and Dacius joined the centurion in the headquarters of the garrison.

"I suppose you're wondering why we didn't greet you with open arms," Lucius Catullus said. "But I have always followed the principle of *si pacem vis habere para bellum.*"

"If you want peace, be ready for war," Constantine repeated approvingly. "It is an excellent motto."

"True, the fighting is somewhere to the north of us, if there is still any war," Lucius Catullus continued. "But with the Persians on our doorstep, it's just as well not to let them know I have emptied the garrison of all but a few household troops and sent them north to help Caesar Galerius."

"Then he *is* in trouble?" Constantine asked quickly. "We heard rumors of it."

"If the gossip in the market place is to be believed—and it's usually several days ahead of official dispatches—the Emperor's son-in-law is about to be routed," Lucius Catullus said. "I expect any day to be forced to retreat toward Antioch to save the skins of the few men I have left, to say nothing of my own."

"Was it Carrhae all over again?" Dacius asked.

"Something like it, from what I hear. The Persian soothsayers have always been wiser than ours. They must have told Narses that Galerius would strike at the center instead of retaking Armenia. But why were you sent here?"

"The Emperor was concerned about the arsenal at Damascus," Constantine explained. "And he wanted to know what is really happening on the Persian frontier."

"The arsenal should be safe, for the moment. Narses will be busy for a while; the Roman retreat began only a few days ago."

"Retreat!" Constantine exclaimed. "Where?"

"To Antioch, if rumors are true," said Lucius Catullus grimly. "Perhaps even to the port of Seleucia, or into the sea. The way I heard it, Galerius was in such a hurry to win a victory in Persia that he used green troops from Cilicia and Syria Palaestina to make up his army, leaving his veterans behind to hold the Danube fortifications, lest the Goths decide to visit Greece again. As an old veteran, Dacius—no offense meant, Tribune—you can imagine what happened when such a rabble began the march from Carrhae to the Euphrates."

"It would have been a kindness to cut their throats first," Dacius agreed. "Those curved swords the Persian cavalrymen use can slit a man's gullet before he knows what's happening to him, so I imagine plenty have been cut since."

"Then you have no idea where the battle lines really are?" Constantine asked.

"Or if any line exists," Lucius Catullus said. "We have been waiting here for the Persians to come, after they finish with Galerius. My advice to you, Tribune, is to recross the river and ride for Antioch."

"Out of the fighting entirely?"

"But alive," the centurion said and added earnestly, "Don't risk five hundred horse on a battle that is lost already; they may be needed to save Antioch." He turned to Dacius. "Don't you agree?"

"The decision is Tribune Constantine's," Dacius said, his eyes never leaving the younger man's face. "He alone is responsible to Diocletian for our *ala*."

"But discretion is still the—"

"Unroll the map, Dacius, and let me see what lies north of here," Constantine interrupted crisply.

Dacius opened the map and the three of them studied it. "I thought I remembered two roads to the north," Constantine said after a moment. "But I see only one leaving here."

"The way forks about two or three hours' ride to the north," Lucius Catullus explained. "One route goes eastward, the other westward to Antioch."

"Can we cross the Euphrates at a point where the Persians might not be in force? I don't want to be caught with the river between me and Antioch and no way to cross."

Lucius Catullus put a finger on the map. "There is a ruined town here at Dura—it's sometimes called Europos nowadays. I'm sure you can cross there, though you may have to swim a bit."

"We will turn northwest when we leave here in the morning then and try to learn more about where Galerius' main force is located."

"You'll need grain for your horses and men and extra skins for carrying water in that country," Catullus said. "I will have everything ready for you at dawn."

"Good," Constantine told him. "I will see that word of your help here is entered on your record of service."

"Whoever delivers my eulogy will thank you." Lucius Catullus' smile was without mirth. "He will have precious little to go on as it is."

Two days of hard riding later, Constantine learned what he had been dreading to hear. The Roman army, which had launched what was to be a lightning attack at the heart of the Persian Empire only a few weeks earlier was now in full retreat toward the Euphrates and Antioch. Long before they reached the area of the Roman retreat, columns of smoke rising in the air and vultures wheeling in the morning sky told a graphic story.

II

Two roads connected Antioch with the heart of the Persian Empire. Galerius had chosen the southern and most direct for his drive into Persia, Constantine and his troop saw when they crossed it east of the Euphrates. The scene of almost indescribable carnage and horror that met their eyes proved beyond doubt that Galerius' army had passed that way recently, in full retreat.

Baggage and weapons had been cast aside by the fleeing Romans. Banners lay in the dust, often stained with the blood of the men who had carried them. Bodies lay everywhere, many already beginning to decay in the hot sun, bellies distended, skin darkened and flesh torn by the vultures that rose in clouds, when Constantine and his troop rode across what had been the line of retreat.

There was no sign of any fighting, or of the "Stand Till Death" motto of seasoned Roman troops. Only here and there could a Persian body be distinguished by dark skin and strange weapons, for this had obviously been an utter rout under a vicious slashing attack by an enemy who had shown no mercy. Mercifully for the wounded, the throats of most of those who had fallen had been slashed with the deadly Persian scimitar.

"This must have been Carrhae all over again," Dacius said. "I only hope Galerius suffered the same fate."

For a moment Constantine was too much in the grip of the horror he was witnessing to risk speech. Finally, however, he forced himself to look away to where the scene of death and plunder stretched westward toward Antioch along the route the retreating army had followed.

"You know this means we're behind the Persians following Galerius, don't you?" he said.

"By the gods of Rome!" the centurion exclaimed. "We have ridden into a trap without knowing it. What shall we do?"

It was a measure of the way Constantine had matured as a leader of men, since they had left Nicomedia for the war against the Egyptian rebels, that Dacius asked for a decision instead of offering advice.

"If the trapper doesn't know we're in the trap, we may be able to get out before he can spring it." Constantine's mind was working rapidly while he spoke his thoughts aloud, testing them, so to speak, against the battle wisdom Dacius had gained through decades of service. "Do you know how far it is to Europos or Dura, that Lucius Catullus spoke about?"

"Only a short distance, as I remember it from the map."

"The retreating column wasn't very wide here," Constantine pointed out, "so we might be able to circle the enemy's south flank unobserved and cross the river to join what is left of our forces."

"It's probably our only chance to get past the Persians with whole skins," Dacius agreed. "And not much of a chance at that."

"Pass the order," Constantine told him. "And warn the men to be quiet. We don't want to give the enemy's rear guard any warning that we are behind them."

It proved to be less than two hours' ride to the Euphrates and, as Constantine had hoped, they did not see any sign of the enemy on the way. But when Constantine and Dacius at the head of the column topped a low rise and found the river flowing placidly before them in the light of the setting sun, there was no mistaking the meaning of the scene that met their eyes.

A squadron of perhaps two hundred soldiers led by a tall man whose armor shone so brightly in the rays of the setting sun that it appeared to have been burnished, was attempting to make an orderly crossing of the river. Their banners were held high and their ranks were still solid, even though some were wounded and a number were being carried by others inside the square they had formed for their defense. Nor was there any sign of panic, though fully twice their number of Persian cavalry were harrying them in the typical slashing attack favored by those superb horsemen.

The chances of very many of those under attack getting safely across the broad flood, here almost half a mile in width, appeared hopeless. The Persian cavalry were quite busy and had not yet noticed Constantine and Dacius, so there was plenty of time to withdraw, but Constantine did not consider such a possibility. Even as his eyes quickly evaluated the situation, he was giving orders to his second-in-command.

"Take half the troops and swing upstream to encircle the Persians," he directed. "I will close the other half of the noose with the rest."

"Standards to the front!" Dacius ordered, drawing his sword. Alternate *turmae* wheel into position. Attack!"

The trumpeter sounded the call to charge and, as Constantine's half of the *ala* executed the same move, a flying double line of horsemen swept down upon the enemy. Intent on destroying their intended victims, the Persians did not realize what was happening until the Roman cavalry were upon them, jabbing with their sharp javelins before the enemy could wheel to meet the new attack. The swarthy face of the leader of the beleaguered band lit up at the appearance of the Roman column and he shook his bloody sword aloft in a gesture of victory.

"Start your men across before it is dark," Constantine shouted to him. "We can handle the enemy."

The tall man nodded, and as Constantine turned to thrust his lance into the body of a Persian officer started to wade into the muddy water, heading toward the opposite shore and calling for his men to follow. They were happy enough to obey. Under their commander's direction, they joined hands to form a human chain and support the shorter ones, who might otherwise be swept beneath the surface in deeper water.

The falling body of the Persian officer almost twisted Constantine's lance from his grasp, but he managed to tear it loose in time to counter the attack of another. Across the seething melee of fighting men, he saw Dacius slashing about him expertly as he shouted orders and encouragement to his column. Then, almost as quickly as the engagement had begun, the Persians who remained alive managed to break through the noose formed by Constantine's troops and went racing away, ending the engagement.

Constantine's men would have followed the fleeing enemy but he shouted an order to reform the column and, urging his horse into the brown flood of the Euphrates, began to cross the river.

The tall man was near midstream now, wading at the head of his troops, but the river was deepening rapidly and his armor made the going heavy. Calling to him to seize hold of his stirrup when he came abreast, Constantine ordered his own men to follow his example and, with each of the little band of foot soldiers hanging on to the stirrup of a cavalryman in the center where the current was swiftest, they managed the crossing without too much difficulty. Only once did the line break momentarily, allowing several men and two horses to be swept downstream, but the chain was quickly restored and the crossing completed.

On the west bank, the leader of the band staggered up the slope with water streaming from his clothing and from the recesses of his armor. Constantine was busy getting his own men out of the river, but he noted with approval that the other officer did not stop to rest until all of his command, except the few who had drowned, were safely on the shore. Only then did he turn over command to a centurion and come striding back to where Constantine and Dacius had dismounted.

"I owe you my life, Tribune," he said, speaking in excellent Latin, though his dark skin and broad cheekbones—Constantine was sure —meant that he was other than a Roman by birth. "My name is Tiridates."

Constantine snapped to attention. "Flavius Valerius Constantinus salutes the King of Armenia," he said formally.

"That title I'm afraid I no longer hold," Tiridates said with a wry smile. "The Persians have driven me out of my domain, just as they have driven the army I was part of out of this area."

"Is Caesar Galerius safe?" Constantine asked.

"He was the last time I saw him," said Tiridates a bit dryly. "My command was acting as a rear guard, while the main part of the army retreated across the river. But the Persian cavalry managed to cut us off from the rest of the column and drove us here to the neighborhood of Dura."

"You know the town?"

"There's not much left of it, I'm afraid. One of my men is from this area and remembered that the river could be crossed here, so we were making for this spot. The Persians would have cut us off, though, if you hadn't arrived when you did." Tiridates gave Constantine a quick probing glance. "Are you the son of Constantius Chlorus?"

"Yes, Your Majesty."

"I should have recognized you from your resemblance to your father, but I was otherwise occupied. Caesar Constantius and I served together once in Pannonia. He is a great general and a brave soldier." His eyes suddenly twinkled. "But no greater, I am sure, than his son. The way you encircled those Persians and cut them to pieces was something to see. I wish I could have spared the time to really enjoy it."

Constantine flushed at the words of praise from this subject king, who had earned the respect and admiration of the entire Roman Empire. But more than that, he felt an immediate liking for Tiridates, much the same sort of affection he felt toward Dacius.

"We are at your command, noble Tiridates," he said.

"Nay, let us share responsibility, particularly since neither of us knows where to go just now." The Armenian king glanced up at the sky where the sun was about to set. "Dura is only a little distance away. Perhaps we can find shelter in the ruins there and in the morning we can decide how to go about finding General Galerius and his command, if any of them are left alive."

"From the looks of the route of retreat, I would say not," Dacius observed. "It's too bad Galerius didn't wait until Emperor Diocletian could reach Antioch and take charge of this venture. Then the attack would have been launched through Armenia, Your Majesty, as I'm sure you advised."

"We'd better get on to Dura while we still have light enough to find out whether any Persians are waiting for us there," Tiridates said. "There will be time enough later to analyze the campaign."

Dura proved to be largely a mass of ruins, but a number of the houses possessed walls that provided shelter for the weary soldiers and there was an ample water supply for both men and horses from a spring and brook that emptied into the Euphrates. The men of Tiridates' command were exhausted from their hazardous retreat and the strain of swimming the river, so Constantine ordered his own troops to undertake the chores of preparing camp and stationing pickets to warn of attack under the cover of darkness.

Night had already fallen by the time the camp was established. While some of the men ate, others took torches and explored what remained of the buildings of the town, in case any Persians were hiding there. Constantine and King Tiridates were eating the usual evening meal of Roman soldiers on the march, cakes of grain and oil washed down with sour wine, when a shout came from one of the searching parties. They went immediately to where the soldier who had shouted was standing before one of the larger ruins. In the light of the torch he carried, his face was as pale as if he had seen a ghost.

"What is it, soldier?" Dacius demanded.

"I think I saw a spirit in there, sir."

Dacius took the torch from the man's trembling hand and drew his sword, as did Constantine and Tiridates. Gingerly they entered through a broken section of wall what had apparently been a large Roman-style house, from the looks of what remained. It was built around the usual open court, now grown up with brambles and reeds, and they had gone only a few paces inside the main part of the structure when ahead of them they saw revealed in the flaming light of the torch, the thing that had so startled the soldier.

It was a large picture painted on a wall of one of the rooms —or rather two which had been thrown together by tearing out an intervening wall, from the looks of it—a painting of a shepherd with his flock around him and carrying a lamb in his arms.

"By the thunderbolts of Jove!" Dacius exclaimed. "What is it?"

Tiridates gave the answer. "This house must have been used as a church by the Christians. I've seen paintings like this in my own kingdom. The shepherd is the man they call Jesus of Nazareth."

"The son of their god?" Constantine exclaimed.

"Yes."

Dacius whistled softly. "I hear that the Christians claim he can save people from death. If he saves us from the Persians tomorrow, I'll make a sacrifice to him when we get back to Nicomedia."

III

"Many Christians live in my country," Tiridates said as they stood in the ruins studying the painting. "They are a peaceful people and harm no one so I don't trouble them. Dura—or Europos as it is often called now—has been a ruin for at least a hundred years, so these pictures must have been painted before that."

Constantine noticed a number of his own command among the soldiers looking into the ruined building. "Are any of you Christians?" he asked.

No one answered for a moment, then the trooper called Josiah from Philadelphia came into the room. "I was raised in a Christian family, sir," he said. "I remember hearing my grandfather speak of churches like this; the Christians were persecuted often, so they used homes as meeting places. You can see where the wall was torn out between two rooms to make a larger room for the services."

Constantine raised his torch and picked his way through the rubble to the other end of the room. The floor was raised there to form an elevated rostrum or dais, and when he looked through the open doorway of a smaller room he saw a sunken bowl, as if the space had been used for washing.

"This room must have been used for baptizing," Josiah said.

"Baptizing?"

"A sacrament, sir, whereby the sins of those who believe are washed away and they are made pure."

"Like the *taurobolium!*" Dacius exclaimed. "I went through that a long time ago."

Above the bowl was a painting of a man and a woman in a garden representing, Josiah said, Adam and Eve, the first man and woman on earth. On another wall of the same room, two soldiers in ancient clothing and armor were about to engage in battle. Josiah named them David and Goliath, the latter a mighty Philistine whom the smaller David was said to have bested with a stone flung by a sling.

On the north wall a sepulcher was depicted with three women

beside it; Josiah explained that this was the tomb of Jesus, from which his followers believed he had risen after death. On the upper part of the small wall, there was a strange scene depicting a group of men in a boat on the water. The same figure of the shepherd was walking toward them on the surface and another, apparently having tried to walk on the water but failed, was sinking and reaching out his hand imploringly to the walking figure.

"Jesus walked on the water of the Sea of Galilee," Josiah said. "But when Simon Peter tried to do the same, his faith failed him and he sank, until Jesus lifted him up."

Even though the colors were faded by time and weather, the paintings were strangely compelling, particularly those depicting the slender shepherd. His eyes, in the flickering light of the torches, seemed almost to be alive, and seeing them Constantine felt again the same warmth of friendship and liking which he'd experienced toward King Tiridates that afternoon on the river bank and which he felt for Dacius.

Whether carrying a lamb or holding out his arms in a gesture of welcome, the man called Jesus seemed to be waiting to receive any who were troubled or ill in his comforting embrace. In fact, one of the pictures portrayed him in the act of healing a man who lay at full length upon a small bed, while another, obviously part of the same scene, showed the paralyzed man now walking with his pallet rolled up and carried upon his back.

On the wall above the head of Jesus, Constantine noticed a strange symbol that he remembered seeing in the old Temple of Asklepios at Naissus. He had no idea what it meant, though somehow the pattern seemed familiar.

"Those markings over the shepherd's head, Josiah," he said. "What are they?"

Josiah held his torch higher, illuminating brightly the strange pattern painted on the stone. "They are Greek letters marking the initials of Christ's name, sir, two of them—*Chi* and *Rho*—superimposed."

"Ingenious!" Tiridates exclaimed. "I suppose they have some magical significance."

"The Son of God has no need of magic, Your Majesty," Josiah said. "All power is his, over men and over earth and in heaven."

IV

Constantine made himself as comfortable as he could for the night, rolled up in his long heavy cloak beside the coals of the campfire, for it was cool on the banks of the great river. When perhaps an hour passed and his troubled thoughts would not allow him to sleep, he got up and, going to the coals of the campfire, blew upon them and put on another piece of wood.

The warmth of the flames lightened somewhat the vague sense of depression he'd felt since they had returned from inspecting the ruins of the old church earlier that evening, but it could not entirely remove it. Nor was he unaware of its cause.

For the first time in his life, he had experienced a moment of real panic that afternoon when they had come upon the wreckage of what had been an army scattered across the plain and he'd realized that he and the five hundred, for whom he was responsible, were behind the enemy lines. In the excitement of attacking the Persian forces that had been about to destroy the little band led by Tiridates, and the subsequent crossing of the river, he had forgotten his own fear. But now, surrounded by the ruins of the old city—in themselves a reminder of death—he felt them flooding in upon him once again.

Antioch—and safety—were still at least three days or more of hard riding away through an area that was certain to be heavily infested with Persian troops. And since those who had escaped the brief battle at the river crossing were certain to report the presence of both his five hundred and the remnants of King Tiridates' command in the area, the enemy was certain to come looking for them in force as soon as it was light.

For some strange reason, which he could not explain at the moment, Constantine found himself remembering the paintings on the walls of the ruined church nearby, particularly the slender figure of the shepherd cradling the lamb in his arms and protecting it from harm. He too was a shepherd he thought, with a flock of nearly seven hundred, now that Tiridates' command had been joined with his. But he felt none of the assurance and confidence that seemed to shine in the eyes of the slender shepherd in the painting. Remembering that look, Constantine felt a strange desire to study the painting again, to discover whether the confidence and assurance depicted in the shepherd's eyes were real and not a trick of lighting, brought about by the torches they had used in examining the ruins.

Only a moment was required to pick up a dry faggot and hold it in the coals until it burst into flames. Carrying the burning stick as a torch, he entered the ruins of the old church once again. The face of the shepherd had the same quiet look of peace and certainty of purpose. And strangely enough, as Constantine stood looking at the somewhat stylized figure, he felt his own doubts begin to ebb away and a new certainty of purpose flood through him like a warm protecting mantle. Leaving the ruined church, he returned to his place by the dry coals of the campfire and fell asleep instantly, to be awakened only when the camp began to stir at dawn.

8

WHILE THE HORSES were being fed and the men were eating a hasty and frugal morning meal, Constantine, Tiridates and Dacius held an informal council of war. Only one subject needed to be discussed—how they might extricate themselves from their extremely hazardous position behind the enemy line.

"Your cavalry can move much faster than my foot soldiers," Tiridates told Constantine. "It isn't fair to ask you to risk five hundred men to preserve our safety. Why don't you ride on and overtake Caesar Galerius?"

"From what we saw yesterday, I would say he's still running," Dacius observed.

"We will gain nothing by dividing our forces." At the note of assurance in Constantine's voice Dacius glanced at him sharply. The old soldier had not missed the moment of panic yesterday when, sickened by the carnage on the plain, Constantine had felt a perfectly human urge to flight. But no sign of that panic showed in his manner now, though their position could hardly be termed less than desperate.

"Many of my band are wounded," Tiridates said. "Shall we leave them behind so the rest can march faster?"

"Together we number close to seven hundred, about a fourth of a legion of experienced fighting men and, as far as we know, the only organized body of Roman soldiers existing in this region," Constantine said. "It will not help the morale of the troops if we leave the wounded behind. And by staying together, we may win our way clear of the Persians. After all, the farther west they go, the more scattered their forces will become."

"What is your plan of action?" Dacius asked.

"What a shepherd does when his flock is ravaged by wolves."

"The hunted becomes the hunter!" Tiridates' eyes suddenly began to glow. "It is a daring idea, especially for so small a band—"

"If I were the Persian general," Constantine said, "I would expect us to turn north and would send forces in that direction. So we will turn south and perhaps be able to fall on those who are following our army. That way we can gain time for Caesar Galerius to gather his troops and make a stand somewhere between here and Antioch." He looked at the other two. "Are we agreed as to the overall strategy?"

"My vote is in favor," Tiridates said promptly.

"And mine," said Dacius.

"Sound the call to get under way then, Dacius. We don't want to be here when the Persians arrive."

Since both were made up of experienced soldiers, the detachments were soon on the move. Those able to march went on foot, while the wounded who could ride were boosted up behind Constantine's cavalrymen. The few not able to travel that way were carried on improvised horseborne litters. All waterskins were filled, since some barren country must still be crossed, and a scouting party of a dozen men was sent ahead under the command of Dacius. Soon the great river was left behind, for Dura was on the western side of a huge curve in its course and their route of march was now directly toward Antioch. It was almost noon when Dacius and one of his scouts appeared ahead.

"You were right," he reported to Constantine, who rode out to meet him. Tiridates, at his own insistence, was marching toward the back of the column with his own men. "The Persians split their forces and sent a large body of cavalry back to the river early this morning."

"How far ahead are the others?"

"No more than an hour's march."

"Then we should be able to attack before the band sent to destroy us returns."

"If we lose no time," Dacius agreed.

"What about Galerius' army?"

"The stragglers must not be far beyond where we turned back. Many of the bodies we saw on the field were still warm."

"Is there any high ground between us and the Persians?"

"I saw a low hill ahead. They should be past it by the time we catch up with them."

"We'll give them a little time, to be sure."

Tiridates caught up just then and Constantine gave him a quick review of the situation. "I propose that we march for another half hour and let the Persians get beyond the hill Dacius saw ahead," he said. "That will give us the advantage of surprise when my cavalry attacks the rear of the Persian forces while your infantry backs us up. Agreed?"

"Leave a few for us," Tiridates said grimly. "That's all I ask."

A half hour later, Constantine and Dacius rode ahead of the column to the hillock the centurion had seen. Beyond it the view was blocked and, halting the men in the protection of the elevated ground, the two officers rode almost to the top, dismounting and climbing the rest of the way. Ahead they saw a plain where the Persians appeared to have trapped part of the Roman rear guard and were now in the process of cutting them to pieces, as they had been with Tiridates and his troops the afternoon before. The action seemed about over and many of the enemy horsemen had already dismounted to loot weapons and other booty from those who had fallen.

"We have them in a trap," Constantine said exultantly. "You take the right flank, Dacius, while I take the left. And tell the trumpeters to make a lot of noise."

"Narses' scavengers will think the whole Roman army is upon them," Dacius promised as they descended to where their mounts waited. "But be careful. I'm beginning to think you are too good a general to be wasted in this sort of fighting."

It was a repetition of the engagement the previous afternoon, though on a considerably larger scale. Like a sandstorm sweeping everything before it, the two wings of Roman cavalry crossed and recrossed the field, breaking up every formation the Persians tried to make. Many of the enemy were caught on foot and cut down before they could remount. The rest were soon in full retreat eastward, not knowing that King Tiridates and his band were waiting just behind the hill to scourge them once again.

At the sight of a Roman force appearing seemingly from nowhere to rescue them, the fleeing rear guard of Galerius' army took courage and began to make a stand, something they had apparently not been able to do since Carrhae. Tiridates' troops, their weapons bloody but their spirits high at having been given a chance to revenge themselves, soon appeared over the crest of the hillock, marching proudly in formation. And as Constantine's forces continued their westward progress, more and more stragglers who had been cut off by the Persian cavalry and left to be destroyed joined them.

By the fourth hour after the brief but bloody battle on the plain, some two thousand men had been formed into a ragged but identifiable military formation, marching behind Constantine and Tiridates, who had at last agreed to accept a mount. The rest of Constantine's forces acted as a rear guard, but, when another hour passed with an additional thousand increase in the ragged and dirty army, it was obvious that the Persian skirmishers had no intention of renewing the attack upon the Roman rear.

Four days later Constantine's army, now increased to more than an entire legion in numbers, and considerably more than that in spirit, marched into the small Syrian city of Beroea, just across the border from the province of Augusta Euphratensia, and less than two days' ride from Antioch itself. Here, at last, they found a Roman military headquarters, distinguishable by its standards and banners, located in a large house of the town. Constantine dismounted and, followed by Tiridates and Dacius, marched into the room and gave the salute of the legions to a startled Caesar Galerius and his staff.

"Flavius Valerius Constantinus," the young officer reported solemnly. "Tribune of the Im—"

"I know who you are, Tribune," Galerius snapped. "How dare you thrust yourself before the King of Armenia?"

Tiridates spoke and the whiplash of his voice made even Galerius stiffen. "I placed myself and my men under the command of Tribune Constantine, Caesar," he said. "I am proud to be serving under him."

"This is most irregular," spluttered Galerius.

"So was our retreat from Carrhae, Caesar," Tiridates said bluntly.

"But for the tribune here and his five hundred cavalry, my blood would long since have been diluted by the Euphrates."

Galerius' eyes narrowed. "Where did you get five hundred cavalry, Tribune?" he demanded.

"In Alexandria, sir. The Emperor sent me north to reinforce your army. I regret that we arrived too late."

"Insolent dog!" Maximin Daia was standing behind Galerius.

"Enough!" The Caesar of the East shut his nephew up before he could say more. "You know Tribune Constantinus belongs to the Imperial Guard and you heard him say the Emperor sent him to reinforce us. Who are we to say he has not carried out his orders?" Then his eyes narrowed. "How far are the Persians behind you?"

"We lured those who were following your army into splitting their forces and destroyed more than half of them," Constantine explained. "I think the rest decided they were too far west for comfort."

"I am in your debt, Tribune." The words obviously caused Galerius considerable effort.

"You would have done as much for me, sir," Constantine said quietly. "Have I leave to billet my men and their mounts? We have come a long way."

Galerius looked at him for a moment, and to Constantine it seemed that his shoulders drooped a little, as if the burden of ignominy put upon them by this defeat was proving very heavy indeed. Then he straightened, like the veteran soldier he was.

"You have my leave, Tribune," he said, then added almost as if he were speaking to himself, "You *have* come a long way, a very long way indeed!"

II

When two days passed without any evidence that the Persians intended to attack the shattered remnants of the Roman army, which had marched so boldly eastward from Antioch hardly a month earlier, Galerius decided to return to the Syrian capital and report to Diocletian, who had recently arrived there by ship from Alexandria. Resplendent in polished silver armor and wearing the purple cloak of a Caesar, he rode at the head of the troops who had not been left behind to hold a hastily erected line of fortifications at Beroea.

Just behind Galerius rode Maximin Daia, who, as Caesar's nephew, was already regarded as the heir to his position in the East. In the next rank were Flavius Valerius Severus, who had commanded the Imperial Guard while Constantine was a cadet, Licinius Licinianus and, over his objections, King Tiridates of Armenia. Constantine had not expected an invitation to ride with the leaders and received none. Instead he rode at the head of the column of his own cavalry, well back in the line of march.

The sun was shining brightly as the long column approached Antioch from the east and turned into the broad colonnaded street —the Via Caesarea—bisecting the city. It was Constantine's first visit to the Syrian capital and, as they rode along, he looked about him with interest at this ancient crossroads of the eastern world which—with its seaport city of Seleucia about an hour's ride away along the banks of the mighty Orontes River that divided Antioch in half—was one of the richest and most important cities of the Roman world.

The broad, column-lined street ended among the foothills of Mount Silpius in a road that wound upward toward the craggy peaks of the mountain overlooking the city. To the east a dense grove of bay trees marked the location of the suburb of Daphne with the gleaming marble Temple of Diana in its midst. The most infamous part of Antioch, the suburb was favored by much of the populace, Constantine had heard, because of the lustful rites practiced there in the worship of the goddess.

On the summit of one of the crags stood a magnificent castle, built long ago as a protection for the city from the eastern hordes that had sought for centuries to wrest it from Roman control. Another crag was surmounted by a lovely temple of Jupiter Capitolinus and, a little to the east, he could see the aqueduct constructed by Julius Caesar after his defeat of Pompey, as well as the magnificent baths. Not far away was the great stadium, only a little smaller in size than the theater for the games at Rome. Above its topmost story Constantine could see the bright colored canvas awnings that protected those of the audience willing to pay extra from both sun and rain.

The streets were lined with people, but it was a strangely silent crowd. As the front ranks of the procession headed by Galerius turned into the Via Caesarea, a golden chariot drawn by six perfectly matched white horses approached along the stone-paved boulevard. Just in front of the advancing column it wheeled and came to a halt, forcing the column to do the same. Diocletian himself stood in the chariot beside the driver, but the grim, erect figure showed no sign of welcome.

Galerius had raised his hand for the column to halt, when the imperial chariot blocked its way; now he dismounted and went forward to kneel before the Emperor. Only a few words passed between Diocletian and his son-in-law. Constantine was not near enough to hear any of them, but he saw Galerius suddenly stiffen. And, when he rose to his feet, the Caesar of the East did not remount his horse. Instead, he reached out to take hold of the golden chariot, the Emperor himself gave the order to march and the imperial vehicle began to move along the broad avenue, with Galerius walking beside it, his face set like a mask carved from granite, and his purple cloak billowing out behind him in the breeze that swept up the street from the river.

"No Caesar was ever so humiliated before," Dacius said from where he rode beside Constantine. "This is truly a triumph in reverse."

For the entire length of the Via Caesarea, the golden chariot continued its stately tour with Galerius walking beside it like a lackey at his master's stirrup. Only when the city had been completely crossed did Diocletian, who had stood erect in the vehicle the whole way, never glancing once at the silent crowds lining the street on either side, allow the humiliated Caesar to resume his mount.

Though the other officers followed the imperial chariot across a bridge to the island, or *insula,* in the center of the Orontes, where the palace of the legate, which had been taken over by Diocletian as headquarters, was located, Constantine was not invited to accompany them. Instead, he rode with Dacius to the stables to see that his men and their mounts were adequately quartered. But he

knew Diocletian well enough now to be sure his feat in saving
King Tiridates' command and the stragglers of Galerius' army from
destruction would not go unrecognized. And he was not surprised
when a centurion wearing the purple crest and helmet of the Imperial Guard, sought him out and saluted.

"By order of the Emperor," the centurion announced. "Tribune
Flavius Valerius Constantinus will this day assume the post of
Commander of the Imperial Guard and the household troops."

In his new capacity Constantine attended the military staff conference presided over by Diocletian that same afternoon. Present
also were Galerius, Maximin Daia, Severus, Licinius, and a number
of other high-ranking officers. But though he was no longer in uniform and now wore the rich robe and the pearl-set circlet of an
emperor upon his brow, no one could doubt that Diocletian was
in complete command.

"How many legions will you need to undo what has been done
in the past few weeks?" the Emperor asked Galerius.

"Ten, with twice the normal complement of cavalry from the
auxiliary."

Diocletian's eyebrows rose at the figure, for it was almost twice
the number with which Galerius had launched his ill-fated thrust
into Persian territory, but he did not comment.

"My army from Egypt will arrive here soon and will set about
preparing for the next Persian campaign," Diocletian said. "Meanwhile, you will leave for the Danube frontier tomorrow to raise
the rest of what you will need." He paused, then added pointedly,
"King Tiridates tells me that when you reach his territory he will
be able to raise additional auxiliary levies as you retake his land."

No one there failed to understand that Diocletian had given an
order for the new attack to be launched through the domain of
Tiridates. Nor did Galerius object, for his folly in making a direct
thrust into enemy territory had already cost Rome several legions
and earned him humiliation at the hand of the Emperor.

"Have I your leave to bring veterans from the frontier posts,
Dominus?" Galerius asked.

"No more than half the complement holding them now."

"But will you be safe in Nico—"

"I shall remain in Antioch, Caesar, until the war against Narses is finished."

Once again the point had been made that even though Galerius would be in command of the new army sent to punish King Narses of Persia, he would be under the eye of Diocletian himself all the while, to be summarily removed from command if he showed any sign of repeating the mistakes he had so recently made.

"You and your staff have my leave to depart," Diocletian told Galerius as the party filed from the room, leaving only Constantine and two legionaries from the Imperial Guard. As their commander, Constantine was required to remain in the presence of the Emperor until personally relieved, so he did not join the others.

"I received no reports from you, Tribune," Diocletian said.

"There was no time, Dominus. When we reached the scene of battle—"

"You mean the rout, don't you?"

"—we found ourselves behind the enemy lines," Constantine explained. "After that I was too busy to send a courier and, besides, he would probably not have gotten through."

"King Tiridates has told me of your meeting. Do you find battle exciting?"

"Yes, but sickening, too."

Diocletian's eyebrows lifted once again. "Not many soldiers would admit that, though all of us have felt it. But I'm glad you had the experience; it should make you appreciate the virtues of a peaceful rule."

"I have a few scores to settle with the Persians, Dominus," Constantine dared to say. "With your permission I would like to be assigned to a command with the force that goes against them."

"You have a task already, to see that I am not murdered in my bed, as poor Numerian was. By the way, I had another request just this morning for your presence during the coming attack on Narses."

"Surely not from Caesar Galerius."

"Hardly," Diocletian said dryly. "My son-in-law considers you and your remarkable resemblance to your father—in ability as well as in appearance—a threat to his own rule as Senior Augustus, when I abdicate. Which is hardly surprising, since he aspires to be sole Augustus then, with his own lackeys as Caesars. This request came from King Tiridates."

"We became good friends on the march. I admire him very much."

"Tiridates says he owes you his life. He wishes to make you general of all the forces in his kingdom when he is restored to rule."

Constantine was startled but by now had learned to hide his feelings. "It is an honor, sire," he said carefully, without committing himself.

"And something Galerius should welcome, if he were a statesman, instead of simply a soldier. Occupied maintaining the frontier, in one of the farthest corners of the Empire, you would no longer be a threat to him and that scowling nephew he plans to appoint as Caesar of the Eastern district."

"Are you going to assign me to King Tiridates, Dominus?"

"And lose the only officer I can depend upon to see that I live to abdicate at the end of twenty years and enjoy Maximian's discomfiture, when I make him join me?" Diocletian gave a short bark of a laugh. "No, Tribune, you are going to stay here."

Constantine drew a quick sigh of relief, for his ambition was considerably higher than the position of a general commanding troops in a subject kingdom like Armenia, in spite of the fact that it would mean a considerable elevation in rank.

"One task I do have for you here in Antioch—that of guarding my wife and daughter," Diocletian continued. "The city has always been a center for the Christians and I hear that a very eloquent priest has recently come here from Caesarea and Tyre. Both Prisca and Valeria imagine they favor that stubborn faith, so they are certain to want to hear him." Diocletian gave him a searching glance. "Wasn't your wife a Christian?"

"Yes, Dominus."

"And you?"

Constantine shrugged. "Rome's gods are my gods—though I see no harm in these people."

"I wouldn't be so sure," said Diocletian. "In troublous times like these the Empire needs only one loyalty—to the Emperor. These Christians claim a higher one—to a man they worship as the son

THE MIRACLE OF THE FLAMING CROSS 107

of a god they say no one has ever seen. They are growing in number every day, so I may have to destroy them lest they convince the people that I am not a god and destroy me. Meanwhile, I shall depend on you to watch over my wife and daughter."

"The Lady Valeria is the wife of Caesar Galerius," Constantine reminded him. "He may not approve."

"Galerius does what I tell him and Valeria is my daughter. You are responsible to me alone, Tribune."

III

Dacius had been relieved of his duties as Constantine's second-in-command with the cavalry detachment and was now in command of a section of the Imperial Guard. When he had escorted the Emperor to his private quarters, Constantine sought the grizzled centurion. Dacius listened in silence to the account of the conversation with Diocletian but when Constantine came to the request from King Tiridates, he whistled softly to himself.

"It's all over the *insula* that Diocletian has ordered Galerius to restore Tiridates to his throne. If you accept the offer, you will become a general overnight."

"The Emperor refused it for me. I had no choice."

"Would you have accepted, if the opportunity had offered?"

"I think not."

"Why?"

"The Emperor gave me the answer when he said Galerius would be well advised to encourage Tiridates, so I would be hidden away in Armenia outside the main current of political events."

"I wouldn't be too sure of that," Dacius told him. "Galerius intends to make Maximin Daia the Caesar of the East, but he'd be no match for you, even in Armenia. As cadets, you always could best him at everything except treachery. And with Tiridates behind you, Augusta Euphratensia, Mesopotamia and perhaps even Syria would fall into your hands like ripe plums."

"You're dreaming again," Constantine told him with a smile. "Anyway the Emperor refused to let me go."

"He'd relent, if you really want the post and asked Constantius to plead your cause."

"Perhaps. But I'm not going to ask my father for help."

Dacius subjected him to a moment of scrutiny with the wise and wintry eyes that had seen so many years of Roman history in the making. "So you're going to gamble for even higher stakes than being a general, though you're not even twenty-five yet? What will it be—the purple of a Caesar?"

Constantine smiled. "Why not the robe and crown of an Augustus?"

"East—or West?"

"No real reason exists for having two, you know." Constantine's voice was serious now. "Firmly ruled, the Empire would be better off with only one court and one army ready to move rapidly wherever trouble develops."

Dacius got up quickly and went to open the door. When he saw that the corridor outside was empty, he drew a sigh of relief and shut it again.

"I've already forgotten what you just said," he told Constantine, and now his face was very grave. "See that you don't repeat it again, until you are ready to put the whole plan into effect."

9

CONSTANTINE had come to know and admire Empress Prisca during his stay in Nicomedia. Her daughter, Valeria, wife of the Caesar of the East, he had not seen before, since Galerius held court for the most part at Sirmium near the Danube frontier. When he was called a few days later to escort the Empress and her daughter to the games and then into the city, he took a small contingent of men to the palace courtyard where two chairs waited, borne by husky Nubian slaves Diocletian had imported from Egypt.

After the carnage he had witnessed along the path of retreat by Galerius' army, Constantine found little excitement in the gladiatorial games of Antioch. The circular arena in the center of the stadium was surrounded by a metal fence, in order to protect the spectators from the animals during the *venatio,* or wild beast hunt, a frequent part of such spectacles. Above the arena rose tiers of seats, the first fifteen rows, called the *cavea,* enclosed by walls and reached by special corridors, or *vomitoria,* so the nobility, members of the Equestrian Order and highly-placed civil and military officials occupying them need not mix with the masses in reaching their places.

Directly above the arena were several thronelike seats, reserved for the Emperor and his party when he attended the games. The royal visitors were ushered to their seats by the *editor,* who financed and staged the performances. A murmur of interest and some applause rose from the crowd when they saw the Empress and the wife of Caesar Galerius, but it was drowned out quickly by the cries of hawkers selling sweetened beverages, pastries,

sweetmeats, small skins of wine and cushions for the hard stone
seats.

It was mid-afternoon before the games were over, but Empress
Prisca and her daughter were not yet ready to return to the palace.
Instead, the chairs and their guards proceeded to the older section
of the city, some distance from the *insula* with its magnificent public structures. Before a building located on a shabby street not far
from the river, the chairs stopped at the order of the Empress and
were lowered to the ground.

"There are no shops in this area, Domina," Constantine protested,
when both Prisca and Lady Valeria stepped down to the stone-
paved street.

"The Bishop of Antioch dwells here and his congregation uses
the building for a meeting place," Prisca explained.

"Christians!"

"I shall not ask you to go inside, Tribune. My daughter and I
will be perfectly safe."

"I must not leave your presence," Constantine said firmly. "My
orders are to guard you at all times."

The building was a converted dwelling, in which the walls between several rooms had been torn away to form a fairly large
meeting chamber, very much like the one Constantine had seen at
Dura on the Euphrates. Nor was he surprised to see on the walls
many of the same sort of paintings, depicting the man the Christians worshiped as a shepherd, as a sower of seed and, in a scene
which seemed to be typical of all such paintings, rising from his
sepulcher.

A venerable man with a long beard, wearing the robes of a priest
and a sort of high headdress Constantine had never seen before,
came to greet the Empress and her daughter. The service had already begun and the meeting room was almost filled with people,
sitting upon benches and listening to a younger priest, who stood
behind the lectern or pulpit on the raised dais across the far end
of the room. He was reading to the rapt audience from a small
scroll that was open before him on the lectern. And so intent were
the audience upon his words that there was hardly any stir when
the Empress and her daughter, followed by Constantine, took a
seat on one of the back benches.

Constantine was startled to realize that he already knew the speaker. It was Eusebius Pamphilus, whom he had last seen at Caesarea somewhat over a year before.

"Finally, my brethren," the priest read, "be strong in the Lord and in the power of his might. Put on the whole armor of God that you may be able to stand against the wiles of the devil. For we do not wrestle against flesh and blood, but against principalities, against powers, against the rulers of the darkness of this world, against spiritual wickedness in high places.

"Wherefore, take unto you the whole armor of God that you may be able to stand in the evil day, having your loins girt about with truth and wearing the breastplate of righteousness, and your feet shod with the preparation of the gospel of peace. Above all, take the shield of faith, wherewith you shall be able to quench all the fiery darts of the wicked. And take the helmet of salvation and the sword of the spirit which is the word of God; praying always with all prayer and supplication in the spirit and watching thereunto with all perseverance and supplication for all the saints—and for me, that utterance may be given unto me, that I may open my mouth boldly to make known the mystery of the gospel, for which I am an ambassador in bonds, that therein I may speak boldly, as I ought to speak."

Eusebius put down the scroll and began to address the congregation.

"Dearly beloved," he said, "you have just heard read to you the words of the Apostle Paul, written to the church at Ephesus at a time when he was in prison, awaiting trial before Emperor Nero and uncertain of his own fate. Yet you heard him charge all who read or hear his words not to be uncertain, but to be strong in the faith and knowledge of God and of his Son, our Lord Jesus Christ.

"Most of you have heard many times the story of how Paul came to be an apostle and a servant of the Lord. He admits to having been a persecutor of the Christians in Jerusalem, seeking to destroy the church. But when, in his zeal, he journeyed to Damascus in order to persecute our people there, he was struck blind by a great light on the road and heard a voice say, 'Saul, Saul'—for that was the name he bore until he was called by Jesus to follow him—

'why persecutest thou me?' And when he asked, 'Who are you, Lord?' the voice answered, 'I am Jesus whom thou persecutest. It is hard for you to kick against the goad.'

"In that very moment this man, who the instant before had been eager to reach Damascus and destroy those who served the Lord, was changed, just as many of us have been changed by the grace of God and his Son, who came to earth, suffered and gave his life for us, yet rose from the dead to give us the assurance of immortality with him in heaven, if only we will believe and accept him as our Savior.

"You have all heard many times too the story of how the followers of Christ were persecuted in Jerusalem and because of it began to spread abroad, sowing fresh seed wherever they went. In time, churches like this one were found as far to the West as Britain and in the East even to the borders of the land of the yellow men. We have as our guides not only the words of our Lord himself set down in the Scriptures and in the Acts of the Holy Apostles, written by the physician Luke, but also the letters of Paul to churches everywhere. In them, he exhorts us to stand fast, as in the passage I have just read you, putting on armor that is not forged in the heat of the furnace and taking up weapons that are not made from steel, yet which can turn men's hearts and conquer them without the shedding of blood.

"Beloved, the Apostle Paul was not afraid, in the terrible persecution by the Emperor Nero following the burning of Rome, to suffer the same martyr's death that was meted out to the Apostle Peter and to so many others. He was not afraid, nor must we be, for, as he wrote to the church at Philippi, 'Our conversation is in heaven, from whence also we look for the Saviour, the Lord Jesus Christ, who shall change our vile body that it may be fashioned like unto his glorious body.'"

The sermon was quickly finished and the people filed out. The Empress and Lady Valeria went down an aisle along one side of the almost empty room, however, and knelt in prayer before the altar with the bearded priest who had greeted them, so Constantine moved out into the foyer or vestibule to wait for them. As he stood there, wondering why the words he had just heard should fill him with a strange unease, he saw the priest called Eusebius enter the foyer from the other side and hurry across it.

"Tribune Constantinus!" he cried, a smile of welcome on his face. "Have you become one of us?"

"No. The Empress and Lady Valeria are inside."

"I saw you come in, and was glad."

"Why?"

"I am vain enough to want you to hear my sermon, of course," Eusebius admitted, "but that was not the real reason. I have just come to Antioch from Caesarea. When I learned that you were here, I planned to seek you out and thank you for what you did for our people in Alexandria."

"For your people? I don't remember it."

"When the Emperor's horse slipped, you reminded him that blood had touched its knees."

"But that was the fulfillment of a prophecy by the priests of Apollo at Caesarea."

"Or an act of God through you as his agent, to keep thousands of innocent people from being killed?"

"I have heard that you Christians speak ill of pagan priests who twist events to fit their own soothsaying," Constantine said somewhat rudely. "Yet here you are doing the same thing."

Eusebius gave him a quick probing glance. "So you too have felt the pull," he said. "And you too are kicking against the goad."

Perhaps because it had been a long day and he was tired, or because Eusebius' sermon had moved him in a way he could not understand, Constantine found himself resenting the implication that he was being used—even by the man the Christians claimed to be the son of their god—like a piece being moved about on a board during a game, with no volition of his own.

"I suppose you will be telling me next that I shall see a vision, like your man Paul," he said harshly.

"I am no soothsayer, as the priests of Apollo claim to be." Eusebius appeared to take no umbrage at his words or manner. "But I can tell you this: whatever God's purpose for you may be, you cannot pull away from it any more than the ox can escape the goad." Then he smiled. "All of Syria is talking about your remarkable exploit in saving the King of Armenia and stopping the Persian army almost at the gates of Antioch. You are the hero of the day, and the honor is well deserved."

It was hard to be angry at one so warm and obviously sincere, and Constantine found his irritation ebbing away. "Are you located in Antioch now?" he asked.

"Only for a little while. Most of my time is spent in writing the story of the whole church, since the birth of our Lord was announced by the angels in Bethlehem. When the apostles and other leaders were forced to flee Jerusalem because of persecution, they established a new church here at Antioch. And with Jerusalem now a pagan city by order of the authorities, it is our most important center in the East, just as Rome is in the West—though the Bishop of Alexandria is also gaining new churches daily."

"Did you say you were writing the history of your religion?"

"Not writing yet, only gathering material before the oldest documents fall to pieces. Many valuable ones have already been lost and we know of them only through references by others."

"We found one of your old churches on the Euphrates."

"Where?"

"At a place called Dura, or Europos."

"I have seen some references to it in the old documents," Eusebius said. "Is much of the church left?"

"A good part of the original building and many of the wall paintings."

"Do they portray Jesus?"

"Yes, as a shepherd carrying a ram that was lost or perhaps injured. And also the tomb you see here on the walls of this building."

"We are trying to preserve as many of the old paintings of the Saviour as we can," Eusebius said. "The church at Dura must be very old, perhaps as old as the time of St. Paul. Do you think the Persians will destroy it?"

"With the army Galerius will lead against them this time, they will be too busy to destroy abandoned buildings," Constantine assured him. "In less than a year, the place should be back in Roman hands."

"Then I will plan to go there and study the paintings," Eusebius said. "Perhaps I can discover some new information about the Christians in the very early period of the church."

"Is that really so important? I should think you would either just believe in your god or not believe in him."

"Our faith is not based simply upon belief in a god, even one who is all powerful," Eusebius explained. "After all, the Greeks have Jove, the Romans have Jupiter and, wherever you go, men instinctively look to a god who is above all others."

"Some people say your god has three faces and that you sometimes worship one and sometimes another."

"We worship God the Father, God the Son, and God the Holy Spirit," Eusebius explained. "But the important thing in our faith is that the Father loved mankind enough to send his Son, to be born as a babe in the humble surroundings of a stable. He let Jesus live and teach on earth—"

"And be crucified? What father could subject his son to such a painful death?"

"It was because he was subjected to such a painful death, yet rose above it, that we know he can give us all the gift of erternal life," Eusebius said earnestly. "From the cross Christ forgave those who had him killed, so we who follow him can do no less."

"If you are persecuted again, will you not hate your persecutors?"

Eusebius shook his head. "Jesus said, 'Love your enemies, do good to them which hate you. Bless them that curse you and pray for them which despitefully use you. To him who smites you on one cheek, offer the other. . . . And as you would that men should do to you, do you also likewise to them.'"

"What man is so perfect that he could follow such rules?" Constantine scoffed.

"Only one in all of history," Eusebius admitted. "They crucified him long ago, but he sends the gift of the Holy Spirit to all who believe in him today, as proof that we too shall live again, with him."

The Empress and her daughter came out just then and Constantine went to call the litter bearers. But from then on, he assigned to Dacius the task of guarding them, for somehow the things he had heard in the Christian church at Antioch and also at Drepanum, and his strange experience in the ruins at Dura-Europos, disturbed him —by raising questions for which he could not find the answer.

II

Having been given a second chance, and realizing that he would most certainly not be given a third, should he fail in the war against the Persians, Galerius prepared carefully. When finally he was ready to leave Antioch some six months after his arrival there in disgrace, he rode at the head of a large and well-disciplined army that headed northeastward toward Armenia. Before leaving King Tiridates came to tell Constantine goodbye.

"I'm sorry you chose not to take command of my forces, once my kingdom is free again," he said. "But I can understand the son of Constantius Chlorus having higher ambitions."

"They may do me no good," Constantine admitted, "but a caravan master who guided us across the desert to Palmyra told me that a man can find his way anywhere in the world if he chooses a particular star and follows it."

"No one can do less than fulfill his destiny," Tiridates agreed. "Years ago a nobleman named Mamgo and his people left the Empire of China and settled in Armenia. I remember listening many times to tales of the yellow people of the East, the vastness of their domain, and the many things they possessed that we do not have. We may still fight together against these yellow men, friend Constantine. And you may live to rule an empire greater than the world has ever known."

From the door, Tiridates turned for a final word. "Beware of Galerius. He will seek to destroy you at the first opportunity."

"But I have done him no harm."

"He blames you for the humiliation he was subjected to by the Emperor."

"I had nothing to do with that."

"The way Galerius sees it, you did, by stopping the Persian army while his rabble were still fleeing."

"Narses would never have been such a fool as to approach Antioch, with our army from Egypt only a few days' march away. What we stopped were scavengers; the main Persian advance never crossed the Euphrates."

"Don't let Galerius learn how much you know, then. Scavengers or not, his men were still running."

"Except you."

Tiridates' laugh boomed out. "How could I, with my back to the river?"

III

Dispatches from the Persian campaign soon began to arrive daily, telling of new victories. As Galerius pushed into Armenia, the people there fell in solidly behind their popular monarch, while ahead of the battle lines small bands of horsemen from the Scythian steppes, many of them descendants of the tribe led by Mamgo, of which Tiridates had spoken, harried the Persian supply lines, cutting out small bands of the enemy wherever they could and destroying them mercilessly.

The sturdy Illyrian veterans whom Galerius had taken from the Danube strongpoints, plus a large body of mounted Gothic auxiliaries, were a far more disciplined and dependable force than the largely untrained levies he had thrown against the Persians in his earlier campaign. When finally the Roman army turned southward from Armenia into the fertile Tigris-Euphrates basin, it swept everything before it. The climax of the campaign came when the Persian monarch was caught at his headquarters in a swift night attack, wounded slightly and forced to flee to the fastnesses of the desert, where Galerius prudently refused to follow. There was more than enough booty and glory for all, however, since all of Narses' belongings, including his wives, his sisters and his children, were captured. And with this stunning stroke of victory, the enemy's resistance largely collapsed.

Only when the eastern frontier was at last secure and its limits extended almost to those established for a brief while by Alexander the Great, did Diocletian leave Antioch for Nicomedia. And then it was only to pause there for a brief period, before going to Rome to celebrate with the ceremony known as a "triumph" this high point in the history of the Empire.

And a high point it was indeed. In the West, Constantius had all but finished subduing the rebels who had followed the upstart Carausius and his lieutenant, Allectus, bringing the fertile and important province of Britain once again into the confines of the Empire. To the North, Constantius had also brought peace to the Rhine frontier by displacing many of the rebellious tribes into the interior of Gaul, settling them in areas where they could no longer join together into a force large enough to cause trouble.

The rebellion in Africa had long since been ended by the forthright action of Maximian and Maxentius. And with the Vicennalia, the twentieth anniversary of Diocletian's reign, approaching close on the heels of the great Persian victory, it was no more than fitting that both be celebrated in the ancient city which—even though Maximian had established his capital at Milan—would always be the symbolic heart of the Empire.

As soon as he could obtain leave after the arrival of the court at Nicomedia, Constantine rode the short distance to Drepanum and his mother's modest cottage there. Helena ran to embrace him as soon as he dismounted. For a long moment she clasped him in her arms, then finally held him off with her hands upon his shoulders while she studied his face with eyes that shone with pride and joy.

"You have changed," she said.

"I'm almost two years older than when you saw me last," Constantine reminded her. "But I am still a tribune and," he added with a slight touch of bitterness in his voice, "still the Emperor's lackey."

"The change goes deeper than that. You've become a man, and more like your father."

"You haven't changed, Mother. If anything, you look younger."

"Having a baby to care for again brings youth to a grandmother. Come inside and see your son."

The baby was sleeping. Constantine had somehow expected him to be a miniature of his mother, but he saw instead a sturdy infant whose resemblance to himself—and his own father—was startling. If Minervina had given Crispus anything save life—thereby losing her own—it was his hair, which was light in color like hers.

"He's the image of you when you were that age," Helena said happily. "I only pray God that he will grow up to be the fine man you have become."

"Pray God," he repeated. "You haven't become a Christian, have you, Mother?"

"Not yet. But they are a kind and harmless people and much in their teachings appeal to me. Why do you ask?"

"The Emperor dislikes them, I think because Empress Prisca and Lady Valeria have taken up that faith. Galerius is already purging his army of Christians and I hear that Maximian is doing the same. Diocletian is certain to follow."

"Minervina was a Christian. She was baptized just before death and I'm sure it gave her the strength to die happily."

Constantine remembered the basin or font in the small room off the meeting chamber in the ruins of the church at Dura-Europos and Josiah's explanation of its use. Ever since his conversation with Eusebius in the vestibule of the church at Antioch, he had resolutely put all thoughts of the faith built around the figure of the man called Christ from his mind. Nor did he let it enter now, after warning his mother, but turned to touch the tiny hand of the baby sleeping in his crib. The small fingers curled about his own with a surprisingly strong grip, and having one so small and helpless unconsciously show its confidence in his protection and care somehow warmed him through and through, making him feel that he was home at last.

"Your father writes whenever he can," Helena said as they moved to the cushioned couch and low table, where the old servant who had been with them in Naissus had laid out a light supper of meat, bread, fruit and wine in silver goblets hammered with the Phoenician symbol of the star, a present Constantine had bought in Antioch and sent to his mother.

"Is all well with him?"

"The campaign in Britain is over, except for a few rebellious towns that his lieutenants can control. Constantius has left Eboracum,* where he made his headquarters in Britain, and returned to Treves in Gaul."

"It was a brilliant campaign. I read about it in the imperial dispatches."

"You have three stepbrothers, you know. Their names are Constantinus, Hannibalianus and Constantius."

* York

"Which puts the *nothus* that much farther away from the purple."

"Don't say that word!" his mother cried sharply. "Your birth is as legitimate as theirs."

"Forgive me, please, Mother." Constantine reached over to touch the arm of the beautiful and stately woman who, though she had been an innkeeper's daughter, had never lost her pride that a Caesar had chosen her for his mate. "I've been in a bad mood lately."

"Something wrong at the court?"

"No. The Emperor trusts me and favors me, but sometimes I wonder whether I took a wrong turn of the road in Antioch. King Tiridates offered me the command of his kingdom's military forces."

"And you refused? Is that what troubles you?"

"I suppose so."

"Why did you do it, then?"

"Because my two strong parents gave me ambition," he said wryly. "Because I am vain. Because of perhaps a hundred other reasons. Who can say?"

"Wasn't it really because you are looking to something higher?"

"How did you know?"

"A woman doesn't suckle a child without knowing just from the way he demands her breast what kind of a man he will be, or that he is born to command. I have never doubted that you will one day have high position."

"As high as a Caesar, like Father?"

"Or Augustus, the position your father will soon hold. Do you really doubt it in your heart?"

"No," he admitted. "I don't think I do."

"Diocletian has sworn to rule no more than twenty years. He will celebrate his Vicennalia soon, but he has never had any use for Rome, so he is obviously going there to tell Maximian he must abdicate too. Then your father will become Augustus of the West and you may be his Caesar."

"Maximian has a son."

"Maxentius is nothing but a cruel and oppressive libertine," Helena said with scorn. "In Africa he put thousands of innocent people to the sword, for no reason at all. The common people of the Empire hate him, and the Praetorians only support him because they

think he might make Rome the capital again, after Maximian abdicates."

"The Emperor told me himself that he will not name a son of any
Caesar or Augustus to succeed his father."

"Only because none except you are fit for the post. You stand high
in Diocletian's favor, with access to his innermost chamber. Surely
you can convince him that he should change his mind."

"We shall see." Constantine finished his wine and got to his feet.
"If you don't mind, I'll go to bed now. When does the young
man wake up?"

"Leave him to me," Helena said. "I've placed you in the farthest
room from his crib and will try to keep him quiet until you awaken."

Constantine enjoyed the best night's sleep he could remember
since leaving Drepanum to start the expedition into Egypt. When
he awoke, he heard the gurgling laugh of the baby in another part
of the house and went to pick Crispus up from his crib and hold
him high in the air. The child showed no sign of fear but laughed
and demanded more. When Constantine departed three days later
for the short ride to Nicomedia, it was with a renewed feeling of
purpose and no more doubts about whether he had been wrong in
not going to Armenia.

High in the heavens above Drepanum he had seen what he was
sure was his star once again and now he had every reason to follow
it without any slackening of the faith in his own destiny. For another would soon be walking in his own steps, as he had walked
proudly in those of Constantius.

10

I T HAD BEEN fully twenty years since a triumph had been celebrated in Rome. During that time the once proud capital of the world's greatest empire had been reduced to hardly more than a hollow shell of its former position of authority, though retaining some semblance of its traditional glory.

With the accession of Diocletian, the Empire had taken on the character of an oriental monarchy, ruled largely from the East. And though authority was shared with Maximian, the more or less constant state of rebellion on the Rhine frontier and across the Fretum Gallicum in Britain had forced the Augustus of the West to move his court to Milan in order to be nearer the fighting.

Now, though Rome clung desperately to its former glory, and the Senate continued to meet there, its pronouncements and decisions turned out to be little more than sound and fury—the sound of words that were largely meaningless and the fury of proud men, whose importance was no longer recognized even by the plebes, the common people of the packed slums called the *subura*.

It was true that the highest civil offices of Consul, Proconsul, Censor and Tribune were still filled by the Senate each year, as they had been for centuries. And when these officers appeared in public for the token carrying-out of their duties, the Consul still headed the procession of the Senate—the *praetors*, the *aedes*, the *lictors*, with their *fasces*, the heralds with their trumpets, the *apparitors*, and the Praetorian Guards with the standards of Rome— as it moved through the streets, often to the jeers of crowds. But everyone knew the real laws were made, and the real authority exercised, in a formerly insignificant town called Nicomedia, located on a gulf of the Sea of Marmara far to the east, by a stocky, bullet-headed, graying Illyrian peasant's son who, but for the military accomplishments that had eventually led the army to name him Emperor, would have been given hardly a glance by even the least in the train of the Consul.

In truth, Rome had become little more than a theater where mimes of ancient tales were still acted out, but with as little reality as the divinity of the actor who, in Greek tragedies, played the part of the *deus ex machina*, the god who was lowered at the end of a long lever or boom at an appropriate point in the play to set everything aright again. Nothing would ever be set aright in Rome again, however, and the Romans, always a practical people, knew it all too well.

Where the Republic had protected the rights of every man, a monarch, oriental in splendor and magnificence, if not in origin, now ruled. And like an oriental monarch visiting some less important city of his domain, Diocletian journeyed to Rome during the late weeks of the fall in the twentieth year of his reign to celebrate the great victories in all quarters of the Empire which had, for the moment at least, brought a repetition of the Pax Romana of the olden days.

The triumph of Diocletian and Maximian could hardly bear comparison with previous ceremonials marking the entry of Rome's great heroes into the city after some of their spectacular victories. Aurelian, for example, had forced the Warrior-Queen Zenobia of Palmyra, whose revolt had spread like wildfire even to the borders of Egypt before he subdued her, to march in golden chains before his chariot. And more than once, proud Teuton kings had been forced to crawl in harness on hands and knees like draft animals, dragging the chariots of their conquerors. In fact, compared to these, the triumph of Diocletian and Maximian was almost spartan in character.

The two Augusti, splendidly arrayed in the traditional robes of the *triumphator*, stood in Diocletian's golden chariot drawn by six spirited white horses. The long procession moved through the city from the Triumphator's Arch to the temple of Rome's patron god, Jupiter Capitolinus, where a sacrifice thanking the god for his favor would be celebrated.

Constantine, with six of his tallest and strongest men, marched just behind the chariot, while outside them on either side marched a ceremonial file of *lictors,* who always accompanied the highest authority when he went abroad. Next came the white ox for the sacrifice, its horns covered with gold leaf and a crown of flowers beneath them; then a long line of dignitaries. But where normally there would have been a file of carts and wagons carrying booty and followed by prisoners in chains, a series of floats, or representations, had been constructed to show the people the reality of the Persian conquest.

First was a great relief map of Persia depicting the terrain, with mountains, rivers and even cities and towns produced in miniature, a float so huge that it had to be borne on three wagons hitched in tandem and guided by men walking beneath it. Next came a file of carts bearing amazingly lifelike effigies of Narses' wives and children, though they had been returned to him in the final settlement whereby the eastern frontier was moved to the banks of the river Tigris. And after them was a train of cartloads filled with booty which Diocletian, in honor of his twentieth year, had given to the people of Rome. Bringing up the rear was a marching column of the Praetorian Guards, whose task it had been in Rome's more glorious days to guard the person of the Emperor.

Through the crowd-lined streets of the city, many of whose people had never even seen the Senior Augustus, the procession moved at a majestic slow pace. At the Temple of Jupiter, Diocletian dismounted from the chariot and, followed one step to the rear by Maximian, entered the temple and approached the altar where the High Priest waited. While the Emperor scattered the traditional incense upon the altar itself, the white ox was brought in through another door by the *victimarii,* whose job it was to carry out the actual sacrifice.

Seizing the ox by one ear and by the muzzle, one of the *victimarii* pulled its head down quickly while another struck an expert blow with an axe, stunning the animal so the priest could move in with the ceremonial knife and slash its throat. As the blood poured out, drenching the altar, all those gathered around it lifted their eyes heavenward, calling upon Jupiter Capitolinus to bless them, the city, and the Empire.

II

The visit of Diocletian coincided with one of the festivals commonly celebrated in Rome, the *ludi plebeii*, in which commoners and nobility alike mingled in the streets and in many balls and entertainments held throughout the city. As Diocletian's favorite among the military officers at his court, Constantine was naturally invited to these. Since a great ball was held on the evening of the triumph, he left Dacius to choose the guard detail for the night and, dressed in his finest tunic, attended the ceremony.

One of the first people he saw was his former fellow cadet from the corps at Nicomedia, Maxentius. The son of the Augustus of the West was chatting with a group of young men and women, but since he knew none of them Constantine did not break in. Instead, he fortified himself with a glass of wine and some sweetmeats from a platter carried by a slave, while he studied the surging mass of richly dressed people. He was gratified to see that Maxentius, in spite of the magnificence of his dress, was still of no higher rank than a tribune and he would have passed on, searching for some of the court chamberlains from Nicomedia, had not Maxentius seen him.

"Hail to the Emperor's lackey," he announced, raising the goblet he held in his hand high in a mock salute, "guardian of the imperial bedchamber and, who knows, probably the imperial chamberpot, too."

There was a round of laughter, but none, Constantine noticed, from a slender girl with light hair on which was perched a small jeweled circlet, betraying her high position.

"Please forgive my brother for being a bore, Tribune," she said with a dazzling smile. "Word of how you stopped the whole army of Narses before Antioch has reached us, so naturally he is envious of your fame."

Maxentius flushed. "My sister Fausta, Tribune Constantine," he said with mock courtesy. "And my friends."

He did not name them, a deliberate act of discourtesy, Constantine was sure. But the girl took his arm and went in turn to each of the others, introducing him. He spoke the conventional words of greeting, and several of the young women responded eagerly, but Fausta made it quite clear that she had taken him under her personal wing. She was, he guessed, about sixteen but, though slender, already mature for her age.

"Maxentius chased a few Moors into the desert during the recent trouble in Mauretania," Fausta said with a malicious smile. "Since then he hasn't been fit to live with—not that he was before either."

"What were you and Diocletian doing so long in Alexandria, Constantine?" Maxentius asked loudly and Constantine realized that he was quite drunk. "Fishing, I suppose?"

A round of laughter followed, which Constantine joined, but not Fausta. "Silence, fool!" she snapped. "Do you want to bring the wrath of Diocletian upon your head?"

"There are two Emperors, dear sister," Maxentius said. "And in a few years there will be only one. Then we will move the capital back to Rome, where it should be."

Fausta took Constantine's arm and led him away, as much, he suspected, to get him away from her brother, before Maxentius revealed too much of what Maximian was planning for the future, as from any desire for his company.

"My brother always babbles foolishness when he's drunk," she confided. "Is this your first visit to Rome?"

"Yes."

"Then you must see more of it. Milan is so new and rough as an imperial capital; I'm always happy to be back in Rome where the shops really have something to see. I'm going shopping tomorrow. Will you go with me?"

"The Emperor of the East may have other plans for me. I'm a soldier, you know."

"And Diocletian's favorite; everybody knows that. Just leave it to me," she assured him. "I shall see that you are free tomorrow afternoon. Then there is a theater tomorrow night and another ball. We shall be very busy."

"Aren't you taking a lot for granted?"

"You mean you don't want to be with me?" Her eyes began to take fire. "I never lack for escorts, you know."

"I am sure of that," he said hastily, for this oddly exciting creature had already begun to seize his fancy. "But I also have work to do."

"Then it's all settled," she said airily. "I need a bodyguard far more than Diocletian does; you have no idea how many men have designs upon me. You will be assigned to me while we are in Rome and then we can be together all the time." She stood on tiptoe to look into his eyes for a moment, as if searching for something there, then dropped back upon her heels, obviously satisfied with what she saw.

"Some day I'm going to marry you, Constantine," she announced as she took his arm again. "So you might as well get accustomed to being with me."

He could not help laughing at her impudence, until he realized suddenly that she was deadly serious.

"How old are you?" he asked.

"Fifteen, but I have been a woman since I was twelve. The women in my family mature early. Of course, we cannot marry just now," Fausta continued. "The daughters of Augusti are not like other girls. Their marriages have to be arranged for the good of the state, as your father's marriage was arranged to my stepsister, Theodora. Tell me, did your mother mind much when your father divorced her?"

Constantine had stiffened a little at the question, but he saw only curiosity, and perhaps a certain concern, in the piquant little face upturned to his.

"She did mind," he confessed. "But she loved my father enough not to stand in the way of his being made Caesar of the West."

"I wouldn't give up my rights without a fight," Fausta assured him. "I want everything that is mine in the world, and perhaps a little more."

"I have no doubt that you will get it."

"I saw your father at Theodora's wedding," she told him. "The two of you are very much alike."

"Everybody else says so and, since you do, it must be true."

"Don't make fun of me, Constantine," she warned and he saw that she was very serious again. "People who do usually regret it."

"I wasn't making fun," he assured her. "And I'm sure you told the truth when you said you always get your way."

"Now about our marriage. You will have to become at least a Caesar before Father will give me to you. The daughters of the Augusti are used to make important alliances or to bind treaties."

"Emperor Diocletian doesn't intend to make me a Caesar."

"Why not? Maxentius expects to be one."

Constantine looked away quickly, lest she realize that she had revealed what he had come strongly to suspect, since he had come to Rome—namely that the Augustus of the West, being younger and in much better health than Diocletian, had little intention of abdicating soon after the Vicennalia and turning over the purple robe of an Augustus to Constantius Chlorus, even though the Caesar of the West had already been designated in Diocletian's plan of empire for promotion to that rank.

"You haven't answered me." Fausta's cheeks were beginning to turn pink with anger. "Are you afraid to stand up for your rights as the son of Caesar Constantius?"

"No, of course not," he said. "But Emperor Diocletian believes the best interest of Rome will not be served unless each Augustus names a Caesar from outside his own family to succeed him."

"Pooh! That's foolish. What man would build up a fortune or an empire, and then not want his son to inherit it? But since you're being kept at Diocletian's court as a hostage—"

"Who told you that?"

"Maxentius. Didn't you know it?"

"Well—yes."

"They're keeping you away from your father because they fear that when Diocletian does abdicate, or dies, the two of you might seize control of the Empire, especially since the legions all know you saved the neck of Galerius in Persia."

Constantine realized that he was hearing something of what must be common talk in the household of Maximian and could not help feeling a little guilty, for somehow it was almost like eavesdropping. But Fausta was untroubled.

"I wouldn't tell you all this if I weren't going to marry you," she assured him. "You see we have to make our plans ahead, if you are going to be a Caesar and later on Augustus, with me as your Augusta."

"What are these plans?" he asked.

"It's no secret that Galerius hates you." Her forehead was wrinkled in a frown, as she considered the question, and he saw that she was deadly serious. "He will probably try to have you killed after Diocletian names him Augustus and gives up the throne, but your father is a very strong man and will certainly guard his own rights in the West. And now that you know what is liable to happen, you can look after yourself. That's it." Her face suddenly cleared. "As soon as Diocletian abdicates, you must flee and join your father at Treves. Then he can name you Caesar and my family will want me married to you, so they can bind you to us."

"I'm beginning to think it is you who should be Augustus."

"What man would ever admit that a woman could rule an empire?"

"Queen Zenobia did. She almost took the eastern half of it away from us."

"And ended up by being paraded through the streets of Rome in chains. I wouldn't like for anyone to see me in chains, even if they were golden ones."

"You'd manage to make them look like a badge of honor," he assured her. "Unless I miss my guess, you're like a cat, always able to land on its feet."

"Women don't like to be called cats either," she said, a little tartly.

"Not even those from Persia? The most regal cats in the world are found there."

"We will tour Persia on our wedding trip and I shall see," Fausta decided. "Father never lets me go anywhere; he says I'm too young. But you will take me with you, won't you?"

"Who wouldn't want all his subjects to see so lovely an empress?" he asked, then added hastily, "Not that I ever expect to be Emperor."

"You gave yourself away!" she cried triumphantly. "Of course you expect to be Emperor of Rome one day; I wouldn't have decided to fall in love with you, if you weren't ambitious." Before he could quite recover from this startling statement, she added, "Now I must go, or father will be angry again. Don't forget that you are going with me to the shops tomorrow."

"And don't forget that I have a job to do."

"You will be free. I promise it."

And free he was—not entirely to his surprise—to meet her chair the next afternoon, according to a note brought to him that morning by a slave from the imperial household. Fausta was quite as lovely and entrancing in the daylight as she had been the night before and, even in a typically narrow Roman street, the people gave way to the sedan chair bearing the emblem of Maximian Augustus.

In order to reach the better shops of the city, they had to traverse an area of what was called the *subura,* where many of the lower classes of Rome lived. Constantine had never seen houses like those, often with as many as seven stories, that jammed the narrow streets on every side. There were taverns everywhere, too, with people going in and out constantly, as well as all kind of shops—those for the sale of food, barbershops, crowded bazaars in which discarded clothing and almost anything else one might wish to buy was for sale, small sidewalk booths where fortune tellers, soothsayers, money changers, street peddlers, and others held forth. And beggars, of course, were everywhere.

At the Septa Julia inside the Via Lata, Fausta stopped the chair and took Constantine's arm, while they strolled through the shaded arcades where the finest shops of Rome were located. Exquisite crystal from Alexandria reminded him of the sorry state in which he had last seen that once lovely city, so he moved on to where Fausta was exclaiming over necklaces, earrings, jeweled combs and silver-mounted mirrors eagerly offered for her inspection by the merchants, along with rich embroideries from Babylon, emeralds from Egypt and silk from China.

Another stall displayed carved trinkets of ivory from the Nubian lands far to the south in Africa, delicate colored tile inlays from Syria and the Phoenician cities, as well as fabrics of all hues and colors. Everything the heart of a woman could want—for these shops catered to feminine taste—was on display, while in another area, booksellers offered scrolls in every tongue known to man, maps of far-off lands and the detailed descriptions of the geographer Strabo, whose works encompassed the entire world.

Fausta soon tired of shopping and, when they resumed their chair, ordered the slaves to carry them to the pleasure park given the people of Rome by the statesman Agrippa in honor of the Pax Romana. Here the chair was stopped again, while its mistress and her escort walked along paths that wound between rose arbors, finely trimmed hedges and beneath the shade of towering trees. In the portico of Europa, they paused before a large map of the world which Agrippa had ordered chiseled from marble, so that all Romans might see the extent of the Empire.

"This will be ours one day," Fausta assured him, running her finger across the marble boundaries of nations and seas. "The whole of it, and even more."

"How can you be so sure?"

"I know myself and I'm beginning to know you," she told him. "When I saw you for the first time last night, Constantine, I knew that a great and deep ambition burns within you, just as it does within me. I must be Augusta and, since a woman cannot rule Rome, it must be as the wife of an Augustus. You should be proud that I chose you."

"I still find it a little dazzling."

"It takes a woman to show a man what he can really do. Between us we shall go far."

Constantine looked at the great sun dial of Augustus, which had stood in this place for almost three hundred years. Already the sun was so low that its shadow was hardly discernible from the surrounding marble pavement.

"We had better find your bearers," he said. "In an hour I'm supposed to accompany the Emperor to the great feast your father is giving in his honor."

"I shall see you there," she promised. "Be sure to wear your handsomest uniform, for I shall be very proud of you."

In the week that followed, Constantine saw Fausta almost every day and each time was even more entranced. He quickly learned that she was quite serious in her ambition to become Augusta through him and, in truth, he was not at all disheartened by the prospect. He was not so dazzled even by love, however, that he failed to keep his eyes and ears open; and nothing he saw or heard in Rome made him feel that accomplishing his ambition would be either easy or soon. Powerful factions were obviously already plotting against the day when Diocletian would doff the purple for the role he had confided often to Constantine that he longed for most—that of gardener in his beautiful palace of Salonae overlooking the Adriatic Sea. And none of the plotting in Rome —Constantine was sure—included a place for him.

Maxentius' obvious desire to centralize all power at Rome once again and—Constantine did not doubt—the ambition of the Senate and the Praetorian Guard to regain much of its former power through encouraging him, was discarded as the sort of thing he would expect from a boaster and a wastrel. But the Co-Emperor Maximian, Fausta's father, he quickly realized, planned nothing less than to succeed both Diocletian and himself—as sole Augustus.

III

Constantine had no reason to suspect that Maximian regarded him as anything other than simply the tribune who headed Diocletian's personal guard, until he was startled at the beginning of their second week of residence in Rome to receive a peremptory summons from Maximian himself. Shortly he was ushered into a small audience chamber in the palace where the Emperor of the West and his family were staying upon their state visit to Rome for the triumph and the celebration of the Vicennalia, as well as the beginning of Diocletian's official year as Consul.

Constantine had not seen Maximian at close hand before, but he knew him to be a soldier of considerable reputation whom his father respected. To his surprise he saw evidence of softness in the man's face, the corpulence of his body and even the stain of wine upon his tunic, although it was still fairly early in the morning. When Constantine saluted, Maximian did not even bother to return it.

"So you are Constantius' bastard," he said. "No one could doubt that he is your father, no matter who your mother was."

"You will find that my birth was quite legitimate, Augustus." By now he had become so accustomed to unjustified slurs upon his legitimacy that he had learned to control himself, particularly when they came from a source which he could not force to swallow the slur. "You have only to ask the Emper—"

"Rome has two Emperors," Maximian snapped. "We rule together and neither has authority over the other."

Constantine did not dispute the assertion, though even the veriest plebe in the *subura* knew Diocletian's orders were obeyed without question by Maximian and both the Caesars.

"Maxentius has told me how you won favor with Diocletian by almost killing the Frankish prince, who was master of horse at Nicomedia," Maximian continued. "And I have heard from Caesar Galerius of your trickery in claiming victory over the Persians when, in actual fact, he had already turned back the forces of King Narses."

Constantine did not bother to dispute the lies, since Maximian had quite obviously decided already what he wished to believe.

"Everybody knows, too, how you insinuated yourself into the favor of Empress Prisca and Lady Valeria by supporting them in their Christian heresy," Maximian continued. "But I must warn you that you shall not worm your way into my household through my daughter. Fausta is still a child and only a scoundrel would use her in the hope of gaining my approval for his ambitions, whatever they are."

"My sole ambition is to do my duty as a soldier and a Roman, Augustus," Constantine said evenly.

"Do you deny trying to turn Fausta's head, for purposes of your own?"

"Lady Fausta has been very kind to me, since I have been in Rome," Constantine said. "I will admit to having developed a considerable affection for her and, in time, I plan to ask your permission for us to be wed."

"Wed!" Maximian sat up straight in his chair and his face became so suffused that, for a moment, Constantine was afraid he would topple over in a faint. But he recovered himself with an effort and, seizing a flask of wine from a tray on the table, drank great gulps from it. Finally he sank back in his chair and stared at Constantine, his eyes cold with hostility.

"What has Rome come to when the bastard son of an Illyrian peasant can aspire to marry the daughter of an emperor?" he demanded.

Constantine could have reminded Maximian that he had been nothing but a common soldier, before rising through the ranks to become a general and, solely because of his friendship with Diocletian, an Augustus. Or that Constantine himself was descended from an emperor. But he realized that he had already made a major blunder in admitting his affection for Fausta and wisely kept silent, lest he make another.

"If you weren't Diocletian's favorite, you can be sure you would be breaking stones on the roads tomorrow as a military prisoner, or hanging from a cross beside the Via Appia," Maximian added. "But you are still a soldier, and I order you now not to force yourself upon my daughter again."

Nothing was to be gained by arguing, Constantine realized, so he merely saluted. When Maximian automatically returned the salute, he marched from the room, expecting at any moment for a string of curses to spatter his retiring back. In the room he shared with Dacius in the barracks that had been turned over temporarily to Diocletian's personal troops, he took off his helmet and, sinking into a chair, stared at the blank wall while he considered the situation in which he found himself.

In the week he had been in Rome, he and Fausta had spent every possible moment together and his desire for her had risen to a point where he could hardly think of anything else. The thought of not seeing her again was like an eclipse, shutting out the sight of the sun. But he also knew that if he went against her father's order and met her again—however innocently, for they had hardly spoken of love to each other yet—Maximian would demand that Diocletian break him. And the Emperor of the East was too much of a soldier to pardon one who did not obey the command of a superior officer.

While he was staring hopelessly at the wall, Dacius came in from a tour of duty. The centurion removed his crested helmet, hung it carefully on a peg, poured himself a goblet of wine and drank it before he spoke.

"You look like Mount Vesuvius erupted on you," he said finally.

"Aren't you supposed to be spending the afternoon with Lady Fausta?"

"I just came from the presence of the Emperor Maximian. He ordered me never to see her again."

"The other officers and I have been wagering on when the axe would be wielded. So today was the day?"

"But why? We love each other."

"Love has little to do with royal marriages. You should know that."

"I am not royal, or ever will be."

"If Maximian could be sure of that, you might be welcomed into the family with open arms, instead of being cast into what I believe the Christians call the 'outer darkness.'"

"Am I a pariah, then? Or a leper to be avoided?"

"You are the strong son of a strong father and the grandson, once or twice removed—I forget which—of a great emperor," Dacius told him. "What better credentials could you have to become ruler of the Roman Empire?"

Constantine managed a wry smile. "Well at least I have two supporters for my candidacy—you and Fausta."

"The girl has more sense than her father and Maxentius put together. If they had any, they would ally you with themselves and, when Diocletian abdicates, the three of you and Constantius could divide the Empire between you, leaving out Galerius and his lackeys Licinius, Daia and Severus—no, not Severus; he's only an honest soldier who obeys orders."

"Are you sure you aren't spinning daydreams again?"

"Centurions run the army and through it the Empire; you should know that by now. I have many friends among the cohorts stationed here in Rome and those that came from Milan with Maximian. They say it is common knowledge that he doesn't plan to abdicate —unless Diocletian forces him to keep his promise—but will try to make himself sole Augustus. Your father is already married to Maximian's stepdaughter and in that way is tied to the family. If you were to marry Fausta, it would be two very strong men against one moderately strong—I'll give Maximian that much— and a drunken braggart, Maxentius. You can imagine how long Maximian and Maxentius would last under those circumstances."

"What do I do then?"

"Obey orders like the soldier you are."

"It was all much simpler when we were riding north into Persian territory," Constantine said a little wistfully. "Battle is a lot better than politics."

"True. But success in the first leads to an involvement in the latter." Dacius shrugged. "Call it destiny, the will of the gods, or whatever you will, the result is always the same. My advice to you is to find another girl, one you can buy, and Rome is the place for it. I've never seen such a variety of slaves as they have here."

"I'm not interested in another woman."

"Have you told Lady Fausta that you are a widower, with an infant son?"

"Why should that make any difference? The boy is with my mother."

"Crispus is still your son, just as you are still Constantius' son and a stumbling block to the dream Maximian has of ruling the whole Empire."

"Well, I can obviously never become an Augustus with so many forces arrayed against me," Constantine said with a shrug. "So my son shall not have the same worries I'm having."

"You aren't going to try and see the girl again, are you?"

"No. Why?"

"I'd wager Maximian is hoping you will, and give him an excuse to break you. And, of course, Maxentius would like nothing better. Now cheer up and let's get something to eat."

But neither Dacius nor Constantine had properly evaluated the stubbornness of Fausta's will. Barely had they returned from the noontime meal, when the door burst open and the girl herself ran into the room. Her cheeks were aflame, she was breathing quickly, and at first Constantine thought she was weeping. Only when angry words began to pour from her in a torrent, did he realize that rage, not sorrow at his going, had driven her to the unprecedented step of visiting his quarters.

Dacius took a quick look at her and reached for his helmet. "I'll maintain a guard outside," he said. "In the name of Jupiter, make this quick, or word of it will spread all over Rome."

"Why did you have to ruin everything?" Fausta demanded angrily of Constantine.

"What are you talking about?" Constantine had already endured more than enough trouble to try his patience that day and this was the final stroke.

"Asking my father for permission to marry me. You should have known the time is not yet. Much is to be arranged first."

"It was your father who sent for me," Constantine told her. "He accused me of trying to worm my way into your family by turning your head—"

"Turning my head. Why—"

"Those were his words, not mine," he said shortly. "And he warned me that the bastard of a Caesar could never aspire to marry the daughter of an Augustus."

"The bastard of a Caesar? That's one of Maxentius' lies."

"Your father seemed to believe it."

"He was only goading you, trying to make you do something he could have you broken for. Don't you see that they are afraid of you, Constantine?" By now her anger had visibly diminished.

"I'm beginning to believe it."

"The first time Maxentius told that lie about your birth, I had a scribe in Nicomedia copy the certificate of your father's marriage from his military record."

"Why?" It was Constantine's turn to be stunned.

"Because I had decided to marry you. Why else?"

"When was this decision made?"

"Oh, a long time ago, when I was only a child, maybe thirteen or so. It was in Nicomedia, when you and Maxentius finished your military training and I saw you ride and fight the Frankish master of horse."

"Crocus?"

"I don't remember his name."

"He's the king of one of the Frankish kingdoms on the Rhine frontier now. My father wrote me about it when I was in Syria."

She seemed suddenly to remember what had brought her to his quarters, for her eyes became stormy again. "How could you be so foolish as to ask Father to marry me?"

"It was when he accused me of using you to gain favor with him."

"And being honorable, you told him the truth?"

"Of course," he said stiffly. "I love you and want to marry you. Why should I be ashamed of that?"

Her face softened again. "You never told me that before."

"You were so busy telling me you were going to marry me and become Augusta that I never had a chance," he retorted. "What do you want me to do now? Tell your father I've changed my mind?"

"Of course not." She came over to stand on tiptoe and kiss him. "There—we are betrothed. But don't tell anyone else about it, until I say the word."

"And when will that be?"

"Not for a while yet." She dimpled suddenly in a smile, one of the changes of expression that made her so adorable. "I've waited this long, I can wait longer."

"But can I?" Constantine said hoarsely. "Sometimes I want you so much I can hardly bear it. Don't you ever want me?"

"Certainly I do. But that must wait too."

"Why?"

"We're not like ordinary people, dearest." It was as if she were a teacher, lecturing to a child. "We have the Empire to think about and our own part in it."

"I'm better at battles than at politics," Constantine said doubtfully. "Maybe I should remain only a soldier."

"You'll learn how it's done," she assured him. "Father wants to remain Emperor after Diocletian abdicates, but I'm sure he will not be allowed to do it, unless we all work together."

"We?"

"Your father is already tied to my family through Theodora," she reminded him. "When you and I are married, we can make a common front against Galerius; he doesn't really deserve to be an Augustus after that shameful defeat in Persia. The Illyrian soldiers in the eastern army will follow you and your father and, with them behind us, we can make Father the Emperor of the East, too, and keep it all in the family."

"What about Maxentius?"

"He can become a Caesar, or go to Africa," she said airily.

"You have it all planned, don't you? Did all this come to you at once?"

"Of course not. I started on it before we returned from Nicomedia, as soon as I decided to marry you. Goodbye, dearest." She kissed him quickly on the lips and was gone before he could take her in his arms for a more ardent embrace.

When the door had closed behind her, Constantine stood looking at it for a long moment. It was hard to believe that such an enchanting little creature could have drawn up a plan of empire and, what was more, embarked already upon putting it into effect. But somehow he couldn't escape the strange feeling that it would all work out just as she had planned and was suddenly a little afraid, as anyone would be at discovering that he was destined to be a puppet—like the painted dolls he'd seen in the street shows since coming to Rome—whose every movement was controlled by a woman.

Dacius came in and wiped the sweat from his forehead with his forearm, although the air outside was not warm. "Well, she's safely out of the way," he said. "But don't ever get into this sort of trouble again if you value your life."

"I had nothing to do with it," Constantine reminded him. "When do you think she decided she would marry me?"

"The first time she saw you, of course. That was about a week ago."

"She did decide the first time she saw me," Constantine agreed. "But it was the day I almost killed Crocus in Nicomedia."

"By the blood of the sacred bull!" Dacius exclaimed. "I remember now that Maximian and his family were there, on account of Maxentius. But Fausta was a mere child then."

"I don't think Fausta was ever a mere child," Constantine said with a note of awe in his voice. "She's determined for me to be Emperor, Dacius."

"And you?"

"I don't like the idea of being led around by the nose."

"No married man does, but it happens just the same."

"Not to me," Constantine said, with suddenly rising confidence. "I'm going to take matters into my own hands."

"How?"

"I want Fausta and there's no need for us to wait. If I ask Emperor Diocletian to demand her from Maximian for my wife, I'm sure he will do it."

"He might, sometime," Dacius agreed. "But not right now."

"Why?"

"I saw one of the Emperor's eunuchs outside just now. Diocletian has been seized by a fever and his physician has advised him to get out of Rome. You know how bad the fevers are here."

"Where are we going?"

"To Salonae.* It's on the way back to Nicomedia. We leave in the morning and this is no time to talk to him about personal affairs."

"That leaves everything undecided," Constantine protested, but Dacius shook his head.

"It leaves you exactly where you were before. Fausta has determined to make you Emperor, so Emperor you shall be. And I hope I'm not the one ever to stand in her way."

* Split or Solin

11

T HE SUMMER was almost past when Constantine saw Nicomedia again. But long before they left Salonae, where Diocletian had paused when the fever returned, he learned that
things had changed markedly in the eastern capital during their
absence. The Emperor's attempt to remedy the Empire's economic
difficulties by a rigid system of wage and price controls, with some
reforms in currency, had been in effect for nearly two years but,
if anything, conditions were worse than they had been before. Few
goods were available at the prices set by the government and buy-
ers were forced to purchase in secret at much higher figures. In
fact, the only group who seemed to have profited under the new
order was the army of civil servants required to collect the taxes
and enforce the edicts.

Galerius had become emperor in fact, if not in name, during
Diocletian's absence. With the old ruler still ailing, he continued
to control the government and thus was able to cast blame for the
chaotic conditions where he knew it would please many people
most—upon the hated Christians. Only an excuse was needed to
begin a full-scale persecution that would allow the Caesar of the
East and the hierarchy of his appointees who now ruled in Nicomedia to seize the property and wealth of the Christians for themselves. It came in January following Diocletian's return.

The day had been hot for winter and all afternoon dark clouds
had hung over the mountains to the south, accompanied by mutter-
ings of thunder and occasional flashes of lightning. The air was
crackling with the threat of a storm when Constantine posted the
guards for the night. A sudden shower of rain forced him to seek

shelter in a summerhouse as he was returning from the farther-most guard post to his quarters in the palace. Morosely watching the storm clouds, which seemed a portent of his own prospects since the interview with Maximian in Rome, he was blinded momentarily by a bolt of lightning so near that it struck a tree and glanced off to the corner of the roof covering a wing of the palace, causing a sudden burst of flame.

Shouting the alarm as he ran through the courtyard, Constantine paused to soak his cloak in water at a nearby fountain and started beating at the flames. Moments later servants came pouring from the palace with jars and buckets to douse the burning wood with water, quickly extinguishing the fire. The second incident happened while he was off duty one evening, a fire in another wing that burned briskly for about half an hour before it was extinguished.

In the tense atmosphere of the palace, Constantine was not surprised when he was ordered to attend a court of inquiry into the fire. It was presided over by the Chief Chamberlain, a eunuch named Carinus, who had been appointed to the position by Galerius. Constantine had more than once had differences of opinion with the portly and swarthy chamberlain and did not doubt that his every activity was being faithfully reported by the eunuch to Galerius.

"We have met to consider the latest crime of the Christians in setting fire twice to the palace and attempting to kill our beloved ruler," Carinus announced at the beginning, giving sentence of guilt even before any evidence was heard.

"Does the Christian god wield thunderbolts?" Constantine asked caustically. "I thought they were the property of Jove."

Carinus ignored him and began to take testimony. A servant swore that the odor of brimstone had filled the air at the time of both fires and several others corroborated his testimony.

"It is well known that the Christians believe in an evil spirit named Lucifer, or the devil, who dwells in a place called Hades, where fires of brimstone are always burning," Carinus said smugly. "I think the connection here is quite obvious to everyone."

"Then is it your belief that this evil spirit set fire to the palace twice in order to cause the persecution of the Christian sect?" Constantine asked.

"It is our contention that the Christians invoked the power of the Evil One against the person and property of the Emperor," Carinus said.

"Invoked?" Constantine raised his eyebrows. "When the one you call Lucifer is the enemy of the Christians?"

"You seem to know much about this accursed sect, Tribune," Carinus snapped. "Perhaps you can tell us what happened!"

"I have already told you I was almost struck by the lightning bolt that set fire to the palace the first time. I did notice an odor in the air, but it was only the pungent smell that is always present when lightning strikes close by. As for the second fire, I was not in the city—"

"There were no clouds that night," Carinus interrupted. "And no thunderclaps."

Constantine shrugged. "Then no doubt there was no odor either, so your witnesses must be lying."

The hearing ended quickly but Constantine did not doubt that the story told to Diocletian would name the Christians as criminals. Or that, in the Emperor's present low state of both spirits and health, he could be persuaded easily that the hated sect was to blame. Nor was Constantine surprised to receive an order to marshal the household troops in the square before the palace the following morning for the purpose of carrying out an edict of the Emperor which would be announced at that time.

A scapegoat had obviously been found, only the formality of naming it publicly remained.

II

It was late afternoon before Constantine was able to turn over command of the palace to Dacius and ride to the estate of his Uncle Marios overlooking the Gulf of Nicomedia a few miles beyond the boundaries of the capital.

"We see too little of you these days, nephew," Marios greeted him warmly. "Are your duties so onerous?"

"Not so much my duties as my cares," Constantine admitted. "I suppose you are familiar with what is happening in the palace."

"A flock of vultures—serving only Galerius—have come to roost there. Have they attacked you?"

"Not directly—yet. It's Mother I'm troubled about, her and her Christian friends."

"Helena is too close to the Christians of Drepanum for her own welfare," Marios agreed. "But we are a family of strong-minded people and I haven't been able to persuade her to give them up."

"Is she a Christian herself?"

"I asked her that question not over a month ago and she assured me she is not." Marios looked at him keenly. "What about you? Dacius told me about the young priest of Caesarea and Antioch."

"Eusebius?" Constantine smiled. "He is naïve enough to believe their god is working through me."

"Then you are not tempted to follow the man they call Christ?"

A familiar picture came into Constantine's mind at his uncle's words, the first time it had been there in many months. It was the face of the slender shepherd with the wise and understanding eyes that seemed not only able to penetrate one's soul but also to bring assurance and comfort in times of uncertainty.

"I saw a painting of the man they worship on the wall of a ruined church at Dura on the Euphrates," he said. "He must have been quite different from other men."

"Different enough to invite his own death on the cross and the deaths of thousands who have followed him since," Marios said shortly. "Put his face from your mind and choose some easy faith, like the worship of Mithras."

"Why?"

"Diocletian might die any day; for all I know, Carinus may be poisoning him slowly with some subtle medicine on the orders of Galerius. When that happens, you will be the son of an Augustus and probably a Caesar."

"Fausta thinks Galerius will try to have me killed when the Emperor abdicates."

"She is probably right," Marios said soberly. "An alliance with the house of Maximian would do you no harm. Of course their blood line is weak but yours is strong enough to overcome it. Do you expect either Maximian or Galerius to favor the match?"

Constantine shook his head glumly. "Emperor Maximian made that clear before I left Rome. Only Diocletian could force him to give Fausta to me, and they are pushing me farther from him every day. Unless I'm wrong, a decree will be issued tomorrow starting a new campaign of persecution against the Christians and I shall be charged with carrying it out, at least in Nicomedia. I'm sure Carinus arranged it, hoping I will refuse."

"You will obey, of course?"

"I can do nothing else, though I had enough of that in Alexandria. But I wanted to be sure no one could trump up a charge and harm Mother and Crispus."

"They are safe," Marios assured him. "It's you that Dacius and I are concerned about."

"Why?"

"Diocletian will not be Emperor much longer. I'm satisfied that he is tired of ruling and ready to give up the throne."

"He told me as much at Salonae," Constantine agreed. "Right now his main ambition is to grow cabbages there larger than any others in all of Illyricum."

"That means Galerius will soon become Augustus of the East and your father of the West. When that happens, you must be on your way to Gaul at once."

"If they let me leave."

"Two powerful horses will be stabled here at all times and others will be in readiness no more than a day's journey apart between here and the Alps at the villas of men I can trust," Marios assured him. "Once there, you can lose any pursuers. Dacius knows the passes like he knows the streets of Nicomedia."

"If I succeed in getting away and your part in my escape is discovered, you may forfeit your life," Constantine reminded him.

"Your father saved my life by staying back to stanch the flow of blood when my leg was thrust through by a spear, so I owe him that much at least. Besides"—Marios grinned—"with a nephew as Emperor of Rome one day, I shall be a powerful man."

By the time a detail of the Imperial Guards, with Constantine at its head, marched from the military compound behind the palace the next morning and took up a position on either side of the portico leading up to the palace, the square before it was packed with people. The central section between the palace and the Christian church that stood upon a little elevation across from it had been cleared, and shortly two thrones were carried out by the black Nubians Diocletian had brought from Egypt as bearers.

Constantine had not known Galerius was in the city until he saw the stocky figure of the Caesar of the East follow the much frailer form of Diocletian from the palace. He was not surprised, however, for little went on in Nicomedia without Galerius' knowledge, and he had a habit of turning up when least expected. The two took their seats upon the thrones with a considerable array of high officials massed behind them.

The crowd set up a roar of approval at the sight of the Emperor, who had not appeared publicly for months. In fact, Constantine had not even seen him for several weeks, since Diocletian spent most of the time in his private quarters, where only his personal servants and the chamberlains who administered the several departments of the government were allowed to go. Though still rather pale from his long illness, Diocletian appeared stronger than at any time since their abrupt departure from Rome and Constantine felt his hopes kindle a little at the thought that he might still persuade the old Emperor to intercede for him with Maximian.

Carinus, the Chief Chamberlain, stood beside Galerius. When the cheering died away, he handed a scroll to the Caesar of the East and Galerius began to read. His first words—after the usual formal invocation of favor from the gods—told Constantine the reason for the gathering.

The imperial edict was brief and to the point. As of that day, images of the Christian deity, or the man called Jesus Christ, found in churches or houses were to be destroyed, as were all writings considered holy by them. The furnishings and property of churches everywhere were also to become public property, granting an open license for pillage and rapine.

The reading of the edict completed, Galerius turned to Constantine. "Search the building for any proscribed image or writing, Tribune," he commanded, pointing to the church. "Let them be burnt publicly here in the square."

Constantine had been dreading the moment when he must open the doors of the church and face another painting of the gentle shepherd of Galilee. Knowing that Galerius and many others were watching, however, he gave the order and, at the head of a small detail of troops, marched across the square and up the steps to the doors of the church. Two of the soldiers threw open the doors and, as he stepped through into the interior of the building, a tremendous surge of relief swept through him.

The interior arrangement was somewhat like those he had seen at Drepanum and Dura, consisting of a single large room with benches for the worshipers to sit upon and a lectern or pulpit upon a raised dais at the end. But there were no paintings upon the walls; nor did he see any when he looked through the open doorway of the small adjoining room in which stood a marble font where, he had learned, the rite of baptism so highly prized by the Christians was carried out.

As he strode down the middle aisle of the room Constantine saw, partially unrolled upon the lectern, one of the scrolls from which it was the custom during the services of the Christians to read the teachings of their leader and the apostles who had been next beneath him in order of power. A tall man wearing a white robe and an embroidered dalmatic—such as he had seen in Antioch—stood before the lectern with his hand resting quietly upon it. The priest showed no sign of fear and, when Constantine raised his hand, the soldiers behind him came to a halt.

"Tribune Constantinus, bearing the orders from the Emperor to seize all images of your god," he announced.

"You will find no images here, Tribune," the priest said. "Our faith forbids them."

"All holy writings are also to be destroyed."

"These are the Scriptures." The priest pointed to the scroll upon the pulpit. "But be sure that for every scroll you destroy a hundred shall spring up—like the seeds in the parables of our Lord."

"Hand them over," Constantine ordered.

"Nay, you must seize them if you wish to destroy them," the priest said firmly.

A decurion, who was just behind Constantine, started to push forward toward the priest at this show of defiance, but Constantine barred his way with an outstretched arm.

"Our orders said nothing about harming people," he said sharply.

"But he has refuse—"

Before the sentence could be completed, Constantine stepped forward and reached for the parchment roll, but as his fingers touched it he found himself recalling the words he had heard Theognis of Nicaea read years before in a little church at Drepanum. The memory of their beauty and simplicity made him want to draw back and, even now, refuse to carry out the order he had been given. But he knew such an act would put him at the mercy of Galerius and, with an effort, forced his fingers to obey his will and close over the scroll.

"Search the building," he ordered the men behind him. "Take out the benches and set them afire in the square with whatever other furniture and furnishings you can find. And Decurion Paulos," he directed, "take a detail and search the floor beneath. Bring out anything you find that can be destroyed."

The decurion's eyes brightened at the thought of possible loot small enough to be hidden in his clothing, or in a safe place until it could be recovered. As Paulos hurried toward the doorway leading to the lower floor, Constantine spoke quickly to the priest in a low voice.

"You will gain nothing by staying here, sir," he said. "The Emperor may order the church burned and it will only be your pyre. Leave by the back entrance; I cannot be responsible for what will happen if you appear in the square."

"May God bless you, Tribune Constantine." The priest turned toward a door behind the altar. "You are a worthy son of your father."

As the priest disappeared through another door, Constantine marched up the aisle and through the entrance of the church with the scroll of the Scriptures held high in his hands. He was followed by a file of soldiers carrying benches, tables, and other articles of wood which they piled upon a fire that had been kindled in the square. Constantine, however, continued past the fire and up the steps to the throne of Diocletian.

"The Christian Scriptures, Dominus," he reported. "Seized as you commanded."

"What of the images?" Galerius demanded. "Where are they?"

"There were no images," Constantine said. "During our march to Egypt I was in the country from which the man called Christ came. I learned there that neither they nor the Jews allow any graven images to be worshiped in their churches."

The reminder of his own difficulties not long after the event of which Constantine spoke sent a red tide of anger surging into Galerius' face. "Burn the building then," he snapped. "Destroy every vestige of their cursed faith."

"Many wooden buildings are located near the church, Dominus." Constantine spoke earnestly to Diocletian. "If it is burned, much of the city may go with it."

"Nonsense," Galerius exclaimed. "With so many people here, we can contain the fire."

"And the mob rushing to escape the flames?" Constantine was still speaking to Diocletian. "Who will contain them?"

"Constantine is right, Galerius," Diocletian said. "It would be too dangerous to set fire to the church now. Burn the cursed writings upon the fire, Constantine, and be sure everything related to their sect is removed from the building and destroyed."

IV

The fire that consumed the scrolls and furnishings of the Christian church at Nicomedia marked the beginning of a holocaust that soon swept from one end of the Empire to the other. That same day, word spread through the city that Empress Prisca and Lady Valeria had been forced to recant, and the next brought publication of a second edict decreeing the destruction of Christian churches everywhere. In addition, Christians were deprived of all honors and dignities they had enjoyed until now, while those who failed to recant and publicly serve the old gods, were to be tortured. Every suit at law against them was also accepted without question by the courts, insuring that their property could be seized upon the slightest pretext. They were further forbidden recourse to the courts in all questions of wrong, adultery or theft, assuring their tormentors of freedom from any punishment. Finally they were forbidden all the freedoms normally belonging to citizens of Rome, including the right to vote guaranteed to all citizens by law.

Troops under Constantine's command were given the task of posting copies of the decree upon the doors of all public buildings and in other conspicuous places throughout the city. Before he was halffinished, two soldiers came to him, dragging by the scruff of his robe an elderly man whose white hair was matted with blood. A dark swelling was already forming over one cheek, too, mute evidence that the prisoner had received rough treatment at the hands of his captors, who now thrust him forward so violently that he fell at Constantine's feet.

"This man was caught removing one of the edicts the moment we finished putting it up, sir," the first soldier reported.

"And he tore it to pieces," the second added.

Constantine reached down and lifted the elderly man to his feet. "What is your name?" he asked gently.

"Amianus, noble Tribune." The man showed no sign of fear, although he had difficulty in standing.

"Are you a Christian?"

At the word, Amianus straightened himself until he stood proudly erect. "I am an elder in the church of Nicomedia, sir."

"Why did you tear down an imperial decree?"

"Because Caesar Galerius persuaded the Emperor to publish these edicts, so he can seize the possessions of Christians everywhere. He even had the second fire set in the palace, so he could blame it upon us."

Constantine had heard the rumor before. Nor did he put it beyond Galerius to adopt such a strategy, for it was no secret in the East that, through the persecutions he had already ordered in areas under his command, he had amassed a considerable fortune in money and articles seized from Christians. But Galerius was not on trial; nor was it Constantine's duty to do more than finish posting the imperial decrees and turn Amianus over to the proper legal authorities.

"Take him before a magistrate so he can be properly charged and imprisoned to await trial," he ordered, and the three marched off, the older man managing to remain proudly erect, though stumbling every now and then.

Most of the day was required for the detail to finish posting copies of the imperial decrees throughout the city. As he was approaching the square before the palace at the head of his detail late that afternoon—already savoring the pleasure of the bath and a glass of wine—Constantine heard shouting ahead and shortly found further progress barred by a mass of people filling every street leading to the square.

"What's happening?" he called to a man, who had climbed to a second floor balcony from which he had a view of the square.

"They are going to put the Christian to death, sir."

"What Christian?"

"The one called Amianus, who tore down the decree this morning. They say that at his trial he accused Caesar Galerius of arresting Christians and seizing their property for himself."

"At least he was telling the truth," someone said, and a laugh came from the crowd. "Galerius will soon be the richest man in the East, unless he runs out of Christians."

"Decurion," Constantine ordered the petty officer who was second-in-command of the detail, "set four men to force a way through here with the shafts of their spears."

The soldiers obeyed immediately, paying no attention to the curses and cries of people who were thrust aside, bruised and occasionally cracked over the head if they did not move quickly. An aisle was soon opened and Constantine moved through the crowd to the edge of the square. Dacius was standing at the head of a detail of the guards a little distance away and he moved to join the centurion.

"What's going on here?" he demanded. "This morning I ordered a man taken before a magistrate and now they tell me he's being executed."

"Justice is swift these days, for Christians. Look over there in front of the church."

The ashes and cinders of the fire that had consumed the benches and furnishings of the church the day before had not yet been cleaned up. Wood was now being piled around a post which had been erected there and Galerius sat upon his portable throne at the edge of the open space perhaps ten paces from the post. Beside him two brawny soldiers held Amianus.

At Galerius' word the battered prisoner was half-marched, half-dragged across the cobblestoned square and up the slight elevation upon which the church stood. There he was quickly bound to the post and faggots of dry wood were piled about his feet. A hush fell over the square as the crowd waited for the next act in the drama, but Galerius had no intention of hurrying it. Rising to his feet, he addressed the people.

"You see before you a condemned heretic," he said, "worshiper of a false god who demands a loyalty greater even than to the Emperor and to the gods of Rome. He has been tried for his crime by me, a magistrate according to Roman law, and found guilty. But Emperor Diocletian is merciful and the flames that consume his body will be a swifter death than the one he deserves, which is to be nailed to a cross until the vultures pluck out his eyes and the flesh begins to drop from his body. Let everyone watch the flames, so any who would follow the false god of the Christians may recant before the patience of our beloved Augustus is tried beyond its limits."

Galerius paused and swept the square with his eyes, giving his words time to sink into the minds of those who were watching before ordering the next act in this grim drama. A soldier bearing a flaming torch had stepped forward and, when Galerius' gaze came to rest upon Constantine, the young officer tensed himself, for he knew what was coming next.

"I am told that Tribune Constantinus of the Imperial Guard ordered the arrest of this miscreant," Galerius said. "Let his be the honor of applying the torch that will carry out the sentence of the court."

For a moment Constantine felt as he had on the body-strewn battlefield that day east of the Euphrates, with the evidence of a Roman defeat before his eyes and the knowledge that he had possibly led his men into a trap from which they might not escape.

It was a feeling of panic, a powerful impulse to run away, and his muscles actually tensed in readiness, until a familiar voice spoke beside him.

"Galerius is hoping you will draw back," Dacius warned. "Seize the torch. If your hand doesn't set the fire, another will."

The moment of indecision passed as quickly as it had come and Constantine stepped out to meet the soldier. Taking the torch he strode forward to thrust the flaming end deep into the pile of wood, holding it there until the faggots caught fire well and the flames licked up to scorch his hand before he dropped the torch.

Only when he stepped back, did he dare look directly at Amianus, but saw no fear in the Christian's face. In fact, the eyes of the condemned man burned with a light fully as bright as the torch Constantine had used to set the flame. And his look was one of such eagerness that Constantine could believe he would run to meet death, were he not bound to the stake.

A great "Ah" went up from the crowd as the flames from the burning faggots leaped up to envelop the slender form standing so erectly against the stake. The acrid smell of burning cloth floated across the square as his clothing caught fire, but not even a whisper of agony came from him, only a shout of exultation:

"Lord Christ, to Thee I commend my spirit! Not my will but Thine be done!"

As the flames and smoke from his burning clothing suffocated the condemned man, the frail body sagged forward loosely within its bonds, and a cry of disappointment went up from the crowd. Galerius, who had half-risen from his throne when the faggots took fire, sank back upon it and shouted for the bearers to carry the chair up the steps into the palace. Constantine remained only until the massive doors of the palace had closed behind Galerius. Then signaling the decurion to take command, he turned and plunged through the crowd toward the military compound and his own quarters. He was bending over the copper bucket in the corner of his room, retching, when Dacius entered.

"Drink this!" The old soldier handed him a cup of wine which he drank gratefully, feeling its warmth course through his middle and bring stability where only turmoil had been moments before. Wiping his face with a wet towel Dacius handed him, he staggered to the small table and sank into a chair beside it, while the centurion hung his helmet on a peg and straddled the second chair.

"So the sight of a burning man makes you retch," Dacius said. "I'm glad to see you are thoroughly human, in spite of your ambition."

"Did you—?"

"Almost puked my guts out the first time," Dacius said cheerfully. "I remember the whole thing well. It was—"

"Spare me, please."

"You get used to it in time. Actually Galerius was right—burning *is* a far more merciful form of execution than, say, crucifixion. With the flames, suffocation comes early, especially if they are well kindled as they were today, so the victim experiences little agony. Beheading is merciful too, if expertly done. But if the executioner is not skilled, or if he enjoys watching the victim suffer, he may take two strokes when one would do. Believe me, I've seen them all and crucifixion is the worst. Those poor devils sometimes hang for days before death comes."

"The son of the god this fellow Amianus died for was crucified," Constantine said.

"I know, but he was lucky. A Roman soldier gave him a merciful thrust in the side with a spear, so his agony was short." Seeing Constantine's look of surprise, he explained: "I once read through the Christian Scriptures to see whether there was anything in their faith for me. The scene is described there."

"And was there anything in them—for you, I mean?"

"Nothing to get yourself burned at the stake for, or beheaded."

"But they promise immortality."

"So does Mithras, and you don't have to torture yourself to achieve it." The old soldier's voice was suddenly sober. "I know you're pulled many ways, boy, especially with your mother almost a Christian and Constantius perhaps having gone equally far. It's no secret that he hasn't been carrying out the persecutions in Gaul and Britain as avidly as Galerius has in the East. But take my advice and stay away from the Christians and their beliefs."

"Is there likely to be any of them left, after the decrees are carried out?"

"History shows that the Nazarene faith comes from the fire like metal in the tempering, harder and sharper than before. My guess is that the same thing will happen again and it will emerge stronger than ever."

Constantine did not speak for a long moment and, when he did, his words were thoughtful: "If that is true, then a man like me, with little chance of realizing his chief ambition otherwise, might profit from the support of the Christians and their god."

12

D IOCLETIAN'S FIRST EDICT had called for the destruction of
Christian churches and Christian books; a second and a
third ordered Christian priests to offer sacrifices to the gods of the
state upon pain of death. As a result, the Christians themselves became sharply divided. Some, in order to save their lives, surrendered the Holy Scriptures to be burned and made at least a token
sacrifice before the state gods; others, however, zealously chose
death rather than compromise their belief. Nor was the situation
helped when many Christian bishops privately urged the clergy under their jurisdiction to make a token acknowledgment, certain
that, as had been the case with other persecutions, this one too
would wane and the church would emerge once again to a position
of influence.

One group of people Constantine was never able to understand
—the fanatics. Amianus, he realized, could easily have avoided being executed that day in the square. And in the months that followed, he saw many others deliberately choose death by going out
of their way to resist the decrees. Trained as a soldier and practical to the highest degree, he found it difficult to understand what
appeared to him to be a needless sacrifice of life.

Then one day, as he was playing in the garden at Drepanum
with Crispus—now a fine healthy boy who promised to be everything Constantine himself had been as a stripling in Naissus—he
looked up to see beside him the tall form of the priest-philosopher
Theognis of Nicaea, who had performed the simple wedding ceremony in which he and Minervina had been married. He rose at
once and gave Theognis the Roman grip of greeting while

Crispus, protesting, was bundled off to supper with the promise that his father would romp with him again at bedtime.

"I am pleased to find you unharmed, sir," Constantine said warmly.

"Others are not," the priest admitted with a wry smile. "They call me a traitor to my faith."

"Why?"

"I gave up the Holy Scriptures, as the Emperor decreed, and made a token sacrifice to Jupiter. The military commander of the district where Nicaea lies is an old friend from my own days as a soldier and required no more of me."

"Isn't it dangerous for you to come here? The commander of this district is a crony of Caesar Galerius and reports to him on everything that happens."

"I shall not be here long. Your Uncle Marios and Centurion Dacius asked me to talk to you. They are comrades from my days as a soldier and know we are friends."

"Surely they don't expect you to convert me to your faith?"

"Rather the opposite," Theognis assured him. "Many times since the Ascension of our Lord it has been best for Christians to remain in hiding. This is one of them."

"But many of your people seem to want to be tortured, sir. I know governors who have tried to keep them from denouncing the Emperor and Rome, but to no avail."

"Alas, we are only human and more often moved by emotions than reason," Theognis admitted. "Christ himself ordered us to render unto Caesar what is Caesar's and unto God what is God's. He was never disobedient to civil authority, though the priests of that day sought to make it appear that he was, so they could destroy him when he threatened their hold over the common people. And the Apostle Paul explicitly commanded us to be obedient to authority."

"I heard a sermon on his teachings in Antioch, when I accompanied Empress Prisca and Lady Valeria to one of your churches. But I don't remember much, except that it concerned armor and breastplates."

"The breastplates of righteousness and the armor of God?"

"Yes. That was it."

"The passage is from Paul's letter to the church at Ephesus, written while he was in prison. He came near to being killed there, when the silversmiths joined against him because many people who listened to his preaching turned away from the worship of Artemis and stopped buying the images they made and sold."

"Some people claim we Romans are only persecuting Christians in order to seize their possessions."

"The charge contains a great deal of truth, I am sure," Theognis said. "You asked just now why it is that some of us seem to court death while others, like myself, compromise their principles in order to stay alive."

"I was not censuring you, sir," Constantine protested.

"You could hardly censure me more than I have already condemned myself," Theognis told him. "Being both philosopher and priest, I am perhaps—as some have claimed—more of the former than the latter. Rigidly interpreted, our faith teaches that those who believe in the Lord Jesus Christ as our Saviour go immediately at death to dwell in heaven with the Father."

"Minervina believed it. My mother told me that by baptizing her, you gave her the courage to face death happily. I have always been grateful to you."

"She was a lovely child and her dying so young was a tragic thing," Theognis said. "But she gave you a strong son, so her death was not in vain. I hope you will always remember her for that."

"How could I forget, with Crispus growing daily into a fine, handsome boy?"

"You asked why so many Christians seem to seek death," Theognis continued. "It is because if they die affirming Christ against oppression, they consider themselves certain of immortal life."

"Do you believe that?"

"I believe it, yes." Theognis' face was drawn, as if from an inner torment. "Emotion urges that no greater proof of loyalty to Jesus could be required than to die because of him with his name on your lips. But Jesus also returned from death and appeared to Simon Peter and some others on the Sea of Galilee, after they had fled from Jerusalem. And when he told Peter, 'Feed my sheep,' Peter understood that he must go back to Jerusalem and face the threat of death at the hands of the high court, the Sanhedrin. The

Christian Church was built upon the rock of Peter's faith and presence but particularly upon his acknowledgment of Christ as the Son of God."

"This Peter was put to death, too, wasn't he? I seem to remember Minervina speaking of it."

"He was crucified by Nero—we believe head down at his own request because he felt himself unworthy to die as Jesus had died. But by then the teachings of our Lord had been spread abroad and new churches had been established all over the world, so Peter could feel that his work was finished and go willingly to his reward. I have not been able to convince myself that my usefulness to Christ is over." Theognis smiled wryly. "But I also wonder whether I tell myself that because I would not have the courage to die as Amianus did in the flames."

"What does your heart tell you?"

Theognis gave him a quick surprised look, as if he had not expected such a question. "It tells me that an even greater work will need to be done after this holocaust has burned itself out. It reminds me that all seemed lost after Jesus was crucified, yet when Peter and the others took up the work again, it prospered."

"Then listen to it."

Theognis looked deep into the eyes of the younger man, as if searching for a reason to believe Constantine was speaking the truth. Finally he smiled. "I came here to advise you because I told myself I was wiser than you, yet you have shown me the way I should go. I think Dacius and Marios are right—in believing you are the man who will one day heal the division between the East and the West and make the Empire whole again."

"How can you work for the welfare of Rome, when it is burning your comrades alive?"

"God's purpose never prospers in a state of anarchy," Theognis said. "Paul, the wisest man in our faith after Christ himself, saw that clearly. We need a government where all men are free to worship whatever gods they choose. My task, and I see it clearly now, is to show them our way is best." He turned and picked up the cloak he had dropped upon a bench. "May God go with you and guard you in all your endeavors, my son."

"Even though I am not of your faith?"

"The ways of the Lord are mysterious and wonderful." Theognis'
smile was warm. "When it is time for you to know his purpose for
you, be sure he will make it known. I must go now before the spies
of Caesar Galerius report that I have been here."

As he watched the tall form of the philosopher priest disappear
into the dusk of the street, Constantine could not help remembering
his conversation with Eusebius of Caesarea almost two years ago
in Antioch. For Eusebius had said then almost exactly what Theognis had said tonight, that the Christian god would one day make
his will known in a way Constantine could not at the moment possibly foresee.

II

In Gaul and Britain, Constantine learned from letters written to
Helena by Constantius, his father had enforced only the first edict
of persecution requiring that the Christians give up for destruction
whatever holy writings they were not able to hide and that their
churches should be torn down. None of these actions prevented the
members of the tormented sect from meeting in small groups in
homes and elsewhere, however, as they had been forced to do
many times before in the history of their faith. And when Constantius gave only a token enforcement to the remaining edicts,
the church managed to stay alive in the West, and even flourish
in a small way.

All of this was known, of course, to Galerius and Maximian
through the spies they maintained in the territory of Constantius,
as well as to Diocletian. But the Senior Emperor was troubled by
illness again and Constantius, in the course of setting new boundaries restraining the Frankish kings north of the Rhine and bringing Britain back into the Empire, had built up the largest, best
equipped and trained army in the whole expanse of the Roman
Empire. Even Maximian, therefore, felt little inclination to force
his considerably more powerful son-in-law into any action of which
Constantius himself did not approve. Meanwhile Galerius was busy
forming his own clique—centered around himself, his nephew,
Maximin Daia, and General Severus, a well-liked officer—insuring

absolute control of the entire East when Diocletian decided to abdicate.

Following the dedication of the Great Circus, which had been building at Nicomedia for almost two years, the Senior Augustus suffered a relapse. On the Ides of December it was even reported that he was dead and the city began to mourn, but early the next morning the Emperor's physician published a bulletin stating that the beloved ruler had taken a turn for the better and now appeared to be on the road to recovery.

The rumor was enough to bring Galerius back to Nicomedia from his capital of Sirmium, however, and the Caesar of the East now took up residence in the palace, allegedly to lighten the burdens of his father-in-law, but in reality to take over as many of the imperial functions as he could. As a result Constantine found himself practically cut off from any contact with Diocletian and was surprised when he received a summons to the bedside of the Emperor.

Carinus, the Chief Chamberlain, stood beside the bed. With him was the physician, who said importantly, "You can stay only a few moments, Tribune—"

"He will stay until I give him leave to depart." The voice of Diocletian, still with some of its old vigor, spoke from the pillow. "Leave us, both of you."

The physician looked at Carinus, who hesitated, obviously not desiring to leave. "I can still order the axe for both of you," Diocletian warned and they scuttled out, leaving the door slightly ajar. Constantine looked at the old man propped up on the pillow and, seeing a gleam of mischief and enjoyment in the rheumy eyes, stepped to the door and shut it firmly.

"I'm glad to see my son-in-law has not cowed you," said Diocletian.

"My first duty is to you, Dominus."

"Not unless you're a fool, which I don't think you are. Every man's first duty is to himself, boy. If I hadn't followed that rule, how do you think the son of an Illyrian peasant could have gotten to be Emperor of Rome?"

"In your case I'm sure it was through the will of the gods, Dominus."

"Perhaps." Diocletian shrugged. "I have ruled as wisely as I could and the Empire is prosperous and peaceful, so I shouldn't ask for more. You're a fine officer, Constantine," he continued. "If the gods had given me a son, I couldn't want him to be different from you."

"Thank you, sir."

"Perhaps you're a bit too tenderhearted and concerned about others for your own good, but in time you will change. All of us do, as we grow older and discover that the world is like a dark forest filled with wild beasts seeking to destroy each other, and us. Only the strong survive in such a world, Constantine, but I believe you have the strength for it."

"At least I can follow your example, Dominus."

"You could do worse, particularly if you discover the virtue of waiting. Galerius has never learned that and I suppose he never will. You have served me well, Constantine, so I felt I should tell you that I have finally decided to abdicate, at the beginning of May. I am sending word to my gardener at Salonae to plant the cabbages as soon as the winter frosts are over." Diocletian's eyes kindled at the thought. "The twenty-year reign I promised myself and the people has already passed. I think the Empire will remain at peace now, with your father and Galerius as rulers."

He had said nothing about the Caesars, Constantine noted, and dared to let his hopes rise a little. For if Diocletian were leaving to Galerius the selection of the Caesar of the East, the choice of one for the West would very likely be left to Constantius. And he was quite sure who his father would select.

"Of the two Caesars your father is the stronger," Diocletian continued. "He has a considerably stronger army, too, so my son-in-law is not likely to realize his ambition to rule the whole Empire."

"Are you sure my father will not be so tempted?" Constantine asked.

"Constantius and I were comrades-in-arms, so I know he places honor above every other virtue. As Augustus of the West he can hold a checkrein upon Galerius and keep the Empire from being torn apart."

Constantine was far from agreeing with the old Emperor's evaluation of Galerius, having seen the Caesar of the East face defeat in the disastrous Persian campaign and build back stubbornly, profiting from his mistakes to win an even greater victory and cement his own position more strongly, until now he almost held Diocletian prisoner in the palace.

"Galerius has no son." Diocletian's voice broke into his thoughts. "Maximian is a brave soldier but an indifferent ruler and his line has run out in Maxentius, a bloodthirsty beast who should have been destroyed at birth. Naturally I shall not appoint Maxentius Caesar in the West, knowing he would seize the first opportunity to stab your father in the back. And since I cannot appoint Maximian's son as Caesar, obviously I cannot appoint Constantius' son to a similar position."

"You warned me long ago not to aspire to rule, Dominus."

"And I was wrong, for you would make a fine ruler. But you can see now that it is impossible. I have already written your father telling him of my decision."

"Will you let me go to Treves then?" He did not add that, if he stayed in Nicomedia, Galerius would break him at the first opportunity.

"I shall not be so foolish as to leave myself unprotected when I am no longer Emperor," Diocletian said. "You will stay with me. Salonae is not far from Nicomedia and, if I should discover that what I have spent twenty years building up is in danger of being destroyed, duty could always call me back to the throne, with you in command of my personal troops."

Constantine could hardly repress a shudder, when he remembered the dark corridors, the massive walls and the cold rooms of the great palace at Salonae.

"You will command my personal bodyguard after I abdicate, so during the next few months I want you to select men you can trust." Diocletian smiled wryly. "I've worked hard for the peace of my garden at Salonae and I intend to enjoy it."

"And the new Caesars?"

"They will be selected by Galerius. Your father has agreed to this, rather than accept Maxentius. But you will be well rewarded, Constantine. When I die you will be one of the richest men in the Empire." Diocletian's voice was warm, but it could not take away the chill that had settled over Constantine's heart. "I know how you must feel now and I wouldn't blame you for hating me, though I hope not for long."

"Not ever, Dominus. What I have become I owe to you."

Diocletian shook his head. "Not to me but to the seed that kindled life in your mother's womb. I merely furnished fertile soil so the transplanted slip could grow into a strong and healthy tree. I know you find it hard to believe now but I am doing you a favor, Constantine. The purple cloak of an Augustus can be the heaviest burden any man is asked to bear."

"At least I shall not have that trouble, Dominus." Constantine managed to smile, but he was only putting up a front to keep from hurting the old man who, he knew, was genuinely concerned about his welfare. For it would do no good now to remind Diocletian that, by closing any avenue to either of the two thrones of Rome, all possibility had also been shut away of his ever marrying the girl with whose elfish charm and impudence he had fallen so violently in love in Rome.

13

THE PROSPECT of seeing his beloved cabbages soon seemed to bring new strength to Diocletian, and to his determination to abdicate. On the first day of May the ceremony of abdication was carried out. And in order that no question should arise concerning the proper release of power, Maximian was required to go through a similar procedure in his own capital of Milan upon the very same day.

Almost an hour's march outside Nicomedia, there was a small rounded eminence that formed a natural platform. Here the largest crowd ever to gather in that region came together to witness the ceremony. Representatives of all the subject rulers of the East were there: pro-consuls, praetorian prefects, vicars, or governors, of the more important cities and provinces with their retinues, and many thousands of ordinary citizens, eager to see the colorful ceremony.

The imperial throne had been erected upon a platform at the very summit of the hill, just in front of a pillar upon which stood a statue of Hercules with a small altar before it, where the priests would perform the traditional offerings of sacrifice. Galerius sat upon a lower platform, robed in the purple of a Caesar. Gathered about him were the generals who were his favorites, notably Flavius Severus and Maximin Daia.

Only the picked group of Imperial Guards Constantine had selected to accompany the Emperor into retirement occupied the top platform besides Diocletian and Carinus, whose duty it would be to read the proclamation connected with the abdication. Constantine commanded the troops, with Dacius as his lieutenant. At his appearance a spontaneous cheer broke out from the crowd lining the slopes of the knoll, for he was very popular in Nicomedia and many of his mother's kinspeople were from the area around Drepanum. He saw a frown of displeasure crease the forehead of Galerius at this evidence of popular acclaim but did not let it trouble him, for nothing, he was sure, could make the living entombment to which he was going with Diocletian any worse than it already was.

The ceremony began with a sacrifice carried out upon the altar before the pedestal and the statue of Jupiter. When it was finished, Diocletian took his seat upon the throne, with the purple cloak about his shoulders and the pearl-set circlet upon his head, while Carinus read the royal proclamation of abdication. It was long and boring—as such documents usually were—beginning with salutations to the most important of the subject kings present and ending with the announcement of the new Augustus of the East. As the words died away, a detail of trumpeters sounded the "Call of the Emperor" and Galerius, resplendent in ceremonial uniform and armor, rose and dropped his cloak to the throne upon which he had been sitting. Diocletian, meanwhile, had moved away from his own throne so Galerius could take a position before it.

"Caius Galerius Valerius Maximianus, I name you Augustus of the East in my stead," Diocletian announced in a voice loud enough for the crowd to hear. "May your hands be more vigorous and more able than mine have been and may Rome ever prosper under your rule."

A roar came from the people at the words, not so much in pleasure at the crowning of Galerius, for he was not well liked, but because each man knew that if he did not show enthusiasm for the new Augustus, word of his lack might shortly find its way to the ears of the spies who were known to be everywhere.

With his own hands Diocletian placed upon Galerius' head a pearl-studded circlet and draped a robe of rich purple about the shoulders of the new Augustus. The old Emperor had kept his own circlet of pearls upon his head and his own robe about his shoulders, however, as a reminder, Constantine was sure, to the new ruler that he could emerge from retirement and renew the purple whenever he wished.

"At this moment," Diocletian announced as Galerius was taking his seat upon the highest throne, "my fellow Augustus, Marcus

Aurelius Valerius Maximianus Herculius, is abdicating his royal position in accordance with a promise made by both of us twenty years ago. In his stead, I appoint to rule as Augustus of the West, Flavius Valerius Constantius Chlorus."

A roar of applause far greater than that which had marked the ascent of Galerius to the throne greeted this announcement. Constantine felt his heart swell with pride at the spontaneous tribute to his father, but when he glanced at Galerius' scowling face, he could see that the new Augustus felt no pleasure at the popularity of his colleague in the West.

Diocletian had made no attempt to silence the tribute to Constantius; only when the applause had died away, did he announce: "The naming of the new Caesars who, as *Filii Augusti,* will share rule with the new Emperors, I have left to Augustus Galerius."

Galerius did not rise but nodded to Carinus, who unrolled a second scroll. "As Caesar of the West," he read, "it pleases us to appoint"—Carinus paused momentarily, conscious of the eagerness with which the crowd was awaiting the name—"Flavius Valerius Severus."

Severus had been standing with other high-ranking officers back of Galerius' throne upon the lower level. Now he stepped from the group and ascended to the higher platform, where Galerius sat with Diocletian standing beside him. Constantine had always respected Severus, in spite of his close ties with Galerius. But he was human enough to envy the other man the purple cloak of a Caesar that Diocletian now draped about his shoulders.

As Severus moved to his place behind Galerius, Carinus picked up the scroll and began to read from it again: "As Caesar of the East, it pleases us to appoint—"

When he paused once again for effect, shouts began to arise from the crowd and, startled, Carinus lost his place. While he fumbled for it, shouts of "Constantine! Constantine!" came from the crowd.

"Read on!" Galerius snapped angrily and the chamberlain, abandoning any attempt to find his place, announced: "As Caesar of the East, Maximin Daia."

A roar of indignation came from the crowd, many of whom knew Daia as a lackey, and nephew, of Galerius. Daia himself ignored the shouting and, stepping from among the group of officers on the lower platform, moved up to a position before Diocletian, where the purple cloak of a Caesar was draped about his shoulders.

There was an awkward moment, for the space on the dais was now filled, but Constantine did not give up the place that was rightfully his beside Diocletian. Galerius, however, solved the matter by casually throwing out his arm and pushing Constantine so strongly that he stumbled and was forced to step down to a lower level. A blaze of indignation at the deliberate affront made Constantine instinctively drop his hand to the sword at his side, but he conquered it immediately and drew his hand away. For an instant he felt the terrible loneliness of being shut out from everything toward which he had worked; then Diocletian stepped down to the lower level beside him and spoke almost in his ear.

"Let us go," the old man said in a somewhat shaky voice and, without waiting for permission from the new Augustus, they marched down the knoll to where the golden chariot waited under the trees with the horses of the troops that would accompany Diocletian to Salonae tethered close by.

II

If Diocletian's almost precipitate flight from Nicomedia following his abdication betrayed his distrust of his son-in-law, the character of the palace at Salonae was proof of it. Located with a lovely view of the Mare Adriaticum, the coast of which was studded with small islands in this region to form almost an enclosed lake, it was one of the most beautiful spots on the entire coast and also the greatest citadel.

The main structure was in the form of a somewhat irregular quadrangle, whose east and west sides were over seven hundred feet long, the north being slightly shorter. The south face looked out over the sea at a height of some eighty feet and was roughly six hundred feet in length. Built into the side facing the water, and some thirty feet above the rocky shore, was a lovely pillared gallery of twenty-four arches with an underground passage leading to the water. Several galleys were always at anchor there, affording a route of escape should the nearly seven-foot masonry walls of the castle ever be breached by an invader.

Diocletian's living quarters were in the south face of the palace, with a *triclinium, cubiculae* for sleeping, a hall of pools and statues, numerous baths and every comfort a Roman accustomed to luxurious living could wish. Breezes from the sea kept the palace pleasantly cool, and the water supply came fresh and cold from the heights above through an aqueduct some five miles in length. There was even a small private Temple of Jupiter within the walls and, of course, the gardens for which Diocletian had longed.

Loving the old man as he did, Constantine was pleased with the way Diocletian's health improved, once he was away from the cares of the court and the tasks of ruling. The beloved cabbages were already flourishing when they arrived at Salonae at the beginning of the second week in May. The sun was warm, flowers were beginning to bloom everywhere, and the whole verdant countryside redounded with the lush aroma of freshly turned earth and growing things.

Diocletian insisted that Constantine join him and Empress Prisca for their meals, treating the young officer in every way like one of the family. Actually the task of managing the small detachment of guard was handled easily by Dacius, so Constantine had little else to do. Being naturally vigorous, however, the young officer spent his energies in the manifold training duties every Roman soldier performed wherever he was: wrestling with the troops, throwing the spear, engaging in mock sword battles, and finishing off each period of vigorous action with a pleasant swim in the waters of the sea that lapped at the foundation of the palace.

In spite of all the beauty around him, the peaceful and almost bucolic life of Salonae held no lure to an active and ambitious man like Constantine, who saw himself banished there for the life span of the old Emperor. Diocletian, paradoxically, seemed to grow younger every day as he puttered about among his gardens. Nor did the fact that Fausta was much nearer to him now at her father's palace outside Milan improve Constantine's feelings about the present. With no future, it seemed, except as a military nursemaid, he could hardly hope for a better reception at the hands of Maximian than had been given him in Rome. And he knew Galerius would never approve a marriage uniting any closer the Praetorian Guard of Rome—for centuries emperor-makers themselves—commanded by Maxentius, with the powerful armies controlled by Constantius as Augustus of the West.

Then suddenly Constantine's whole situation changed abruptly with the arrival of an Imperial Courier bearing an official order, returning both him and Dacius to Nicomedia for reassignment with the legions. It was signed by Caius Flavius Valerius Licinianus Licinius, General of the Armies.

"You've been pining for a change," Dacius told Constantine. "Now you shall have it."

"Unless Diocletian refuses to let me go."

"You and I are needed around here about as much as a worm in one of his cabbages, but Galerius should be happy to have you buried here."

"Unless someone in Nicomedia has suddenly realized how much closer I am to my father here at Salonae than I was in Nicomedia."

"It took them long enough to see it, but I suspect that's why they suddenly decided to move us eastward. Anyway I'm glad to see Licinius coming up in the world. He's a good man; knows how to obey orders and keep his mouth shut."

"Which should make him valuable to Galerius."

Dacius shrugged. "Severus is Caesar now for the same reason. And if perchance Daia gets drunk enough one night to fall off a pier at Caesarea or Alexandria, Licinius could become Caesar."

"Are you saying I'll get no help from him?"

"Or from Severus. But you can at least be sure neither of them will strike a dagger into your back some dark night, which is more than I can say for Galerius. When are you going to tell Diocletian?"

"Tonight, at dinner. After all, Galerius is his son-in-law and if he insists that we stay here, even the Augustus of the East will hardly refuse."

"Don't tell me you want to stay, after moping around like a lovesick swain for three months."

"I intend to go to Nicomedia, if only to see what is behind the order," Constantine said. "But there's no reason for you to share whatever fate they've devised for me. After all—"

"I'm an old man and not able to keep up? Is that it?"

"For God's sake, no! You can outlast me in a cross-country run any day, but I don't see why you should get yourself killed—"

"Are you planning to commit suicide?"

"Of course not."

"Neither am I." Dacius smiled. "I remember the first day I saw you back in Nicomedia. You've got some of the same look on you now, like a man uncertain of what's going to happen but determined to make the best of it." Dacius' hand dropped to Constantine's shoulder in a warm gesture. "But be careful, lad. Don't make the same mistake before Galerius that you made here just now."

"Mistake?"

"You swore an oath, in the name of the Christian god."

14

Y RIDING HARD, Constantine and Dacius made the journey to Nicomedia in four days. General Licinius looked surprised when they presented themselves before him.

"You made good time I see, Tribune," he said. "How did you leave Emperor Diocletian?"

"Well, and happy."

Licinius smiled. "And the cabbages?"

"Thriving. No one near Salonae dares to grow any larger than his. May I ask where I'm being sent, sir?"

"You have been ordered to the Persian frontier, in the realm of Caesar Maximin Daia," Licinius told him. "I believe you have been through that area."

"Some years ago, at the time of the Persian War."

"Then you no doubt know the territory along the Euphrates, and the fortress of Callinicum."

"Callinicum?" It was Dacius who spoke, the words jolted from him by surprise. "When I was there, Callinicum was commanded by a centurion."

"Both Caesar Maximin Daia and Augustus Galerius feel the post is important enough now to justify stationing a tribune there," Licinius explained. "And since both of you are already familiar with the region guarded by the fortress, it seemed a logical place for you to serve."

It was a clever scheme, Constantine conceded. By burying him in the East, Galerius would avoid the trouble with Constantius that would surely come, if he simply arranged an execution. But there was also the possibility that, in his cleverness, Galerius had defeated his own purpose. Only a few days' journey to the northeast lay the province of Armenia and the kingdom of Tiridates, who was not only one of the most powerful independent monarchs in the Empire but also Constantine's close friend. And he was certain that, if he called upon Tiridates for help in escaping from the living burial of Callinicum, even Galerius could hardly refuse the request of so important a monarch that a new commander be assigned to his troops.

"Do you share the centurion's feeling about Callinicum, Tribune?" The odd note in Licinius' voice warned Constantine that he was expected to object, possibly opening the way for an even worse assignment.

"I am a soldier of the Empire, General Licinius. I will serve wherever I am ordered."

"And I likewise," Dacius added.

"When do we proceed to our new post?" Constantine asked.

"You may have a few days' leave if you wish," Licinius said. "I believe your mother's family lives in this region."

"At Drepanum," Constantine confirmed. "With your permission I shall ride there tonight."

II

Depressed though he was by the assignment that would put half the Roman world between him and Fausta, Constantine's spirits were buoyed up by the delight of his mother and Crispus at seeing him again. The boy was almost ten, a sturdy lad who could already hurl a light spear and handle smaller versions of the weighted darts called *plumbatae* that were favorite weapons with the Illyrian soldiers. He had taken to horsemanship as naturally as he had to walking, when Marios had provided him with a pony. Together father and son spent the mornings galloping over the rolling hills beside the gulf and, for a while, Constantine was able to forget the bleak future ahead of him. But when they came back to the house at Drepanum from one of their rides, he found Marios there and sensed from his uncle's grave expression that more trouble must be brewing.

"I was going to visit you tomorrow, before Dacius and I leave for the Euphrates," Constantine said. "Is anything wrong?"

"Wrong enough that it seemed better to tell you of it here instead of in Nicomedia, where Galerius' spies might overhear. A man cannot even trust his servants any more when they can be sure of a reward by denouncing their owner."

"Not as a Christian. You were never that."

"No. For a while people were denouncing each other for selling under the table, but Galerius had the good sense—I'll give him that much—to let the wage and price laws of Diocletian die unsung. It was a disastrous experiment that did nothing but create an army of thieves and spies."

"What about the coinage?"

"Rumors say he is adding base metal again, but so far he is moving slowly and the people still have confidence in the value of Roman money."

"Then the experiment, as you call it, was not a total loss?"

"In that way, perhaps not," Marios admitted. "But when half the people are encouraged to spy on the rest, instead of working, new crimes have to be invented to keep them busy. Galerius created a number of them with vague edicts covering what he calls 'offenses against the state,' allowing him to imprison those lucky enough to have any possessions left. But enough of that," he added briskly. "Fortunately none of your mother's family is likely to suffer at his hands as long as your father has the finest army in the Empire ready beyond the Alps. Actually, it's you I'm concerned about."

"What could possibly happen to me in the East? The Persians have been at peace now for several years."

"You aren't going there."

"How do you know that?"

"Galerius is not the only one with spies, though he would have my head if he could prove it. When you went to Salonae with Diocletian, I wrote to Constantius and suggested that he ask for you to be sent to Gaul. A letter came about a month ago with the request! That's why Galerius sent for you so hurriedly and planned to bury you on the Euphrates."

"You mean he dared to ignore Father's letter?"

"Most likely he was going to pretend that it was not received before you were safely dispatched to the East. And he might have gotten away with it, if a second letter from Constantius hadn't arrived last night demanding in words that even Galerius can't wriggle out of that you be sent to Gaul at once."

"How did you learn so soon—about the second letter, I mean?" Constantine felt a surge of excitement rising within him at the thought that at long last he might be joining his father.

"You can thank Dacius for that; the noncommissioned officers of the Roman army have a spy system of their own. Most of them worship your father and dislike Galerius and Daia intensely, so almost before Galerius finished reading the letter, Dacius knew about it. When you get back to Nicomedia tomorrow, you will be greeted with news that you are going to Gaul carrying dispatches for Constantius."

"But that is exactly what I want!" Constantine cried. Then a thought struck him. "Why did father write a second time so soon after his first letter?"

"According to Dacius' information, he pleaded illness."

"Of what nature?" Constantine asked quickly.

"Constantius gave no details, but I hope for a letter in a few days with more information."

"Could it be a device to get Emperor Galerius to release me?"

"I doubt it. Your father is so honest that he rarely dissembles, even in a matter as important as this. My guess is that he really is ill and wants you with him on the expedition to Britain."

"I didn't know of any such campaign," Constantine admitted.

"Your father mentioned another campaign in his last letter," Helena said from the doorway where she stood with Crispus, looking like a small blond bear in a nubby towel draped about him like a toga, the ceremonial garment that was rarely seen in the East and was worn in Rome now only upon state occasions. "He doesn't trust Maximian and Maxentius, so he has concluded treaties of peace with two Germanic kings—I think their names are Ascaricus and Regaisus. As soon as he can put down a minor uprising of the Picts in Britain, he hopes to move his capital to Milan." She turned to Marios. "Did I hear you say that Constantius is ill?"

"So he said in a letter Galerius received last night. He wants Constantine to join him."

"He wouldn't say it unless he were." Helena turned quickly to her son. "He needs you, Constantine. You must go to him at once —tonight."

"If I leave without a military order, Galerius could have me killed on sight," Constantine reminded her.

"But he will never let you go to Gaul. Not with your father ill."

"My information is that Galerius intends to let Constantine go," Marios interposed. "Or at least start."

All of them understood the significance of Marios' words, so there was no need for explanation. It was a long ride to Gaul and almost anywhere along the route an assassin could be waiting.

III

Constantine barely had time to dismount in the military compound behind the palace at Nicomedia the next afternoon when an aide of Emperor Galerius appeared. "Tribune Constantinus is ordered to report at once to Augustus Galerius," he said.

When Constantine had left Nicomedia for Salonae a few months before, Galerius had been a hard-muscled, obviously fit fighting man. But already—he saw, when he saluted the Augustus of the East in the same audience chamber where he had so often stood beside Diocletian—the role of Emperor had put its mark upon the latest wearer of the purple robe and pearl circlet. Galerius had thickened noticeably about the middle, and the cold eyes that had always had something of the hooded look of an eagle or a falcon about them were pouched now and dull.

"Your promptness in obeying orders does you credit, Tribune Constantinus," the Emperor said with the nearest to warmth—even if feigned—Constantine had ever heard in his grating voice. "How did you leave my father-in-law in Salonae?"

"His health improves each day, Augustus—perhaps because he is happy."

"He and his precious cabbages." Galerius appeared not to notice that Constantine had addressed him only as Augustus, not with the title of Dominus—Lord—he had always given to Diocletian. "How is your mother?"

"Very well."

"And your son?"

"Looking ahead to his seventeenth birthday, Augustus—and the beginning of his military training."

Galerius looked surprised. "How old is he now?"

"Nearly eleven, and well developed for his age."

The old hooded look came and went for a moment and Constantine was sure he could read the thought behind it. With both Constantius and himself as thorns in Galerius' side, the Senior Emperor could take little pleasure in the knowledge that still another of that family was reaching toward manhood.

"I believe General Licinius gave you new orders day before yesterday."

"Yes, Augustus."

"We badly need men in the East who know that country and, since you once traveled from Alexandria to the Euphrates, few should know it better than you." The memory of the circumstances attending that ride seemed unpleasant to the speaker, for his jaw tightened briefly. "I am sorry we will not have the benefit of your experience."

"Are my orders being changed, Augustus?" Constantine hoped the note of surprise he feigned seemed genuine enough to convince Galerius that he had not heard of it before.

"You are to join your father in Gaul. I'm sure the news will please you."

"I've not seen him for a long time—during which he has married again and fathered three sons and some daughters."

"Then you will no doubt want to make sure of your own standing with him. Did you know he was ill?"

The question had been designed to catch him off guard, Constantine was sure. But knowing Galerius, he had been expecting some sudden thrust in this verbal fencing match and was ready to parry it.

"I have had no letter from my father in many months." He was telling the strict truth, but nothing more. "I hope his illness is not severe."

"It's probably only a recurrent fever; all of us who have fought in other parts of the world get them occasionally. Your father is preparing to cross the *Fretum Gallicum* again and punish some rebels among the Picts, a stiff-minded people with hiding places among the hills and chasms of northern Britain. Constantius probably feels that younger legs can chase them better."

Galerius reached for a scroll lying on a small table beside him and handed it to Constantine. "Here are your orders. They authorize you and Centurion Dacius to obtain horses at the stations of the Imperial Post and draw rations and lodging at the *mutationes* along the way." His voice became studiedly casual. "How soon would you like to leave?"

"At once, Augustus. Dacius and I have hardly unpacked since we came from Salonae."

"Tomorrow will be soon enough," Galerius assured him. "My scribes are busy preparing some letters for you to take to Constantius. They will be delivered to you as soon as they are ready. By the way," he added, "Emperor Maximian didn't clear the Alpine passes of brigands too well, when he ruled from Milan, and Caesar Severus has not yet had time to finish the job. Be careful in that area."

"Dacius and I will be on our guard all the way," Constantine promised.

In their quarters, Constantine seized Dacius by the shoulders and danced him around. "I have orders for both of us!" he cried. "We're going to join Father in Gaul and accompany him on an expedition to Britain to put down an uprising among the Picts."

"You'll not be quite so happy after a month or two in that climate with winter coming on," Dacius warned. "In the morning the fog is so thick you have to feel your way through it. And your clothes rarely get a chance to dry, except when they freeze."

"I don't mind, just so I can be with my father and have a chance to do something besides act as a nursemaid."

"You'll see enough fighting to please you," Dacius promised. "When Constantius discovers how able you are, he's sure to make you a general and then your future in the West will be assured."

"We're not there yet." Constantine forced himself to be calm. "Uncle Marios thinks an attempt will be made to kill us on the way

and Galerius himself just warned me against the danger of brigands in the Alpine passes."

Dacius had been reaching for a flagon of wine to pour a cup
for himself. He halted now with his hand still short of its mark.
"Was anyone else there?"

"An aide and two scribes. Why?"

"Just enough witnesses to absolve Galerius of any accusations,
when we are set upon and killed," Dacius said crisply. "Let me see
the orders."

He read carefully the scroll Constantine handed him, then rolled
it up and tied it with the purple ribbon identifying it as an imperial order. "Just as I thought, they specify no route. How soon
do we leave?"

"Tomorrow, as soon as the clerks finish some letters I'm to carry
to father. Why?"

"Unless I miss my guess those letters will express Galerius' concern for your safe arrival in Gaul and mention his warning about
the Alpine passes to your father. And you can wager that, after
we are set upon and killed by what look like brigands, the letters
will somehow find their way to Constantius, absolving Galerius of
any blame in our deaths."

"The whole thing does fit into a pattern," Constantine admitted.

"Fortunately we've been warned, so we have a chance to escape
the trap." Dacius rubbed the gray stubble on his chin thoughtfully.
"The Alpine passes are bad on horses, so we can only be sure of
remounts by staying on the roads of the Imperial Post, where the
ambush is sure to occur. Galerius is no doubt counting on just that;
the question now is how to outwit him?"

"At the Euphrates with King Tiridates and his band, our situation
appeared hopeless when we were behind advance parties of the
Persian cavalry," Constantine reminded him. "So we decided to attack."

"*You* decided to attack. The rest of us only agreed."

"The point is that we did what the enemy didn't expect us to
do."

Dacius' grim face began to lighten. "So we follow a route the
enemy—in this case Galerius and his assassins—don't expect. But
which way is that?"

"You're the one who's supposed to know the country," Constantine said. "I'm counting on you to tell me."

"Then we'd better start with the maps." Dacius went to the corner where the cylindrical container in which he always carried his maps was standing. An hour later the two of them looked up from the map they had spread on the floor, the same look of satisfaction and excitement in their eyes.

"Then it's settled?" Dacius asked.

Constantine nodded. "Galerius expects us to take the route northeast to his old capital of Sirmium on the river Save, near where it joins the Danube, and thence almost directly westward through the Alpine passes into Gaul and on to Treves. Right now he's probably sending word to his henchmen in Sirmium to arrange our assassination somewhere west of that city."

"It will be well planned, you can wager on that," Dacius agreed. "But that's a game two can play. Now we'd better get a good night's sleep; we'll have a long ride tomorrow."

Constantine had no idea what time it was when he was awakened by the touch of a hand upon his shoulder. He turned over quickly, instinctively reaching for the wall peg upon which he had hung his sword before retiring, but he let his hand fall when he recognized the face of General Licinius, revealed by a shaft of moonlight pouring through the single window of the *cubicula*. Licinius was unarmed, he saw, and, realizing that whatever the reason for the nocturnal visit it was not an attack, he sat up on the sleeping pallet.

"Speak only in a whisper," Licinius warned. "I have the letters you are to take to your father. Augustus Galerius drank a great deal of wine before he retired tonight and will be sure to sleep late tomorrow. I thought you ought to get an early start."

"How early?" Constantine had not missed the emphasis on the word "ought."

"Now, if I were you. Centurion Longinus is saddling two horses; they will be ready as soon as you are. May Jupiter and Mithras guard you."

The visitor's hand was on the door when Constantine asked, "Why are you doing this for me, sir?"

"Your father and I have been friends for a long time." He was

gone and Constantine wasted no time in waking Dacius and telling him of the visit.

"Licinius is an honorable man," the centurion said, as he dressed
hurriedly. "Galerius no doubt intended to hold you here another
day with the pretext of the letters, so the messengers he sent ahead
to arrange our deaths would be sure of reaching Sirmium in time."

"I would like to see his face when he learns the route we have
chosen," Constantine said, as he buckled on his sword and took
his cloak from a peg. "But by that time we should be safe at
Treves."

IV

Only a little over two weeks later Constantine stood in an upper
room of an inn on the outskirts of the Italian city of Neapolis,*
waiting impatiently for Dacius to return from the errand he had
sent him on—that of discovering whether the Lady Fausta was in
residence at her father's country home in the lovely Campana district nearby. As he had expected, Dacius had exploded into anger
when he revealed his real reason for including Neapolis in their
route to Gaul, arguing—with considerable reason—that it would be
nothing short of foolish for him to try to see Fausta after Maximian
had expressly forbidden it.

In the end Constantine had been left no choice except to order
Dacius to find Fausta, or at least try to learn where she was, and
the grizzled centurion had departed with his back as rigid as the
shaft of a *pilum*. To make matters worse, Constantine knew in his
heart that Dacius was right, yet he could no more have been this
near Fausta without trying to see her than he could have taken
wings and flown northward over the Alps.

To take his mind off the question of Fausta, Constantine re-
viewed the events of the past few weeks, since he and Dacius
had departed so precipitately from Nicomedia in the middle of
the night after the visit of General Licinius. By keeping to back
roads and largely unpaved streets while leaving the capital, lest

* Naples

the sound of hooves on the cobblestones bring out the guard, they
had managed to leave undetected.

In the first part of the journey, they had followed the route of
the Imperial Post by which mail and official documents were trans-
ported rapidly between Nicomedia and Sirmium. Known as the
Cursus Publicus, the official network of roads was studded about
every twelve Roman miles by *mutationes,* where horses could be
exchanged and food obtained. In general, two *mutationes* were located between each two *mansiones,* or inns, where travelers could
spend the night. But since wagons bearing beds for sleeping and
coaches with cushions upon which the occupants could rest were
freely available, many people traveled both night and day when
on urgent business.

The roads were carefully marked with the standard milestones,
cylindrical in form and set into square bases. They were policed
by senior noncommissioned officers, known as *beneficiarii,* so that
in general travelers were safe in moving along them except in areas
like the Alps. Each milestone bore the name, title and year of the
emperor in whose reign it was put up, along with a figure indicating
the distance from the nearest town, so it was quite difficult for
travelers to become lost upon these highways.

Having changed horses several times at posthouses along the
way, they had been ferried over the narrow neck of water called
the Bosporus—or Ox-Ford—after the Greek legend of Io, who
was supposed to have crossed there in the form of a heifer. Taking
fresh horses at one of the *mansiones* on the northern shore, they
had ridden on toward Hadrianopolis that night and slept for a
while toward morning, wrapped in their cloaks beside a spring
that furnished both water and lush grass for the horses.

By dawn they were off again and on the evening of the fourth
day applied for a room at a *mansion* in Hadrianopolis. There they
ate hugely, making up for the rather sparse rations they had consumed on the way. After announcing to the crowd filling the *mansion* that they would travel on northwestward toward Sirmium the
next day, they had retired to their pallets, leaving orders to be
awakened an hour before dawn.

The mists of the night had still not lifted from the countryside
when they had taken to the fields in a southward direction out-

side Hadrianopolis and shortly found themselves on the Via Egnatia, one of the Empire's main thoroughfares leading westward toward Rome. The passage of the two travelers across the mouth of the Mare Adriaticum, just north of the straits of Otranto that formed its mouth, had been easy for the winds had been fair—an omen, Constantine hoped, for the success of the remainder of the trip. The fishing boat they hired had made it in little more than a day and night of sailing, with Dacius seasick much of the time. When they had shown their orders at the port of Brundisium* they had been furnished horses for the ride across the lower part of the boot-shaped peninsula to Neapolis.

Impatient at Dacius' delay in returning, although he had been gone little more than an hour, Constantine stepped out upon the balcony outside his window and breathed deeply of the salt-tinged air that came from the harbor with the freshening evening breeze. It was his first visit to the thriving new center called Neapolis, and his first glimpse of the area—as they had ridden into the city from the east—had impressed him greatly.

The fertility of the land around it was attested by rich groves of olives and grape arbors lush with heavy fruit, furnishing, Dacius said, some of the finest wine in the Empire. Villas, often almost hidden by the trees, studded the hills and dotted the seashore. And not far from the city itself was the thriving Roman port of Puteoli, where Constantine and Dacius hoped to find a galley bound for the mouth of the river Rhodanus—or Rhône, as it was more often called—near the city of Massilia,† from whence they could follow that broad water highway into the very heart of Gaul.

The sound of footsteps in the hall outside brought Constantine from the balcony into the room. When they stopped before the door, he rushed to open it before Dacius could knock with the agreed-upon signal. Dacius' frown told him the centurion did not approve of his impetuousness, but whatever guilt he felt was dissipated when Fausta hurled herself into his arms.

"You have an hour, and this time leave the door locked until I give you the signal." Dacius closed it, leaving the two lovers to-

* Brindisi
† Marseille

gether, and for a long, precious moment, while they kissed passionately and clung to each other, there was no need for words. Then Fausta pushed herself away until she could look into his eyes.

"Why are you hiding like a criminal, Constantine?" she demanded.

"Didn't Dacius tell you?"

She wrinkled her nose in a wry expression. "Dacius doesn't approve of me. He would tell me nothing, except that he was bringing me to you."

Constantine gave her a quick summary of his difficulties with Galerius and his escape from Nicomedia.

"Maxentius was furious when he wasn't named Caesar and that stupid Maximin Daia was," she said.

"I was passed over too. Don't forget that."

"We all knew you wouldn't be named Caesar," she assured him. "After all, Galerius can't afford to have your family and ours any more closely connected than we already are."

"Where is Maxentius now?"

"In Rome, busy plotting against Severus."

"If I ask your father for you, is there any chance that he will agree?"

"Not now, darling, I'm too valuable for him to let me go so cheaply. Father has sworn to rule again, when Galerius and Maximin Daia make a mess of things in the East. And there's no better way to gain the support of important men than to use the lure of a beautiful daughter."

Looking at her now as she sat beside him on one of the couches in the room, he was sure she was right. For she *was* beautiful, even more beautiful than when he'd last seen her. But the thought brought him no satisfaction, for it seemed that she was still as far away from becoming his now as she had ever been.

"If you really loved me, you would go to Gaul with me," he said.

"But darling!" she cried. "Love has little to do with royal marriages. I told you that in Rome."

"You also said you made up your mind to marry me, when you first saw me fighting Crocus in Nicomedia."

"I did. But I also made up my mind to be an Augusta some day. Make me one and I'll be yours tomorrow."

"Why do you have to torment me?" he demanded angrily. "You know perfectly well I'm further from the throne now than I ever was."

"Ever since you saved so many men in the retreat from Persia, the legions have worshiped you," she said. "You could have made yourself Augustus of the East by appealing to them in the name of your father when Diocletian abdicated."

"How could I have destroyed Galerius?"

"The same way emperors have been destroyed before, by death," she said calmly. "After all, the people called for you at Diocletian's abdication. They would have supported you if you'd gotten rid of Galerius and named yourself in his place."

"What about Diocletian's plan to keep the Empire stable?"

"The forces that will tear it apart are already building up," Fausta said with a shrug. "Maxentius plots against Severus while my father plots against Galerius and Maximin Daia. If he thinks the East is in danger of being lost, Diocletian might come back to the throne; then Father could proclaim himself Emperor of the West again."

"You forget that my father is Augustus now."

"There's room for three: your father in Gaul, Britain and Spain, with you as Caesar; my father in Italy, Africa and Pannonia; and Maxentius in Egypt and Syria. It's a much more sensible division than the one we had under Diocletian. Surely you can see that."

She came into his arms again with the words and he was so excited to discover that she had become considerably more womanly than when they'd said goodbye that day in his quarters at Rome, he quite forgot everything else. When she kissed him, the softness of her mouth against his set up a flame of desire that threatened to overcome him. But even as she nestled against him—fully conscious, he suspected, of the effect she was having upon him—he could not help wondering how much of her partial yielding was based on real emotion and how much on furthering her own schemes.

"Now that you have left Nicomedia, your only course is to make such a name for yourself in Gaul and Britain that the legions will follow you anywhere." She pushed him away just when he was becoming really ardent. "After all, Carausius once made himself Augustus of Britain."

"He was a rebel!"

"Before he was a rebel he was a hero—when he cleared the pirates from the channel. My father and Diocletian even acknowledged him as Augustus of Britain."

"Only because Gaul was in a ferment from the revolt of the *bagaudae* and the Germans were threatening from the north."

"Gaul is always in a ferment," she said airily. "And the Germans are only waiting for another chance to cross the Rhine. The Picts are in revolt again in Britain and I heard Father say only yesterday that Constantius is going to have to cross the Fretum Gallicum again to put them down."

"He did it before," Constantine reminded her, with some pride.

"But only because *my* father moved from Milan into Gaul, when yours took his army to Britain, and secured the Rhine crossing at Colonia Agrippina and Mogontiacum."*

"That is true," Constantine admitted. "I suppose he would like to do it again."

"He might, if Severus doesn't support your father. Now that Constantius is married to Theodora, all of us in the family must help each other." She gave him a quick, teasing kiss. "So you see you have every reason to make a name for yourself in Britain. Conquer the Picts and push on north to the Antonine Wall; then cross over to seize Hibernia—and you will rule an area worthy to name its own Augustus."

"How do you know these things?" he demanded, fascinated by her familiarity with cities of which he had hardly even heard.

"By learning them, of course. As soon as I decided to become Augusta of Britain a few months ago—"

"A few months ago!"

"Mother had a letter from Theodora saying your father had demanded that Galerius send you to Gaul to help him put down the Picts," she explained patiently. "I remembered then that Carausius had once been Augustus of Britain, so I started reading about it."

* Cologne and Mainz

"You've forgotten that Carausius was only allowed to rule because your father and mine were busy making Gaul safe for Rome. When that task was finished, he was destroyed."

"Only because Carausius sought to extend his rule to Gaul," she corrected him. "Surely you knew that."

Constantine was not too clear, history never having been his strongest point, but had no intention of letting her know it. "You see what happens to people who become too ambitious?" he said triumphantly.

"We're not going to take Gaul!" Fausta's voice was a little sharp; the teacher was obviously beginning to lose patience with her pupil. "You're already a hero from the Persian campaign and Theodora's sons are much too young to rule. For the time being, you can become Caesar of Britain and later Augustus. Then, when your father abdicates at the end of twenty years, you will rule Gaul, too. And, with the two greatest armies in the Empire at your back, you can march across the Alps and make yourself ruler of Italy, and Europe in a few months—to say nothing of the rest of the Empire."

Constantine felt somewhat the same sensation he remembered experiencing once, when he had watched a swaying serpent in the process of being charmed out of its basket by the wailing notes of a flute in the hands of an old magician in the East. Then an alien sound intruded into his consciousness—two quick raps on the door, followed by a brief pause and a third. It was the signal from Dacius that Fausta should go.

"Be as daring in Britain as you were against the Persians, dearest," she said, standing on tiptoe to kiss him goodbye. "Before you know it, you will be proclaimed Augustus there and I will hasten to your side."

"What if your father still refuses?"

"Don't worry; I can always get around him. If I have to, I'll even run away."

"Then why not go with me now?"

"But darling!" Her eyes opened wide. "Who would trouble to run a race, if the prize were his before he started?"

15

T HE BITE OF WINTER was already in the salt air when Constantine and Dacius topped a rise one afternoon and looked down upon the bustling port city of Gesoriacum. A swift military galley had brought them from Neapolis to the mouth of the river Rhône, where they had transferred to an almost equally swift vessel for the upstream trip to Lugdunum,* military headquarters of central Gaul and a major city in its own right.

Had he not known his father's capabilities as a ruler, Constantine might have been amazed at the evidence of prosperity and peace everywhere. Growing towns lined the river, with fertile farms and groves between, and a fine network of Roman roads connected those centers not joined by the water artery and its tributaries. These latter, he was told by the galley's captain, were so extensive that goods and passengers could be carried upon them to within thirty miles of a tributary of the other great river in the north, the Rhenus, or Rhine, there to be transshipped for further passage by water. At least half the traffic on the river was military and at the cities along its banks where they stopped, they learned that more men and goods were moving across country by land, all directed toward the coast, where Constantius was building up an army for the campaign in Britain.

The city of Gesoriacum was the most important port on the channel called the Fretum Gallicum, because of its location near the narrowest part of that vital water barrier. It ranged along some hills beside a river mouth, but the water of the harbor could barely be seen for the large number of galleys and merchantmen anchored there. A passing soldier directed them to Roman headquarters in a

* Lyon

building overlooking the port, and the purple ribbons with which Constantine's orders were tied opened every door, so he and his father were soon embracing each other in greeting.

"Marios and Helena spoke truly in their letters." Constantius held his tall son away from him, examining him with eyes that were, like Constantine's own, a little misted over. "You have grown into a man."

"I'm nearly thirty, Father. My growing was finished long ago."

"I'm not talking of stature but of mind. Marios says your wisdom equals your skill as a soldier."

"I hope it excels, Father."

"You're right, of course. Anyone strong and agile can learn to fight well, but a special wisdom is required of those who would rule."

"We saw much evidence in Gaul that you possess such wisdom," Dacius said. "Many changes have been made since I was here last, all for the better."

"Tell me about your journey," Constantius urged them. "I see that Galerius lost no time in granting my request."

Constantine began the account with the receipt of the orders at Salonae, relieving him from his assignment as commander of Diocletian's guard. When he came to where Dacius had foretold that the letters from Galerius would contain a warning about the dangers of the Alpine passes, Constantius stopped him and broke the seal upon one of them. While he read, Constantine studied him more closely than he had been able to do in the first excitement of their greeting each other, but what he saw gave him no pleasure.

The strong ruddy man who had ridden away from Naissus that day—leaving an angry and tearful boy behind—had aged much in slightly more than a decade. His color was less healthy, Constantine saw, and the broad shoulders drooped a little. His face, too, was beginning to show gaunt lines and the looseness with which the uniform tunic hung upon his body made Constantine suspect that the illness mentioned in the letter to Galerius was much more severe than any of them had thought.

"Ha!" Constantius held up the scroll, marking with his thumb a spot he wanted them to read.

Dacius had prophesied truly when he had warned against taking the northern route directly to Treves, Constantine saw. The warning against the Alpine passes was in the letter, confirming that a trap had been planned for that area and that, after the two of them were killed, the letters would somehow have found their way to Constantius, seemingly absolving the writer of any blame.

"Galerius shall pay for this!" Constantius said grimly. "I let him name Severus Caesar in Italy to avoid any controversy with Maxentius, while I was busy putting down the Pict rebellion. But as soon as the campaign in Britain is over, I shall move my capital to Milan and send Severus to Gaul. Go on with your story, Constantine."

"There's not much more to be told, sir. We rode out of Hadrianopolis as if we were going by the northern route but cut across the fields to the Via Egnatia. In Italy we went to Neapolis and were lucky to find a military galley ready to leave for Lugdunum."

"You were wise in not going to Rome," Constantius agreed. "Severus reports to Galerius before he does to me and Maxentius has no love for you."

"I had another reason for going to Neapolis," Constantine confessed. "It was the hope of seeing Fausta."

"Fausta?" Constantine frowned. "Maximian's youngest daughter, isn't she? I didn't know you even knew her."

"We met in Rome at the Vicennalia, and fell in love."

"Isn't she rather young?"

"But very mature for her age."

"I remember her now. She was at Treves for a visit last year —you know, of course, that my wife, Theodora, is her stepsister? A pretty little thing, isn't she?"

"And very determined. She told me a number of things that might interest you."

"Oh?"

Constantine gave a brief resume of his conversation with Fausta, omitting the part where he was to be appointed Caesar of Britain and make himself Augustus.

"Most of this isn't exactly news to me," Constantius said when he finished. "Theodora isn't fond of her stepfather and word comes to her frequently of what goes on in his household. I know Maximian hopes to assume the purple once more and that Maxentius is equally ambitious. But I will give you an important lesson— No, I will let Dacius do it. After all, he has been your tutor since I left the East."

"Whoever controls the army rules the country," Dacius said promptly. "And the army of Gaul is worth any two in the rest of the Empire."

"Exactly as I would have put it, old comrade," Constantius said warmly. "You have been a good teacher."

"With an apt pupil."

"I can see that. What would you like to do here, Son?"

"Cross over to Britain with you and help subdue the Picts."

"As my second-in-command? You've been kept from your just dues long enough."

Constantine knew his father well enough to be sure the offer was tendered sincerely. Nevertheless, he did not consider yielding to the temptation to accept.

"If I am advanced over the heads of your regular commanders, it will only breed discord," he pointed out. "As a tribune, I am entitled to command a legion. Give me one and let me see if I can prove myself."

The light of approval in both his father's and Dacius' eyes told him he had made a wise choice. Constantius struck a small bell on the table beside him and the door opened almost immediately to admit a plump man of middle age, wearing the robe of a scholar.

"This is Eumenius, my *magister memoriae*," Constantius said. "My son, Tribune Constantinus and Centurion Dacius."

"I shall order a sacrifice of thanks to Jupiter for your safe arrival, Tribune," Eumenius said warmly. "And for yours, Centurion. We have been awaiting your coming with some anxiety."

"Have an order issued today assigning my son to command the Twenty-second Legion, Eumenius," Constantius directed the secretary and turned back to his son. "You will like this command. The best of the Gallic horse among the auxiliaries belong to it. I remember that you did well with such troops in Augusta Euphratensia. Dacius will be your aide, of course."

"It's time for you to rest, Augustus," Eumenius said firmly. "I will find quarters for the new commander of the Twenty-second Legion and his aide and return to give you your medicine."

"It's a good thing you're here to protect me from this tyrant,

Flavius," Constantius said, but from his tone the younger man realized that his father was genuinely fond of the plump secretary. "We will have the evening meal here later and talk about the campaign against the Picts."

"Just how ill is my father?" Constantine asked the secretary when they were outside the room.

Eumenius gave him a quick, appraising glance. "He had a serious attack two months ago, but is much better now. That's why the expedition to Britain comes so late in the year."

"But he will recover completely?"

"Your father is fifty-five years old and the years since he came to Gaul have been a strain, even for a strong man. I cannot say what caused the attack he suffered a few months ago. It may have been a recurrence of an old fever, or an ailment of the liver, which could be more serious. Just now he is improving, but you could see that he has lost a good deal of weight."

"His color is not as good as I remember it either," Constantine said.

"The burdens of maintaining the peace are always heavy," Eumenius told him. "I am pleased that strong shoulders are here to share them."

They had hardly left the building and started up the street, when Constantine heard his name shouted and turned to be engulfed in the embrace of Crocus, his old companion from the training days at Nicomedia. The Gallic prince had reverted to the customs of his people. His rich blond hair was combed back and hung almost to his shoulders, being held there by a narrow band about his head. A tremendous moustache curled at both ends of his upper lip. His tunic was dyed a half dozen colors and the breeches beneath, ending in leather boots, were embroidered with flowers that were quite as colorful as the tunic. A cloak hung from his shoulders by a golden chain, golden bracelets were on his wrists, and golden earrings in his ears.

"Your Majesty." Eumenius' words brought Constantine up short and for the first time he noticed that the silver band on Crocus' head was actually a narrow jeweled coronet, while the cloak that hung from his shoulders was dyed purple.

"You're a king!" he cried.

"It's only a small kingdom, left me by my father at his death," his friend assured him. "Augustus Constantius confirmed me as its ruler, but my real work is with the army and the Gallic horse."

"Then my letter—"

"Opened every door for me after Galerius—may his name be forever a curse—sent me home in disgrace. When your father discovered that I had some small knowledge of horses and horsemanship—"

"And was the best cavalryman in the Empire—"

"Oh no, my friend! That honor is yours," Crocus corrected him. "It was won on the field at Nicomedia and confirmed—from what I hear—on the banks of the Euphrates."

"Your Majesty," Eumenius' voice interrupted firmly. "It is time for the Emperor's medicine; I was taking the tribune and the centurion to find quarters."

"They will live with me," Crocus said at once. "I would not hear of it being otherwise."

"Perhaps that is just as well," Eumenius agreed. "Tribune Constantine will be commanding the Twenty-second Legion."

"My best horse are with the Twenty-second," Crocus exclaimed. "You are very lucky, my friend." Then his face sobered. "But such a command is not worthy of the son of an Augustus, who saved an entire army in the Persian revolt. I'm surprised that your father didn't make you his deputy."

"He offered to, but I asked for a legion," Constantine admitted. "After all, my last command was less than fifty men. I shall have to prove myself, as you did."

"One battle will do it," Crocus assured him. "We'll have plenty of fighting when we go against the Picts. Come along and I'll find quarters for you."

Constantine and Dacius were soon comfortably ensconced in a house at the edge of the town that had been taken over by Crocus. It overlooked a field where horses were tethered by the hundreds, awaiting transfer across the channel, and bands of mounted men were in training. A servant brought meat, bread and wine—the Gauls, Constantine remembered, were always mighty trenchermen.

While they ate, he sounded out Crocus concerning affairs in Gaul and particularly about his father's health.

"Augustus Constantius was very ill earlier this year," Crocus told him. "Some of us felt then that you should be sent for, but he feared that Galerius would hear of his condition and refuse to let you come, lest you seize the reins of power if—if anything happened."

"I almost didn't come this time," Constantine admitted. "Orders had already been issued sending me to the Euphrates. Galerius only released me because he planned to have us killed by assassins in the Alpine passes."

Crocus swore a colorful oath. "Then you only got out of the East in time. How that beast Daia would have loved having you under his command. But you will enjoy fighting the Picts," he continued. "They are great rough fellows wielding huge broadswords and speaking a tongue that sounds like a saw biting into an oaken log. A giant named Bonar leads them into battle shouting a cry calculated to paralyze all but trained troops with fear. It's truly a pity their chiefs don't have the good sense to sign a treaty of peace and become Roman citizens, as did the rest of Britain."

"Then you think it may be possible to pacify all of the island?"

"Why not, if Bonar can be brought to terms? After all, Carausius ruled for a while there. If he hadn't wanted Gaul too, and seized Gesoriacum, he might still be Augustus of Britain."

Crocus' words were a striking confirmation of what Fausta had said. And having studied the map of Britain from Dacius' precious roll during the voyage from Neapolis to Gaul, Constantine was inclined to agree. If he distinguished himself during the coming campaign, Constantius would be quite ready to appoint his eldest son as Caesar of this area and send Severus packing, when the move from Treves to Milan was consummated. And then only a few years might be needed for the whole plan—which had seemed so fantastic when Fausta outlined it—to come true.

"What about the Germanic tribes north of the Rhine?" he asked Crocus.

"Your father secured that frontier first through treaties with Ascaricus and Regaisus, the two most important and Germanic kings. I suppose you know why this campaign against the Picts is being carried out just now, even though your father's illness forced us to postpone it until the best season for crossing the channel to Britain is almost gone."

"I can guess," Constantine said. "If Galerius should try to put Italy under his own rule, our rear and flanks will already have been secured so we can move eastward in force."

"You've come a long way from the boy who came to Nicomedia for training some ten years ago," his friend said admiringly.

"And so have you."

"No," Crocus demurred. "I was a king's son already, so Galerius could hardly do much to me for fear of stirring up an uprising in Gaul. But even while you were a hostage in Nicomedia for your father's good behavior here in the West, you managed to become a hero of the legions and take a long stride toward earning the purple cloak of a Caesar for yourself."

"Now who's dreaming?" Constantine scoffed.

"I'd wager my kingdom on it." Crocus was all seriousness now. "And on your becoming Augustus of the West one day."

"You're a little late on two counts, Your Majesty," Dacius said dryly. "The day he came to Nicomedia he'd already decided to rule the Empire—alone."

Crocus gave Constantine a startled look. "Is that true?"

"I was a boy—groping for the moon."

"How is it then that you have already chosen your Empress?" Dacius retorted. "Or should I say she's chosen you?"

II

The evening meal, which Constantine had been invited to share with his father, turned out to be a staff conference of the leading commanders in the coming expedition against Britain. Crocus was there, as staff commander of all mounted *alae* attached to the several legions making up the expedition. So was Eumenius, who, Constantine had realized by now, was much more than just a secretary to his father, serving actually as trusted aide and adviser in matters of government and policy. Constantine listened carefully to the plans for the campaign and studied the maps with others.

He spoke but little, however, preferring to learn as much as he could first. As the dinner was drawing to an end, Constantius turned to him.

"You've spoken but little tonight, Flavius," he said. "I don't remember that as being one of your virtues."

Constantine smiled. "Dacius taught me to keep my mouth closed, unless I had something to say, sir."

"Do you approve the plans of the campaign?"

"To a point. As I see it, your main project is to repair and rebuild the wall constructed by Emperor Hadrian across northern Britain. But why not the wall of Antoninus Pius north of it?"

"Hadrian's Wall has always been the stronger, but lately it has fallen into disrepair," Constantius explained. "We plan to repair it first and then use it as the base for a move north to the second wall."

"Do you really expect these walls to hold back the Picts, when they've never been able to do it?" Constantine asked.

"They've never been heavily garrisoned before."

"They could still be bypassed easily by a coastal fleet," Constantine pointed out. "Those who were snug and warm in the shelter of the walls wouldn't even know the enemy was at their rear, until the swords of the Picts were at their throats."

A flush of annoyance had risen in Constantius' cheeks when Constantine began to question the value of the wall. Before he could say anything, however, Eumenius spoke.

"There is a precedent for Tribune Constantine's objection to the wall, Augustus," the scholar said. "You no doubt remember how Asclepiodotus got lost in the fog and drifted into the mouth of the river Thamesis, when we first invaded Britain a few years ago. He was able to capture Londinium and outflank Allectus, who then surrendered, allowing you to come ashore at the foot of the cliffs without any opposition at all."

"This flanking maneuver seems to be a favorite of yours, Flavius." Constantius had regained his good humor. "What do you have in mind? To re-establish the Antonine Wall as our northernmost defense line?"

"Why not go beyond it?" Constantine bent over the map that occupied the top of the table. "Just north of a line drawn eastward at the northern tip of the island of Hibernia there appears to be a deep inlet in the coast of Britain. Unless the map is wrong, it narrows the country into a corridor there not much wider than the one where the Antonine Wall is located."

The others were bending over the map looking at the point he had put his finger upon, a spot where the jagged outline of the coast was cut by many deep inlets and rivers.

"Why not land there in the first place?" one of the legion commanders, a brawny soldier named Cornelius Cella, asked.

"The channel between Britain and Hibernia is often stormy," Constantius objected. "We will be lucky to get the two fair days in succession we need to ship the horses across. Besides, we can move troops easily by land, since all the major cities of Britain are connected with fine roads. We've been building them since the time of Julius Caesar."

"But not in the far north where Crocus tells me the stronghold of the Pict leader, Bonar, is located," Constantine said.

Eumenius stepped into the breach again. "You might be able to use the coastal fleet that guards Britain and the channel from pirates for some sort of waterborne invasion such as Tribune Constantine seems to have in mind. Remember the patrol galleys you ordered built, Augustus? The soldiers call them Picts because their sides are painted green like the sea and the crews wear green clothing. They are excellent for slipping along the coast undetected at night."

"By the thunderbolts of Jove!" Constantius exclaimed. "I'd forgotten about them."

"Could these boats carry troops?" Constantine asked.

"Not very many," Eumenius admitted. "But the crews are familiar with the coast, so they could guide a fleet of larger vessels in landing troops north of the Antonine Wall, near where Bonar's villa is located. We know it's the most important rallying place for the Picts in that area and, if it could be destroyed in a surprise attack, they would be dealt a body blow."

"It's a daring scheme," Constantius agreed. "And with winter coming on, we need to make the campaign as short as possible. We'll put the whole thing in your hands, Flavius."

"I'll do my best, sir."

"You'll be commanding a varied force, including a naval fleet, so it will not be enough that you are merely the commander of a legion. To demand the allegiance of all elements of the army, you need to be named my deputy."

"I, for one, am ready to acclaim him Caesar," Cornelius Cella said.

"And I," Crocus agreed.

Constantine, however, spoke before his father could answer. "I still say I must earn whatever honor shall come to me," he insisted. "Name me your deputy for now, Father; we will let the future take care of itself."

16

ONSTANTINE was far north of the Antonine Wall, at the villa of Bonar, the Pict chieftain, when an urgent message arrived from Eumenius at Eboracum, the capital of northern Britain. Constantius, the message said, was gravely ill and might not last until his arrival there. Taking horse less than an hour later, Constantine rode southward with a small bodyguard, for the Pict chieftain and his people were now at peace with Britain, a feat which many considered no less remarkable than Constantine's daring dash by water and land a few months earlier into the heart of Bonar's domain to capture the rebel leader.

The plan Constantine had outlined to his father and the assembled commanders the day of his arrival at Gesoriacum had gone off almost without a hitch. While the main body of the troops rode northward to the provincial capital at Eboracum—following the crossing of the channel and the landing in Britain itself—Constantine's picked band had angled northwestward across Britain. There they had joined a fleet of galleys dispatched on the long seaward run around the island's southwestern tip and northward along the coast facing the green island called Hibernia. Embarking far to the north and guided by the green painted boats of the coastal patrol, they had gone ashore deep in the territory of Bonar, the Pict chieftain, and, after a forced march inland, had captured both the villa and the person of the rebel leader.

The Picts, powerful warriors who often wore the skins of animals and went into battle with fierce cries, had fought well, but the element of surprise, plus their antiquated weapons, had proved their undoing. After burning the villa, Constantine had retreated southward, with Bonar in chains, to meet a force under the command of Crocus riding northward from Eboracum.

Constantius and the generals had thought only of executing Bonar, but Constantine had insisted upon carrying out the second portion of a plan by which he hoped to remove northern Britain as a trouble spot in the Empire. And, with such a spectacular victory behind him, even his father had not opposed the move.

Scrupulously treating the giant Bonar with the respect due a local king, he had taken him on a tour of the countryside, letting him see the manifold blessings Roman rule had brought to Britain: the busy mines where lead, silver and other ores were dug, the smelters where the metal was extracted, the prosperous shops of the artisans, the rich life of the lords in their great country villas, where all kinds of produce were grown for their own use, sold in the cities, or exported in the thriving trade conducted between Britain and the rest of the Empire.

In the end the intelligence of the Pict leader, which Constantine had been counting on, had seen the advantages of a treaty of peace over execution. Once the treaty was signed, Constantine himself had ridden northward with only the small bodyguard as a token of good faith to install Bonar officially as ruler under Rome of the farthest northwest corner of the Empire, just as King Tiridates ruled the farthest northeast corner.

These activities had consumed much of the winter and had been very tiresome, so Constantine had remained with Bonar for a while, enjoying the hunting and feasting and training the Pict chieftain's men in using the new weapons Rome supplied them. He had barely finished that pleasant chore when Eumenius' urgent letter had arrived.

II

When he came into the room at Eboracum where his father lay, a quick glance told Constantine that Eumenius had not been wrong in sending for him. The waxy pallor of Constantius' cheeks, the shallow hurried breathing, the grave faces of the men gathered about the couch—all testified to the fact that the Emperor of the

West was dying. Eumenius got up quickly and went to meet Constantine, who had come directly to the sick room in his muddy boots, pausing only to drop the heavy cloak from his shoulders.

"Thank Jupiter you are here," the plump secretary said in a low voice, for the sick man was sleeping. "The attack was sudden, and severe. I think there is bleeding within his body."

"Then there is no hope?"

"Only a miracle could save him. The priests have been praying for him."

For the first time Constantine noticed that one of the men standing beside the couch wore an embroidered dalmatic over his robe and a high-crowned headgear, such as he'd seen worn by Christian leaders in Antioch. Eumenius noticed the direction of his gaze and said, "This is Eborius, Bishop of Eboracum. Your father asked for him."

"A Christian!" The word was louder than Constantine had intended and he saw Eborius turn his head.

"Surely you knew your father has been sympathetic to Christians," Eumenius said.

"Of course. Have the proper sacrifices also been made to Jupiter Capitolinus?"

"Yes. And to Mithras."

"Flavius!" It was his father's voice.

"Yes, Father." Constantine moved to the couch and took the almost colorless hand lying upon the cushion.

"Thank God, you got here. I was afraid—"

"You're going to be all right, Father, Eumenius says—"

"You're both too honest to make good liars." Constantius managed to smile. "I'm dying. I knew it would come after the first attack; that's why I sent to Nicomedia for you. Is it well in the north?"

"The frontier is secure, Father. I'm sure Bonar will keep his word."

"Then I can die in peace, knowing I am passing it all to you with everything in order. One thing more—"

"Yes, Father."

"Keep a close watch on Ascaricus and Regaisus in Gaul. I don't entirely trust them."

"I will," Constantine promised. "Now you should get some rest."

"There is much to tell you, and too little time. Take care of Theodora and the children."

"I will guard them as I would Crispus."

"I wish I could have seen the lad."

"He looks like you, Father."

"Assure your mother of my devotion when you see her again. And don't trust Maximian or Maxentius; they will try to cheat you out of your birthright. Beware of Galerius too; he would rule the Empire alone. But you know that already."

"Yes, Father."

"You have wise counselors in Eumenius, Crocus and Dacius, and in my good friend Eborius here. Be kind to his people. They can be depended on and will harm no one."

Constantius' eyes closed and for a moment Constantine thought he was gone. Then he saw that the broad chest was still moving with breathing, though only faintly, and realized that his father had lapsed again into unconsciousness. When Eumenius spoke his name softly, he turned away and followed the *magister memoriae* from the room and down the corridor to Eumenius' own quarters.

"The servants will call us if he awakens again," Eumenius assured him. "You heard him say just now that you are to rule in his stead?"

"Yes, but he did not name me Caesar."

"No one can doubt that he intends for you to succeed him." At the note of intensity in Eumenius' voice Constantine looked at him sharply. "It is never good for a monarch to die without naming his successor, especially with two frontiers and rebels waiting to cause trouble. Your father was no doubt thinking of the peace in this region when he named you his deputy in Gesoriacum, so an order must be issued today insuring that a strong hand will be kept at the steering oar."

"Do you think I am qualified?" Constantine asked.

"You are qualified to rule the whole Empire, and some day you will. But only if you act forthrightly to hold everything your father is handing on to you."

"What do we do first?"

"I shall prepare the order and sign it in your father's name, designating you to succeed him. You must also be proclaimed

Caesar by the army, but we shall have no trouble there. The difficulty will come if Galerius tries to spread his own rule and include the West as well as the East."

"Whatever happens, I shall hold Britain, Gaul and Spain," Constantine said firmly. "My father made them secure and I shall not let them go to anyone else."

"Good! We can go back to your father now."

Constantius was still unconscious, however, so Constantine went in search of Dacius. He had never made a major move so far in his career without consulting the grizzled veteran and he hoped Dacius could ease his mind on one point that still troubled him.

"They tell me Constantius is dying," Dacius said, when Constantine found him. "Is it true?"

"Yes. Eumenius is sure of it."

"Did he name you Caesar?"

"Not in so many words, but he obviously expects me to succeed him here and in Gaul."

"You *must* succeed him," Dacius said firmly. "If Constantius is not able to name you his successor, then the army must do it."

"Eumenius says the same thing. But doesn't it smack of treason to make such plans while my father is still alive?"

"It is never treason to make sure a country will be governed properly. If Constantius dies without signing the order, I shall acclaim you Caesar myself. You can be sure the army will follow."

Constantius died during the night without gaining consciousness. Constantine was at his bedside and afterwards took the Bishop of Eboracum aside. "I beg you to pray to your god for my father's soul, sir," he said. "If there is any—"

"No Christian would accept pay for such a prayer. Actually, we have been praying for the Emperor ever since illness struck him." He gave Constantine a probing look. "Are you going to continue his policies, now that you are ruler here?"

"Your people need fear no harm at my hands," Constantine promised. "Was my father a Christian, sir?"

Eborius shook his head. "I was hoping he would let himself be baptized before he died, but he said he had sworn allegiance to the Empire in the name of Jupiter, so he could not renounce it and continue to rule. All Christians in Britain will be glad to learn that you are to succeed your father."

"Then you agree that I should?"

"It was his will. All of us heard it and will testify to it."

III

In final tribute to his father, Constantine himself put the torch to the dry wood of the traditional funeral pyre and stood rigidly erect until the flames began to die down.

"The troops are awaiting your orders." Dacius touched his elbow, then added, "Your duty is to the future now, not to the past."

Dacius and Eumenius had worked out very carefully the sequence of events that would take place after the funeral. Constantine now fell into step beside Dacius and marched toward the platform bearing the imperial colors which had been erected at the edge of the field, where the cremation had taken place in the sight of a large crowd of people. As he mounted the steps leading up to the platform, a hush fell over the massed ranks of the army on either side of the pyre and the sea of heads and upturned faces of the people crowding the rest of the field.

"On behalf of myself and my family, I thank you for the honor you have done my father in death," Constantine said to the crowd. "He loved this land to which his rule brought peace and security. We shall all miss him, but we know he died happy in the knowledge that the struggle in the north is over and that peace once again reigns throughout the land."

His brief speech finished—the official panegyrists had spent hours earlier delivering the customary final orations in honor of the dead—Constantine turned toward the steps. Dacius, however, was before him.

"Hail, Constantine! Caesar!" he shouted from the platform and below him the soldiers began to take up the cry. It subsided, however, when Crocus raced up the steps of the platform and, seizing Constantine's arm, held it high.

"Hail, Constantine! Imperator and Augustus!" the Gallic king shouted. Whipping off his own purple cloak, he draped it about

Constantine's shoulders and knelt to lift Constantine's hand and place it upon his forehead in the traditional gesture of fealty.

The sudden appearance of the colorful Gallic king and his dramatic gesture was the spark needed to ignite a tremendous flame of enthusiasm in the crowd.

"Hail, Constantine! Imperator and Augustus!" They seized the cry and sent it echoing back to the edge of the field again and again, until finally Constantine threw up his arms in a gesture of acknowledgment, and acceptance.

Fausta had been right, he told himself exultantly. He could be Augustus of Britain here and now, if he wished. But a larger goal was still unattained and he did not let what was happening today obscure his vision of tomorrow.

IV

The burdens of a ruler, Constantine learned in the first few hours of his reign, were many and varied. First there were the ceremonial duties, receiving and confirming in his old position the Governor General of the province of Britain, who ruled there as viceroy, and confirming the commissions of the commanders of the three military districts, whose duty it was to protect the people and put down any flare-up of rebellion. Next came the renaming —for the moment at least—of the leading judges, who would dispense the famous Roman justice in their various districts.

It was midnight before Constantine was able to step down from the throne chair of the audience chamber in his father's—now his own—palace and turn his attention to perhaps the most important of his first official duties. This was the writing of the letter that would be sent by a waiting Imperial Courier to Galerius in Nicomedia, informing the Emperor of the East of Constantius' death and the designation of Constantine himself as ruler by popular acclaim of both army and people in that area. For this task Eumenius, Dacius and Crocus gathered with him in the palace, where food and wine had been placed upon a table. But there was no time tonight for the leisurely dining and lounging upon couches that characterized Roman social life. This was a council of war, with Galerius the enemy.

"Are you going to tell Galerius of your acclamation as Augustus?" Dacius asked.

"We must decide that first," Constantine said, then added with a smile, "General Dacius."

The former centurion was too hard-bitten a soldier to break down, or even show much emotion. But Constantine did not miss the sudden warm glow of gratitude in the wise old eyes.

"You shall be my major military adviser," Constantine told him, but Dacius shook his head.

"You have a special genius for such things," he said. "I am only a soldier, not a tactician."

"We four will make the decisions together, then. What comes first?"

"After the letter is sent to Galerius, you must go to Gaul and be acclaimed there," Crocus said.

"What about Spain?"

"That can come later," Eumenius said. "The army and people of Britain and Gaul must be behind you by the time Galerius receives the letter we will send him." He glanced quickly at Constantine. "Forgive me, Augustus. Your father and I were very close and I developed a habit of speaking my thoughts without invitation."

"Nor will you need an invitation from me," Constantine assured him. "I agree completely with everything you say."

"What title will you claim?" Dacius asked.

"I named him Augustus," Crocus protested. "With the army of Gaul behind us we can easily—"

"I must accept only the lesser title, until I can prove myself as a ruler, Crocus," Constantine said firmly. "I'm sure Eumenius understands this—and Dacius."

"We know Britain is behind their new Augustus and will accept him as sole ruler," Dacius agreed. "But it will not help to precipitate a civil war with Galerius and Severus by claiming half the Empire, and then have to fight the other half for it."

"Dacius is right," Eumenius agreed. "Your father always said a man should never bite off more than he could digest, else he would find himself with a bellyache and lose what he had eaten."

"Call yourself what you will," Crocus said, "you will be my people's ruler as soon as I can get back to Gaul and proclaim you there."

"I'm counting on you to help me convince all the people of Gaul that my father intended for me to rule them," Constantine assured him, "but in good time. Shall we get on with the letter?"

More than an hour was required to draft the message to Galerius. In the end, thanks to Eumenius' scholarship and his skill with words, it said everything Constantine wished it to say and implied a great deal more. First, the letter informed Galerius, as Senior Augustus, of Constantius' death at Eboracum, emphasizing, though subtly, that Constantius had appointed Constantine deputy commander of the army of Britain before they left Gaul and that upon his death, Constantine had naturally taken command of the troops there.

While giving proper deference to Galerius' position, the letter reported that the affectionate violence of the troops had named Constantine their leader in spite of his protests of unworthiness and acclaimed him to the purple before he had an opportunity to consult Galerius about the matter. Without pointing out that his accession to the position of ruler—at least in Britain—was already a fact, Constantine humbly begged Galerius' approval of the army's action. And finally, the letter pointed out that Crocus, as king of a large section of the Alemanni, the most powerful tribe in Gaul, had himself named Constantine to the purple in Britain and intended to fill a similar function in Gaul upon their return there.

"Galerius will be angry enough to order your execution," Dacius told Crocus, when he read over the final draft of the letter. "But he knows the strength of the army in Gaul, so he will have to accept an already accomplished fact."

"What next?" Crocus asked. "Remember Gaul is waiting to acclaim our new Augustus."

"It will take several weeks for the letter to reach Galerius," Constantine said. "That will give Eumenius and me time to visit the major cities in Britain and secure our position here. Meanwhile you and Dacius can prepare the army to embark at Londinium for Gaul."

The tour of Britain by the new Augustus—only in the letter to Galerius had Constantine intimated that he might officially accept the lesser title of Caesar—was a succession of triumphs. At the newly repaired fortifications of Hadrian's Wall in the north, he was cheered by the army and the people. And in a meeting with Bonar, who had marched south to meet him there, he received anew a promise of loyalty from that doughty chieftain, whose friendship and respect Constantine had earned by the daring raid into the country of the Picts.

Moving southward along the westward side of the island, which was not so highly developed as the central and eastern section, he visited an area where the smoke from coal fires, as ore dug from the hills was roasted to separate the lead and silver it contained, lay heavy upon the air. And pigs of lead were piled in every market, awaiting the wagons that would haul them to seaports for shipment to all parts of the Empire.

Not far from Aquae Sulis,* which, because of its bitter mineral springs, had been a favorite watering place for Romans even in the time of Julius Caesar, Constantine rode through the lake country. There he saw a wattle-walled church with a thatched roof, which Eumenius told him Constantius had once visited because of the story that Joseph of Arimathea from the land of Judaea, a follower of Jesus Christ, had fled there after the crucifixion and established the first Christian church† in Britain. But when he was still a half day's ride from Londinium and the military transports waiting there, he was met by Crocus and Dacius, who had heard of his coming from couriers racing along the excellent roads of Britain with mail and official communications.

"A messenger arrived last night from Gaul," Dacius said.

"With news of treachery!" Crocus spluttered angrily. "Ascaricus and Regaisus have broken the treaty of peace made with your father. They crossed the Rhine nearly a month ago and have been raiding south of the river."

Constantine's first thought was that the Germanic revolt was the

* Bath
† Glastonbury

worst thing that could possibly have happened now, but on its heels came another. It was true that the revolt of the Germanic kings posed a threat to the fertile province south of the Rhine, with its busy and prosperous cities, great villas, farms and factories. But he now commanded a mighty army waiting to embark at Londinium for the return to Gaul and the revolt might also give him the opportunity he needed to achieve a striking victory. Such a victory would not only entrench him as master of his father's old domain but also rally the army and people behind him, increasing tremendously his bargaining position, should Galerius try to deny him the title of Caesar of Gaul and Britain.

"How far into your country have the Germanic forces penetrated?" he asked Crocus.

"The dispatch said they are besieging Augusta Treverorum." It was the full name of Constantius' capital in Gaul—ordinarily called by the shorter name of Treves.

"Is my father's family in danger?"

"The city is well fortified and should be in no danger," Crocus assured him. "But they are pillaging the countryside and telling the people the Roman armies have been defeated in Britain."

"Where did they cross the Rhine?"

"At Colonia Agrippina. Your father built a bridge there some time ago, so the Germans could sell their products in Gaul. A party of them pretending to be farmers selling produce somehow managed to seize the bridgehead and let a large force cross."

"What other bridges cross the Rhine?" Constantine asked.

"None of any importance. What do you have in mind?"

"If the Germans crossed at Colonia Agrippina to enter Gaul, they will have to cross there going out, and we will be waiting for them. How many additional levies can you raise on short notice in Gaul, Crocus?"

"Every farmer in my kingdom has horses and all can ride and fight. But we already have enough of an army to drive the renegades back across the Rhine."

"If we let them cross it."

Dacius chuckled. "Remember how a youth on foot once catapulted you from the saddle, using only a spear, Crocus? I suspect our Germanic friends are in for much the same sort of a surprise."

17

IN SPITE OF a forced march across country from their debarkation
point at Gesoriacum, Constantine failed to trap the German
kings south of the Rhine, as he had hoped. Crocus had been sent
ahead with a considerable force of mounted auxiliaries to hold the
bridgehead until Constantine could arrive with the foot soldiers, but
it was a crestfallen cavalry commander who rode out to meet him,
when he approached the Gallic river crossing.

"They must have had lookouts posted on the heights above the
Fretum Gallicum," Crocus reported. "When they got word that our
fleet was in the channel, the main body of the enemy retreated
across the river without even giving battle."

"How long ago did they pass over?" Constantine asked.

"The last of their troops crossed yesterday," Crocus told him. "We
got here in time to seize this end of the bridge, but they cut the
other end before we could ride across." He pointed to where a
ribbon of logs had spanned the current of the Rhine to form a
pontoon bridge. The chains that bound the logs together had been
severed and little more than half of them remained now, scattered
along the banks of the river where they had washed ashore.

"What about Empress Theodora and her children?"

"They are safe at Treves. I had a dispatch to that effect only a
few hours ago. Shall we ride on there and have you acclaimed
Augustus, as we planned?"

"That can wait," Constantine decided. "Our first task is to capture
the two rulers who broke their vows to my father and take them
with us to Treves in chains."

"Where do we start?" By now Crocus too had come to expect unorthodox actions from his new ruler.

"Put five hundred men across in boats and have them scour the countryside for five or ten miles up and down the river bank and the same distance inland," Constantine directed. "We don't want the enemy to know we're building another bridge."

To no one's surprise, except the Germans, who were caught unawares, the whole affair went exactly as Constantine planned. With every man of the large force working and using dry logs from the woodyards that supplied the city with fuel, plus those which had washed ashore along the river bank for several miles downstream, they were able to fashion a new bridge, larger and stronger than the old, in about two days. The morning after its completion, Constantine and Crocus led the mounted troops across at dawn, followed by the foot soldiers under Dacius.

The cavalry did not remain with the foot, but launched a wide swing eastward and then south, trapping the unsuspecting enemy against the river which, with no major bridges in this area except the one controlled by Constantine, now formed one jaw of the trap he had forged. The carnage was considerable and at the end of the three-day engagement, the renegade kings, Ascaricus and Regaisus, with their advisers and chief commanders, were prisoners.

Constantine refused to see the captive kings or treat with them in any way, but ordered them sent to Treves in chains. The soldiers of their command who had been captured, he instructed Crocus to send farther south, to be parceled out among the Gallic people as slaves, a procedure Diocletian had successfully used against the Goths along the Danube and which Constantius had employed here in Gaul. Constantine and Dacius crossed the river by boat at Mogontiacum with a small force and rode directly to Treves. There Eumenius, who had gone directly to the capital from Gesoriacum, was already taking over the reins of government in Constantine's name.

Word of the smashing victory over the Germanic renegades had spread rapidly through the countryside, and Constantine's progress toward the capital was a triumph in itself, proving the correctness of his assumption that a major victory would do more to solidify the people of Gaul behind him as their ruler than anything he could do. He had never seen Augusta Treverorum before, though he knew it was the greatest city in northern Gaul, and was hardly prepared to find its streets paved and its great buildings comparing favorably with older cities of the Empire.

Located on a major tributary of the Rhine, a short distance below the confluence with another flowing from the northwest and still another from the south, Treves had excellent communications by road and water with the rest of Gaul, as well as eastward with the rest of the Empire by way of the Alpine passes and southward through the same land with Italy. A well-built stone bridge across the river gave access to Treves from the west and a strong wall, penetrated on the north by what was called the Porto Nigra, surrounded the entire capital.

A little east of the Forum at the center of the city were the magnificent imperial baths, called the *barbarathermen*. Consisting of three stories, they compared favorably with any Constantine had seen elsewhere. Beyond them, the entire northeastern quarter of the city was devoted largely to government offices, including the imperial palace and the buildings of state. South of the baths was the temple area, with a large shrine of Rome's patron god, Jupiter Capitolinus. And since the people of Gaul were particularly devoted to the games, a large amphitheater had been built against the wall on the east side of the city with, a little north of it, a Circus for chariot races and other public functions.

Constantine approached the palace on foot, a little awed by what his father had been able to accomplish here in this land so far from the Dalmatian hills in which he had grown up. He did not enter the living quarters of the palace immediately but went instead to the great audience hall, the *Aula Palatina*. It was paved and tiled with a mosaic effect and the walls were elaborately decorated with the rich colors loved by the Gauls.

The sound of his footfalls was loud in the silence of the building, echoing back to him from the walls as he crossed the chamber to the elevated dais at the end, where stood the throne. A little hesitantly, he approached the steps and stood looking up at the empty chair, feeling somewhat the same sense of awe he'd experienced when, as a boy, he had first seen his father in the magnificent uniform of a Roman general. Slowly he ascended the steps and seated himself, looking down into the great hall and imagining it as it must often have been during his father's audiences—packed with people in the colorful garb favored by Gallic nobles and peasantry alike. And suddenly overcome by the magnitude of the task that faced him in filling his father's footprints, he spoke a silent prayer—to a god he did not name—asking that he be given the strength and the wisdom to rule well.

A light footfall on the dais startled him, and he turned quickly to see a slender woman robed in white, with the pearl-studded silver band of a coronet upon her head, looking at him with startled eyes. Constantine would have been sure of her identity, even without the coronet, for there was a regal dignity about the Empress Theodora and a quiet pride which his mother had also possessed. Here, he recognized, was a woman of stature: nor would he have expected less, for he knew his father had been devoted to her.

"Augusta," he said, stepping down from the dais, upon which the throne chair stood, and moving toward her.

"The title is no longer mine," she protested.

"You must keep it always. I wish I could have brought you the news of his death myself, but there was much to be done in Britain before I could leave. And after that the rebel kings here in Gaul had to be put down."

"Is it true that they are your prisoners?"

"Yes. I hope you were not troubled by the siege."

"We were well protected. Your father fortified Treves against just such an attack." She hesitated, then spoke again. "Tell me. Was his death painful?"

"Not at all," he assured her. "He suffered another attack and weakened rapidly. I barely got back from the north in time to speak to him before he died. His last thought was of you and the children."

Actually, Constantius' last words had been of Helena, but he didn't hesitate to stretch the truth a little, knowing that the assurance she had been in the dying emperor's thoughts would be comforting to this tall woman who had loved his father. "I promised him that I would guard you and your children as I would my own," he added.

"Thank you. I had forgotten that you have a son." She hesitated again. "Would you like to speak to the children?"

Constantine had not thought of what it would be like to face his father's children by another wife. But he felt an instant liking and respect for Theodora and experienced no awkwardness when she presented her six children, three boys and three girls. The oldest was a boy of about thirteen bearing Constantine's own name; after him they ranged in ages down to the youngest, who was still a toddler. The other boys were named Hannibalianus and Constantius, while the girls were Constantia, Anastasia, and Eutropia. The six regarded him with wide-eyed solemnity, until the oldest boy broke the ice in a rush of words.

"Is it true that you defeated the giant Pict called Bonar in single combat?" he asked.

Constantine laughed. "He was not a giant, though he is a large man. And he was giving me some trouble, until Dacius brought him down with the butt of a spear."

"Why didn't you kill him?"

"Bonar is a brave man and much beloved by his people," Constantine explained. "It was better to make him my friend, so he would rule them for the Empire."

"Your father would have done the same," Theodora assured her son. "Don't forget that he made a treaty of peace with Ascaricus and Regaisus."

"But they broke it and tried to capture us here at Treves." The boy turned back to Constantine. "You did capture them, didn't you —by a quick march into their own country?"

"Yes."

"Will you make them pay for their treachery?"

"They shall pay," Constantine promised and turned to Theodora. "I must go now, Augusta."

"We will move from the palace at once," she told him. "After all, it is yours now."

"There is no reason for you to leave your home. I require but little and I shall be away much of the time, visiting Spain and organizing other legions."

"Then you expect trouble from Emperor Galerius?"

"Let us say I plan that there shall be no trouble. My father taught me one thing above others—that the strong rule until they cease to be strong. I intend to be strong, Augusta, for a long time."

She studied him for a moment, then nodded slowly. "You are a worthy son of your father and you will always have my loyalty. But beware of my stepfather and Maxentius. You are now one of the most powerful men in the Empire and I am sure they are already working to cut you down."

II

"We must arrange a triumph to celebrate your victory over Ascaricus and Regaisus," Eumenius said, as the four were eating dinner that evening in the suite of a half dozen rooms which Constantine had chosen for his own quarters in the palace.

"And allow Crocus' people to acclaim you Augustus before you hear from Galerius," Dacius added.

"Don't forget that your father left another son with the same name as you," Eumenius reminded Constantine. "Empress Theodora would not push his claim to become ruler of Gaul over yours. But Maximian and Maxentius would like nothing better than an excuse to name themselves regents, until he is of age and could be proclaimed Caesar."

"If he lived that long," Crocus said with a shrug. "Heirs to thrones have a habit of dying early, especially if the regent is strong and ambitious."

"I gave Empress Theodora my promise that she and her children will be protected as I would protect my own son," Constantine said.

"When did you see her?" Crocus asked.

"This afternoon, in the audience chamber. I went there to meditate and she came in. We agreed that she will retain the title of Augusta and I plan to turn enough of my father's wealth over to her to assure that she and the children can live in comfort here, or wherever they choose."

"You made no commitment for the future of the oldest boy, did you?" Crocus asked quickly.

"None, nor did she ask. Besides, the throne is no longer handed down from father to son. Diocletian stopped all that."

"The custom can always be revived," Dacius reminded him.

Constantine smiled as he reached for a hunk of meat and a piece of bread. "I'm not even a Caesar officially, yet you are all busy deciding my successor. Let us get to more important things—the triumph Eumenius mentioned. How about five days from now? Galerius can hardly get a letter back to us by then and it will give time for Crocus' relatives to get here. With all of them behind me, I should be able to conquer the rest of Europe."

Although quickly arranged, the gala celebrating the capture of the rebel kings and Constantine's return to Gaul was the largest affair ever staged in Treves, or for that matter in Gaul itself. It was held in the great Circus in the northeastern section of the city and long before it was to begin, the huge arena was packed with people. Knowing the excitable Gauls well, Crocus and Eumenius had arranged the affair carefully. It began with a set of exciting chariot races followed by gladiatorial contests. After a few hours of preliminaries, the crowd was in a frenzy of excitement in preparation for the real purpose of the event.

Constantine rode into the Circus in a chariot which had been hastily covered with gold leaf. It was drawn by six white horses selected and driven by Crocus. And since the dashing Gallic king was well known in his native land, his public acknowledgment of Constantine's sovereignty impressed the people more than any words Crocus might have uttered.

Slowly the shining vehicle moved around the circular track where a short time before chariot drivers and horses had strained in exciting races. Behind the chariot rode the cavalry, followed by the legions from Britain and the Gallic levies, who defended the capital nobly against the Germanic thrust southward. After them, standing in open wagons, came the bound German kings, while their advisers and generals plodded along behind, likewise in bonds.

The procession having circled the arena, Constantine dismounted and ascended to the first tier of seats where a massive throne chair stood in the imperial box. Empress Theodora and the three oldest of her children were already there, as were the nobles of the court. Constantine did not immediately take his seat, however, but remained standing beside the throne, waiting for the cheering of the thousands to subside.

"People of Gaul," he addressed them, when the Circus was finally quiet. "You have heard of my father's death in Britain, but you do not know that he was ill for some time before his departure.

In fact he risked the hazardous journey across the sea and endured the rigors of a winter in Britain against the advice of his physicians because, if that land is kept secure and free, Gaul itself will never again be threatened from across the Fretum Gallicum, as it was in the time of the rebel Carausius."

A roar of applause forced him to stop for a moment.

"My father died in the service of the Empire," he continued. "And I, his designated deputy, will not hesitate to give my life in the same service." Few could doubt that he was making a personal claim to his father's throne, though not spoken in so many words. The crowd took it as such and raised a tremendous shout of approval.

"Long live Augustus Constantine!" Crocus led the cheering and the people took up the cry, shouting and throwing hats, the small wineskins sold as refreshment in the amphitheater, and whatever else was loose into the air. During the resulting din, Constantine glanced at Eumenius, who was sitting behind him in the royal box, and saw by the pleased smile on the face of the *magister memoriae* that all was going just as planned. When the shouting began to subside, he once more raised his hand for silence.

"I thank you for honoring me," he said. "I pledge you that my rule shall be just and fair and that I shall do everything I can to protect you from your enemies and insure that no man shall go hungry for lack of work with which to earn his bread.

"But let no man think he can break faith with the authority of Rome and go unpunished." He looked down at the wagons where the Germanic kings were standing. "These one-time kings made a solemn treaty not long ago with my father, promising to respect our borders, as we promised to respect theirs. Yet no sooner had he left the country on business connected with the welfare of the Empire than they broke their vows and began to pillage and rape. Do such men deserve mercy?"

"No!" the crowd thundered.

"They have attacked you in your homes, perhaps killed those you love. What shall be their punishment?"

"Throw them to the beasts!" a voice from the crowd shouted and immediately a hundred, then a thousand, then ten thousand voices took up the cry.

"So be it," Constantine announced. "The people who suffered most at their hands have spoken. Let the prisoners be thrown to the beasts."

Behind him, Constantine heard Dacius' familiar low whistle. "Our fears were needless, scholar," the old soldier said to Eumenius. "There stands an Augustus who will rule Rome with an iron hand."

"And a just one." Eumenius' words sounded like a prayer. "May Jupiter—and all the gods—grant us that boon."

III

During the next month, Constantine spent most of the time riding around the countryside, as he had done in Britain after his father's death. In the lovely town called Lutetia* in the district of the Parisii, in Lugdunum and in Massilia, he received the plaudits of thousands acclaiming him Augustus of the West. Had time allowed, he would have ridden through the mountain passes into Spain, but he was expecting a letter from Galerius to arrive at Treves almost any day. So after making a swing eastward to the headwaters of the Rhine, he turned again to Treves, where he found the expected letter waiting.

It was brief and he could imagine Galerius' white-lipped fury as he had dictated it to a clerk.

Constantine's claim to the title of Augustus was ignored. But since Galerius could hardly ignore the largest and best army in the Empire, he had confirmed the young ruler in the title of Caesar, with sovereignty—under himself as Senior Augustus—over Gaul, Britain and Spain. What was not mentioned, but which the courier who brought the letter reported, was that even as it was being sent westward to Treves, Galerius, Maximian and Severus were converging upon the palace of Diocletian at Salonae to beg the old Emperor to take up once again the robes of office and put the young upstart in the West in his place.

As reported to Constantine later by his spies, the plea did not move Diocletian. Instead Galerius appointed Caesar Severus the Augustus of the West and sent word of his action to Constantine,

* Paris

who was busy bringing his army up to the greatest strength he could attain against the day when some of the others might move against him in the next act of the grim drama for control of the Roman world. Meanwhile, he prepared to make a move of his own which he had been contemplating on the journey through prosperous and wealthy Gaul. He voiced his decision at one of the almost daily conferences of state.

"I am sending you to Italy," he told Dacius. "A military galley will take you from Lugdunum to Neapolis."

"For what purpose?"

"To bring back my betrothed, the Lady Fausta."

"Are you going to demand her of Maximian?" Eumenius asked.

"I suppose it amounts to that."

"I know you are eager to claim your bride," Dacius said. "But is this the time?"

"Maximian went to Salonae hoping to resume the purple of an Augustus, but he failed and Severus was given it instead," Constantine reminded him. "Maximian cannot turn to the East, so he is certain to look to the West to support his ambition. What could give him greater hope than to have me as his son-in-law?"

"What about Maxentius?"

"My spies tell me he has promised the Praetorians to return their old glory, if they support him when he tries to seize power from Severus. Naturally he would welcome the knowledge that I would not interfere."

"What will you do, if Maximian lets Lady Fausta marry you and then demands your support against Severus?" Eumenius asked.

"What any sensible man would do—let them both weaken themselves by fighting each other, then move in to restore stability."

"With yourself as Augustus of the West?"

"Why not—if there is no strong power in Italy?"

"For that the army of Gaul must be stronger than any two the others can bring against us, which means more taxes," Eumenius warned.

"And more trouble," Dacius said bluntly. "Don't forget the *bagaudae*."

"I've been thinking about them," Constantine said. "They rebelled because they were oppressed by the great landowners. But if I force those who own much land to share with the serfs, those who now pay no taxes will be able to pay—from the sale of what they produce."

"Surely you don't intend to determine prices and wages, as Diocletian did," Dacius protested.

"No, that scheme was a failure. But a plan that makes men proud of themselves and gives them a reasonable share of what they produce with their own hands should succeed. What say you to that, Eumenius?"

"The principle is above reproach," the scholar agreed. "Its success will depend on how well it is carried out."

"Then it will be sure to succeed," Constantine said with a smile. "I am this day appointing you Chief Chamberlain with the task of putting my plan into effect, while I take steps to make the frontier safe."

"How do you propose to do that?" Dacius asked.

"By building bridges across the Rhine that cannot be easily destroyed, starting at Colonia Agrippina. And by putting a fleet of war galleys on the river to patrol it."

Eumenius shook his head slowly, and admiringly. "Sometimes I wish you had less ambition, Augustus," he admitted. "I was looking forward to returning to my old post as teacher of rhetoric at Autun."

"That will wait. My task now is to rule Gaul so well that other parts of the Empire will be envious."

"And desire you for their ruler," Dacius added.

"Perhaps that too. I have one more step in mind. What do you think of letting the Christians rebuild their churches?"

"It would be a good move," Eumenius said promptly. "They were intensely loyal to your father and are sure to transfer that loyalty to you. Let me pass the word quietly to the bishops that the churches will not be torn down again and no edict will be necessary. That way Galerius cannot use it against you."

Thus it happened that the Christians quietly rebuilt their churches throughout Gaul and resumed public services of worship. And with the spreading of word that the young ruler—though not a Christian himself—looked with favor upon their faith, the church grew rapidly, further entrenching Constantine in the favor of a substantial section of the people of Gaul and Britain.

The building of the great bridge across the Rhine at Colonia Agrippina served notice upon the Germanic tribes that any rebellion would be put down swiftly with the sort of punitive raids into their territory for which Constantine was already famous. And with Britain and Gaul safe and prosperous, tax funds flowed steadily into the treasury, to be administered carefully and even austerely by Eumenius, as Chief Chamberlain.

Constantine himself led an austere life and there was a minimum of luxury in the palace, so the major part of the accumulation in the treasury was distributed to pay the additional legions and auxiliaries being raised and trained at Treves and other centers throughout Gaul. Meanwhile, several months had passed since Dacius' departure for Rome to bring Constantine his bride; then one day he rode into Treves—alone.

18

ONSTANTINE'S FACE was suffused by a sudden flood of rage. "Did Maximian dare refuse me again?"

"No one has refused you." Dacius raised his hand, as if to ward off the force of the younger man's anger.

"Then why didn't you bring Fausta with you?"

"The lady herself agrees that the time is not yet ripe."

"Does she want someone more important than the Augustus of Gaul, Britain and Spain?" Constantine demanded.

"In the eyes of her family you are a Caesar—not an Augustus," Dacius reminded him. "Maximian and Maxentius hope to keep you in the lesser place, but Lady Fausta has other plans—and you know how determined she can be."

Constantine did know very well. "Suppose you tell me the whole story," he suggested.

"When I discovered that the galley I was sailing on contained cargo for Rome, I ordered the shipmaster to go there first," Dacius said. "Fortunately you made me a general, so he could not refuse."

Constantine found that he could smile, in spite of his anger and disappointment.

"At Rome I learned several interesting things," Dacius continued. "Severus seems to be afraid to come into Italy. Even though he was appointed Augustus, he still remains at the border in the neighborhood of Aquileia."

"Why?"

"He is Galerius' puppet. Apparently both of them fear to lengthen the strings that make him dance."

"Doesn't he know he's playing into the hands of Maxentius and Maximian?"

Dacius grinned. "If he doesn't, we shall certainly not tell him and defeat our own purpose."

"Go on," Constantine urged.

"Galerius has revoked the freedom from taxation the people of Rome have always enjoyed."

"That should cause a real upheaval," Eumenius observed.

"More like Vesuvius in eruption," Dacius said dryly. "Rome is angry enough to leave the Empire, if it could, but Maxentius and Maximian have other ideas. They will soon name themselves joint Augusti and move north—with the Praetorians and legions of southern Italy at their backs—to seize the Alpine provinces between the Rhine and Danube."

"That will put them on my eastern border!" Constantine exclaimed.

"And force them to treat with you," Dacius reminded him. "Else they will be caught between your armies and those of Galerius."

"Did you learn all this during a brief stop in Rome?" Constantine asked.

"I'll admit I didn't see through the whole scheme until I got to Neapolis and Lady Fausta told me her father is joining Maxentius in the venture," Dacius admitted. "She thinks that if you play the game right, you will come out the winner—with the title of Augustus for yourself."

"And I suppose she refuses to marry me until I am officially named Emperor."

"No," Dacius said. "But she does think that if you wait, both will soon be handed to you—in her own words—'on a golden platter.'"

"What a queen she will make!" Crocus cried. "Like that one in the East—what was her name?"

"Zenobia," Constantine said shortly. "But don't forget that she wound up in chains."

"As I remember it, the bonds were made of gold," Eumenius said, "and the lady lived a long and honorable life in Rome afterwards. Even married a senator."

"Enough!" Constantine was still having trouble keeping his anger over Fausta within bounds. "What did you learn about Galerius?"

"When Severus was made Augustus of Italy and Africa, Daia demanded equal rank," Dacius said. "Galerius talked him out of it apparently, with the asurance that Severus would have no authority in the East, only in the territory formerly ruled by your father."

"But not in Gaul!" Crocus looked quickly at Constantine. "Surely you will not allow that."

"Would the Gallic legions and auxiliaries bow meekly to Severus?" Constantine asked him.

"No, of course not."

"There is your answer. You yourself named me Augustus and I have no intention of relinquishing the title, whether the rest of the Empire acknowledges it or not."

II

Reading the reports of his spies in the rest of the Empire, Constantine sometimes felt like an observer perched high above some giant circus, watching a grim drama of struggle for power being waged in the arena below. In the months that followed, Dacius'— and Fausta's—shrewd assay of the future course of events proved accurate.

First, Galerius tried to assuage somewhat the indignation of the citizens of Rome at being taxed like the lowliest provinces of the Empire by dedicating the magnificent *thermae,* or baths, which Diocletian had begun toward the end of his reign. But the costly structure only served to remind them that they were paying for the baths, bringing to a head the boil of their resentment.

Nor was Maxentius loath to capitalize upon the public unrest. Promising to restore Rome to its traditional place as the Empire's capital, he let himself be named Augustus of Italy and Rome by the angry Senate. The few officials loyal to Severus were quickly massacred and, when Maxentius invited his father to join him, Maximian avidly seized the opportunity to regain at least part of his former glory.

In a ceremony of solemn mockery, the people, the Senate, and Maxentius persuaded the former Augustus to accept the purple cloak once again and reign as Co-Emperor with his son. And when the Praetorian Prefect—chief administrative officer of Rome itself— judiciously threw in his lot with Maximian and Maxentius rather than lose his head, and the troops garrisoned in Rome and southern Italy did the same, the feat was accomplished without bloodshed.

Faced with the loss of both his title and his territory, Severus moved at last, but by now supporters of Maximian and Maxentius were largely in control of Milan and other northern cities. When Severus marched into Italy, he found every city fortified against him and managed to advance no nearer than a point about sixty miles from Rome. By then, however, agents of the usurpers had succeeded in buying off units of his army with promises of gold and, with the triple threat of Maxentius' troops before him, a hostile populace in fortified cities behind him, and serious defections within the ranks of his own army, Severus prudently withdrew to Ravenna, where he had ample support by sea and provisions for a long siege. Spies sent by the wily Maximian convinced him, however, that the populace of the town was about to yield him and his army up to the besiegers and that he would be much better off to sue for an honorable peace. Yielding, he discovered too late that Maximian's generosity extended only to letting him choose the means of his own death, so he opened his veins.

Galerius naturally could not stand idly by and see the very heart of the Empire wrested from his grasp, even though the new conquerors insisted they were loyal to him as Senior Augustus. Gathering an army, he marched from Nicomedia into Italy, only to find town after town fortified and garrisoned so strongly that, had he stopped to conquer them, his forces would have been exhausted before reaching Rome.

Once again Maximian and Maxentius poured out Roman gold to buy off the Illyrian legions who followed Galerius. And since the Emperor of the East was generally hated because of an edict decreeing a census of persons and property and payment of taxes in the area, he shortly found himself in the same position Severus had been in hostile territory with fortified strongposts at his back and a steady rate of defection in his own ranks. Remembering his experience during the hasty dash into Persia, Galerius chose the wiser course of retreat and, fuming but impotent, returned to Nicomedia, leaving Maximian and Maxentius in clear possession of the field.

While Galerius was still in northern Italy, the wily Maximian made a third move, designed to insure that he and Maxentius would be free to advance eastward whenever they chose. A letter, couched in flowery terms and borne by an imperial ambassador, was delivered at Treves, inviting Constantine to meet the father of his beloved at Arles on the southern coast of Gaul, not far from Massilia. The avowed purposes of the meeting were twofold: first to invest the Caesar of Britain, Gaul and Spain with his rightful title of Augustus, and second to celebrate the wedding of Fausta and Constantine.

Constantine was natually overjoyed with the news from Rome and at once dispatched a courier with a message of acceptance and a magnificent necklace of emeralds he had purchased in Spain for Fausta. These pleasant duties finished, he went to the apartment of the Empress Theodora to notify her of his coming alliance with her family.

He found the Empress talking to an olive-skinned man whose features had a Spanish cast and whose dark eyes were bright with intelligence. He reminded Constantine somewhat of Eusebius of Caesarea—perhaps because, like Eusebius, he wore the robe of a priest, though without the headgear of a cleric of high rank. Theodora came to greet Constantine, her hands outstretched in greeting, her eyes bright with welcome.

"We have seen too little of you in Treves, Augustus," she said. "The children were asking about you today; your stepbrothers and stepsisters are very fond of you."

"And I of them," he assured her. "May I take them to the games tomorrow?"

"Of course—except Eutropia. I'm afraid she's still too much of a baby for such affairs. May I present my confessor, Bishop Hosius of Córdoba?"

Hosius bowed in acknowledgment of the introduction. "As one of your subjects, I pray daily for your welfare, Augustus," he said.

"But I am not a Christian."

"You are a man of principle, like your father. And because you are, our people in Gaul, Spain and Britain have been freed from persecution and our churches rebuilt."

"Bishop Hosius is from Spain and was a close friend of your father's," Theodora explained to Constantine. "I asked him to remain at Treves and act as my confessor, but I'm afraid I have imposed upon him."

"Not at all." Hosius' fine eyes glowed in a smile. "Your chamberlain, Eumenius, and I are old opponents in debate and discussion, Augustus. Seldom have I spent more pleasant months than I have here."

"I didn't know you were a Christian, Augusta," Constantine said when the churchman had departed to hear the prayers of the children.

"Do you disapprove?"

"Not at all; I have many Christian friends. Tell me, was my father a Christian? Eborius in Britain said he was not."

"It's true that Constantius never professed to the Christian belief," Theodora said. "I think in his heart he was one of us though, and eventually would have acknowledged it publicly. But with the edicts of Diocletian still in force and persecution going on in the East and in Egypt, it didn't seem a good idea at the time. And then"—her voice broke a little—"it was too late."

"You spoke just now of Hosius as your confessor. I'm not familiar with the word."

"We Christians try to live our lives according to the teachings of Jesus Christ, but we are only human and therefore certain to sin," she explained. "Forgiveness of our sins has been promised us if we confess them freely and publicly, so most of us confess to a priest and are assigned some deed to be done in penance before we can be forgiven."

"I thought the rite of baptism was supposed to wash away all sin."

"It is, but being human we are sure to sin again. That's why many Christians choose to be baptized only in the hours just preceding death."

"A priest named Eusebius of Caesarea tried to explain some of these things to me once," Constantine admitted. "But I'm afraid I understand them no better now than I did then—especially a god who is not one but three." He changed the subject. "I had a letter today from Emperor Maximian. He wants me to meet him at Arles so he can invest me with the purple of an Augustus."

"I am happy for you," Theodora said warmly. "And your father would be too if he were alive. It is no more than you deserve." Then her face grew sober. "But why is my stepfather doing this just now?"

"To make sure I shall be behind him in any trouble he has with Galerius, Maximin Daia and Licinius."

"Licinius? I don't know him."

"He was a general on the staff of Emperor Galerius when I was in Nicomedia and once did me a great favor. Word came today that Galerius had named both him and Maximin Daia Augusti. Licinius is to govern Illyria, Galerius Greece and the Asian provinces, and Daia, Syria and Egypt—with Galerius Senior Emperor over all."

"So with three Augusti in the East, my stepfather naturally wishes to be sure you are on his side?"

"Can you blame him?"

"No, I suppose not—so long as you know why he is courting your favor."

"I have no illusions concerning my future father-in-law," he assured her.

"Then you and Fausta—"

"Emperor Maximian has finally agreed to our marriage. He is bringing her to Arles with him."

"I am happy for you both." She gave him her hands in a warm gesture of pleasure. "Fausta is a lovely little thing and I know you love her dearly. The children and I will move to your father's country villa outside Treves. With your own family now, you will need the palace for yourself."

"There is no hurry," he assured her. "I plan to remain in Arles for a while; it will be easier to keep in touch with events in Italy from there." Both of them understood that with Maximian and Maxentius not to be trusted, it would be prudent for him to be in a position where he could march into Italy quickly by way of the passes through what were sometimes called the Maritime Alps.

19

T HE WEDDING of Constantine and Fausta at Arles was the most
elaborate ceremony ever staged in southern Gaul. His in-
vestment with the imperial purple and the official title of Augustus—which most of his subjects thought he already possessed—
took place a day later and was patterned after a Roman triumph.
Subject kings from the territory along the Rhine were present with
their retinues and even the German lords who—after the example
he'd made of the rebel kings, Ascaricus and Regaisus—had decided to support the Pax Romana.

Constantine and Maximian rode together in the golden chariot
to the Temple of Apollo where, at Maximian's insistence—perhaps
because he knew of Constantius' leaning toward the Christians—
the new Augustus presided at the usual sacrifice of a young bull.
Only then did Maximian officially name Constantine ruler of Gaul,
Britain and Spain and drape the rich purple cloak he had brought
from Rome about the younger man's shoulders.

The division of the Empire was now complete and six Augusti
—Constantine, Maximian and Maxentius in the West and Galerius,
Licinius and Maximin Daia in the East—each theoretically of equal
power, ruled it. What had been a united nation under Diocletian,
was now broken into six parts, but the prospect of conflict, inevitable though it seemed, did not trouble Constantine. With the
strongest army and one of the most populous and prosperous ter-
ritories of the Empire under his rule, he was now ready to move
on to wider spheres of activity when the occasion presented itself.
Nor was it long in coming.

Enchanted with love for his bride though he was, Constantine
did not fail to keep a close watch on the dramatic battle for

control being waged in Rome and Italy, the ancient center of the Empire. For that purpose, to say nothing of a pleasant place to spend a prolonged honeymoon, he could not possibly have chosen better than the sun-drenched city—on the banks of the Rhône near its mouth—known to citizens of the province everywhere as the "little Rome of Gaul."

At Arles the Massilotes had built an important trading station in the time of the early Phoenicians, before the luckless Queen Dido of Tyre had founded Carthage on the African coast to the south. Julius Caesar had constructed galleys on the banks of the river in preparation for the assault on nearby Massilia, and much of Arles's commercial importance was linked with its role as a port where river vessels transshipped their cargoes to seagoing bottoms.

The center for Roman administration in Arles lay in the western part of the city, not far from the river, while between it and the broad sluggish stream stood a giant arch completed by Constantius shortly before his death. The climate was hot in spring and summer, but a huge structure called the *Cryptoporticus,* with a network of underground passages, formed a cool retreat as well as a storage place for perishable goods. All in all, Arles was a happy place, far removed from the constant threat of invasion from across the Rhine that made Treves—for all its magnificence—a frontier city.

When Fausta became pregnant with their first child, Constantine was overjoyed. And when the baby proved to be a girl, he felt a sense of relief, for he knew Fausta would fight to preserve the succession for her own progeny, while he had always considered Crispus his successor in line of rule.

Helena had not come to the wedding, though Constantine had notified her of the date and offered to place the resources of the Imperial Post at her disposal. She did not mention it in her letter telling him she could not come but he was sure her absence was dictated by her distrust of Fausta because she was Maximian's daughter. Bewitched with love for his young bride, he could not sympathize with that view, but he could understand his mother's not wanting to meet Maximian, who had been responsible—with Diocletian—for her divorce from Constantius. His mother did report that Crispus was growing tall and strong and was eagerly looking forward to beginning his military training.

The uneasy accord between Maximian and Maxentius was not long in being disrupted by the unstable tempers of its two adherents. Maximian considered that his position as Ex-Emperor had provided Maxentius with backing to seize control of Italy. The son, on the other hand, cited the support of the Senate and the Praetorian Guard in his election to the post of Augustus. The controversy between them—faithfully reported to Constantine in Arles by his spies—finally resulted in the flight of Maximian from Rome to Illyricum.

Galerius, however, had no intention of offering refuge to the old troublemaker, so Maximian was forced to flee again, this time to Arles, where Constantine received his father-in-law with all the deference due his rank. Maximian settled down with his daughter and her husband, confident that he was aligning himself with the strongest force of the Empire—as no doubt he was.

While Constantine was playing the game of watchful waiting at Arles, however, a coalition of Germanic chiefs decided to take advantage of the fact that much of his army was in the south and launch one of their recurrent raids into Gaul. Crocus countered the attack promptly but Constantine decided to move swiftly northward and put down the revolt before it had time to weaken his own position in the Empire. He was at Argentoratum, a city near the headwaters of a major tributary of the Rhône, when he received startling news from Arles.

Maximian, the dispatch from Dacius said, had declared Constantine dead and named himself Augustus of Gaul, Spain and Britain. Furthermore, he had seized the considerable treasury Constantine had built up at Arles during his stay there and was pouring out gifts to the legions in an obvious attempt to buy their loyalty. Dacius himself had been imprisoned when he refused to turn over command to Maximian, but the old soldier had managed to send word of the treachery at Arles to Constantine by friends in the army, along with the assurance that Fausta and her little daughter were safe.

Constantine read the letter with some difficulty, the words blurred by the red haze of anger before his eyes. Tossing it to

Crocus, he went to the window and stared unseeingly out upon the bustling activity of the garrison while he fought for control.

"So this is how your father-in-law repays you for giving him refuge!" Crocus spat out a curse. "What are you going to do?"

"Go to Arles as quickly as possible. We march southward tomorrow."

"There's a quicker way—the river. In its upper reaches the Rhône is a swift-flowing stream and you will be traveling with the current. If Maximian really thinks you're dead, a rapid descent by water will catch him unawares."

"The river is the best road," Constantine agreed. "Commandeer everything that will float; my father-in-law is going to be in for a surprise."

II

There was every reason for Constantine to move swiftly with all the troops he could safely take from duty along the Rhine, since Maximian's next move would undoubtedly be the formation of a pact with Maxentius in Rome, giving the two of them control of the entire western half of the Empire. That accomplished, they could then attack Licinius and seize the fertile provinces of Illyricum before Galerius would be in a position to mount any serious opposition.

Less than a week was required for the descent by water to Arles, but word of Constantine's coming reached Maximian when someone along the river saw the giant armada floating southward and rode night and day to warn him, sure of gaining a reward. By the time Constantine reached Arles, his father-in-law had retreated to Massilia on the coast, taking Fausta and her little daughter with him.

Since Massilia was heavily fortified Constantine decided upon a different tactic than the usual direct assault. Accompanied only by a driver and a trumpeter, he was driven back and forth in his golden chariot before the walls of the city, standing in the vehicle with his cloak of imperial purple billowing out behind him, while he shouted a command for the legions in Massilia to seize the city in his name. When there was no immediate response from Massilia, he reluctantly ordered preparations for an attack the following day. But just before midnight there was a stir in the camp and a cloaked feminine figure, accompanied by a detail of soldiers and a servant bearing a blanket-wrapped bundle, came to his tent. It was Fausta with their little daughter.

"You've not been harmed?" Constantine asked quickly.

"By my own father?" she demanded, apparently blaming him because she had been routed out in the middle of the night. "What kind of monsters do you think we are in my family?"

Constantine knew well from actual experience what kind of monsters there were in her family, and that they must be destroyed. But happy to have her and the child back, he ignored the sharp note in her voice.

"Thank God, you're safe anyway," he said.

"The gods deserve no thanks," she said tartly. "Father sent me to you."

"Why?"

"What else would you expect? He only seized control because we received word that you were dead. He was afraid some of your generals might have the same idea."

"Like Dacius?" He could imagine the story Maximian had told her—and which she seemed to have believed.

"Or some others." She had missed entirely the irony in his voice. "Father says he will yield up Massilia to you, so there will be no bloodshed."

"On what terms?"

"Why must you be so suspicious, when he is only trying to help you? At least show some gratitude to him for guarding your realm when you were reported to have been killed while chasing Germans."

"This courier who brought word of my death," Constantine said. "Did you see him?"

"Of course. Do you think I would have accepted the report, if I hadn't heard it with my own ears?"

"No, I suppose not," he admitted.

"Then you're going to accept Father's offer?"

"You and the baby—plus the city of Massilia—in return for his life? I would be less than grateful if I didn't."

"I told him you would be generous."

From outside came the sound of marching men and Dacius soon appeared, at the head of a detail of troops. The old soldier looked somewhat the worse for wear and his face was grim. Behind him, a prisoner, stumbled Maximian looking small and insignificant without his purple cloak.

Dacius halted the detail and saluted. "The city is yours, Augustus," he reported. "And one prisoner."

"I demand the arrest of General Dacius for seizing me when I was preparing to surrender Massilia to you." Maximian stepped forward to embrace his son-in-law, but something in Constantine's gaze stopped him. "Thank Hercules you are safe, my son!" he said lamely. "We were told that you were dead."

"Thank you for looking after my family and my kingdom," Constantine said coldly, and ordered a detail to take Fausta, the baby and Maximian to Arles by chariot. He watched the little party disappear into the night toward where the chariots were located, then turned and, putting his arm about Dacius' shoulder, guided his old friend into the tent and poured him a cup of wine.

"You look as if you were roughly treated," he said. "Who unloosed your bonds? Maximian?"

Dacius swore a purple oath. "Don't tell me you were taken in by that play-acting just now."

"Of course not. My guess is that the legions turned against Maximian, after they saw me in the chariot this afternoon and learned that I am alive."

"The Twenty-second, your old command, was first. I was still in my cell, but I'll wager the old fox realized the dogs were too close and sent your wife and child to bargain with you for his life."

"Tell me exactly what happened."

"About a month ago a courier came to Arles with word that you had been killed. He said he had been caught by the enemy and his papers taken away, but he'd managed to escape. I was so grieved that I failed to question him myself. When Maximian moved to seize the throne, it occurred to me that the message might be false, but by then the courier had disappeared. Soon after that, I was arrested."

"How did you manage to get word to me from prison?"

"A decurion among the guards owed me a favor; I saved his skin once when he was in training at Nicomedia and broke a rule. What are you going to do with Maximian?"

"I shall make him my pensioner." Constantine's voice had a grim note. "To one as ambitious as he is, that should be punishment enough."

"Death would be more merciful," Dacius agreed. "But I'll have him watched just the same. Even a dead scorpion can sting, if you step on his tail hard enough."

III

After the treachery of Maximian at Arles and the humiliating necessity for Constantine to reclaim part of his own kingdom by force, some months were required to assert again his full authority there. Pockets of resistance, which had caught fire during the brief rebellion, had to be put down by force and, though Constantine would have preferred to move to Treves, his presence in the south was required for some time.

Fausta was pregnant with their second child now and kept much to her quarters because she did not like others to see her swollen condition. She slept in a room adjoining Constantine's own chamber and he was surprised one night, upon his return from a four days' journey of inspection in southern Gaul, when she came into his room as he was preparing for bed. He saw that she had been weeping and went at once to take her in his arms.

"What is it, dearest?" he asked.

"I almost betrayed you by believing Father was sincere, when he seized control here," she admitted.

"I knew you had no part in his plan," Constantine assured her. "What changed your mind about him?"

"I just discovered that he plans to assassinate you and seize control again."

"How do you know this?"

"My maid learned of the plot from her lover. He's my father's manservant."

"Did he give her any details?"

"The attempt is set for tonight. Father knows that once we go to Treves, it will be hard for him to join up with Maxentius, so he has to kill you before we leave."

"Are you sure of your source?"

"Absolutely. My maid and her lover have both been promised their freedom if he succeeds in killing you, but she thought they could make a better bargain by revealing the plot to me."

"They shall both be suitably rewarded," Constantine promised. "Now get back to your room, so I can arrange a welcome for my assassin."

"Please don't kill him," she begged. "He's just an old man eaten with vanity and ambition."

"He shall not die at my hands," Constantine promised her, but said no more.

The arrangements were quickly made. A eunuch, warned to remain awake because of the expected attack, was assigned to Constantine's bed. Because he could not be sure just how many people Maximian had been able to bribe in connection with the assassination attempt, Constantine took only Dacius into his confidence. The two took up a post in Fausta's bedchamber adjoining Constantine's, with the door barely cracked so they could hear sounds from the adjoining rooms.

It was after midnight when they heard the outer door from the chamber into the corridor open, proving Constantine's wisdom in not revealing his knowledge of the assassination attempt to any of the regular palace guards. For Maximian could not have gained access to the bedchamber without having bribed the guard stationed outside the entrance to the imperial apartment at all times. The intruder carried no light, obviously having familiarized himself with the room to a point where he could make his way to the bed unseen.

Before Constantine could shout a warning to the eunuch who had taken his place in the bed, he heard a muted cry of triumph from the assassin followed by a moan from the bed. Jerking open the door, he allowed Dacius to run past him to secure the corridor door, while Fausta brought a candle from the closet in which she had hidden it, so there would be no sign of light beneath the door to warn the assassin.

They were too late to help the unwary eunuch, who had apparently made the mistake of falling asleep, in spite of Constantine's warning. The glow of the burning candle showed Maximian bending over the bed, stabbing again at the inert body lying there. When he stood up with the bloody dagger in his hand, Fausta screamed, dropping the candle. Taking advantage of the confusion as Constantine stooped to pick up the still-burning candle, Maximian darted like a cornered animal toward the outer door, but Dacius was there, sword in hand, so the old Emperor turned toward Constantine again. Seeing the dagger in his son-in-law's hand, he realized he was trapped and dropped his bloody weapon.

"Your daughter has interceded for you, even though you are a murderer," Constantine said coldly. "You shall have the same leniency you gave Severus, and I trust you will have the dignity not to disgrace the purple you once wore."

Shortly after dawn, Dacius came with news that Maximian had hanged himself in his own quarters. But though the story of the old Emperor's treachery was widely known by now, Constantine ordered that his body be given every honor to which a former Augustus was entitled. When the funeral pyre had burned out, the ashes were gathered up and sent to Maxentius—ostensibly to be placed, as was the custom in Roman households, in an alcove of the family home called the *columbarium* set aside for the remains of the dead. Actually, however, Constantine meant them to be a pointed reminder to his brother-in-law that treachery earned its own swift—and ruthless—reward.

20

THE SECOND CHILD of Constantine and Fausta was born soon after they moved from Arles to Treves. It was a girl and though he assured Fausta that its sex made no difference to him, Constantine could see that she was depressed by her inability, so far, to bear him a son. Nor did the presence of the Empress Theodora so near Treves with her three sons and three daughters do anything to soothe Fausta's rather mercurial temper. When Theodora came to pay a courtesy call upon Constantine and Fausta and have a look at the new baby, her stepsister gave her a frosty reception. Afterwards, Constantine took his young wife to task for her coolness.

"Why does she have to stay here at Treves?" Fausta retorted. "It was her home long before it was ours."

"But now it's ours. Isn't it enough that you let her keep the title of Augusta, without her always reminding us that your father's children are older than ours? Let something happen to you in one of those battles you're always fighting with the Germans and she'll be shoving that pale son of hers forward as your successor."

"I already have a son older than my stepbrother Constantine," he reminded her.

"And I suppose you plan for him to succeed you."

"Why not? Crispus is my firstborn."

"By a peasant girl! And a Christian!"

"Minervina was a merchant's daughter of Drepanum."

"As your mother was a barmaid!"

For the first time in his life Constantine felt like striking a woman, and that woman his own wife. "My mother's family operated an accommodation on the Imperial Post in Bithynia," he said coldly. "They were not assassins and liars like yours."

His tone told Fausta she had gone too far and, as mercurial as one of the lizards he'd seen in the East that could change its color with the locale in which it found itself, she was suddenly all sweetness and affection.

"Of course I want you to love your firstborn, darling," she assured him. "It's just that I'm jealous of any other woman who has borne you a child, especially a boy."

The quarrel ended on that note, but it started a train of thought in Constantine's mind. He'd been too preoccupied with matters of state lately to think much about Crispus, but he remembered now that the boy was almost as old as he had been when he'd begun his military training at Nicomedia. And with that memory he came to a decision.

"I want you to go to Drepanum and bring Crispus to Gaul," he told Dacius when they finished inspecting the household troops the next morning.

"When did you decide that?"

"Yesterday."

"The Empress Fausta will not like having him here."

Constantine shrugged. "Fausta resents anything that poses what she considers a threat to her own children."

"You can hardly blame her for that, but Crispus *is* your firstborn."

"And it's time he began his military education."

"Surely not here at Treves," Dacius protested. "That would be throwing him into the Augusta's face."

"I have no desire to affront Fausta," Constantine admitted. "But Crispus needs to learn about Gaul and its people, if he is going to be Caesar when I move on to Rome."

"Rome?" Dacius' eyebrows lifted. "Is that our next goal?"

"Hasn't it always been?"

"From what I hear about Maxentius, many there would welcome you. The Senate and the nobles wanted him, but now that he has imposed the tax he calls a 'free gift' on them, they're wailing louder than a merchant of Greece or Syria who thinks he's been cheated. When do you want me to go to Bithynia?"

"As soon as you can get ready. Licinius has always been our friend, so it should be safe for you to travel by the northern route through Illyricum. I will give you a letter to Galerius."

"Is that wise? After all he might choose to hold Crispus as he tried to hold you."

"I think not," Constantine said. "Just yesterday, Eumenius showed me some reports from our spies in his capital. Galerius is ill, perhaps with a mortal disease. It will do no harm to assure both him and Licinius that I have no territorial ambitions against them."

Dacius raised his eyebrows. "But is that true?"

"I'm still young. There's plenty of time to consider the East, after I secure the West."

II

Constantine's swift campaign against the Germanic invaders and the even swifter move by water to Arles in the face of Maximian's attempt to seize Gaul, had not given him time to inspect the work of his deputies. The vicars of the several divisions of Gaul had been supervised by Eumenius as Chief Chamberlain and Crocus as military commander, but Eumenius was anxious to return to the *Scholae Maenianae* at Autun in central Gaul, where he had taught before becoming Constantius' *magister memoriae* and Constantine planned to turn Crispus' further education over to him there.

While waiting for Dacius to return from Bithynia with Crispus, he made a close inspection of the territory and found the country prosperous, though there was the usual grumbling about the taxes necessary to maintain the large army he had been developing— ostensibly as a defense against the frequent German attacks but actually in preparation for the inevitable contest with Maxentius.

During this period, he also made a quick journey to Britain to inspect the defenses there and found the country stable and at peace. One thing was particularly noticeable in both Britain and Gaul: the Christians had taken him at his word and had rebuilt churches everywhere. In city after city, the bishops came to thank him for his tolerance and he could not fail to notice how well organized their congregations were, proving once again his wisdom in freeing them from persecution.

His inspection in Britain finished, Constantine hurried back to Gaul, certain that by now Dacius would have arrived with Crispus. But remembering the sturdy lad of ten with whom he had ridden across the hills around Drepanum, he was startled to find his son a tall, rather serious-looking young man, whose eyes were remarkably like his mother's. In almost every other way, however, he was a smaller duplicate of his grandfather Constantius, with fair hair, broad shoulders and a quiet assurance of manner belying his youth.

"Is your grandmother well?" Constantine asked.

"Very well, sir. She sent you her love."

"And Lactantius? Has he kept you at your books?"

Crispus grinned and Constantine laughed, the reserve between them broken.

"I remember feeling the same way, when I was your age," Constantine admitted. "But I hope you're a better scholar than I was. Tell me, do you still ride?"

Crispus' eyes lit up eagerly. "Uncle Marios gave me a horse of my own after I grew too large for the pony. I ride every day at home."

"And you will here in Gaul," Constantine assured him. "I'm going to send you to the *Scholae Maenianae* at Autun. My chamberlain, Eumenius, will be your tutor."

"But I want to be a soldier like you," Crispus protested.

"We maintain the school at Autun for training young officers to join the legions later," Constantine explained. "The men of Gaul are fine horsemen and we put great emphasis on the cavalry."

"I would like that, sir. When do I go?"

"Whenever Eumenius is ready. It shouldn't be long."

Dacius came in just then, a smile warming his craggy face as he put a hand on the boy's shoulder in a gesture of affection. "You have a fine son, here, Augustus," he said. "With the makings of a good soldier."

"Dacius himself planned the military training program at Autun," Constantine told Crispus.

"Then I know I shall like it," the boy said eagerly. "Will you excuse me now, Father? King Crocus has invited me to go with him to the chariot races."

"By all means do. Dacius and I have much to talk about."

"He is just such another as you were at his age," the old soldier said, when the door closed behind the boy. "Your mother has done a fine job of bringing him up."

"Did she object to letting him come? I explained to her in my letter that it was time for him to begin his military training."

"She hated to lose him, but she knows he is old enough now to leave the nest."

"What about your mission to Licinius and Galerius?"

"Licinius is playing a waiting game, but I'm sure he will come over to your side once you win control of Italy."

"And Galerius?"

"Our old enemy suffers much from a plague that has afflicted his whole body. You'll find this hard to believe, but he is obsessed with the conviction that he has offended the Christian god and is being punished because of it."

"I don't know anyone who deserves it more."

"I suspect Galerius realizes that. But having filled his treasury with Christian gold and enriched himself with their property, he now wants to make peace with them. He has even published an edict of tolerance, allowing Christians all the rights they enjoyed before the persecutions." Dacius took a parchment scroll from a pocket in his tunic and handed it to Constantine. "Here, read it for yourself."

The document was simply worded, informing all officials that henceforth members of the Christain faith were to be allowed to worship as they pleased, to rebuild their churches and to regain the honors many of them had enjoyed before the edicts of Diocletian.

"What about Maximin Daia?" Constantine asked. "Will he obey this edict?"

"Daia does as he pleases, from what I heard. As long as a single gold coin can be extorted from the Christians for his own purse, he will continue to afflict them. What are you going to do about Galerius' edict?"

"Publish it, of course. After all, I've been doing the same thing in Gaul and Britain for several years."

"Your mother will be happy to hear it."

"Then she has really become one of them?"

"Yes. She couldn't join the Christians before for fear of embarrassing you while laws were in effect ordering their persecution."

Something in Dacius' tone told Constantine he had not heard the whole story. "Is something wrong with Mother?"

"Not her, but it is with the Christians. They claim to be set apart by their god, but they're proving to be frail vessels indeed."

"What do you mean?"

"As soon as the edicts of persecution were rescinded in the Asian provinces and in Illyria, the Christians began fighting among themselves. Those who let themselves be tortured rather than give up the Scriptures to be burned refuse to recognize the ones who pretended to obey the edicts in order to stay alive. They now claim that only they are the rightful priests and, as a result, bishops are damning other bishops. Even churches that kept together are beginning to split over who is pure and who is not."

"Do you blame them?"

"Not if they admitted they were like other men and subject to the same weaknesses," Dacius said. "But those who resisted the edicts now claim to possess a special holiness and have even set themselves up as a court to judge those whose faith may not have been quite as strong as theirs. I've read the teachings of the man they call Christ more than once, and I found nothing there to support this sort of an idea."

"We will have none of it here in Gaul either," Constantine said firmly. "Properly controlled, I believe Christianity can be a powerful force for keeping order. If one day I am to rule from Persia to Britain and from Germany to Egypt, I must control it everywhere."

"When did you decide that?"

"These past few months, while I was traveling through my own realm and saw how the sect has grown. Do you know Hosius of Córdoba?"

"The Spanish priest who is confessor to Empress Theodora?"

"Yes."

"Only by sight, but he and Eumenius are close friends."

"Hosius is actually a Christian bishop," Constantine explained. "I'm thinking of making him one of my chief advisers, when Eumenius goes with Crispus to Autun."

"Why not become a Christian yourself?"

"I may, some day. The old gods and the old days are dying, Dacius, and Christianity may one day be the strongest religion in the Empire. Diocletian made enemies of them when he issued the edicts of persecution and Rome has suffered because of it. I shall not make that mistake."

III

Constantine had expected Fausta to be difficult while Crispus was in Treves. The boy was less than a decade younger than she and posed a definite threat to her ambitions for the sons she hoped one day to bear. But to his surprise, she was cordial to the youth and even gave a magnificent royal reception for him the evening before he was to depart with Eumenius for Autun. She was in one of her gayest moods and Constantine could see that Crispus was quite bewitched with her, just as he remembered being on a similar occasion in Rome. Afterwards, when they were preparing for bed, he thanked her for her kindness to Crispus.

"Why shouldn't I be nice to your son, darling?" she asked.

"I—I was afraid you would be jealous of him."

"For what?"

"When I move on to rule the rest of the Empire, I hope to name Crispus Caesar in Gaul, Britain and Spain."

"The Empire is large enough for all your sons," she assured him. "Not only Crispus, but the ones I shall bear you, too."

Constantine drew a long sigh of relief for Fausta could be quite difficult when it suited her—as in the matter of Theodora and her children. And the last thing he wanted during the days of crisis which would surely come with the death of Galerius was domestic quarreling.

"We may not be far from the time when my realm will increase," he told her. "Dacius says Galerius is dying and Licinius will probably not be able to stand against your brother very long."

"It will be good to get back to Rome again!" The fact that he could hardly gain control of Rome without first destroying her brother seemed not to trouble her. "You don't know how I miss it."

"Both of us have always known our stay in Gaul would not be permanent."

"You weren't so sure when I first met you in Rome," she reminded him. "Or when you tried to persuade me to run away with you at Neapolis. You see how wrong it would have been to set Father and Maxentius against you then? Everything has worked out just as I planned."

"Even your father's death?"

"Not the way it happened, of course. But Father could never have become Emperor of the West again. Neither you nor Maxentius would have allowed it."

"And now only Maxentius stands in my way—"

"*Our* way, darling. Remember, I started planning all this when I saw you fight Crocus at Nicomedia."

"Our way then," he added, smiling. "But what shall I do with Maxentius?"

"Banish him to Africa or somewhere else when you take control of Italy. My brother isn't fit to rule; he's proved that by the mess of things he has made in Rome. Stop worrying about him and come to bed. I'll decide what to do when the time comes."

Constantine was too pleased at having Fausta in a good mood to argue about the role she had played in his success. Besides, he would have been the first to admit that there was much truth in what she had said. But had he taken the trouble to think about it, he might have wondered whether, having so easily disposed of her own brother, she might just as easily one day dispose of his son—should Crispus ever stand in the way of her ruthless ambition.

IV

Riding with Eumenius and Crispus as far as the villa of Empress Theodora the next morning, Constantine welcomed the chance for a final chat with the plump scholar who had left his tasks as a teacher years before to serve first father and then son well. Eume-

CONSTANTINE

nius had delivered an oration at the funeral of Constantius and another on the marriage of Constantine and Fausta, recounting in the usual flowery terms of the panegyrists the accomplishments of both father and son. And his wise counsel had been invaluable to a young ruler thrust suddenly into a position of grave responsibility.

"We have come a long way together, old friend," Constantine said as they rode along, with Crispus galloping ahead through the countryside, impatient to reach Autun and begin his military training. "I shall miss you very much."

"And I you, Augustus," Eumenius said. "But a scholar should not absent himself too long from the halls of learning, else he may lose his ability to think, when no end is in view."

"Why would a man think to no purpose?"

"You are a soldier, so such may seem foolish to you, but some of the greatest discoveries in history have been that way. Are you familiar with the story of how Archimedes discovered a way of measuring the volume of an irregular object?"

"No. Is it important?"

Eumenius chuckled. "So important that the principle explains how a ship floats. According to the story, the king of the Greek city where Archimedes lived gave some pure silver to a silversmith to make a crown. When it was delivered, he suspected that the silversmith might have mixed base metal with the silver, keeping the rest for himself, and gave Archimedes the task of deciding the question. At first Archimedes could find no answer because he could not measure the crown. Then one day his servant filled his bath to the top of the tub and when he got in, the water ran over."

"What is so unique about that?"

"To most people nothing. But to Archimedes it meant that a body immersed in water displaces a volume equal to its own."

"But that is obvious."

"Perhaps, though no one had set it down as a principle before. Anyway, it told Archimedes how to measure the volume of the crown, simply by immersing it in a container filled with water and placed in a pan to catch what ran over. When he measured the amount in the pan, he knew the volume of the crown and its weight was easily determined with an ordinary pair of scales. Then by using a block of pure silver, he was able to determine the density of silver and solve his problem."

"What was the answer?"

"The silversmith kept his head. Since then any mathematician who knows the density of an object can tell whether or not it will float. Remember when you used dry logs to cross the Rhine and capture Ascaricus and Regaisus? You were utilizing the principle Archimedes discovered."

"If I give you all the money you need to support your school at Autun, will you guarantee to solve all my knotty problems for me?" Constantine asked with a smile.

"Not guarantee—no one can do that. But scholars must eat and be protected from harm like anyone else. You have brought peace and prosperity to Gaul and with it a climate favoring the search for knowledge. Be sure that our minds will always be available to you."

"Then tell me whether I'm right in encouraging the Christians."

"You ask me, when you know I am not one of them?"

"I ask you *because* you are not one of them," Constantine told him. "And because I trust you to give me an honest answer."

"I think you are right," Eumenius assured him. "The uprising of the *bagaudae* here in Gaul showed that the day when great landowners can disregard the welfare of those who till the land is over, but we will always have the poor with us. Christianity appeals to the poor, the downtrodden and the hopeless more than to any other group, so it is certain to grow—until it too becomes rich and powerful, as did the priests and temples of Jupiter in Rome."

"Will it go the way of the other religions then?"

"Yes, unless their god is really stronger than all others, as they claim. And unless his son really did come to earth to give men the gift of eternal life."

"If you think that might be true, why aren't you a Christian, Eumenius?"

"Perhaps I'm too old to change."

"You're younger in spirit and thought than I am."

"Perhaps that's a reason too," Eumenius admitted. "Logic tells me what the Christians claim is impossible. After all, many religions include belief in a god who becomes a man, is killed, and then rises

again. But none of them give men the courage to die willingly for
their faith, as many thousands of Christians did during the persecution. And I have friends who swear they have heard the man they
call Christ speak to them in their hearts, as he is supposed to have
done to their Apostle Paul on the road to Damascus."

"Would you believe if he appeared to you in a dream, or a vision?"

"Yes, I think I would, if I could be sure my mind had not con-
jured up something that wasn't there, as men see visions in the
desert when dying of thirst. Why do you ask?"

Constantine told of his visit to Dura on the Euphrates; the strange
effect the painting of the shepherd on the wall there had had upon
him; and the comfort and assurance he'd received when he'd taken
the torch later that night and gone to look into the eyes, which had
somehow seemed not to have been painted at all but to be alive.

"You may have had a vision of the man called Christ," Eumenius
admitted. "Others have had much the same experience."

"Then you cannot give me the answer?"

"No, Augustus. If I could, perhaps I would no longer doubt myself."

v

Hosius of Córdoba read carefully the edict Constantine planned
to publish, then handed it back. "This is a great thing for the
followers of Christ throughout the Empire, Augustus," he said. "I
will send a letter to the other bishops, asking them to pray for the
soul of Emperor Galerius."

"But Galerius was the one who instigated the persecution and
sent so many to their deaths."

"How much a man sinned is not important, Augustus, but whether
he truly repents."

"Even when he is only seeking to purchase peace for his soul?"

"Why else would a man change his ways? The peace that comes
from God is beyond the understanding of those who have not experienced it. The Lord Christ puts no barriers in the way of any
who would seek it."

"Eumenius has recommended you as one of my close advisers," Constantine told him. "Will you accept the post?"

Hosius did not answer for a moment. "Was it only because of my friend's recommendation that you chose me?" he asked finally.

"No. Eumenius only encouraged me in the decision. More than anything else I want Gaul to be stable and prosperous and I think your church can help me keep it that way, if we work together. Besides, I would know more about this faith of yours myself."

Many eyebrows were raised when a Christian—and a Spaniard —took up residence in the palace at Treves as a close adviser to the Emperor, but Constantine did not trouble himself about them. Important things were happening on two fronts, neither concerning directly his own province, or prefecture, of Gaul, it was true, but both of great importance to the Empire.

As Dacius had predicted, Galerius continued to go downhill and died some months later. Both Licinius and Maximin Daia moved at once to claim the territory he had governed and in a few weeks their armies faced each other at the Bosporus and the Hellespont, with the watery barrier of the Sea of Marmara between them. Here wisdom prevailed, however, and the rival Augusti of the East prudently decided that if they dissipated each other's strength in a civil war, neither would benefit and either Maxentius or Constantine would then be able to move in and take control. The two therefore made a pact to divide Galerius' old holdings between them—the provinces of Asia falling to the lot of Maximin Daia, while those of Europe went to Licinius. And since the Hellespont, the Sea of Marmara, and the Bosporus formed a natural barrier between Europe and Asia, the watercourse they formed was named as the boundary between the two Emperors.

Licinius chose to remain at Galerius' old capital of Sirmium in the Danube country, while Daia ruled mainly from Antioch in Syria. Meanwhile, a minor uprising in one of the African provinces gave Maxentius an opportunity to replenish his treasury and gain further power. Moving quickly across the narrow strait separating Sicily from Carthage on the Libyan coast, he laid waste to that fertile and rich province, seizing all riches that came into his hands and killing the owners.

During the subsequent triumph celebrated when he returned to

Rome, Maxentius flaunted his spoils. But, in spite of his new-found wealth, he did nothing to lessen the heavy tribute demanded each year from Rome and, in order to satisfy his passion for luxury and sybaritic living, sold consulships and preceptorships to the highest bidders, who then enriched themselves by oppressing the areas they ruled. Nor were the Senators themselves exempt from oppression, the so-called "Free Gifts" being demanded of them at every opportunity. Even worse, wives and daughters of prominent men were forced to yield to Maxentius and the licentious group of sycophants surrounding him, or see the men of their family hauled before the courts, executed, and their possessions appropriated by the State.

Watching closely from his capital at Treves the steady disintegration of the Prefecture of Italy, Constantine made two important moves in regard to it. First he sent a friendly letter to Licinius suggesting that emissaries representing each of them meet near Vindobona* on the northern frontier to discuss matters of common importance. And when Licinius sent a favorable reply Dacius, now a general and known everywhere as the personal representative of the most powerful among the four Augusti ruling the Roman Empire, was dispatched to Vindobona. In addition to the fact that Dacius and Licinius had both been centurions and thus in a sense spoke the same language, Constantine had not forgotten that Licinius had been a friend of his father and had warned him to flee on the night when Galerius had planned his death.

"At first Licinius would not commit himself to an alliance between you," Dacius reported upon his return to Treves. "He is afraid of an attack by Daia."

"Then you had to play the second card?"

"Yes. As your representative, I offered him Princess Constantia in marriage."

"And he agreed?"

"He was as eager as any bridegroom, when I described her to him," Dacius said dryly. "After all, she is a very beautiful girl. But will she agree?"

"Constantia is my father's daughter and knows her duty as a prin-

* Vienna

cess in the royal family. Besides, she will become an Augusta when she marries Licinius."

"*She* may gain by it, but I doubt if *you* will," Dacius said. "Licinius is a poor ally; he's so afraid of Maximin Daia that he will hardly make a move. Besides, Maxentius has been making overtures to Daia, suggesting that they join together against you and Licinius."

"It's a logical move."

"Licinius' spies report that Maxentius offered Daia help in gaining all of the East for himself, if Daia will keep Licinius from attacking Maxentius, when he goes against you."

"Then Maxentius must have decided to attack through Raetia, hoping to arouse the Germans against me. This information could be more important than anything else you discovered, Dacius."

"I am sure it is," Dacius agreed. "With Licinius' fear of Daia keeping him anchored in Illyricum, you will be free to rid the world of a viper named Maxentius."

"And then on to Rome! He who has the city holds the key to the Empire."

"Tell me," Dacius said. "Has there ever been a time—since Marios left you with me in Nicomedia—when you doubted that you would one day rule the whole Empire?"

"Yes, once." Constantine's face sobered.

"When was that?"

"At Dura, when we were behind the Persian lines."

"I remember it well. But you couldn't have been in doubt very long, for the next morning you had a whole plan of action outlined. What gave you confidence?"

"I'm not sure, but I think it was a sign—from heaven."

21

Busy BUILDING the prosperity of Gaul to the highest possible level and forging a powerful military machine there, Constantine nevertheless kept a close watch upon events in Italy through his spies. With the wealth he had seized in Libya at his command, Maxentius was not long in taking the first crucial step in the deadly game of intrigue and war being played out for control of the Roman Empire. He ordered all statues of the Augustus of Gaul torn down and degraded publicly and Constantine's name erased from public buildings in Rome and throughout Italy—twin insults obviously intended to provoke Constantine into starting the war that had now become inevitable.

Constantine, however, was biding his time, waiting for Maxentius to make a move that would give him the advantage he so badly needed because of the inferiority in numbers of the Gallic legions. He had been busy building up his army for two years since the death of Maximian, but it still numbered only some ninety thousand men and eight thousand of the fleet and highly trained Gallic horse commanded by Crocus. And since at least a fourth of these were required at all times to hold the frontier of the Rhine against the Germanic chieftains, the eighty thousand men Maxentius was reported able to put into the field, along with forty thousand Carthaginian troops raised in the Libyan provinces, outnumbered Constantine's forces nearly four to one.

Several things were in Constantine's favor, however. One was the fact that his army was a highly trained fighting machine, veteran of many border clashes and commanded by experienced officers, while Maxentius' troops had been softened by idleness and debauchery and the newer levies had never been tried in battle at all. In the political sphere Constantine had moved to tie Licinius closer to him by officially announcing the betrothal of Princess Constantia to his fellow Augustus. Another move was made for him when, unexpectedly, a delegation of Senators and noblemen from Rome appeared at Treves, asking for an audience.

"We come at the peril of our lives and the certain loss of our positions and possessions, Augustus," said the spokesman for the delegation, a venerable and highly respected Senator named Marcellinus. "But we could not remain inactive while a wild beast named Maxentius ravages the city we love and reduces Italy to poverty."

"Only a few months ago, a wealthy matron named Sophronia plunged a dagger into her heart rather than yield to the embraces of lustful men on the order of the Augustus of Rome," another of the visitors added. He was a plump man with shrewd gray eyes who gave his name as Adrian and in whom, Constantine suspected, there was more than a trace of Greek blood.

Constantine did not doubt the truth of what he was hearing, for his own spies in Rome had sent him similar accounts. But he could not risk his vastly smaller army against the might of Maxentius merely to rescue the Senate which had, not so long ago, invited Maxentius to seize control in the hope of seeing Rome's former glories—and particularly their own privileges—restored. He did not, however, remind the men before him of their fatal error, for he already saw how he could use the presence of the Senators in Treves to legalize his own descent upon Rome, when the proper time came.

"How many of the Senate would vote to depose the Emperor Maxentius, noble Marcellinus?" he asked.

"All of us, for each has suffered at his hands," Marcellinus said promptly. "I myself have often heard him give his soldiers the orders: 'Fruimini! Dissipate! Prodiget!'"

"Drink, wine and debauch," said Dacius, who was standing at Constantine's elbow. "You'll have trouble weaning any legions away from him, if Maxentius gives them that much license."

Constantine was thinking the same thing and the thought brought him no comfort. He had insured the neutrality of Licinius in the coming struggle through the projected marriage with Constantia, which he intended to postpone until Rome was in his hands. But that still left him outnumbered at least three to one.

"I can understand your indignation, noble Marcellinus," he said soothingly. "The glorious name of Rome has indeed been besmirched by its ruler. But has the Senate ever voted to remove him from office?"

"How could we, when it would mean our death?" the old nobleman cried. "We only managed to escape by smuggling ourselves aboard a galley owned by Adrian here."

"I am a merchant trading with the East, so I was not watched as closely as the others," Adrian explained. "Augustus Maxentius maintains a connection with Augustus Maximin Daia, who has his own warehouses in Antioch and Caesarea, and ships of my fleet sometimes took part in that trade. We escaped by pretending to be bound for Caesarea."

"How strong is the political alliance between Maxentius and Maximin Daia?" Constantine asked.

"In my opinion, it is only a marriage of convenience in order to exert pressure on Augustus Licinius to remain neutral," Adrian said. "In doing business, I have talked to many Senators and I can tell you that privately the majority of them have expressed their intention to welcome you, when you free Rome from its tyrant."

This was what Constantine had been wanting—a vote by the Senate, however unorthodox the method of its taking, that he could claim as constituting an invitation to unseat Maxentius.

"Will you swear that such a vote was taken?" he asked Adrian. "And that the result was as you described?"

The merchant's eyes met Constantine's while each weighed the other. Constantine knew perfectly well what he was asking of the merchant-Senator and he was sure that Adrian too understood. If he became Emperor of Rome, the merchant could profit in many ways, not the least through acting as a factor in Constantine's personal trading ventures with the rest of the Empire. But if he failed, Adrian would go down with him and could hope for no mercy from Maxentius.

When Adrian smiled, Constantine knew he had judged his man well. Like a bettor assaying the chances of a chariot in winning a race, the other man had made the final decision by evaluating the most important single factor—the driver.

"I will swear to it, Augustus. And I will affix my name to the scroll upon which it is written."

Just behind him, Constantine heard Dacius give the short tuneless whistle he used to express approval of a particularly clever move. "I will do what I can to free Rome," he promised the Senators. "But I shall expect all of you to follow my armies and assure other Senators of my respect for their noble counsel, when finally we reach the capital."

"One thing, Augustus." It was Marcellinus. "Is it true that you have become a Christian?"

In his chair on the front row of seats in the audience chamber, where the visitors were being received, Constantine saw Hosius of Córdoba look up sharply. "No, I have not," he answered without hesitation. "Why do you ask?"

"It is rumored in Rome that you favor them, as your father did."

"All the Augusti signed the edict of toleration published by Emperor Galerius." The frosty note in Constantine's voice might have intimidated a younger man, but Marcellinus was a veteran of many years in the Senate. He had faced emperors and would-be emperors before and, like most of the Senators, clung to the old privileges and customs, even though they had been largely nullified by such as Maxentius and Maximian.

"The Empire was built on the favor of its gods and, if it is to thrive again, we must return to them," the old man said. "Will you sacrifice to Apollo and ask the favor of Rome's gods upon your venture into Italy?"

"I shall sacrifice to both Apollo and Jupiter before starting to liberate Rome, noble Marcellinus," Constantine promised. "And I beg your prayers for my success."

The public audience ended then, but Constantine asked Dacius to bring Adrian to his quarters for a continuation of the discussion.

"Did you say you are a merchant?" he asked the plump Senator, when the three of them were alone.

"Yes, Augustus."

"Then you must have business connections in the north—perhaps in Raetia and Venetia?"

"Lately I have been sending some supplies there," Adrian said.

"On whose orders?"

"Augustus Maxentius. He feels that he can trust me because of my trading connections with Augustus Maximin Daia."

"Can he?" Constantine asked bluntly.

Adrian's eyes suddenly took on a bleak look. "A month ago my niece, a beautiful girl just entering womanhood, attracted the attention of a tribune in the Praetorian Guard. She was seized in her own house that night and taken to the barracks of the guard."

"Say no more," Constantine told him. "I ask your forgiveness for my question."

"You were right to ask, Augustus." Adrian forced his voice under control. "After three days in the hands of the Praetorians, my niece threw herself into the Tiber. I gave up everything I possessed to come here, hoping you would avenge her."

"She shall be avenged," Constantine promised. "And your possessions shall be returned to you."

"The first will be enough, Augustus."

"Is it your belief that Maxentius intends to attack me through Raetia?"

"No, Augustus."

"Why do you say that?"

"Because larger amounts of supplies are being stocked in the area around Susa and Mediolanum—Milan."

"Then Raetia is to be a feint!" Dacius exclaimed. "The main attack will be delivered by way of Mount Cenis."

The three principal passages between Gaul and Italy were: the northern route through the passes of Mount St. Bernard, the central by way of Mount Cenis, and the extreme southern route by way of Mount Geneva. If Maxentius, by a feint in the north, managed to lure Constantine's forces into concentrating there, he could then drive almost unopposed through the region of Mount Cenis by way of Taurinum* and Segusio or Susa. From there he could strike a dagger into the very heart of Gaul, capturing Lugdunum and paralyzing trade between the northern districts along the Rhine and the populous and fertile areas to the south.

* Turin

"We shall have to watch Maxentius more closely, Dacius," Constantine said thoughtfully. "I hadn't given him credit for being so clever."

"It isn't Maxentius but his generals, Augustus—particularly Pompeianus," Adrian said. "He has charge of the forces in the north."

"I remember Pompeianus," said Dacius. "He's probably the second best man I ever trained." Then he grinned. "So what is the first going to do?"

Constantine went to the window and looked out upon the bustling city. Once again he had to make a decision to commit his forces in a single attack, since to divide them any more than it had already been necessary to divide them, in order to protect the Rhine frontier, could be sheer suicide.

"I shall do what I have always done when the odds are against me," he said, when he turned back to the others. "Carry the battle to the enemy."

"And give up your resolve not to attack Maxentius until he attacks you?" Dacius asked.

"No. We will make Maxentius attack us by launching his feint through Raetia."

"Make?" Dacius' eyebrows rose in an unspoken question.

"Lure then. Tomorrow I shall sacrifice to Apollo and Jupiter in the new temples here and announce that I am sending the army to counter an attack expected through Raetia. Maxentius must have spies here—I have enough of them in Rome. They will send word of my decision to him and he will launch his feint in the north to hold me there."

"While we move south to Mount Cenis." Dacius shook his head admiringly. "I would give a lot to see Maxentius' face, when we suddenly appear on the plains before Susa and Taurinum."

22

TRUE TO HIS PROMISE to Marcellinus, Constantine took part in solemn ceremonies of sacrifice to Apollo and Jupiter before his army marched leisurely toward the northernmost of the three routes leading into the Prefecture of Italy by way of the Alpine passes. On the march he was accompanied by Hosius of Córdoba, the Christian leader, upon whose advice he had come more and more to depend since Eumenius had gone to Autun. And each night he found peace after the cares of the day in listening while Hosius read the Christian scriptures aloud.

Couriers had been sent ahead to the border of Raetia to bring back immediate word of any attack there. And just as Constantine had predicted the feint attack was soon delivered.

"Maxentius is playing into your hands," Crocus said happily, when word of the attack in the north came to the main body of the army, still days away from the Alpine passes. "We will descend upon him before he is ready to fight."

"Our forces are still outnumbered," Constantine reminded the Gallic king, but the same note of excitement was in his voice. "Still, the advantage of surprise may make up for that. Be sure to keep Crispus near you."

Knowing from his own experience what the campaign would mean to the boy, Constantine had sent to Autun for Crispus to join them and had arranged for him to serve as an aide to Crocus, who, as usual, commanded the cavalry. Crispus had grown to young manhood almost overnight, since going to Autun for training, and his skill in weaponry and horsemanship was already a legend at the school.

Once news of Maxentius' feint in the north was received, no time was wasted in turning southward to the great highroad leading eastward from Lugdunum by way of Mount Cenis. Constantine set a fast pace, with an advance guard of cavalry ranging ahead to intercept any of Maxentius' forces that might be spearheading the attack upon Gaul and prevent the enemy from learning that their route of march had been changed.

Maxentius, however, acted just as he had foreseen. Entrusting the military leadership to his generals, he remained in Rome, confident that Constantine's army was busy pursuing the small force, which had made the feint against Raetia, ever deeper into the Alpine passes where—even were the ruse discovered—they could never extricate themselves in time to re-form and defend the vital centers along the Rhône.

Long before Maxentius' generals realized what was happening, Constantine's army appeared before Susa. Battering rams and fire carts were pushed up to the city gates, scaling ladders were placed against its walls and, while the garrison was still trying to organize an effective resistance, the fortifications were breached and the city was lost. On Constantine's strict orders, no looting was allowed, however, since he wanted word to go ahead of him that he came not as a conqueror but as a defender, to relieve the oppressed people from the intolerable burden of rule by a monster.

When part of Susa caught fire, Constantine delayed his march eastward for a day while his army fought the flames beside the populace, quelling them and saving the city from destruction. As a result, Maxentius' generals gained the time needed to mobilize a force intended to block the invading army. By the time Constantine's forces reached the plain before Taurinum, some forty miles to the east, they found a considerable body of shock troops drawn up in the wedge formation for which the Italian cavalry were best known.

The effectiveness of the foot soldier, bulwark of the army in the time of Julius Caesar, had been considerably diminished by new tactics in warfare and new weapons borrowed from the East. The traditional armed square of the earlier legions had long since been replaced by heavy cavalry, both men and horses armored with thick plates of metal cleverly jointed so as to give protection from arrows and javelins. The ponderous cavalry was designed to exert its major effect largely by weight, however, since the heaviness of the armor made swift maneuvering impossible.

This massive display of armor Constantine and his army found arrayed before them for the first time when they approached Taurinum at the foot of the Alps through which they had just passed. Crocus came riding back from his first assay of the situation to where Constantine and his staff had gathered on a hill that gave a full view of the plain which would shortly become a bloody battleground.

"They've done just what you predicted," he told Constantine jubilantly. "The gates of the city have been opened so the garrison could come out to help destroy us here on the plain."

"And they might do just that," Constantine warned, "if they were fighting other than Gallic cavalry. Those armored horsemen could crush a line of footmen without incurring a wound."

Below him on the plain, Constantine's forces were beginning to advance in the traditional Roman wall of shields, with Crocus' cavalry equally divided on either flank.

"I can hear their commanders boasting now that we are fit only to fight untrained Germans," Dacius said. "Watch this closely, Crispus, you'll learn more here today than you would at Autun in a year."

Constantine glanced at his son—who was now almost as tall as he—and a surge of pride swelled within him. He must see more of Crispus, he reminded himself; the cares of ruling and trying to anticipate the actions of Maxentius had occupied him too much lately for more than a brief visit to Autun, where Eumenius had reported that the boy possessed an eager and inquisitive mind.

"The enemy is moving, Augustus," Crocus warned.

"Give the order when you're ready." A glance at Crispus told him the boy was fairly bursting with excitement and, though his first impulse was that of a father to protect his son, he knew what a taste of action would mean to the boy.

"And take Crispus with you," he called to Crocus as the Gallic commander was mounting his horse.

"Come on, young Constantine," Crocus shouted. "It will be like the old days when your father and I rode together."

Crispus was on his horse in a single bound, racing down the

slope in the wake of the Gallic king, while behind them Crocus' trumpeter blew a series of quick blasts on his trumpet. As the notes floated out across the field, the swift Gallic cavalry—unencumbered by the armor that made the mounted troops of Maxentius' army resemble a wedge of land turtles advancing ponderously across the field—began a wide flanking movement that took them clear of their heavier counterpart.

Only for a moment was Constantine able to follow the two flying figures on horseback moving down the slope. Then, as they disappeared among the Gallic horse, he turned his attention to the ranks of the legions advancing doggedly with the seeming intention of pitting their puny strength against the wedge of armor moving toward them. On they went, until only a short distance separated the two forces. Then, when Constantine spoke a quiet order to his own trumpeter, a single note sounded, swelled immediately by a mass of sound as the trumpeter of each cohort acknowledged the order. At the same moment, the columns of men marching against the point of the cavalry advance wheeled suddenly and a gap rapidly widened just in front of Maxentius' armored horsemen.

As the impetus of their own movement carried the armored troops of the enemy forward, their very ungainliness proved to be their greatest weakness. Confusion reigned among them as the commander of each *ala* sought to regroup in order to cope with an enemy whose ranks had suddenly melted away. Meanwhile, taking advantage of the confusion, Constantine's foot soldiers attacked on either side where the armor of the cavalry was jointed and therefore the weakest. At the same moment, Crocus' cavalry split into four groups, one of the two on each flank racing on toward the city of Taurinum in order to seize and close the gates, so the army on the field would have no place of safety to which they could retreat.

The other and larger group wheeled to attack the enemy foot who had been advancing behind the armored horse. Caught from both flanks and rear, Maxentius' army was turned in moments from a disciplined and highly organized force into a confused milling mass. With the screams of dying horses and men making it quite impossible to hear the orders by which the unit commanders might have been able to save the day, the battle quickly turned into a rout. By now, too, Crocus' cavalry had burst through the defenses of Taurinum and, making short work of the few men left to guard them, quickly closed the gates, denying to Maxentius' retreating army even that refuge.

The battle had begun in mid-morning and ranged into early afternoon, but at no time was there any doubt concerning the outcome. The clever maneuver designed by Constantine and Crocus to utilize the swift and highly maneuverable cavalry of Gaul more than overcame the advantages in weight and armor possessed by the heavily protected Italian cavalry. By mid-afternoon Maxentius' forces were in full retreat but, with the gates of the city barred against them, they had no choice except to surrender or be cut to pieces. By nightfall the battle was over and the gates were opened again for the triumphant passage of Constantine and his troops into the city.

Though Taurinum was now at his mercy, Constantine continued his role of deliverer rather than conqueror, and the city was forced to provide no tribute other than food and lodging for his army. With the army Maxentius had gathered on the plains for the invasion of Gaul now largely destroyed, no major barrier lay between Constantine and Milan, the former capital of Maximian. A few days later his army marched into that city unopposed, to be greeted joyously by its people while Constantine himself was hailed as Emperor of the West. At his father's side rode Crispus, proud of having bloodied his sword in the first battle of his life.

Rome was an easy southward march of some four hundred miles by way of the Aemilian and Flaminian highways, two of the greatest thoroughfares in Italy. With a jubilant and victorious army at his back and embassies coming in by the hour from the important cities of northern Italy and the Alpine provinces, acclaiming him Augustus and thanking him for deliverance, the temptation was great for Constantine to make the same sort of swift march on Rome that had carried him through the Alps. But even before he reached Milan, he had received news that a large army was at Verona, almost a hundred miles to the west. Moreover, it was now commanded by General Ruricius Pompeianus, who, in spite of the earlier defeats, could be counted on to fight with skill and daring.

Somewhat reluctantly, therefore, Constantine continued east-

ward and spent several weeks in the siege of Verona, before that
stronghold was reduced and Pompeianus' army destroyed. The
time taken up by the campaign was far from a total loss, however,
for now all of northern Italy and the Alpine provinces were in his
hands. Furthermore, Maxentius failed to oppose his brother-in-law's
southward march at the Apennines or in the Umbrian passes and
was reported to be cowering in his palace at Rome, paralyzed with
fear and convinced that the gods who had seemed to favor him
until now had at last deserted him.

Constantine did not make the mistake of believing these reports,
however. According to his evaluation of the situation, Maxentius
had chosen to remain at Rome with the greater part of his forces
because he was confident that the highly trained troops of the Praetorian Guard and the Moorish cavalry raised during his African
expedition would prove equal to any forces Constantine could
bring against him. And since—numerically at least—Maxentius was
correct, Constantine moved carefully down through central Italy,
taking almost two months to reach a point seven miles north of
Rome, where he halted and made camp.

II

Saxa Rubra—where the reddish soft earth of the *tufa*, from which
Rome's underground city of tombs was carved, broke through to
the surface—was the first station of the Imperial Post on the old
Roman Via Flaminia. To the left lay the Silvus Cimininus and to
the south the plains of the Tiber, but Constantine had little hope
of luring Maxentius from the safety of Rome's fortifications to an
open battlefield.

On the day after his army took up a position in Saxa Rubra, he
rode up to the height crowned by the delicately beautiful Villa of
Livia, accompanied by Senators Marcellinus and Adrian and a few
aides. Leaving them, he went a little way by himself, seeking some
peace in the quiet beauty of the castle which had been built during
the golden age of Augustus for the gracious Empress Livia, who
had lived there much of the time.

She had been—he remembered from his small readings of Roman

history—scrupulously chaste, a virtue he was sure his own wife, Fausta, possessed. But Fausta could certainly not lay claim to Livia's second quality, that of never quarreling with her husband's actions. Their increasingly frequent altercations usually ended in reconciliations that were just as violent, making, he was forced to admit, for an exciting married life. Nor did he find it in his heart to condemn her, since he knew the reason for her petulance lay in her failure to bear him a son—for which he was at least equally responsible—although she had given him two fine daughters. But even the quiet beauty of Livia's villa somehow failed to stir him from the strange depression that had gripped his spirit at the prospect of laying siege to Rome.

"Have you sacrificed to the gods asking for victory, Augustus?" Marcellinus had ridden up to where Constantine had reined in his horse and the anxiety in the old Senator's voice broke into the younger man's thoughts like cold water upon a sensitive tooth.

"What gods?" he demanded a little shortly.

"The gods of our fathers! The gods who made Rome great!"

"The proper sacrifices have already been made, noble Marcellinus," Constantine said soothingly, but his mind was busy with something else the old man had said.

The gods of our fathers! Who had been the god of his own father? he asked himself. Was it Apollo of the sun and light, who was widely worshiped in Gaul? Was it Jupiter Capitolinus, patron god of Rome itself? Was it the Christian god? Or his son, of whom Hosius had been reading to him from the Christian scriptures?

The Empress Theodora, he remembered, had said that Constantius had been strongly drawn to the Christian faith, as—Constantine freely admitted—he was himself. And remembering that though he had ordered the proper sacrifices to Apollo and Jupiter, he had said nothing to Hosius about some similar act of devotion to the Christian god, he made a mental note to ask Hosius how one went about invoking the favor of the man called Jesus Christ.

Or was it the Father of Jesus who was the real god of the Christians? Somehow, even though Hosius had tried to explain it, he had never been able to understand just what significance each of them held—or the part played by what they called the Holy Spirit, which he couldn't understand at all. But certainly if gods took a part in human affairs—as most humans devoutly believed they did—he must leave no stone unturned to invoke the favor of all deities upon the undertaking in which he was engaged, the most important one of his life.

Adrian met them as they were riding back to camp. Constantine had found him to be capable and intelligent, especially when it came to dickering for supplies the army required in the cities through which they had passed. A young man in the rough clothing of a peasant rode behind the merchant.

"This is my nephew, Camianus, Augustus," Adrian said. "He escaped from Rome yesterday by disguising himself as a peasant and pretending to be the driver of a food cart. I thought you should hear at once what he can tell us of the happenings inside the city."

"By all means give us any information you have, Camianus," Constantine said kindly to the obviously nervous young man.

"The Emperor Maxentius has invoked the aid of the priests and the soothsayers, Augustus," Camianus said.

"You see, Marcellinus." Constantine turned to the old Senator. "Our enemy invoked the gods too. Who will they support?"

"The side that is right, of course, Augustus. Yours."

"Let us hope so."

"They say the Emperor even sent for the Sibylline Books and had them consulted," Camianus volunteered.

"What was the verdict?" There was no levity in Constantine's tone now, for the recorded oracles of the Sibyl—the priestess of Apollo at Cumae—were considered to be the final decisions of heaven on human affairs.

Camianus hesitated, obviously not wanting to answer.

"Speak up, boy," Constantine ordered. "No one will hurt you."

"It is said in the streets, Augustus, that the books predict the death of the enemy of Rome. Augustus Maxentius gave a great birthday feast to celebrate the verdict."

Beside him, Constantine heard Marcellinus catch his breath and knew what the old man was thinking, in fact what anyone in Rome would almost certainly think of such a prediction by the famed oracles.

"Am I the enemy of Rome, Camianus?" he asked.

"Oh no, Augustus," the young man exclaimed. "The people look to you as their saviour, but the nobles and the Praetorian Guard —" He did not finish the sentence and, looking at the grave faces of Marcellinus and Adrian, Constantine knew they were thinking the same thing. The people of Rome, the masses who thronged the *subura,* subsisting on grain given them through the generosity of the Emperor, shouting for a hero today and crying for his death tomorrow, might look to him as their saviour. But hardly anyone would lift even so much as a dagger to help him capture the city for fear that the gods had already decreed that he would fail.

Nobody spoke as they rode down the hill from the lovely villa toward the immense spread of the camp set against the pinkish background of the *tufa*-tinged earth at Saxa Rubra. Constantine's head was bent, as he racked his brain, seeking some daring feat, some new and untried military tactics that might lure Maxentius to cross the Tiber and leave the protection of Rome's walls.

In his heart, he knew that were he in Maxentius' place, he would not even consider such a move. Instead, secure in the knowledge that the masses of the people would place the same interpretation upon the verdict of the Sibylline Books that Marcellinus, Adrian and Camianus—and in truth himself—had done, he would remain within the walls, while the attackers spent their strength, until finally they were forced to withdraw. Then he would harry them all the way back along the road they had traveled so triumphantly over a period of not much more than four months.

"Did you mention the Sibylline Books in the camp, Camianus?" Constantine asked Adrian's nephew.

"He didn't have to, Augustus," Adrian volunteered. "Some peasants, who brought supplies for sale this morning, heard of it from others who had been in the city. By now it is all over the camp."

So the damage was already done, Constantine thought. Nor could he blame the troops—who until now had considered their young commander almost a god—for being oppressed by the knowledge that a god himself had seemed to predict Constantine's death in the coming battle for Rome. To point out that oracles and soothsayers customarily couched their pronouncements in words that could be interpreted several ways—and thus be proved true whatever the outcome—would be of little avail, he knew. It was first impression that seized hold of the emotions, and that had already been done.

A sudden uproar from the camp ahead brought Constantine upright in his saddle, looking to see its cause. Everywhere he saw men falling on their faces in the reddish earth, crying out a name he did not understand—until suddenly he realized that it was "Apollo!"

"A sign!" Camianus croaked, his voice a hoarse bleat of terror. "A sign! There in the heaven—around the sun!"

III

Constantine turned quickly to look westward where the sun still hung several hours above the distant sea. He saw at once what had caught the attention of the troops—and Camianus. Spread over an arc of the sky that covered perhaps a sixteenth part of its total circumference was a strange pattern of light rays flashing through the thin cloud cover that hid the normal blue of the heavens.

"The radiance of Apollo!" Marcellinus' voice broke on the words. "A warning—"

The strange pattern of light against the skies did resemble the rays of the sun streaming out from a glowing center often depicted on the banners and devices of Apollo. But the bars of light crossed at their center also reminded Constantine of something else that eluded him at the moment, a pattern he was certain he had seen before, though he couldn't remember where.

The shining device in the sky was already beginning to fade and the momentary hysteria it had caused was subsiding as Constantine rode down into the camp. He called an order to Crocus to set the men to work, and the Gallic king lifted his voice in a loud bellow, commanding the troops to add an extra wall of palisades to the southern side of the camp. The soldiers moved to obey, though grumbling at the extra duty.

"Do you need my nephew anymore, Augustus?" Adrian asked.

"No. Thank you for the information you brought, Camianus." When Adrian too started to ride away Constantine called him back. "You're a Greek, aren't you, Adrian?"

"On my mother's side, Augustus."

"What do you make of that pattern there in the sky?" The strange device had almost paled now, though the crossed bars of light could still be seen by one who knew where to look. "Do you think it's really a sign from Apollo—a warning?"

"Such a thing is described in some of the ancient writings of the Greeks, Augustus, under the name of a *parhelion*."

"Was it always interpreted as a sign from the gods?"

"Usually, at least by the common people. Some philosophers claim it is formed by a chance pattern of the sun's rays shining through the clouds, but others say it is seen only when the sun is said to be drawing water."

"Of course!" Constantine exclaimed. "We saw it in the west and the sea is only a few miles away."

"Let us hope they didn't see it in Rome, and consider it a sign of favor from Apollo," Adrian said. "With the verdict of the Sibylline Books—and now this—we cannot hope to gain much help from the people inside the walls, if it comes to a siege."

Constantine ate little at the evening meal. The information brought by Camianus and the strange pattern in the clouds depressed him even more than the prospect of laying siege to Rome. To which was added now the conviction that he had seen the pattern formed by the rays of the sun before—though just where still eluded him—and that then it had possessed an entirely different meaning.

From his servant he learned that opinions in the camp concerning the strange phenomenon in the clouds were almost as varied as there were men in the army. But if any consensus existed, it was in favor of a warning from Apollo, a natural assumption since Apollo was often portrayed as Sol Invictus, the god of the sun, with the rays from the burning planet spreading out in a radiating pattern such as had characterized the vision in the sky. None of this, however, gave Constantine any comfort, and finally he resolutely put the whole question of what he had seen in the sky from his mind and composed himself for sleep.

23

THINKING ABOUT IT later, when he had time for thought after the rapid sequence of events, Constantine was never quite sure whether it had been a dream or a vision. The whole episode was so clearly etched in his mind that it could have been either, but somehow he had felt no surprise when the shepherd of the ruined church at Dura on the Euphrates appeared to him. In fact, it was almost as if he were expecting the man whom the Christians called Jesus Christ and whom they considered to be the son of their god.

The shepherd had been dressed as before, in the short robe of those who tended the flocks. There was the same gentleness of features, the same living warmth in the eyes that looked out at him, the same gentle smile. This time, however, he did not carry a lamb in his arms, as he had in the paintings Constantine had seen on the walls of Christian churches. Instead he bore a banner upon which, so clearly outlined that there could be no doubting its identity, was the pattern Constantine and thousands of others had seen painted in broader strokes that afternoon by the rays of the sun against the clouds.

Looking at the banner, Constantine suddenly knew where he had seen the device before and why the vague sense of its familiarity troubled him so much that afternoon. It was the same cryptic pattern he had seen painted on the wall at Dura above the head of the shepherd, the man called Jesus Christ, who now held the banner aloft in his dream—or vision.

The light glowing from shepherd and banner filled the room with a glory almost blinding the viewer. To Constantine it seemed that his every sense was tuned to such a high degree of perceptiveness that every line, every color, every aspect of the scene was etched indelibly into his mind. In the midst of his awareness that he was indeed in the presence of a divine revelation, the visitor spoke, but his voice was not the sound of thunder, like that of a god. Rather it was gentle, like nothing else—it seemed to the viewer—so much as the voice of a shepherd assuring and calming the fears of a sheep that had been lost.

"In this sign, conquer." The words were a promise and a command in one. And suddenly Constantine understood the meaning of both the visitation in the night and the sign emblazoned upon the sky that afternoon, just as he knew at last who had been his father's god and who would henceforth be his own. He sought words of thanks, of praise, but found himself unable to speak. He tried to throw himself at the feet of the heavenly visitor in resignation to divine will, but was unable to move. And so he could only watch, as the glittering banner with its device of crossed lines grew dim and the voice, fading away, echoed back to him again and again with the words: "In this sign, conquer."

Only when the vision was gone did Constantine discover that once again he could move and speak. Wide awake now, he was filled with a sense of exaltation and conviction that victory would be his, a victory without qualification, save that the banner borne by the shepherd in the vision must go before him. Sweating and trembling from the intensity of the experience through which he had just gone, he got to his feet but swayed and was forced to grasp the center pole of the tent to keep from falling. Staggering to the opening, he threw back the flap and let the cool breeze from the nearby sea caress his body as the sentry posted before the tent stiffened to attention.

"Wake my servant, sentry." Constantine's voice was hoarse. "Tell him to bring Bishop Hosius to me at once and send for General Dacius and General Crocus."

The sentry moved off to obey, as Constantine stepped out into the open space before the tent. The vertigo he'd experienced upon arising was gone now and he looked up to the western sky, half expecting to see the shining cross there, as he had seen it that afternoon, but only the dark velvet background of the night with the stars sprinkled upon it met his eyes. The great camp, too, was asleep, except where lights moved about as the servant went to waken the others.

Stepping back into his tent, Constantine put off his sleeping robe and rubbed his sweaty body with a towel. He was knotting the cord of another robe about his waist when Bishop Hosius came in. The dark eyes of the churchman were concerned, until he saw that Constantine did not appear to be ill.

"I have seen the Son of God, Hosius!" Constantine cried. "Here in this tent just now—in a dream or a vision."

"How did it happen, Augustus?"

"Long ago I saw a device above Jesus' head in a painting on the wall of a church at Dura on the Euphrates," Constantine explained. "It was exactly like the sign in the sky this afternoon and Christ himself bore it upon a banner, when I saw him in my dream just now."

Hosius' eyes brightened. "It could have been the secret sign formed by the initials of the Master's name in Greek—the letters Chi and Rho superimposed."

"That was it!" Constantine cried. "The crossed bars of light painted upon the clouds by the sun this afternoon formed the same pattern."

"Many thought they were seeing the sign of Sol Invictus," Hosius reminded him. "The emblem of Apollo does bear a distinct resemblance to it."

"But Jesus Christ himself showed me the same sign here in my tent a few moments ago," Constantine insisted. "He bore a banner with the same device upon it."

"In a dream, Augustus?"

"A dream? A vision? It was so vivid that it could be either. He was here, I tell you. And he spoke to me."

Dacius and Crocus came in just then and Constantine forced himself to be calm while he recounted the circumstances of the vision and the banner borne by the shepherd. "Here," he said, going to a table and seizing a piece of parchment from the sheets left there by a clerk. "I will draw it for you. Crocus, get me a piece of burnt coal from the sentry's fire outside."

Using the piece of charcoal, Constantine sketched upon the parchment the outlines of the device upon the banner held by the shepherd in the vision. It was roughly the same outline, as Hosius had said, of the Greek letter Chi—two crossed bars or lines—upon which was superimposed the Rho—a vertical bar turned over at the top almost in the shape of a shepherd's crook.

"There!" he cried, standing back to look at the sketch. "This device was on the banner he carried. And when he spoke, the words were repeated over and over again: 'In this sign, conquer.'"

"It must be that the god of the Christians favors you in the attack on Rome." There was a great wonder in Crocus' voice.

"What say you, Hosius?" Constantine asked. "After all, he is your god."

"Nay, Augustus," the priest said quietly. "Our god belongs to everyone who accepts him."

"Many who saw the sign in the sky this afternoon thought it was that of Apollo—or Sol Invictus," Dacius cautioned.

"But the vision of Christ here in the tent tonight identified it without question," Constantine insisted.

"Why would the Christian god give you a sign?" Dacius asked.

"Perhaps I can answer that," Hosius said. "Christ is the only Son of the one true God, in whom Augustus Constantine's father believed. The vision we all saw and the device upon the banner borne by our Lord when he appeared to the Emperor tonight in a dream or a vision, is the symbol of immortality and the victory Christ won over death. I think it means, Augustus, that if you march into battle with the banner of our Lord, the *labarum*, before you, God will deliver Rome into your hands."

"It shall go before me," Constantine said without hesitation. "More than that, the device shall be scratched upon the shield of every man who follows me."

He was all eagerness and enthusiasm as he turned to Dacius. "Order skilled craftsmen brought to me at once and rich cloth for the banner. And have a bar welded to a tall spear, tall enough for all to see when it is borne before us, and broad enough to bear the sign."

"Lift ye up a banner upon the high mountain," Hosius said in an odd voice. "Exalt the voice unto them, shake the hand, that they may go into the gates of the nobles."

"What is that?" Constantine asked.

THE MIRACLE OF THE FLAMING CROSS

"A prophecy from the writings of Isaiah, foretelling both the coming and the death of Christ. The support you ordered made for the banner, Augustus—the tall spear with the crossed bar welded upon it. Do you realize that it is the Sign of the Cross—upon which Jesus himself died?"

II

As finally completed in the early hours just before dawn, the *labarum*, whose rough outlines Constantine had drawn with the charcoal, was striking enough to seize the attention of those who followed and the enemy against which it would be borne. At the top was a gilded sphere, borne on a tall standard to which was attached a crossbar in the form—as Hosius had pointed out—of a cross, from which the banner itself hung. As for the design, artisans had been working on it under Constantine's direction since he had seen the vision, emblazoning in precious stones upon rich cloth the pattern of the superimposed letters Chi and Rho as part of a *labarum* of such a large size that anyone seeing it could not doubt its identity.

The whole was barely finished when one of the scouts posted ahead of the army on a height overlooking Rome came riding furiously up the center street and brought his mount to a plowing stop before Constantine's tent. "The enemy is leaving the city!" he shouted. "Their army is already crossing the Tiber over the Milvian Bridge and the pontoon bridges above and below it."

"The promise of the vision is already being fulfilled," Constantine said to Bishop Hosius in an awed voice. "What else could have brought Maxentius out of Rome to give battle upon the plain?"

The call to arms was sounded, and the troops hurried to their places in the battle formation, a maneuver which could be carried out quite rapidly because of the arrangement of the *castra*, or camp, where each organization was quartered strictly according to its position in the battle line. Crocus rode up and dismounted before Constantine's tent, where the commanders had gathered.

"What tactics do we use?" he asked. "The wide-swinging flank attack as before?"

"No," Constantine said. "This time the enemy's front cannot be very wide, since he has only a few bridges to use in crossing the Tiber. We will pin him against the river as we did the German kings against the Rhine. I shall lead the army into battle myself, with the banner of the Lord before me."

"But Augustus—"

"I can do no less, when victory has been promised us by Divine will," Constantine said firmly. "Whichever part of our forces breaks through first will fan out behind the enemy line and destroy the pontoon bridges across the Tiber to shut the route to retreat. Before the day is past, Rome will be ours."

Word of Constantine's vision had spread quickly through the camp with the order to scratch on each soldier's shield a replica of the cryptic design of Chi and Rho. As Dacius had pointed out, there was considerable similarity between the crossed bars of the superimposed Greek letters and the radiant emblem of Apollo, so many took the new insignia to be that of the Sun god. Not a few of the soldiers were Christians, however, and these understood the symbolism of the banner. Most important of all, what had yesterday been a dejected and dispirited army, was now filled with enthusiasm by Constantine's vision and the tangible evidence of its promise of victory in the great banner going before them.

Toward mid-morning Constantine's army saw the enemy advancing to meet them. It was an impressive force, the center made up of the Praetorian Guards, with the banner of Maxentius himself before them, indicating that for once he had dared to come out with his troops. On each flank rode the Moorish cavalry raised by Maxentius in Africa, tall hawk-faced men on beautiful horses, their white robes contrasting sharply with the brilliant armor of the Praetorians. Behind the first rank were the levies, less well-trained soldiers whose absence from the front line of troops betrayed Maxentius' lack of confidence in them.

Crocus was beside Constantine, when the enemy came into sight, and made a last attempt to dissuade the young commander from leading the troops himself.

"This battle can be lost and our cause can still prevail," he pointed out. "But if you are dead all hope of defeating Maxentius and Maximin Daia will be gone. They will crush Licinius between them, as I would crush a worm underfoot."

Constantine leaned forward in the saddle for a final look at the magnificent banner borne by a trooper riding beside him. The bright morning sunlight turned the globe at its top, the gilded crossarms and the lettering of the banner itself into shining gold. "When a god marches beside you, friend Crocus," he said, "how can you be elsewhere than in the front of the battle? Sound the order to attack," he directed his trumpeter and reached over to punch Crocus affectionately on the shoulder. "Take care, old comrade. This may be the most important battle we shall ever fight together."

Raising his lance in his right hand, Constantine sent his mount racing toward the massed ranks of Maxentius' army, as the blare of trumpets all along the line acknowledged the order to attack. Beside him, he heard Crocus raise his voice in the high-pitched shout of the Gallic cavalry going into action; then seconds later his horse crashed into the front line of the battle and he found himself thrusting and jabbing with the sharp pointed lance as the conflict milled and eddied about him.

Constantine had hoped to meet Maxentius face to face in combat, but the standard of the self-styled Emperor of Italy and Africa remained well back in the massed ranks of the Praetorian Guards. The Praetorians themselves fought gamely, but the debauchery that had characterized their lives during Maxentius' reign shortly began to tell upon them. No match for Constantine's battle-hardened veterans, both on horse and on foot, the elite troops were pushed back. And when their ranks finally broke, the spearhead of Constantine's cavalry was able to penetrate to the levies of the reserves and quickly scatter them.

On the flanks, the Moorish horse were faring no better against the swift-moving Gallic cavalry commanded by Crocus. The curved swords of the Moors, though vicious weapons for close fighting, availed them little against sharp lances that could penetrate a Moorish heart long before the wielder could reach his opponent. Their horses, too, though far handsomer than the wiry mounts favored by the Gallic cavalry, quickly became nervous and hard to control in the heat of the battle.

Hardly two hours after Maxentius marched boldly forth from the safety of Rome's walls, his army was in full retreat toward the bridges leading across the Tiber into the city. Constantine's forces gave them no rest, however, and the plains of the Tiber were covered by a confused melee of men and horses, as the defeated army of Maxentius struggled to cross the bridges and reach the safety of Rome's walls. Meanwhile, Crocus had sent his swift-ranging horse around both flanks of the now almost destroyed enemy forces, keeping most of them from reaching the bridges and concentrating the others in a narrow space, where they could be attacked more effectively by Constantine's steadily advancing legions.

When Constantine reined in his horse upon a little rise overlooking the battlefield, he saw that the attachment of one of the pontoon bridges to the shore had already been cut by Crocus' cavalry. Those of Maxentius' forces who had been scrambling to get across had been thrown into the water when the bridge swung out into the current. And, since no one on the bank could help them, most sank like stones, carried down by the weight of the armor.

The few who managed to reach the shallows on the side nearest to Constantine were either captured or methodically cut down by his soldiers. Some managed to remain on their feet and gain the opposite side, where they clawed at the reddish volcanic earth forming the bank. But water pouring from the recesses of their armor quickly softened the *tufa* into a thick paste and rendered ascent almost impossible.

Crocus appeared by Constantine's side, his hair matted with blood from a cut in his scalp just beneath the flaring rim of his helmet.

"This is a great day in the history of Rome," he cried. "My men are already across the Milvian Bridge and holding one of the gates of Rome for our entrance."

"Look over there!" Constantine raised himself suddenly in his stirrups. "The man climbing the bank on the opposite side—isn't his armor golden?"

"By the gods!" Crocus cried. "It's Maxentius!"

The Emperor of Italy and Africa was indeed making a desperate effort to climb the steep bank on the farther side of the Tiber, clawing at the slippery earth with a desperation that betrayed his fear of death. His grasping fingers almost obtained a secure hold on the edge, but the booted foot he had thrust into the side of the bank to gain a hold tore away the earth that had been supporting it and for a moment all his weight hung on the fingers desperately clutching at the grassy edge. Even a root might have given him the purchase he needed to save himself, but while they watched, the earth spurted from beneath Maxentius' fingertips, as his grip loosened, and he went sliding down into the water.

He thrust feebly against the tug of the current in the shallows but the desperate effort to escape had obviously sapped most of his strength. Twice he managed to struggle to his feet, but each time the force of the current against his legs toppled him over. Finally he disappeared beneath the flood, muddied by the struggling men in the shallows and stained red here and there by the blood of the wounded, who had fallen from the bridges or had been massacred when they sought to leave the river.

"There's one prize that will not get away." Crocus spurred his horse down the bank and into the stream, choosing a course that angled across the flood to take advantage of the current. Constantine watched anxiously as the current swept over the heads of both Crocus and his mount, but the hooves of the wiry Gallic pony finally struck bottom on the other side and it struggled into the shallows, not far from where Maxentius' body, rolled along by the current, had grounded for the moment upon a sandbar.

Unencumbered by the heavy armor that had proved the undoing of Maxentius, Crocus dropped from the saddle into the shallows beside the body, examined it briefly, then rose and shook his clasped hands aloft in a gesture of victory—by which Constantine knew that his enemy was dead. Spotting a lower area along the bank downstream, Crocus began to wade toward it through the shallows, dragging the half-floating body of Maxentius behind him and followed by his horse.

The battle for Rome had ended and the heartland of the Empire was in Constantine's hands, to do with as he wished.

24

Fausta had gone to Arles in southern Gaul when Constantine began the march on Rome. When word of the capital's fall reached her by Imperial Courier, she embarked at once upon a fast military galley and quickly arrived in the capital. The Senate had decreed a round of games and festivals in honor of Constantine's victory and both he and his Empress joined in them, for nothing pleased Fausta more than the gaiety of the capital.

Constantine had long ago given up trying to discuss with her the problems that beset a ruler, since her intense ambition to be called Augusta had apparently gone little deeper than the purple robe setting her apart from other women. Now that she had achieved the title, he was sure she had no ambition to delve deeper into affairs of state—but there, as it happened, he was wrong.

Constantine submitted gracefully to the ceremonies hailing him as Augustus of Italy and Africa and made official appearances at the games and ceremonies staged in his honor, though mainly to please Fausta. Meanwhile, he was busily occupied repairing the damage Maxentius had done during his six-year reign.

The first step toward accomplishing this vitally necessary reform was made when he sent Maxentius' head to Africa, where it was paraded in Carthage and the other cities which had been almost bankrupted by the former Augustus of Italy and Africa. With the grisly proof of his successful conquest of Rome, Constantine also sent assurances to the people of the African provinces that continued allegiance to him and obedience to his decrees would assure peace and prosperity to them. Next, the remainder of the Praetorians were assigned to legions along the Rhine, so distributed that they could never again form a nucleus for rebellion. But though informers were coming forward daily, seeking gain for themselves through naming others as associates of Maxentius, Constantine refused to institute a blood bath such as victorious emperors had customarily done in the past.

The breaking up of the Praetorian Guard, more than any other single event, served as an omen of Rome's descent to a lesser position in the Empire. Since the great days of the city's glory in the time of the early Caesars, the Praetorians had represented privilege and power; now their empty barracks were a promise of what was to come. But Rome, busy celebrating the accession of the new conqueror as Senior Augustus and building a triumphal arch in his honor by tearing away some of the decorations from the Arch of Trajan—hitherto one of its most magnificent monuments— managed to shut its eyes to the future.

In the two months that Constantine remained at Rome, he worked steadily to undo through generosity and leniency the evil Maxentius had accomplished in his six years of rule. He was deferential to the Senate and to its customs, but he also named leading men of the provinces to membership, thereby making the Senate a much more representative body of the western half of the Empire than it had ever been before. He swore to maintain the ancient rights and privileges of the Senate, but at the same time made it obvious to all that he was the absolute ruler and that henceforth the deliberative body would be little more than an echo in his decisions.

To those whose estates had been confiscated during Maxentius' tenure, Constantine returned their property. He also made himself easily accessible to citizens of all levels who felt that they had been wronged, proving so generous and wise in his pronouncements that, when the Triumphal Arch was finished, the Senate ordered inscribed upon one side, "To the Liberator of Our Capital City," and on the other, "To the Founder of Our Repose."

In the usual long and flowery orations dedicating the arch, the panegyrist lauded him because: "At the suggestion of the Divinity and at the prompting of his own magnanimity, he and his army vindicated the republic by striking down the tyrant and all his satellites at a single blow." To the listeners—and no doubt to the speaker—the divinity mentioned was Jupiter Capitolinus, or perhaps Apollo, and Constantine did not correct the speaker. But in his heart, he had already determined upon a revolution in the religious life of the Empire, a revolution that would be no less broad and sweeping than were the changes he was making in its political life. This change, he knew, must be made slowly—just as almost any change had to be made in Rome because of the great part tradition played in every aspect of its life. He therefore celebrated the customary ritual sacrifices to Rome's gods; but quietly, through Hosius of Córdoba, he assured the Christians of his support and gave them the same freedom he had given their brethren in Gaul.

Actually there was much about the Christian faith which even the intelligent Hosius of Córdoba had not been able to explain entirely to the satisfaction of the young Emperor's intensely logical mind. And though he loved the beauty and truth of the Scriptures —having had Hosius give him additional instruction in Greek so he could read them for himself—they, too, often failed to answer queries raised by his ever questing mind. Of one thing, however, he had no doubt—namely that the God of the Christians, or his Son, had marched before his army on the plains of the Tiber south of Saxa Rubra and had given him victory over Maxentius.

Just why Maxentius had chosen to leave the safety of Rome's walls and risk battle on the plains, no one was able to decide for sure. Dacius argued that, convinced by the verdict of the Sibylline Books and perhaps by what he considered the sign of Apollo in the sky, Maxentius had been certain of victory and so had come out to destroy Constantine and his army. Hosius, on the other hand, felt that God had delivered Maxentius into Constantine's hands, as Christ himself had promised in the vision that night in the camp at Saxa Rubra—a view that Constantine shared. But in either case, no one could deny that a miracle had indeed occurred that day.

II

With Rome stabilized once again, Constantine turned to the next step in the plan he had worked out long before leaving Gaul. With half of the Empire now under his control, the next step was to

isolate Maximin Daia in the East. That, of course, meant allying
Licinius actively with himself, and to this end he announced the
coming marriage of his half sister, Constantia, to Emperor Licinius.
The bridegroom-to-be, however, showed some reluctance toward
coming to Rome, so Constantine moved his family and his court,
with most of his army, to the former capital of Maximian at Milan
in the north.

The Senate and citizens of Rome, almost to a man, urged him
to remain and let the marriage of the East and the West be
celebrated in the ancient capital. But there was too much of what
Hosius contemptuously called "paganism" about Rome to further
the purpose in which Constantine wished to persuade Licinius to
join him. And so he turned a deaf ear alike to Fausta's petulant
objections to leaving the luxury of Rome and the Senate's desires
for him to remain there. He did, however, listen when Senator
Adrian begged for an audience.

"You look tired, my friend," Constantine greeted the merchant,
when Adrian was ushered into his private audience chamber. "Can
I offer you some fruit or a glass of wine?"

"I breakfasted long ago, Augustus," Adrian said. "My clients were
clamoring outside my door a little after dawn, the time when sleeping is best."

"You find the life of a Senator hard, then?" Constantine asked
with a smile.

"Harder than you know, Augustus." Adrian sighed gustily. "All
day I scramble to be where I should be on time. In fact, I might
as well be like Trimalchio in Petronius' drama, with a trumpeter
to tell me the hours and how much of my life is gone."

"I remember feeling the same way years ago, when I first came
to Nicomedia as a cadet and Dacius routed us out before dawn
for a cross-country run."

"I go at a run all day, even though I have neither the figure nor
the wind for it anymore. Dawn hardly breaks before my servants
descend upon the house like so many ants, attacking it with mops,
sponges and brooms, to the tune of buckets clattering and the cries
of dolts falling off ladders. Then when I rise, I must put on a *toga*
instead of a *pallium,* and must employ a servant merely to pleat

it. I tell you, Augustus, those garments were invented only to try men's souls."

"That's why I wear a tunic most of the time," Constantine admitted.

"Next I must put myself in the hands of my *tonsor*, though I don't understand how he can take an hour just to shave me and dress my thinning locks," Adrian said plaintively. "The day I consented to my *depositio barbae* was the beginning of my slavery."

Constantine could not help laughing at the plump merchant's tale of woe, particularly because he knew it was only partially true and that Adrian was very proud of being a Senator.

"I'll wager that you looked forward to your first shaving at the hands of a *tonsor* no less than I did," he said. "Why Nero even offered up the first shavings of his beard in a casket of gold to Jupiter Capitolinus."

"And who is all this preparation wasted upon when I open my door?" Adrian asked. "My clients, made up mostly of my wife's impecunious relatives."

"Why not settle a sum upon them?"

"They would only spend it and be back on my doorstep in a month. Do you know that I cannot even go to bed without being sure I have enough coins to go around in the morning? Six and a quarter sesterces I must have every day for each one, else he will scream that he is being starved to death and word will get around that stingy Adrian no longer takes proper care of his clients. Then how can I expect to gain from those richer than I am?"

"I pity you, my friend."

"When I have finished with my clients," Adrian continued, "I must be off to the warehouses to prod my clerks, a lazy lot who don't even appreciate the chance I am giving them. Where else, Augustus, could they become familiar with the prices of oil from Spain's olive groves, or tiles and bricks from Egypt, to say nothing of corn shipments from Alexandria, lumber and wool from Gaul, preserved meat from Bactria, tin from the Isles of the Cassiterides —I will not bore you with the list."

"I find you very entertaining," Constantine said, "especially on the subject of how hard it is upon you to be rich. Now tell me why you came to see me so early this morning."

"I came to ask whether you are going to make your permanent capital at Milan, Augustus."

"I don't know yet." So the old fox has come to pry secrets out of me, Constantine thought, but took no offense. He had become very fond of the plump merchant and knew Adrian's sharpness in driving a bargain had saved both him and the Empire considerable money during the progress of the army from Treves to Rome.

"I'd wager against it," Adrian volunteered.

"Why?"

"Maximin Daia is certainly not going to accept you as Senior Augustus, so he must be dealt with eventually, as you dealt with Maxentius. When that happens, you will find it more convenient to rule from somewhere farther east."

"Where? Nicomedia?"

"Nicomedia is too small and the gulf there is silting up. Byzantium* is not far away at the Bosporus and would be much better. From there you could eventually conquer the territory around the Pontus Euxinus. A whole world is waiting to be seized in that area, but you will need someone you can trust to handle your business affairs here in Rome and the West while you are busy conquering the East."

"Someone like you?"

"Why not? You can be sure I will make the best profit I can for you, and that I will take no more commission for myself than is right under the law."

"I can think of no one better fitted to represent me, Adrian," Constantine said warmly. "A royal commission will be prepared today, naming you my steward."

III

The wedding of Caius Flavius Valerius Licinianus Licinius, Augustus of Illyricum, Greece, Thracia and the provinces along the Danube frontier, to Constantia, sister of the Senior Augustus Constantine, was an event of great magnificence and the most important social affair in the Empire that year. For it there flocked

* Istanbul

to Milan most of the subject kings under Constantine's rule, bringing gifts and magnificent entourages.

Though Fausta had protested bitterly against moving from Rome to Milan—a city she considered fit only for barbarians—she seemed to enjoy the wedding. Watching her with Crispus during the formal reception and seeing the boy's wide-eyed admiration for her, Constantine felt a moment of jealousy for his own son, who was nearer Fausta's age than he was.

Crispus, he decided, should return to Gaul with Empress Theodora and her other children, to resume his studies with Eumenius, and for a moment he found himself wishing—a little wistfully—that Fausta could be as gay with him as she seemed to be with the boy. For his preoccupation with political affairs, since the capture of Rome, had built something of a wall between them, a wall he wished desperately to level, yet which he did not know how to attack.

With Licinius married to Constantia and agreeable to the suggestion that the newly wedded couple remain at Milan through the winter, Constantine was ready to put into effect a project that had been close to his heart since the night at Saxa Rubra, when the shepherd of Dura had appeared to him with the banner which had brought victory over Rome. Licinius, who did not subscribe to Christianity, required some convincing, but on that subject Constantine was finding a new eloquence and finally prevailed. Signed by both Augusti, the Edict of Milan—directed to the governors of each province—was the broadest statement ever issued in the Roman Empire on the subject of the state and religion:

> Inasmuch as we, Constantine Augustus and Licinius Augustus, have met together at Milan on a joyful occasion, and have discussed all that appertains to the public advantage and safety, we have come to the conclusion that, among the steps likely to profit the majority of mankind and demanding immediate attention, nothing is more necessary than to regulate the worship of the Divinity.
>
> We have decided, therefore, to grant both to the Christians and to all others perfect freedom to practice the religion which each has thought best for himself, that whatsoever Divinity

troops and, in the battle that followed, Daia's failure to bring adequate supplies and weapons with him on the forced march across the Galatian uplands told heavily against him. As a result, Licinius' Illyrian veterans put Daia's forces to flight and Daia himself was destroyed.

Reading reports of the downfall of Maximin Daia brought to him by the Imperial Post, Constantine found much to praise in the rapidity with which Licinius had opposed Daia. But of what followed the victory, he could hardly approve. First, Licinius ordered the destruction of Daia's young children, a boy of eight and a girl of seven. Two other refugees, Lady Valeria, the widow of Galerius, and the Empress Prisca, who—being Christians—had been in hiding from persecution in Syria, now came to Licinius' new court at Nicomedia, expecting to be welcomed there, since Galerius had raised Licinius first to the rank of general and then to the purple of a Caesar and Augustus. Instead, they were harshly treated and only managed to escape alive with the help of the Christians of Nicomedia.

Busy putting down the Frankish rebellion during the rest of the winter and early spring, Constantine heard of these melancholy events, but could do nothing at the moment about them. He had thought that Licinius had been convinced by his example of how effectively people could be ruled by the application of justice and fair treatment to all. But it was only too apparent now that, suddenly finding himself ruler of more territory than he had imagined could ever be his, the Emperor of the East had succumbed to the same lust for power that had brought about the downfall of Daia, Maxentius and Maximian. At the moment, however, each of the two remaining Augusti—where once there had been six—needed each other, so the situation was left at that.

IV

The years following the downfall of Maximin Daia were busy ones for Constantine. Forced to move about almost continuously to keep the peace in the huge area now under his rule, he could not long escape the conviction that a dependable deputy was badly needed to governor either the Prefecture of Gaul or that of Italy, leaving him free to supervise both but responsible only for the day-to-day government of one.

Crispus was not yet old enough and experienced enough to be named Caesar of Gaul, but he gave great promise and Constantine had long ago decided to hold that prefecture against the day when the boy could take over its rule. Only Italy and Africa remained and, since he had never liked those areas particularly, Constantine decided to place a deputy in charge of them, under himself as Senior Emperor. After consultation with leading members of the Senate, he chose for this honor a man named Bassianus, who came from a large and wealthy family with wide business interests and the reputation of having furnished Rome with statesmen for many generations. And in order to hold Bassianus close to him, he gave the chosen deputy his half sister Anastasia in marriage and raised him to the rank of Caesar.

It had been less than two years since Constantine had won Italy and Africa from Maxentius at the battle of Saxa Rubra and the Milvian Bridge. Before entrusting a large amount of power to Bassianus, Constantine decided to place him in temporary command of the district, while he observed the way the new deputy handled situations that arose. Bassianus gave no hint of dissatisfaction with this secondary role, but it shortly developed that he was suffering from a disease common to Caesars and would-be Augusti—an acute case of ambition.

Adrian brought the first hint of it when he appeared one day at Constantine's palace at Milan. The countenance of the merchant, usually jolly, was grave and Constantine immediately ended the audience he was holding and retired to a private chamber with Adrian and Dacius, who now commanded his personal troops—Crocus being in Gaul watching the frontier there.

"Have the *mensores frumentarii*"—the measurers of corn—"been cheating me?" Constantine asked the merchant, when the three of them were alone. "Or have the *domini navium*"—builders and operators of fleets—"been leasing rotten bottoms to us for the trade with Britain in lead and silver?"

"If it were anything so minor, Dominus," Adrian said, "I would have haled them before the tribunal of the *praetor urbanus* and brought you their heads as proof that I had no part in it."

"I would need no proof of that," Constantine assured him. "You have served me well, Adrian, and no one knows it better than I. What did bring you to make the long journey from Rome to Milan?"

"Something so grave that I could not trust it to hands other than my own," Adrian told him. "Ten days ago one of our galleys returned from Trapezus at the eastern end of the Pontus Euxinus. During the voyage, our ship rescued the crew of a galley belonging to Senecio, the brother of Bassianus. It was sinking in the Mare Aegeum after a storm."

"Bassianus will no doubt be glad to hear they are safe."

"I haven't told him yet, Dominus," Adrian said. "My nephew Camianus happened to be aboard our ship as supercargo; I am training him to be my deputy. He went aboard Senecio's galley with some men, trying to save her for salvage, but they were forced to leave the ship later—though not before he removed some letters the Captain had failed to destroy."

"You opened them?" Constantine's voice was grave.

"The water had broken the seals, Dominus, and when Camianus saw what was written there, he brought the letters directly to me. The captain of the galley still thinks they were destroyed," he added pointedly, as he opened the package he carried and revealed two small scrolls such as were regularly used for correspondence.

The parchment was stained from exposure to water and the wax seals had broken loose from their attachment, allowing the letters to become unrolled. The seals were still intact, however, even to the deep imprint pressed upon them while the wax had been warm and soft. Constantine needed no second look at the imprint in the wax to recognize it; he'd seen it often enough before.

"What possible need could there be for official correspondence between Bassianus' family and Emperor Licinius?" he asked.

"I asked myself the same question, Dominus," Adrian said. "The answer is there in the scrolls."

Constantine lifted one of them, unrolled it and read it, then rolled it back up again. "So Senecio has been acting as agent in negotiations between Bassianus and Licinius," he said slowly. "But why would Bassianus seek to betray me? I trusted him enough to make him Caesar and to give him my sister in marriage. In a month or more I would even have made him Prefect of Italy and Africa."

"Ambition and impatience have ruined more than one good man," Dacius said. "Remember Julius Caesar."

"Bassianus and Licinius have obviously been plotting to destroy me and take over the Empire for themselves," Constantine said. "So there can be no question of what to do with them. But how can I tell Anastasia that I must execute her husband almost before their marriage bed is cold?"

"Or your other sister, Constantia, that her husband also sought your death," Dacius said. "She has just borne that black traitor, Licinius, a son."

Constantine picked up the scrolls and read through them again. "Licinius says here that he is moving to Sirmium. No doubt he meant to drive eastward from the Danube and join forces with Bassianus, after I was assassinated and the legions bought off with the gold he was sending to Senecio."

"I reached the same conclusion," Adrian agreed.

"Do you think many others in Rome are involved in this plot?"

"I cannot tell, Dominus," the merchant said. "I only learned of this by accident because Camianus was clever enough to discover the scrolls, after the master of the galley tried to jettison them."

"Your nephew shall receive my personal commendation and a generous reward," Constantine promised and turned to Dacius. "Send a tribune you can trust and a hundred men to Rome at once. Tell them to arrest Bassianus and bring him to me here. Meanwhile, I want you to leave at once for Treves to raise an army there and move through the northern passes toward Sirmium."

"Shall I cross over into the territory of Licinius?" Dacius asked.

"Not until I send you word, but be ready on the border." Constantine raised his hands and let them drop in a gesture of defeat. "Why must I fight again, when so much could be done for everyone, if I were only left to rule in peace?"

"There will be no peace, Dominus, until Emperor Licinius is destroyed and you rule the world," Adrian said. "He has been seized by an attack of ambition—the same disease that killed all the others."

"I have tried to improve the lot of the people instead of building a great army to impose my will on all, so it will be a long fight against great odds," Constantine said soberly. "See that the *labarum* goes before you on the march, Dacius."

The old soldier nodded. "I will also sacrifice to Jupiter and Apollo. We need the favor of all the gods we can persuade to help us."

v

Two weeks later, Bassianus stood in chains before Constantine at Milan. Rome had been thrown into a turmoil by the sudden arrest and, seeking to save themselves, informers by the score had come to Adrian, implicating others in the plot to kill Constantine and seize control of the Prefecture of Italy and Rome in the name of Licinius, who would then have become sole Emperor, with Bassianus as his deputy. From his throne, Constantine looked down at the culprit, much as he might examine a worm before crushing it under his heel. The audience chamber was filled with nobles of the court at Milan, including Constantine's personal chamberlain, for he wanted the fate of Bassianus to become a lesson to all.

"Read the letters," he instructed the clerk, without even speaking directly to the culprit.

The clerk opened the scrolls, still marked by the wax seal of Licinius, and began to read. They were not long, but they established beyond doubt the guilt of the prisoner and his brother Senecio in an elaborate plan to seize the government and buy off the army as had been done many times before—with gold furnished by Licinius.

"I took you into my own family and made you Caesar, next in rank below myself, Bassianus," Constantine said, when the reading was finished. "Why did you betray me?"

"The Empire should be governed by those whose blood entitles them to rule—the Senate and the noblemen." A half sneer was on Bassianus' thin lips and his voice was proud, even haughty. "You have already polluted the Senate with people from all walks of life, common men with no qualifications for the high office. I wish to keep Rome as capital of the Empire and hold the power where it belongs, in the hands of men whose noble birth qualify them best to govern."

"Have you no more to say in defense of your treachery?"

"It is not myself I serve, but Rome. What crime can be found in that?"

"The crime of deciding that what is in your own interest is always best for the state," Constantine said gravely. "Emperor Diocletian could have retained the power and glory belonging to a single Augustus, yet he chose to share it because he believed the Empire could be ruled more effectively from several capitals. Under his direction Rome's frontiers were extended from the river Tigris in Persia to the Antonine Wall in Britain, proving him right. The greatness of a ruler is not measured in pride, Bassianus, or in lust for power, but in compassion for those he rules and the desire to improve the lot of the people. You cannot make men free by forging chains of gold; the lowest plebe unchained is far more free than you, bound as you are by the fetters of lust for power that you have forged for yourself."

Constantine nodded to the *magister memoriae* who sat beside him. "Let it be recorded that the prisoner Bassianus is hereby ordered beheaded—"

"But you cannot!" Bassianus protested. "Emperor Licinius—"

"Licinius doesn't rule here!" Constantine snapped. "Your sentence is death."

"Then let me choose—"

"A traitor has no choice. Only consideration for my sister keeps me from ordering your head paraded through Italy, as I did with Maxentius in Africa."

Babbling pleas for mercy, Bassianus was dragged away. As Constantine turned to the door leading to his private cabinet behind the chamber, he ordered the guard who stood there to send for Bishop Hosius, and was standing at the window breathing deeply of the fresh air outside when Hosius of Córdoba entered.

"Are you ill, Augustus?" the priest asked anxiously.

"Only with a nausea of the spirit that became too great for the body to stand." Constantine turned to face the churchman. "I remember feeling this way once after a venomous serpent struck at me when I was walking through the woods. I was seized by such a rage then that I beat the snake to death without knowing what I was doing, but afterwards was so spent from retching that I had to sit upon a log for a while before going on."

"There are similarities between a traitor and a serpent," Hosius agreed. "Are you all right now?"

"Yes. I sent for you to ask how Christ would have treated a man like Bassianus."

"We believe the Master taught us the will of God when he spoke from a mountain in Galilee and said: 'Love your enemies, bless them that curse you, do good to them that hate you and pray for them that despitefully use you and persecute you.'"

"Would Christ have forgiven Bassianus, knowing he would only connive again?"

"Jesus was also a man, Augustus," Hosius said. "One morning on the way to Jerusalem when he was hungry, he came upon a fig tree. The fruit of this tree usually appears before its leaves and, since the tree was full of leaves, its fruit should have been ripe, yet it was barren. The Master cursed the tree that day and it never again bore fruit."

"Then the man you worship as god was no more consistent than an ordinary man would be. He taught us to forgive those who err, yet cursed a tree that failed to bear fruit."

"That passage in the Holy Scriptures has troubled many people," Hosius admitted. "It appears in two of the gospels which we consider authentic, so we believe it really happened."

"You still haven't explained the difference between what Christ said and what he did."

"I remind you again that Jesus was not only the Son of God but also a man, Augustus. Since he was born of woman and therefore mortal, he could act as a man in cursing the fig tree. But he is also God and taught the word of God. We believe the incident of the fig tree really means that when a man has the outward show of a good character, but not the fruit he should bear, he cannot be considered valuable to the kingdom of God and thus should be cast out."

"Bassianus had the outward show of good works but certainly not the inward quality of loyalty," Constantine said. "Does that mean I am justified in executing him as a traitor?"

"I am not a judge, Augustus."

"Nor are you of any help to me now!"

"Would you have me serve as your conscience?"

The question brought Constantine up short, for the churchman had put his finger on a sore spot. He did want Hosius to act as his conscience, and tell him he had been right.

"Hardly two years ago, you triumphed as a leader in battle behind a banner bearing the sacred initials of Jesus Christ," Hosius reminded him. "Is it not reasonable to believe you will triumph as a ruler under the same banner?"

"Are you saying I should end this play-acting of sacrifice and apparent allegiance to Rome's gods and acknowledge only yours," Constantine demanded, "even though you proved just now that his teachings would lead me to do one thing and his actions another?"

"I merely told you the story to point out the choice that is before you as judge," Hosius said. "Bassianus was like the fig tree, all outward show with leaves but no inward fruit. The Scriptures we regard as holy would seem to justify his execution, Augustus, so long as you keep in mind one thing when you pass judgment."

"What is that?"

"If you could look at the records kept by Pontius Pilate as Procurator of Judaea nearly three hundred years ago, you would find that Jesus of Nazareth was actually condemned and executed as a traitor under Roman law."

25

WHEN HE LEARNED that Senecio and many others in the conspiracy to assassinate him and seize the government by force had fled to Licinius, Constantine sent a peremptory demand to his fellow Augustus for their return. Licinius, however, refused to give them up and, what was more, couched his refusal in contemptuous words. Shortly afterwards, too, a number of statues of Constantine erected with those of Licinius along the border between the two Emperors, when they had made their pact of mutual co-operation following the marriage of Constantia, were cast down and degraded by a mob obviously stirred up by agents of Licinius.

With proof of his fellow Emperor's treachery in the shattered statues and the harboring of traitors, Constantine made one of his characteristic swift decisions, followed by equally swift action. The courier service of the Imperial Post had already brought word that Dacius, Crispus and an army of some ten thousand veterans from Gaul were encamped far enough from the border with Licinius for their presence not to be an obvious threat, yet close enough to enter Licinius' domain in a few days of forced marches. A message now went to Dacius by the swift chain of couriers, telling him to move eastward for a junction with Constantine's own forces between Virunum on the headwaters of the river Savus, and Galerius' old capital of Sirmium on the same stream some fifty miles west of the junction of that river with the Danube. At the same time, Constantine himself moved northward with ten thousand troops, mostly cavalry.

When Constantine's spies reported that Licinius' army, now moving westward from Sirmium along the banks of the river Savus, numbered about thirty-five thousand—roughly twice as many as he commanded—he began to seek a field of battle where the terrain would be favorable to his forces, evening somewhat the odds against him. Shortly after joining Dacius and Crispus, Constantine found a spot suitable for his needs not far from a town named Cibalae. It was a defile lying between a deep swamp on one side and a steep hill on the other, enabling him to present a solid front in depth against Licinius' attack in spite of the difference in numbers. His foot soldiers were stationed in the defile, while behind the hill, hidden from observation, he placed a force of nearly five thousand horse. These preparations made, he set up his own command post on top of the elevation.

Licinius' army, under the command of an experienced general named Valens, advanced to attack but were thrown back with—it seemed to Constantine, as he watched from the hilltop—suspicious ease. His suspicion became a certainty, when he saw his eager front rank, ignoring Dacius' fiercely shouted commands, pursue the seemingly fleeing enemy.

Realizing that the initial attack had been only a feint designed to draw him into a trap, Constantine acted swiftly. Ordering his personal trumpeter to sound the command to attack for the five thousand cavalry behind him, he spurred his mount down the hill. Crispus, who was acting as second-in-command, realized the danger at the same moment and Constantine saw the youth's mount flash by and heard his exultant yell, as he led his *ala*, too, in the attack.

The impact of the cavalry, launched at full speed downhill like a battering ram, came at the very moment when Valens ordered his troops to turn and attack Constantine's confidently advancing foot soldiers. As a result, what had been planned as a trap for Constantine's forces suddenly became one for the enemy.

As he had done with the massively armored horse of Maxentius' army before Augustus Taurinum, Constantine sent his cavalry in as wedges from both flanks, splitting the forces commanded by Valens into two parts and leaving the front ranks to be destroyed by his own veteran foot soldiers, while the cavalry went on to sow havoc and confusion among the rear files of Licinius' army.

From that point on, the tide of battle went swiftly against Licinius and long before nightfall his forces were retreating in disorder. The next morning scouts reported that the enemy was withdrawing by way of Sirmium but, though Constantine pursued them, General Valens managed not only to extricate his troops from Sirmium but also to take everything of value from the city as they departed.

Pursuing the retreating army through the Dalmatian uplands, Constantine came one night to Naissus, his old birthplace, and camped outside the city. Crispus had distinguished himself so well upon the battlefield that Constantine had promoted him to the rank of Tribunus Primii Ordinarius. The new tribune was with him as he rode into the city where he had spent his boyhood, and so pleased was Constantine to be in the old surroundings that not even the news that Licinius had advanced General Valens to the rank of Caesar could disturb him.

The house where Constantine had spent his boyhood was little changed by the years and he almost expected Helena to step out and greet them. That night he slept in his own room and felt a lump come into his throat once again, when he remembered getting up for a drink in the night and hearing his father and mother discuss the forthcoming divorce, so Constantius would be free to marry Theodora.

In the morning the troops marched southward toward the crucial battle for which, spies reported, Licinius was gathering a considerable army south of Naissus on the Plain of Mardia in Thrace. Before leaving, Constantine walked with Crispus through the tree-lined streets to the former Temple of Asklepios but found it decrepit and uncared for, with only the small paintings he remembered so well to indicate its former status. These, though dimmed by dust and cobwebs, were still as brilliant as on the day when he had opened the door and stepped inside, then raced away, his heart thumping with the fear that the evil spirits—whose pictures he was certain those upon the wall had been—might be in pursuit of him.

"What has happened here?" he asked the prefect of the town, who accompanied him. "In my boyhood, the Christians worshiped in this temple."

"They did, until the edict of Emperor Diocletian, Augustus," the prefect said. "When the soldiers came, they took it to be still the Temple of Asklepios, so it was spared."

"What happened to the Christians?"

"They were either destroyed or recanted."

"Are none here now?"

"No, Augustus. Few dared to worship the Christian god after Emperor Licinius proscribed it."

"Did you ever hear of the Edict of Milan, signed by both me and Emperor Licinius?"

The prefect—he was an old man—shook his head, proving again that Licinius had never bothered to enforce the edict in his territory.

"Was anything wrong back there, sir?" Crispus asked as they rode out of Naissus in the wake of the army.

"The old temple was once a Christian church. Your grandmother used to go there to pray."

"I remember that she looked after the Christians in Drepanum. We even sheltered my teacher, Lactantius, for a while."

"Did Lactantius teach you about the Christian god?"

"Yes. But it was a long time ago and I've forgotten much of it."

"What does Eumenius teach you about religion at Autun?"

"Not much. He worships Apollo—at least there is a little image in his house and he often reads poems in Greek about Apollo. But he says each man must decide in his own heart who to acknowledge as god."

"Have you decided yet?"

Crispus shook his blond head and the morning sun, touching the ends of his hair where it curled around the rim of the Roman helmet, turned them momentarily into pale gold. Minervina's hair had been the same color, Constantine remembered. It was the first time he'd thought of her in many years and he found himself comparing Minervina's simple pleasures with Fausta's driving ambition and her gentle voice with his wife's strident tongue when she fancied herself affronted—which was often.

Minervina had possessed an inner goodness that gave her a strange luminescence, like a star seen from a mountain top through the clear air of the night. Remembering all these things he suddenly realized how little his position as ruler of half the Roman world had given him over what he had possessed here at Naissus and at Drepanum as a young man and turned his eyes away, lest Crispus see the tears in them.

"I will have Hosius instruct you in the mysteries of the Christian faith," he told his son, when he could control his voice again. "If you are to decide for yourself who is to be your god, you should at least have some knowledge of them all."

"Mithras would be my choice," Crispus said. "He understands battle and danger and the importance of skill in arms. Are you a Christian, sir?"

"Not yet, though I owe much to God. Hosius is instructing me, but I am not a very good pupil."

"Lactantius said the same about me more than once," Crispus admitted. "But Eumenius and I get along very well. He has taught me that if a man is to rule well, he must know much more than how to issue commands and use weapons."

"I might rule better if I had learned that lesson years ago," Constantine admitted.

"Oh no, Father!" The term of affection—little used by the boy because their relationship was most often a military one—brought a warm glow to Constantine's heart. "Eumenius says you are the greatest ruler Rome has ever known. That's why—" He paused.

"Yes?"

"I was going to say you should guard yourself more in battle."

"Dacius is always lecturing me on that subect," Constantine admitted. "You've had a taste yourself of the joy of battle, so you know how hard it will be to give it up, but in the next battle, you will command the horse and Dacius the foot. Don't be surprised though, if you suddenly find me riding beside you, jabbing with my lance and slashing with my sword like any other mounted trooper."

II

The necessity for each of the warring Emperors to raise additional armies delayed the crucial battle for some weeks. This time Licinius had chosen the ground—the Plain of Mardia in Thrace—and the odds were nearer even, though still weighted in his favor.

For hours the two forces were locked in combat, with the wavering battlefront now advancing for one and now for the other. Constantine had planned carefully, however, and not long before the sun went down, when the tired troops were almost ready to disengage, he sent a large body of horse led by Crispus against the enemy's front in a smashing attack that broke through the front line of Valens' troops, forcing him to withdraw toward the hill and leave the front ranks to surrender or be cut to pieces.

When morning came, only the wounded and the dead occupied the plain, Licinius' main army having withdrawn into the mountains of Macedonia to the south. Nor was Constantine surprised to see an emissary approach toward mid-morning, bearing the traditional white banner requesting a parley.

"Tribune Galba," the emissary announced himself stiffly. "Augustus Licinius requests that you receive an ambassador to discuss terms for ending the fighting."

"You may tell my brother, Licinius, that I will receive the ambassador at sunset," Constantine said gravely, ignoring an explosive, but quickly muffled, oath from Crispus at his words.

Tribune Galba saluted and rode away, this time without his banner. When he was clear of the camp, Constantine turned to Dacius. "Order a tent made ready for the parley and one for the ambassador," he directed. "Then join me in my tent with Tribune Crispus."

Dacius came in and, tossing his helmet into a corner of Constantine's luxurious tent, reached for a cup of wine. Crispus, however, exploded into words, when he was barely inside the opening flap.

"Why agree to a parley, when you have beaten the enemy in battle, Father?" he demanded.

Dacius answered and, though the old general was tired, his voice was patient and kind—as Constantine had often heard it, when he had himself exploded prematurely into words on other occasions.

"In the first place, Crispus," he said, "we haven't beaten Licinius."

"But the cavalry—"

"The cavalry turned the tide of battle just when it needed turning and earned you a commendation—if you were anyone but the son of an Emperor."

"He will get that, too," Constantine said.

"We have succeeded in cutting up the front ranks of Licinius' troops and destroying maybe a fourth of his army," Dacius continued. "But in doing it, we have exhausted our reserves. Hardly a town between here and Gaul now has enough of a garrison within its walls to police it against a siege, while Licinius still has Asia, Syria and Egypt to draw from."

Crispus was beginning to look a little crestfallen and Constantine intervened. "What Dacius is saying, Crispus, is that Licinius has been taught a lesson. If we push him too hard now, he will only leave his army to delay us while he flees to the Bosporus. And once across there, he can rebuild his forces in Asia."

"But we could follow."

"Not without a fleet and Licinius controls Macedonia and Achaia, for the time being. While we were building ships—or seizing them from the Greeks—his forces would harry us constantly. Right now his army has been badly beaten, so he may be tricked into believing he is getting a good bargain if we make peace with him—until the time comes when we can defeat him."

"And when will that be?"

"Who can tell?" Constantine shrugged. "But next time we will be the ones who will draw an army from Illyricum, not Licinius."

"And with three-fourths of the Empire behind us," Dacius added, "conquering the other fourth should not be too difficult a task."

Licinius' ambassador, Mistrianus, was tall, with iron-gray hair and aquiline features. A Senator and a nobleman in his own right, he was obviously conscious of his own importance.

"I come before you, Augustus," he said unctuously, "hoping the break between you and your sister's husband, Augustus Licinius, may be healed by the dictates of humanity, moderation and reason. If hostilities are pursued further, naught but harm can come to both sides, harm that is sure to cause delight in the camps of our common enemies on the Rhine and the Danube and perhaps encourage them to attack. Nor," he added with a quick glance at Constantine to see the effect of his words, "is the outcome by any means yet decided."

Constantine let that pass since, as he and Dacius had pointed out to Crispus, it was largely true. What he needed now was a period of relative peace during which to consolidate the gains he would win at the peace table and place them firmly under his own control. And he was willing to make some concession to Licinius in order to gain it.

"I am therefore authorized," Mistrianus continued, "to suggest the following terms of settlement in the names of the two Augusti I represent."

"Augusti!" Constantine exploded angrily, the room suddenly clouded by a red haze before his eyes.

"Emperor Licinius and Emperor Valens," Mistrianus explained, but now with much less assurance.

"After rejecting one ungrateful brother-in-law in Bassianus, shall I now accept as my colleague a contemptible slave?" Constantine demanded frostily.

"Perhaps you did not see the decree naming General Valens an Augustus—"

"Since it was done without my consent the decree is void," Constantine said flatly. "By the way, when was Valens raised to the position of Augustus?"

"Yesterday—after the battle."

"As a price for not yielding up my brother-in-law to me?"

As Mistrianus' mouth dropped open in amazement, Constantine heard Dacius' soft chuckle behind him and was sure he had put his finger upon the heart of the elaborate scheme. In return for not being handed over to Constantine's mercy, Licinius had undoubtedly yielded leadership to the ambitious Valens and the equally ambitious Mistrianus. Now the two of them were trying to get as much out of the peace settlement for themselves as they could.

"Tell Augustus Licinius that the abdication of Valens is the first article of any peace treaty we shall make," Constantine directed. "Notify him also of the terms I will accept: the provinces of Pannonia, Dalmatia, Dacia, Macedonia and Greece shall become part of my realm."

"You drive a hard bargain, Augustus."

"On the contrary. I am being generous in leaving my friend and brother in possession of Thracia, Asia Minor, Syria Palaestina, Egypt and the districts wrested from Persia."

"I will transmit your terms," Mistrianus promised, but Constantine was not yet finished.

"Tell my brother Licinius also that I am today appointing my son, Crispus, Caesar of Gaul, Britain and Spain," he directed.

Crispus was standing near his chair, tall and straight in the uniform of a tribune. He stiffened at the announcement, but did not speak, though Constantine could see the pleased delight in his eyes. Mistrianus departed hastily before further provisions could be added and the officers who were present crowded around Crispus to congratulate him.

"Does that make you happy—Caesar?" Constantine asked with a smile when they had left the tent and he was alone with his son.

"Happy—but unworthy, sir."

"I was unworthy myself when my father died in Britain and the legions proclaimed me Emperor."

"But you proved your worth ten times over."

"As I expect you to do."

Crispus knelt and removed his plumed helmet. Lifting Constantine's hand to place it upon his head, he said, "I swear, by whatever gods there be, to do everything in my power to prove myself worthy of your trust."

With an effort, Constantine resisted the urge to touch the pale golden curls revealed when Crispus removed his helmet. It was a moment of rare warmth and companionship between father and son—whom fate had separated for most of their lives—and he knew he would always treasure it.

"Do you mind if I send Dacius with you to Gaul?" he asked.

"I was going to ask for him. And I hope King Crocus will remain there too."

"Naturally he will; his kingdom is in Gaul."

"What do you think Emperor Licinius will do, Father?"

"Agree to my terms, then plot to regain what he has lost—and more. That's why I need someone I can trust to guard the frontier in Gaul and help me defeat Licinius when the time comes."

The next day a new emissary arrived from Licinius, by which Constantine judged what he learned later to be true—that Valens and his co-conspirators had been sent into exile. The defeated Emperor of the East accepted the terms of peace, harsh though they

were, with only one request—that his son Licinianus be named
Caesar. To this Constantine readily agreed, since the young man
was only an infant of twenty months.

The treaty of peace signed that day by him and Licinius marked
the end of the era begun by Diocletian, when rulers had selected
their successors—at least publicly—on merit and ability. From now
on, occupancy of the throne of Rome would be determined more
by blood descent than by any other single factor.

CONSTANTINE

26

T HE TREATY of the Mardian Plain inaugurated a period of nearly eight years of peace between the two rulers of the Roman Empire, but it could not settle one difficulty that erupted as soon as Constantine returned triumphantly to Milan. Fausta had wanted the pomp and panoply of a triumphal celebration in Rome, but Constantine had come to dislike the city on the Tiber as much as his old master, Diocletian, had done. Besides, he had much to do and could ill afford the time for a ceremonial journey that could have no real purpose except to bring pleasure to his wife.

Storm signals were in Fausta's eyes as he accepted the welcome home and the plaudits of the Prefect of Milan, replying with a gracious speech, promising prosperity as a result of a new peace treaty. The storm erupted as soon as they were alone together in their quarters in the palace.

"You might have told me you planned to name your son a Caesar," Fausta said, when her servant had prepared her for the night and departed.

"It wasn't planned. The boy handled himself well in battle and I need someone I can trust to rule in Gaul and Britain."

"A mere youth—with no experience? Where is the wisdom in that?"

"I was only a youth when I became Caesar of Gaul," he reminded her. "But I had the wise counsel of Eumenius and so will Crispus. Besides, I'm sending Dacius with him to Treves."

"You and Licinius have already made plans for your sons," Fausta flared. "What about mine—when they are born? Will there be any place for them?"

"You once said the Empire is large enough for all my male

offspring—if there are any more," he reminded her. "Give me a son and, when he is christened, I will make him Caesar in Pannonia."

"Christened? What is that?"

"A Christian custom, and a very beautiful one. Hosius has been telling me about it."

"Then you're really becoming a Christian? And not simply using them to help you control the Empire?"

"The Christian Church has more to offer me than any other religion, and no one could deny that it is a considerable influence for stability in the Empire." He put his arm about her and drew her close. "Give me three sons and I will name each to rule a quarter, as in the days of Diocletian."

"I shall make you keep that promise," she warned him. "Our next child will be a boy; I've decided on it."

"As you decided that we would be married when you first saw me at Nicomedia?"

She wrinkled her nose at him and was once more the delightful creature with whom he had fallen so violently in love in Rome. And in his happiness that the growing coolness between them over his refusal to spend much time at Rome seemed to have abated, he found it easy to forget that her father had tried to destroy him twice and her brother once.

II

Originally, Constantine's sponsorship of the Christian Church had been motivated by two convictions. The first was his belief that at two crucial points in his career—at Dura, when he had been unsure of the course he had plotted for his command, and again at Saxa Rubra—Christ himself had guided him to victory. The second was his realization that, highly organized as it was through bishops, local churches and clergy, the Christian faith could help him unify the Empire. To these two had now been added a third factor, a genuine faith and conviction of the truth inherent in Christianity brought to him by his studies of the Scriptures with Hosius.

He and Dacius had spent hours arguing about the vision at Saxa

Rubra and the battle of the Milvian Bridge—with no final conclusion. Dacius had held that the determining factors in the battle had all been military: first, Maxentius' error in leaving the protection of the walls of Rome; second, his tactical stupidity in placing his forces with their backs to the Tiber with the only retreat afforded by the Milvian Bridge and several floating bridges above and below it; and third, Constantine's forthright attack against the center with the full force of his army, breaking through and forcing Maxentius into the disastrous retreat.

Against these arguments Constantine could bring to bear mainly the vividness of the vision in which Jesus of Nazareth had promised him victory behind the *labarum* and the strange flaming cross in the sky the afternoon before—neither of which Dacius conceded as being real. The question of just how much of a role the man the Christians believed to be the Son of God had actually played in Constantine's spectacular career had therefore to be left undecided. But there could be no doubting the practical value of having on his side an organization that was growing rapidly and steadily increasing its hold upon a large section of the people.

Such was Constantine's logic, and his convictions. But he discovered quickly that, being made up of fallible humans, the Christian Church, even with divine guidance, was something less than the dependable ally he'd expected it to be. In fact, evidence soon developed that it could not even govern itself without severe factional struggles and explosive emotional crises that time and again threatened to tear it and the Empire apart.

Seeking to gain the support of the Christians when his own troubles began, Maxentius had wisely eased the persecution in Italy and Africa. When Constantine assumed control, he sought to further strengthen them by making grants of money to the clergy, only to discover that his act of charity set off an explosive chain of events which quickly involved the whole church in a boiling controversy.

During the persecutions, some of the clergy had saved their lives by yielding up the Scriptures, as required by law, knowing that copies had been hidden in many of the monastic centers—often located in the desert or other out-of-the-way places where the persecutors never penetrated. The period of religious freedom inaugurated by the Edict of Milan brought an upsurge of controversy, however, with those of the clergy who had defied imperial power and suffered torture and imprisonment accusing their unpersecuted brothers of mortal sin in making a pact with their persecutors and insisting that they be denied the right to administer the sacraments of holy communion, baptism, marriage and the like.

The controversy had flared briefly in Rome, when Maxentius had liberalized his treatment of the church, and at one time rival factions had even fought in the street, leading Maxentius to seize all church properties there. After some eight years, Miltiades had been elected to the prestigious seat of the Bishop of Rome, however, and the Christians had been given back their property.

In Africa trouble now flared in the district of Carthage. A new bishop, Caecilianus, had recently been consecrated there by one Felix of Aptunga, but the latter was now branded a *traditor*, as those of the clergy who had handed over the Holy Scriptures were called. And since, if the charges were true, Felix was therefore judged guilty of mortal sin in the eyes of the more intransigent portion of the church, he was likewise incapable, in their eyes, of the laying on of hands by which the apostolic power of Peter, gained from Christ himself, was given to the bishops. Refusing to acknowledge the authority of Caecilianus, the dissident faction next named as bishop one Magorionus.

The moving spirit in the controversy was actually a fiery priest named Donatus, known to his followers as Donatus the Great, and the faction opposing Caecilianus soon became known as the Donatists. When Constantine, upon assuming power in Italy and Africa, gave money to the clergy to build up their churches, it was naturally distributed to the regular priests, who were under the jurisdiction of Bishop Caecilianus, and the Donatists were excluded. These promptly appealed to the Emperor, but Constantine, determined to leave church and theological matters strictly alone, left the decision of who was right up to a church council or synod, which convened at Rome that same year.

At the council, the claims of the Donatists were refused and the right of the regular clergy to perform all duties of priesthood was confirmed. The church in Africa continued to boil with controversy, however, so Constantine ordered a council of clerical representatives from throughout his realm to convene at Arles in the year following his victory at the Plain of Mardia.

To make certain that a large number would attend, transport at government expense by way of the Imperial Post was furnished those who were to take part in the council at Arles. And thus, by calling the council and placing the facilities of the government at the disposal of the Christian Church, Constantine publicly committed himself to it for the first time. Moreover, he allied the civil power of the government with the religious power of the church, an alliance which was to exist—though not unbrokenly—for many centuries.

No Eastern bishops attended the Council of Arles, since the questions involved were largely confined to the West. The provinces of Africa, Gaul, Spain, Italy, Sardinia, Britain and Italy were represented. Sylvester, Bishop of Rome, sent two presbyters and two deacons but Constantine himself did not attend. He did, however, furnish the followers of Caecilianus with everything they needed to combat the claims of the Donatists in the form of a detailed report of an investigation of Felix of Aptunga conducted by his personal representative, or vicar, in Africa and buttressed by sworn documents proving the innocence of the accused. Proved false also was the charge that Caecilianus had prevented members of the church of Carthage from helping those who had been imprisoned by the edicts of Diocletian.

The report of the Council of Arles addressed to Bishop Sylvester of Rome, titular head of the church, and to Constantine, its sponsor, completely discredited the claims of the followers of Donatus. Nevertheless they continued to give Constantine trouble from time to time and, some four years after the judgment of the council, he wrote a very remarkable letter to the church in Africa, showing just how far he had gone toward adopting in his own life the teachings of Jesus Christ:

> We must hope, therefore, that Almighty God may show pity and gentleness to his people, as this schism is the work of a few. For it is to God that we should look for a remedy, since all good vows and deeds are requited. But until the healing

comes from above, it behooves us to moderate our councils to practice patience and to bear with the virtue of providence any assault or attack which the depravity of these people prompt them to deliver.

That there be no paying back injury with injury: for it is only the fool who takes into his usurping hands the vengeance which he ought to reserve for God, our faith should be strong enough to feel fully confident that whatever we have to endure from the fury of men like these, will avail with God with all the grace of martyrdom. For what is it in this world to conquer in the name of God, unless it be to bear with fortitude the disordered attack of men who trouble the peaceful followers of the law.

If you will observe my will, you will speedily find that, thanks to the Supreme Power, the designs of the presumptuous standard-bearers of this wretched faction will languish and all men will recognize that they ought not to listen to persuasion of a few and perish everlastingly when, by the grace of penitence, they may correct their errors and be restored to eternal life.

The virtues Constantine recommended to his people were the same that Christ had recommended to the Jews of Palestine in his day, and they fell upon almost equally empty ears. The Donatist heresy—for as such it was condemned by both Constantine and the church—continued to flourish and soon became a refuge and rallying point for all who were dissatisfied with either government or religion. Meanwhile, Constantine counteracted by ignoring the African church and withdrawing most of his support from it.

Perhaps because he never really understood what was at stake, Constantine neglected the real point at issue, namely how severely a man should hold up his conscience as a standard by which to judge his actions and those of others. And where the Donatists might have pointed up an important facet of the Christian faith, their very intransigence not only drove away the man who could have been their greatest adherent—Constantine himself—but also closed the ranks of the church against the very real and important questions upon which they had based their original contentions.

III

True to her promise, Fausta provided Constantine with a son, who was named Constantine—although there was another, the son of Constantius and Theodora. And delighted to have another male heir, the father named the infant a Caesar, though without a domain.

As for the other Caesar, Crispus, the Gallic legions adored him. With Eumenius and Dacius as advisers and Crocus assisting in military affairs, he governed well, putting down any rebellion relentlessly, but treating his people with the same tolerance and understanding that was making his father's rule one of the most successful in Roman history.

Annoyed by the quarreling of the Donatists and by the day-to-day cares of government, which he had never borne very tolerantly, Constantine was almost glad when the Goths, their strength rebuilt by a peace of nearly half a century following their conquest by the Emperors Claudius Gothicus and Aurelian, attacked across the Danube frontier. He put down the revolt with all his old forthrightness and, when military matters claimed his presence in the north for much of the time during nearly two years, Fausta moved to Rome and a new palace he had built for her there, claiming that the climate was better than that at Milan, which she had never liked. She was further delighted when Constantine decreed that the Quinquennalia of the Caesars should be celebrated that year with a great triumph such as the Empire had not seen since the days following his great victory at Saxa Rubra.

27

DACIUS AND CROCUS accompanied Crispus eastward for the Quinquennalia and Constantine embraced his old friends and his son with real fervor. It was the first time he had seen Dacius since Crispus had gone to Gaul some five years earlier, and an even longer time had passed since he had left Crocus behind to watch over Gaul, while he was occupied in the campaign against Licinius. Neither appeared to have aged notably, but Constantine could see in their eyes the shock they felt at the way the toll of the years had etched its pattern into his features, even bringing a considerable sprinkling of gray to his hair, though he was not quite fifty years old.

"Have you been ill, Augustus?" Crocus asked anxiously.

Constantine shook his head. "Diocletian once warned me that the purple cloak grows heavier from year to year. I can understand now why he was so glad to put it off after twenty years."

"Have you started growing cabbages yet?" Dacius asked.

Constantine threw an arm affectionately across the broad shoulders that were as straight as he remembered them on that day, a good thirty years earlier, when he had first stood before the old soldier as an aspiring cadet. "Perhaps I need you here to keep me on the right road," he admitted. "But I shall not grow cabbages. Diocletian found little peace in them, I'm afraid."

"And you?" Dacius asked.

"What peace I need, I find in the teachings of Jesus of Nazareth —when I have time to study them."

Crocus gave him a quick look. "Then it's true that you've become a Christian?"

Constantine nodded. "Everything I am, I owe to the grace of God and his Son. How could I worship any other?"

"When did the knowledge come to you?" Crocus asked. "With the vision at Saxa Rubra?"

"Not for some time afterwards," Constantine admitted. "I think now that God had been preparing my soul for the realization through the years, perhaps beginning even as far back as the day I saw Emperor Diocletian's horse slip on the bloody streets of Alexandria and pronounced it the sign of Apollo. You remember that, don't you, Dacius?"

"I remember it well," the old soldier said. "But any man can look back on his life and find a pattern in it, if he wishes. The gods, whoever they are, have favored you; there's no question of that. But not because of any whim on their part. You gained their favor because you believed in yourself and were not afraid to risk in order to gain."

"Dacius is right," Crocus agreed. "That day when I unhorsed you on the field at Nicomedia, another would have yielded before hopeless odds. But you risked having your body torn by the point of my lance to set the butt of yours against the ground and knock me from the saddle. You've been fighting the same battle ever since, and in the same way."

"Speaking of battles," Dacius said, "when are you going to move against Licinius?"

"It may not be long now. He has begun to oppress the church and God will surely deliver him into my hands soon."

"It's been a long time since I read the Christian scriptures," Dacius said, "but I seem to remember something that applies here."

Constantine smiled. "The passage from the writings of the Apostle Paul about putting on the breastplate of righteousness, the shield of faith and the sword of the spirit? It is one of my favorites."

"That isn't the one." Dacius' face was suddenly grave. "I remember now. It's something Jesus of Nazareth said—but perhaps you would rather not hear it."

"Why not?"

"The words were these: 'What shall it profit a man, if he shall gain the whole world, and lose his own soul?'"

Constantine stared at the old soldier, who had been his friend and mentor for most of his life, while the familiar red haze of explosive anger which seemed to come more and more often nowadays cast a sudden pall between them. Even in his anger, though, he realized it was not Dacius who had changed, but himself, and the realization did not serve to lessen the effect. Without answering, he went to a small table that held a flagon of wine and a silver cup, poured a full cup and drank it down without offering any to the others. When finally he turned back to the other two, his lips were still white with anger.

"If you were not who you are, Dacius," he said stiffly, "you would be on your way to the headsman's axe right now."

"Truth always hurts." Dacius' voice was gentle and sad. "It's when you can no longer face it that you are beyond redemption."

"What do you know of redemption?" Constantine demanded. "You're not even a Christian."

"I was speaking of redemption by another besides the Son of God—if he really were that. By yourself."

"Now you're talking in riddles." Constantine turned to Crocus. "Do you understand him?"

"I know nothing of Christianity," the Gallic king admitted. "But I think I know what he means."

"Then explain it to me—if you please."

"There's no point in becoming angry at Crocus," Dacius said quietly. "Today, when Nazarius was delivering his oration in praise of Crispus at the Quinquennalia and called him the 'most noble Caesar of his august father,' I was watching your face. I saw something reflected there I'd hoped never to see—envy of your own son."

"That's ridiculous." Constantine controlled himself with a great effort. "No, you're right. I do envy Crispus his youth, and what lies before him. I envy him the adoration of the people of Gaul and Britain—that once was mine. Here in Italy and the East, I hardly seem able to please anyone anymore." He turned upon Dacius almost savagely. "You cannot know what it is to bear the responsibilities of government. The endless complaints and bickering can drive a man mad."

"Why listen to them? Crispus leaves such things to Eumenius, while he guards the frontier."

"Crispus has you two and Eumenius, but who can I trust here? Once I put my confidence in Licinius and he failed me. I would have given Bassianus great responsibility, but he tried to assassinate me. You have no conception of what it is to have the whole world look to you for final judgment in all its controversies. Why, the followers of this priest Donatus alone have caused me enough trouble to last a lifetime."

"Destroy them then," Dacius said bluntly. "Or are you so afraid of your new god that you dare not act as the Emperor should?"

"Afraid?" Constantine found that he could examine the word without rancor. "No, not afraid. But if I accept the favor of God, I must try to live according to his laws—and the principles taught by his Son."

"As revealed to you by Jesus himself?" Dacius asked bluntly.

"No. To his priests, who advise me."

"Priests, bah!" The old soldier exclaimed. "Do you know that in Egypt they are squabbling now over whether the Son is equal to the Father or a lesser being?"

"We have had word of it," Constantine admitted. "But the quarrel is still in Licinius' territory."

"Which will soon be yours, if the ambitions of the bishops are not denied."

"Are you saying I should let Licinius destroy the church in the East?" Constantine demanded.

"I am saying you should not let the bishops there trick you into attacking Licinius and throwing the whole Empire into war again, because they think they will fare better under your rule than his. What right have they to guide you, when they cannot even settle their own quarrels?" Dacius threw up his hands in a gesture of disgust. "The clergy are only men and as frail vessels as the rest of us. Your heart has always told you what is right, and best for both you and the Empire, Constantine. Listen to it now instead of the priests. Listen before it is too late."

II

The visit of Dacius and Crocus and especially the old soldier's blunt appraisal of the changes that had taken place in him, stimulated Constantine to begin a reorganization of the government along lines designed to remove many of the petty burdens of rule from his own shoulders. But before he could put this plan into effect, the long expected trouble with Licinius erupted.

Constantine's prompt military action had largely stabilized the section of the frontier across which the Goths had launched their attack. Licinius' own province of Thracia in Europe had been menaced too by the movement southward of the Gothic tribes, but the Augustus of the East had not contributed to its defense. As a result Constantine had been hard put at times to maintain peace on the frontier, especially in an area near the mouth of the Danube, where the territory occupied by a Teutonic tribe called the Bastarnae actually extended southward across the river.

Unable to penetrate Constantine's powerful chain of fortifications along the Danube, the Gothic kings now used the corridor belonging to these Bastarnae in a drive southwestward toward the very heart of Illyricum. Under heavy attack, Constantine's forces in Moesia— the weakest link in the chain of defense due to the proximity of the province to Thracia, which Licinius controlled—were forced to fall back. But when as Senior Emperor Constantine demanded that Licinius launch a flank attack northward to cut off the Gothic advance, the Emperor of the East refused.

To Constantine, tight-lipped with fury at Licinius, only two explanations for his brother-in-law's betrayal seemed likely. Either Licinius intended to move into central Illyricum himself, after both adversaries had exhausted themselves, or he had invited the Gothic chiefs to attack, assuring them that they would be left free to pillage at will in Constantine's territory. Whatever the explanation, immediate action was demanded and, when Licinius refused to do his part, Constantine ordered his forces to converge upon the invaders, even though it meant that one body of his troops would pass through Licinius' territory.

When Constantine's forces unexpectedly appeared on the southern flank and threatened to cut them off entirely, the surprised Goths had no choice except to flee across the Danube as best they could. But Licinius, his plan to cripple Constantine gone awry, decided to declare war against his fellow Augustus on the grounds that Constantine had invaded his territory—something which the Senior Emperor had every right to do in any event. Thus the die was cast for the final struggle, which indeed had been in progress, as Constantine himself discerned, for a long time—the death struggle between Christianity and paganism.

Constantine had been a Christian now for a number of years, though in order to avoid stirring up those who still clung to the worship of the old gods, he had not made Christianity the official religion of the Empire. He had, however, taken an increasingly active part in the strictly religious life of his domain, as witnessed by his calling the Council of Arles and intervening in the recurring struggle with the Donatists.

Licinius, on the other hand, had espoused paganism more and more openly in recent years, rescinding the Edict of Milan and attacking the church in order to seize its wealth for the building of the army with which he planned to destroy his brother wearer of the purple. To this end, he had developed a weapon whose extent he had been able to keep largely secret—a vast fleet recruited from the maritime countries under his rule. At the Hellespont, the mouth of the waterway separating Europe from Asia, he now assembled more than three hundred and fifty ships of war under the command of an admiral named Amandus.

Constantine reacted to the knowledge that the coming conflict would be fought both on land and sea with two swift maneuvers. At Thessalonica, near the head of the Grecian Sea, he ordered that work be carried on night and day in the shipyards to build a fleet of two hundred war galleys and more than a thousand transports. In the meantime, lest Licinius attack the vital shipyards with his superior fleet and cripple this phase of the war, Constantine hastily prepared for a campaign on land designed to keep his opponent busy.

Licinius, however, countered by attacking, seeking to throw Constantine off balance before he could marshal enough land and sea forces for a combined pincers operation against Byzantium, whose fortifications had been rebuilt since the city had fallen to Maximin Daia so easily some ten years ago. Hurriedly mobilizing to meet this new threat, Constantine sent word for Crispus and Dacius to bring as many of the regular legions from Gaul as could be spared, leaving Crocus with a small force to parry any attack across the Rhine by the ever watchful Germanic tribes. From Italy, he also brought the legions ordinarily stationed there, adding them to his

Army of Illyricum, a force of hard-bitten veterans of the campaign against the Goths.

It was a warm June day when Crispus and Dacius, at the head of a small but seasoned army from Gaul, marched into the camp on the plains before the city of Hadrianopolis, where Licinius had chosen to make his stand. Constantine greeted the two warmly and led them to a hill overlooking the area where the crucial battle would soon be fought.

"Dacius and I defeated Emperor Galerius here once—by a trick," he told Crispus. "We were escaping from Nicomedia, after father had demanded that Galerius send me to Gaul. But we were certain that an ambush had been set for us somewhere to the west, either along the main road to Sirmium and the Alpine passes by way of Naissus, or in the passes themselves, so we took evasive action. Dacius knew the country around Hadrianopolis well, so we rode out as if we were going northwestward toward the Alps, then cut back south to the Via Egnatia by way of Philippi and Thessalonica."

"I was the one who knew the country, but your father figured out the strategy, Crispus," Dacius said. "It has always been his strong point."

"What is your strategy now, Father?" Crispus inquired.

"Licinius is counting on the river Hebrus that lies between us and Hadrianopolis to hold us up." Constantine pointed to the winding course of the river east of where they stood. "A river crossing under attack is always a hazardous tactic, unless the force opposing you is small."

"What are the odds this time?" Dacius asked.

"We're still outnumbered," Constantine admitted. "My spies tell me Licinius has a hundred and fifty thousand foot soldiers and fifteen thousand horse, plus the fleet in the Hellespont that will keep us from moving any troops against him by water."

"And against them?"

"We have a hundred and twenty thousand horse and foot, with a fleet not yet half built and far from equal to theirs."

"About the same odds that were against us when we fought Licinius before," Dacius estimated. "But this time he is probably in a better position. I take it that his men occupy the heights on the other side of the river."

"They are in strength there," Constantine conceded.

"So what do we do?"

"The same thing you and I did here almost twenty years ago."

"You can't hide a whole army from an enemy who occupies the heights," Crispus protested.

"Not a whole army," Constantine corrected him, "only part of it. Tomorrow I shall announce publicly—so Licinius will be sure to hear of it—that you are taking five thousand of our troops to Thessalonica to provide fighting men for the ships there, when we force our way through the Hellespont and attack Byzantium from the sea."

"You mean I'll miss this battle?"

"You will be in it," Constantine promised him. "The day after tomorrow you will move southward at the head of your five thousand men, most of them archers—as shipboard fighters should be. You will follow this bank of the Hebrus to where the river bends eastward south of here and wait there. When I send a courier to you with word that the battle is about to be joined here at Hadrianopolis, you will then cross the river by night—on logs if you can't find a shallow enough spot to wade—and invest a heavy wood that lies back of Licinius' battleline. At the right moment, your archers will start peppering the enemy's rear with arrows and create enough confusion for us to cross the river in force here."

"Aren't you overlooking one thing?" Dacius asked. "What will Licinius be doing while Crispus is making a swing into his territory?"

"He will be busy—watching us build a bridge."

Dacius shook his head admiringly. "Just like the old days. What Crocus wouldn't give to be here."

"I'm enjoying it," Constantine admitted and pointed to the river. "We've been hauling dry logs to the bank for several days now and roping them together. If Crispus can create enough confusion for us to gain a foothold on the opposite bank of the river we will slide a bridge into the water and float it across. Then we'll pour men over it so fast that Licinius will swear the angels are transporting us over the stream."

Dacius gave him a quick look. "Does the *labarum* still go before you?"

"Of course." Constantine's voice was suddenly sober. "Licinius supports the old gods and is trying to destroy the Church of Christ. This may be the most important battle ever fought in the history of the world."

28

T HE START OF THE BATTLE for Hadrianopolis was delayed three days, while Crispus and the five thousand carried out Constantine's plan to put archers into position in the thick woods back of Licinius' troops. To keep Licinius from suspecting anything was afoot, Constantine launched feints at several points along the river, forcing the enemy to shift troops constantly, for fear that a crossing was imminent. Meanwhile, his main force worked day and night completing the pontoon bridge.

The first major crisis came late on the first day of active fighting, shortly after Crispus' archers had advanced upon the rear of the enemy to deliver a shower of arrows. The unexpected attack upon the enemy rear turned the tide of battle against Licinius for the moment. But Crispus and the five thousand could easily have been destroyed, when launching the bridge across the river proved more difficult than Constantine had anticipated, because of a cloudburst in the hills where the stream had its source. Constantine was kept from carrying out his part of the two-pronged maneuver as planned and, when he saw a considerable number of Licinius' troops being shifted from the opposite river bank, he realized that Crispus' predicament had been correctly evaluated by the enemy. Unless he moved quickly, the force of archers behind Licinius' lines would be overwhelmed.

"I'm going to take the bridge across," Constantine shouted to Dacius as he ran to mount his horse. "Give us what protection you can with the archers."

Dacius made no protest at the risk Constantine was taking. Both of them realized that, since it had been he who had sent Crispus behind the enemy lines, the responsibility for saving as many of the five thousand as possible rested on Constantine's shoulders.

"Aim high," Dacius ordered the bowmen who were protecting the men standing in the shallows as they worked desperately to start the bridge floating toward the opposite bank. Mounted now, Constantine seized the rope by which the workers were planning to tow the end of the bridge across the stream. He urged his horse into the current, angling upstream to overcome the force of the river's flow. As his trumpeter blew the call to attack, his personal troops followed him into the stream.

Licinius' forces on the opposite bank had not missed the significance of Constantine's maneuver—or the fact that it was led by the Emperor himself, for whose death their commander would reward them hugely. The sharp bark of orders rang out in the morning air as the centurions realigned the troops who had been moving to the rear to attack Crispus and his force. But as the enemy bowmen rushed to the water's edge to concentrate their attack upon the small force making the desperate attempt to float the bridge across the river, they were met by a withering hail of arrows from the archers commanded by Dacius.

The result was a brief period of confusion at the water's edge, giving Constantine some of the time he needed to swim his horse across the main current, dragging the free end of the floating bridge behind him by means of a rope attached to it. Held back by the drag of the bridge, his horse lunged desperately to keep its head above the water, and, seeking to help the hard-pressed animal, Constantine slipped from the saddle and swam beside it. He heard the trumpeter—whose horse was swimming beside him—cry out when an arrow drove through his heart, killing him instantly. And almost in the same instant, Constantine's own mount went under when an arrow drove deep into the animal's body.

Quickly loosening the loop attaching the towrope to his saddle, Constantine used the sinking body of his own mount as a stepping-stone, so to speak, and managed to throw himself across the back of the trumpeter's horse. Seizing the reins, he urged the animal forward, and seconds later they were clear of the main pull of the current. With the horse swimming strongly now, Constantine was able to swing himself into the saddle.

Arrows were whining past him on either side, but his heart took a great leap when he looked back and saw that the bridge was safely across the main part of the current, being steadied by men of his own guard, who swam their mounts beside it. The water was a melee of dying men and horses, for the toll had been heavy, in spite of Dacius' quick thinking in concentrating a hail of arrows against the opposite bank to protect Constantine and the daring band who were swinging the bridge across.

Both above and below the intended anchoring point on the enemy shore, mounted troops were now spurring their horses into the stream, supporting their Emperor. By the time Constantine's second mount stumbled up the opposite bank, a wedge of cavalry had formed behind him, splitting the ranks of the defending forces and enabling some of the attackers to dismount and secure the bridge to trees growing near the water's edge. With the bridge secured, a file of soldiers began to move across it, backing up the forces led by Constantine as he went on to expand the bridgehead he had established.

The cost in men and horses during the maneuver had been high. No more than a dozen of Constantine's one hundred elite guards made it across the river alive. But caught between Crispus' skilled archers attacking from the rear and Constantine's troops spreading out rapidly from their bridgehead on the river bank, Licinius made the mistake of moving his forces from their advantageous position upon the heights. Meanwhile Constantine's veteran legions from Illyricum and Gaul launched a massive attack that sent the enemy reeling back to the safety of the hills, leaving some thirty-four thousand dead or dying on the plain before Hadrianopolis. Nor did Licinius attempt to give battle again. Instead he retreated behind the massive fortifications of the city of Byzantium, overlooking the narrow waterway called the Bosporus.

Except for Byzantium, all of Europe was now in Constantine's hands, but he did not underestimate the difficulty of reducing the most heavily fortified center in the East. Machines of war, sapping tools and the other things necessary for a long siege were concentrated upon the narrow peninsula where the city stood. Meanwhile, Constantine handed the young Caesar of Gaul the most challenging task that remained in the campaign to free all of Europe from the control of Licinius.

II

"Admiral of the Fleet!" Crispus stared at his father in astonishment. "But I know nothing of seafaring, sir."

"Who else do I have? You, Dacius?"

The old general shook his head. "I get seasick crossing a lake. Remember what happened when we sailed from Dyrrhachium to Brundisium?"

"I can't take charge of the naval force myself," Constantine said. "My only experience with naval affairs was when we floated an army through Gaul, after Maximian seized control of the government at Arles. You're younger and more adaptable than either of us, Crispus, so the task will have to be yours."

Constantine went to a large map he'd ordered drawn of the area and indicated the neck of territory serving as a land bridge between Europe and what was ordinarily called Asia Minor. It was cut only in one place—by the narrow waterway known as the Bosporus within sight of Byzantium. "Our major purpose is to take Byzantium and cross the Bosporus into Asia," he said.

"I take it there is no possibility of any further agreement with Licinius?" Dacius asked.

Constantine turned almost savagely upon the old soldier who had been his tutor. "Would you have me give him leave to go on harassing the church? And encouraging the Goths?"

Dacius was not intimidated. "I just want to be sure that religious considerations are not directing military policy."

"What do you mean by that?"

"The territory beyond the Bosporus is large and we both know how quickly an army can be cut to pieces in an area like Augusta Euphratensia. It is one thing to risk an army to gain an important military victory, but quite another to ask men who are not Christians to put their lives in jeopardy so bishops and churches may be preserved."

With an effort, Constantine controlled himself. From the viewpoint of logic alone everything Dacius had said was true. The majority of his subjects, whether in Britain, Gaul, Italy or Illyricum,

THE MIRACLE OF THE FLAMING CROSS

were not Christians. And his obligation as a ruler was as much to them as to those of the church to which he gave allegiance.

"I shall not ask men who followed me across the Rhine and the Danube to die needlessly for any faith," he said and turned back to the map. "Here is the Hellespont, Crispus. You can see that it is narrow and long, but if you succeed in opening it and driving through the Sea of Marmara and the Bosporus, we will cut off any retreat of the enemy across to Asia Minor. Otherwise, if the siege begins to go against Licinius, he will leave Byzantium and go over into Asia."

"Then my task is to push through the water barrier and deny the Bosporus to the enemy?" Crispus asked.

"You've stated it exactly."

"Against a larger fleet, commanded by Admiral Amandus," Dacius reminded Crispus. "He has had a lot of experience in naval warfare. Don't make the mistake of underestimating him."

"Amandus has the advantage of numbers and experience," the young Caesar conceded. "But your spies report that he is showing his age by being overcautious and bottling up his ships in a narrow waterway. That may even the odds to where a much smaller fleet will be able to smash through and open up the Hellespont."

"What do you say to that?" Constantine asked Dacius.

"A thousand years ago the Hebrews had a great general and king named David, who also wrote psalms," Dacius said with a grin. "A verse from one of them seems to be the only comment that fits the present circumstances."

"What is it?"

"Out of the mouth of babes and sucklings hast thou ordained strength because of thine enemies, that thou mightest still the enemy and the avenger."

III

More than a quarter of a century had passed since Constantine had taken part in a siege operation to reduce a major fortified center. In fact, his one and only experience with that static and discouraging type of warfare had been during the almost year-

long siege of Alexandria. Busy supervising the raising of great
mounds of earth by which the huge machines of war were lifted
to a level where they could toss stones over the walls into Byzantium, attacking the morale of the defenders, he received cheering
news from the Hellespont.

Crispus, according to the report, had lost no time in mobilizing
the small fleet gathered at Thessalonica against the much larger
armada of Admiral Amandus blocking the Hellespont. The first day
of the sea battle had been indecisive, with losses on both sides
about equal, but about midday on the second, a south wind had
sprung up. With all sails set, oars put away—since they were not
needed now—and the oarsmen used for fighting, Crispus' galleys
had been driven like battering rams by the force of the wind into
the very mouth of the Hellespont against the enemy fleet massed
there.

With the wind against them, Amandus' ships had not been able
to maneuver in the narrow waterway or use their sails and were
therefore caught at a considerable disadvantage. The rams of the
attacking fleet smashed oars and tore great holes into hulls, destroying a hundred and thirty vessels, somewhat less than half the
entire fleet gathered there by Licinius. Five thousand men—most
of them trained mariners and therefore not easily replaceable—had
been killed, and Amandus himself only escaped by taking to land
on the shore of Asia Minor, while what was left of his fleet retreated through the Sea of Marmara to the Bosporus.

To Constantine, slogging in the mud around Byzantium, the
opening of the Hellespont meant far more than the defeat of a superior naval force, however joyous that news might be. From the
seaports of Greece and the fertile land of Macedonia, a plentiful
supply of food now began to flow to his army, as well as additional
siege machines, sappers, weapons and the other tools needed for a
prolonged military operation. In the meantime, a hail of missiles
poured into the beleaguered city from towers raised outside the
walls, and battering rams, pushed against the walls in the protection of the mobile houses covering them, had started to break holes
in the fortifications.

Licinius was not long in making the move Constantine had been
expecting, since it had never been the custom of the Augustus of

the East to remain with his armies in defeat. With the fall of Byzantium growing daily more certain, he managed to escape with his family and treasures across the western end of the Pontus Euxinus, which was controlled by his own fleet, and gain safety on the other side. To Constantine, busy crushing the hard nut Byzantium had turned out to be, word soon came that Licinius was busy raising an army of some fifty or sixty thousand men in Bithynia, obviously expecting to make a stand there when, his forces weakened by the siege and the necessity of transporting them by water, Constantine moved on to the next phase of the attack.

But here Constantine showed the same daring, the same willingness to risk all in a swift strike for victory that had characterized his military genius from the beginning. Leaving Byzantium to wither on the vine, so to speak, with only enough troops in the sappers' trenches and on the mounds to man the great siege machines, he sent Crispus and his fleet against the remaining armada commanded by Amandus. And once again, though outnumbered in both vessels and men, the genius of the young commander brought victory.

Choosing a day when a following wind filled his sails and drove his vessels on, Crispus smashed through the Bosporus, crushing Licinius' galleys right and left and sending many of them to flounder on the Cyanean rocks just offshore. Meanwhile, the waiting troops of Constantine's army, embarking in everything that would float, negotiated the narrow waterway.

Licinius and his forces were waiting near Chrysopolis, on the southern shore of the Bosporus across from Byzantium, confident that the heights there would give them the advantage they so desperately needed. But with a smashing naval victory and a successful water crossing behind it, Constantine's army could not be denied. Storming ashore before Chrysopolis, the main body held Licinius' forces at bay while flanking parties drove inland on either side, closing the jaws of the great trap that was Constantine's favorite tactic of war.

Licinius' hastily raised levies, cut to pieces by Constantine's flanking columns, began to retreat in disorder. Twenty-five thousand men died on the heights around Chrysopolis, but once again Licinius escaped, this time to Nicomedia. Confident that Constantine would leave him at least part of the Empire which, by his own greed and misgovernment, he had allowed to shrink to almost nothing in less than ten years, he sent his wife, Constantia, to beg mercy for her husband from her brother.

But the victor had no intention of giving the vanquished anything more than his life, and that only in answer to Constantia's prayer. The unlucky Martinianus, who had been second-in-command, was executed summarily, while Licinius was allowed to doff the purple forever, after swearing never again to attempt any seizure of power. Having acknowledged Constantine as Dominus and relinquished all further claim to rule, the former Augustus of the East and his family were banished to Thessalonica.

IV

Constantine, Dacius and Crispus stood upon one of the seven hills making up the peninsula upon which Byzantium stood and looked down at the city, scarred and torn by the siege. It had fallen quickly after Licinius' defeat at Chrysopolis and Constantine's fleet—which Crispus had handled so masterfully—now rode at anchor within the horn-shaped inlet forming a major part of the harbor, an area where fish schooled so often in the sunlight that its inhabitants likened it to the mythical Golden Horn of Plenty.

"I think this is one of the most beautiful spots in the world," Dacius said.

"It could also be the most important to me," Constantine said thoughtfully.

"Why do you say that, Father?" Crispus asked.

"You, Dacius and Crocus should be able to hold the Germanic tribes in check in the West. With troops stationed at Milan and Sirmium, it should not be difficult to maintain the Danube frontier to the north. But the East is another matter. The Sassanid kings of Persia have grown more daring lately, but Licinius seems to have made no attempt to hold them in check. Unless they are put down soon the entire eastern border will be in revolt."

"You've come almost full circle," Dacius reminded him. "Your

first major command was on the Persian frontier when Narses rebelled against Diocletian."

"And I first found Christ there, in a painting on the wall of the
ruined church at Dura. A whole world out there in the East has
never heard of God and his Son. For some reason, certainly not
through any worthiness of my own, God has chosen to favor me
in all my efforts. Perhaps he intends for Persia to be next."

Far to the east, in the haze where sky and water met, an irregular dark line marked the distant shore of the beautiful inland
sea. That line had been a frontier, Constantine remembered, even
in ancient times, when Jason and the Argonauts had sailed there,
seeking the almost legendary fleeces placed by earlier inhabitants
in mountain streams to trap particles of gold washed down from
deposits in the hills above.

Who could say that a new frontier for him did not lie beyond
the Pontus Euxinus, beyond the Euphrates and the Tigris, beyond
even Armenia and Mesopotamia, in the vast territory extending to
the river Indus in far-off India? It had been conquered briefly by
Alexander the Great and called Ariana by him, but Rome had
never extended its domain there. And at the thought that he might
one day rule a greater expanse of the East than even the victorious
Alexander had ever been able to conquer, Constantine felt his
imagination take fire.

"Rome is dying." To Crispus and Dacius, Constantine seemed
to be speaking to himself rather than to them. "I shall leave it
behind me and build here a great city from which to rule an Empire of the East, a Christian Empire greater than the world has
ever known."

Seeing the glowing light in Constantine's eyes Dacius was reminded of another occasion when he had seen that same look in
the camp on the bank of the Euphrates behind the Persian lines,
where Constantine had risen from sleep and revealed his daring
plan of attack. And yet—though Dacius could not see it—one great
difference, besides that of age, separated the youthful commander,
who had risked all that day to gain much, and the Emperor who
stood now with the world at his feet. For while the youth had
been filled with confidence in his own strength, the Emperor freely
acknowledged that another Power, higher than himself, had been

instrumental at every critical point in his life, prescribing by various means the course he would follow.

The change had been a gradual one, it was true. But Constantine himself had already acknowledged it publicly when, in a letter to the Council of Arles two years after he had raised the standard of Christ at Saxa Rubra and gone on to Rome in victory, he had written:

> The inconceivable goodness of our God forbids that mankind should continue to wander in the dark. I have realized this truth from many examples outside myself, but I can also confirm it from my own experience. There were things in my own nature that were devoid of righteousness and I seemed to see no heavenly power that I might have been carrying hidden in my breast. But Almighty God, who watches from the high tower of heaven, had vouchsafed to me what I have not deserved. Verily past numbers are the blessings that he, in his heavenly goodness, has bestowed on me, his servant.

29

W ITH THE FALL of Byzantium, the need for the Army of
Gaul in the East was over, so Crispus and Dacius prepared to leave for home, where Crocus had been hard put at times
to hold back the Germanic tribes. The Gallic troops would take
the overland route, but the young Caesar and his grizzled adviser
who, though past the traditional three score and ten showed hardly
any signs of advancing age, boarded a swift galley for the journey
westward.

Constantine joined them for the first leg of the journey, a very
short one that took them only as far as Drepanum. As the galley
moved over the sunlit waters of the gulf, his memory went back
to the day when he and Marios had paused on a headland overlooking the narrow body of water not far from Nicomedia and he
had watched just such a vessel as this moving up the gulf toward
its berth.

"It has been a long time." Dacius echoed Constantine's unspoken
thought, as each had done so often for the other in the years when
they had been close. Lately, however, more than simply the distance to Gaul had come between them, for Dacius had not espoused Christianity. In fact, he had not hesitated on more than one
occasion to express his feeling that the Christian bishops were ex-
erting too much influence upon Constantine in purely political decisions and, as a result, the two had drifted somewhat apart. Nor
did Constantine doubt that the failure of Crispus to accept his own
faith could be laid largely at the door of Dacius, for Crispus worshiped the old general fully as much as Constantine had in his
own youth.

"It *has* been a long time," Constantine agreed. "And a long road still lies ahead. Eumenius had already organized a stable government in Gaul before I left. Here in the East I must now try to undo the misdeeds of Daia and Licinius."

"I don't envy you," Dacius said. "Especially with the bishops fighting among themselves again in Alexandria."

Constantine ignored the thrust, although he knew what Dacius meant. Rumors of a new religious crisis brewing in Alexandria had come to his ears, but at the moment he preferred to put it out of his mind and enjoy the approach to Drepanum and the prospect of seeing his mother again. The town had changed little, he saw as they descended from the galley and walked along the shore. At the house where Crispus had spent his boyhood, the three of them turned in. Before they could make their presence known, Helena saw them from the garden and ran to seize Crispus in her arms.

Once again as he had occasionally during the recent war, when the soldiers had acclaimed the handsome young Caesar of Gaul for his spectacular victories, Constantine felt a twinge of jealousy for his own son. But he resolutely put the thought from him and went to embrace his mother, reminding himself that, since she had reared Crispus from a baby until he had left for Treves and his military training in Gaul, the boy would naturally seem more like a son to her than would Constantine himself.

"I hope you weren't troubled during the fighting," he said to Helena as they entered the house.

"Why would anyone bother an old woman?" Seeing her again after so long a time, it seemed to him that, like Dacius, she was ageless. For though her face was a little lined by the years, she was still beautiful.

"You may rule the world, Flavius"—it had been so long since Constantine had been addressed by his given name that for a moment he hardly realized his mother was speaking to him—"but your greatest accomplishment was fathering the boy there."

Constantine looked to where Crispus was embracing the old servant, who had looked after him as a child. "He is a man," he admitted. "A Caesar in every way."

"Just such another as you were, though he looks more like Constantius."

"Father thought of you when he was dying," he told her. "In fact his last words were of you."

"I'm glad you could be with him. Tell me, was he happy with—" She hesitated over the name.

"Empress Theodora is a fine woman, Mother. You would like her. She has done a good job of bringing up the children."

"Constantia seems to be very nice. She visited me several times when they were in residence at Nicomedia."

"I didn't know that," Constantine exclaimed. "She never mentioned it."

"It was after Licinius was pushed back into this area. You know her oldest daughter is named for me, don't you?"

"Yes. Empress Theodora didn't mind."

"What of your own children?"

"We have three boys and three daughters. Now that the war has ended, Fausta will be coming to Nicomedia with them."

"Where is she now?"

"In Rome. She prefers it there, so I built her a fine palace. She says the children have better tutors in Rome and I suspect she's right."

"A wife's place is with her husband." Helena's eyes followed Crispus, who was eagerly exploring again the house where he had spent his boyhood. "How does this new wife of yours get along with the boy?"

"They're the best of friends: after all they are not very far apart in age." The words brought to mind the last time he had seen Fausta and Crispus together, at the Quinquennalia of the Caesars celebrating the election of Crispus and of Licinius' son, Licinianus, to that rank. He remembered the eager, excited look on Crispus' face, as he and Fausta chatted together, and the way she had looked up at the youth admiringly—just as, Constantine recalled, she had looked up at him during the reception celebrating the Vicennalia of Diocletian and Maximian.

"Are you sure you're happy with this wife of yours?" His mother's words broke into his thoughts. "She spends so much time in Rome. And there have been rumors—"

"Don't listen to idle gossip." His tone was sharper than he had intended it to be and, suddenly contrite, he reached into the pocket of his tunic and took out a small scroll. "This is for you, Mother, or perhaps I should say Augusta. The title has been yours since yesterday, when I signed the document."

More than a quarter of a century had passed since Helena had signed the bill of divorcement at Naissus, releasing Constantius to marry Theodora and shutting herself away from any of the honors the man she had married when he was a junior officer in the Roman army would gain thereafter. Now, by the decree giving her the title of Augusta, or Empress, Constantine had restored to her, however belatedly, what she had given up so long ago.

"What use have I for titles at my age?" she said huskily, as Crispus and Dacius came up to congratulate her. But her eyes were shining with unshed tears and Constantine knew he had made her very happy.

"You must come and visit me in Gaul, Grandmother," Crispus said. "I will stage a great gala in your honor."

"I'm too old to travel, unless it would be to Galilee and Judea where the Saviour walked." Her voice suddenly kindled with indignation. "Do you know that a pagan temple stands at Jerusalem over the tomb where the body of our Lord was placed, when he was brought down from the cross?"

"I didn't know it," Constantine admitted. "Why don't you go there and find out whether such a thing is true. If it is, the temple shall be torn down and the tomb properly honored."

Crispus and Dacius departed the next morning on a galley that would take them through the Sea of Marmara and the Hellespont, where the youthful Caesar had won the first of his two great naval victories. From there they would take a larger ship for Gaul. Meanwhile, Constantine went on to Nicomedia and the thousands of decisions awaiting him in connection with reorganizing the government along lines he had already decided to put into effect here in the East, based upon reforms first begun by Eumenius in Gaul and later extended to Italy and Illyricum.

Before he could even begin this work, however, he was faced with further treachery on the part of Licinius, who, even from his refuge in Thessalonica, continued to plot against his benefactor. In the end, no choice was left except to execute the former Emperor of the East, while Constantia and her son, the young Caesar

Licinianus, were given refuge at her brother's temporary court of Nicomedia.

Constantine's realm now stretched from the farthest eastern corner of Armenia to the area of the Picts in northern Britain and from the northernmost courses of the Danube and the Rhine southward in Egypt beyond the city of Syene, far up the Nile. For one man to govern so vast an empire was manifestly impossible, and the reorganization of the government was designed to remove much of the burden of day-to-day decisions from his shoulders.

II

Under Constantine's plan the Roman Empire was divided into four Prefectures, each under an officer with the title of Praetorian Prefect. The Prefecture of Gaul, already under the rule of Crispus, comprised the three dioceses—as they were called—of Britain, Spain and Gaul, each governed by a *vicarius*, or vicar. The dioceses were further divided into districts governed by *consulares*. The Prefecture of Italy was made up of three dioceses comprising the City of Rome, Italy itself, and Africa. The Prefecture of Illyricum was divided into the dioceses of Macedonia and Dacia, while that of the East, called the *Praefectura Orientis*, contained five dioceses.

The smaller divisions were governed by officials variously known as *consulares*, presidents, correctors, dukes and counts in descending order of rank. The court, too, was reorganized to make it more efficient and to cut down the political infighting which had so characterized the court of Diocletian and other emperors before him.

At its head were seven major officers: the Grand Chamberlain, with a subordinate Deputy Vicar and a Count of the Bedchamber and Palace; a Chancellor, whose duties were concerned with the courts and with business having to do with foreign powers; a *quaestor*, the final authority in questions of legality, who also composed the imperial edicts; the Treasurer General, who had charge of collection and disbursement of revenue; the Master of the Privy Purse, managing the Emperor's private affairs—a job which devolved upon Adrian, who had handled it so well in the past; and the

Commanders of the Household Troops, one for the cavalry and one for the infantry.

One of the most striking changes Constantine instituted was that of nobility divided into *illustres, spectabiles* and *clarissimi*. Classified as *illustres* were Consuls during their period of office, the Patricians and Life Peers, the Praetorian Prefects governing Rome—and later Byzantium—the Masters of the Cavalry and Infantry and the seven consuls of Asia, Africa and Achaea, the heads of the thirteen dioceses, and various ranks in the army grouped as "Counts" and "Dukes." The army, too, was reorganized into "palatines" and "borderers," the former stationed in the major cities and the latter guarding the frontiers. All were placed under two supreme generals, the *magister equitum*, commanding the cavalry, and the *magister peditum*, the infantry.

Before these reforms were completed, a delegation of Senators and other important nobles arrived from Rome, disturbed by rumors that Constantine might place the center of the Empire farther east than the city which had given it its name. They were led by Marcellinus, the old Senator who had come to Treves to beg Constantine to remove Maxentius. Though almost ten years had passed since the campaign for Italy, Marcellinus hardly seemed to have aged a day. Nor did he hesitate to plunge immediately into the business that had brought him and the delegation to Nicomedia.

"Rome deserves better treatment at your hands than to be left to die on the vine, Augustus," he said. "We welcomed you after the battle of the Milvian Bridge with one of the greatest triumphs in our history. We have given our hearts to the Empress Fausta and your children. And though you chose not to come to Rome after your victory over the base traitor Licinius, the city outdid itself only a few months ago in tribute to your son Caesar Crispus, when he visited there."

Constantine had been listening with half an ear, wondering how he could appease the delegation and send them back without committing himself to further support of a city that had welcomed a tyrant like Maxentius, because its leaders thought to gain from having an Augustus in residence there. But at the mention of Crispus' name, he sat up straight and the familiar red haze of sudden explosive anger drew an almost tangible curtain between him and the old Senator. For Crispus had not even been scheduled to stop at Rome, much less celebrate a triumph there.

"Did you say Caesar Crispus visited Rome?" Someone more observant than Marcellinus would have noticed the sudden change in Constantine's voice and manner.

"Yes, Augustus, on the way home to Gaul. All of us were heartened when he sacrificed to Apollo. You have a worthy son to—"

"How long was he there?"

"Almost a week. The people went wild over him and would not let him go. And now—"

Constantine got suddenly to his feet. "I will talk to you and the delegation again tomorrow, Marcellinus," he said sharply and this time even the old Senator could not fail to see that something was wrong.

"But Aug—"

Constantine left the room before Marcellinus could finish what he was saying and did not stop until he was in his own private quarters and the door was shut. There he poured wine for himself with trembling hands and gulped it down, almost choking from the tension of anger constricting his throat.

So the treachery had not ended with Licinius, he told himself. Now his own son was working behind his back to build favor with the people of Rome, sacrificing to the old gods because he knew it would please them, letting himself be honored and receiving the plaudits of the crowd. What made matters even worse was Constantine's realization that with the whole area east of the Alps almost denuded of veteran troops to build the army that had defeated Licinius and the Army of Gaul fanatically loyal to him, Crsipus could take Italy and Rome if he wished, as Constantine himself had taken it from Maxentius.

Fighting for control, and losing the battle, Constantine brooded over what he considered the ingratitude of his son until finally he fell asleep, only to awaken in the grip of a nightmare in which a gleeful Crispus sacrificed his own father upon the altar of Apollo. When the dawn came, he summoned his *magister memoriae* and dictated a terse order removing Crispus from his position as Caesar of Gaul and Britain and naming his son Constantine II as ruler there—although the boy was not yet in his teens—with Eumenius, whose loyalty it did not occur to him to doubt, as acting Prefect. This done, he sent a peremptory letter to Fausta at Rome, ordering her to come at once to Nicomedia and bring the children with her.

That afternoon, he also ordered Marcellinus and the delegation back to Rome without even giving them a second audience. At the same time, he sent with them an official communication to be published in all major cities of the Empire, a communication whose wording he was to regret more than once in the years that followed. In brief, the open letter to his subjects invited any who might know of a plot against the Emperor or the government to reveal that information, with the assurance that he would be well rewarded.

"Let him come without fear, and let him address himself to me!" Constantine said at the end of the letter. "I will listen to all: I will myself conduct the investigation and, if the accuser does but prove his charge, I will vindicate my wrongs. Only let him speak boldly and be sure of his case!"

It was an open invitation to informers, tellers of tales, and those who sought to attack others for their own benefit. And before long it lighted the fire under a cauldron containing a veritable witch's brew.

III

By the second day following publication of the sweeping edict, Constantine was beginning to have misgivings over the precipitate action he had taken in a fit of anger which—more than anything else he realized now—had lately become his besetting sin. Dispassionate consideration could only lead to the conclusion that there must be a logical explanation for what had happened in the case of Crispus. But when he could not immediately think of one, he lapsed again into the black mood which had seized him at the news of his son's triumph in Rome.

When Helena, who had remained at Drepanum while preparations were going forward for her journey to Syria Palaestina and Jerusalem, came to Nicomedia, he refused to see her. She ignored the order, however, and went to the private apartment where he had sequestered himself. Nor did the guards try to stop her, since the proclamation naming her Augusta had been posted everywhere. Constantine himself looked up at his mother with eyes that were red from loss of sleep, and the tears of one betrayed by someone he loved.

"Is it true that you removed Crispus as Caesar of Gaul?" Helena demanded angrily.

"Yes. How did you learn of it?"

"Constantia sent word to me. Why didn't you tell me yourself, without waiting for me to hear of it through palace gossip?"

"It is done," Constantine said morosely. "What difference does it make now?"

"But why?"

"Because my son has betrayed me!" Constantine's anger boiled over again, as it had while he was listening to Marcellinus. "Do you know that he went to Rome and let the people there celebrate a triumph in his honor?"

"He deserved no less, after winning battles for you." Helena gave him an appraising look. "Is it possible that you are jealous of your own son?"

The question was too close to home not to give Constantine pause; he had asked it of himself more than once during the past several nights, while he had lain awake, feeling his heart break inside him and unable to find a way to heal the wound. What was more he realized what a terrible mistake he had made in publishing the edict inviting informers to betray others, yet was unable to bring himself to a public confession of error.

"I will admit that Crispus earned a triumph, Mother," he said. "In time I would have ordered it myself, perhaps on his Decennalia. But he had no reason to go to Rome now, except for that purpose. And he sacrificed to the old gods."

"How do you know that?"

"Marcellinus told me and he would not lie. Why else would Crispus sacrifice to Apollo than to remind the people of Rome that he is not a Christian, like his father?"

Taken aback by the question, Helena was silent.

"You see, you cannot answer, no more than I. He must be seeking to make Rome support him, so he can take Italy as well as what I have already given him. First Maximian, then Bassianus, then Licinianus, and now my son. Why must the people I trust always betray me?" It was a cry of pain.

"Crispus would not betray you deliberately, I'm sure of that." Helena's eyes suddenly narrowed. "It must be *her* doing."

"Whose?"

"Your wife. Don't forget that she's Maximian's daughter and the blood of traitors runs in her veins. This is the sort of thing Maximian's get would think of."

In the dark hours of the night, wracked by the agony of doubt and the proddings of his conscience Constantine had remembered how much Fausta had been disturbed when he had made Crispus Caesar—until he had assured her that other parts of the Empire would be placed under the rule of her sons, a promise he had just now fulfilled in making Constantine II Caesar of Gaul. But Fausta and Crispus were friendly, too friendly he had even thought on one or two occasions. And there could be no possible gain for her or her sons in Crispus' being acclaimed a hero by the people of Rome —rather the opposite.

"What are you going to do?" Helena asked.

"I have ordered Fausta to come to Nicomedia at once, and the message removing Crispus from the Caesarship of Gaul also ordered him to come here. I shall let him defend himself, if he can."

"But will you give him a fair trial?"

"Can you ask that? My own mother—about my own son?"

Helena came over and put her hand upon his shoulder. "I realize that the cares of a ruler are great," she said. "But should you let them change you as much as you have changed, Flavius?"

With an effort, he resisted the impulse to lash out at her and waited until the instant response of anger had subsided. "Have I changed so much, Mother?" he asked finally.

She nodded soberly. "I didn't believe it at first when others mentioned it—people who love you and have no wish to harm you with idle gossip. Dacius even spoke of it before he left for Gaul and asked me to try to reason with you. But I thought your temper was only short because you had just been under the strain of a military campaign."

"I'm always under a strain! It seems that nothing goes right any-more."

"Perhaps because you demand too much of other people, and of yourself. Not many people have the strength of will to keep a goal constantly before them throughout their lives as you have, Son. Even our Lord begged the Father to take the cup from him, when he knew he was about to be arrested and nailed to the cross."

"Christ still said, 'Not what I will, but what thou wilt,'" he re-minded her.

"Yes, but are you sure it is God's will that has changed you and not your own?"

IV

Sweeping though Constantine's reforms in government were, those in the field of religion went even further. At the time of the Edict of Milan, the *clerici*, or clergy, had been recognized as a separate class of individuals and freed from many of the onerous duties devolving upon Roman citizens. As a result, there had been an immediate rush of wealthy people into the ranks of the clergy and from time to time it had been necessary to issue edicts control-ling this trend.

Some three years before the crucial victory over paganism at Chrysopolis, the Christian Church had been permitted by imperial decree to accept legacies and many congregations in the larger cities and the more populous districts had acquired considerable wealth. As part of his program of reform, Constantine now began to allow regular contributions by the government to the church, including landed revenues and shares in crops. At the same time, certain of the prerogatives of imperial power were relinquished to officers of the church, even to the point of giving the sentences meted out by bishops—when sitting as a court of arbitration in religious contro-versies—the same force as those of judicial officers of the Empire.

Although all were still free to worship whatever gods they pleased, ceremonial sacrifices other than to the Christian deity were discontinued, making it quite apparent to all that Christianity was the religion preferred by their ruler. Ironically enough, however, the force Constantine sought to bring to his aid in governing soon proved to be a veritable thorn in the flesh for that government, even threatening parts of the Empire with revolt.

This time the controversy was not over actions of the clergy as it had been with the Donatist schism. Instead, it involved questions concerning the very nature of God and his son.

30

Constantine first realized that what he had regarded as a local religious controversy had now entered into a wider sphere of involvement when Eusebius of Caesarea appeared at the court in Nicomedia.

"I am pleased to see that you escaped harm at the hands of the persecutors," he said in greeting Eusebius, whose rise to the position of bishop had been rather rapid.

"I was forced to endure imprisonment in Egypt for a while," Eusebius said. "But God released me in time, perhaps so I could continue writing a history of the church."

"I knew you had become Bishop of Caesarea, but I had forgotten about the latter project."

"I feel that it will help others to know the various vicissitudes through which the church has come," Eusebius said, "but lately I have been troubled by matters of the present that make it difficult to write objectively about the past. I hesitate to burden you with them, Dominus, but I have journeyed from Caesarea to speak to you on behalf of a priest named Arius, and his difficulties with Bishop Alexander of Egypt."

"Why must priests bicker, if they are united in the one purpose of serving God?"

"Perhaps our zeal to serve God in the best way makes us differ," Eusebius admitted. "Surely questions of military policy come up among your generals from time to time."

Constantine smiled. "Whenever they do, I resolve them by knocking heads together, until all think as one." Then his face grew sober. "But priestly heads seem harder than soldierly ones; the more

I knock, often the worse they quarrel. I have almost come to believe that government should have no part in religious matters."

"But there must be a final authority," Eusebius protested. "Else how would anything be decided?"

"By prayer and seeking the will of God, as I have sought to settle doubtful questions in my own life. But get on with your own petition, Eusebius. I suppose you are here to ask me to reverse the decision of the synod of bishops from Egypt and Libya who excommunicated Arius two years ago."

Eusebius looked startled. "I had no idea—"

"I kept close watch over happenings here in the East while it was ruled by Emperor Licinius," Constantine assured him. "Still, I must confess that I cannot see what this controversy is about, or why Arius has stirred up so much trouble. Perhaps you can tell me."

"The question of the nature of God has intrigued religious philosophers since the beginning of time."

"I have no time for a sermon, Bishop Eusebius. Save that for the church. Tell me what new thing Arius advocates that has turned so many against him and caused so much controversy."

"He questions the position traditionally accorded Christ in the godhead," Eusebius admitted.

"What is this position you speak of?"

"In his letter to the Galatians, the Apostle Paul says: 'When the fullness of the time was come, God sent forth his Son, made of woman, made under the law, to redeem them that were under the law, that we might receive the adoption of sons. And because you are sons, God has sent forth the Spirit of his Son into your hearts. . . . Wherefore you are no more a servant, but a son; and if a son, then an heir of God through Christ.'"

"That seems simple enough for anyone to understand, without argument. I have often felt Christ's spirit in my own heart and I believe I have seen him as well."

"You have been doubly blessed, Dominus, for the personal revelation is not given to all. Most of us must be content with the infusion of the Holy Spirit sent by Christ to lift us toward him and, as Paul said, make us heirs of God through him."

"But if the revelation to the Apostle Paul was so clear, why the difference in interpretation?"

"Perhaps because so many of us who follow Christ these days are Greeks," Eusebius admitted. "And being Greeks, we like to apply logic, even to religion."

"Why not? It applies to everything else."

"I wish it were that simple, but in matters of the spirit, the hard core of logic is often difficult to find. Almost a hundred years ago Origen stated the fundamental Christian belief that there is one God, who is the Father eternal, and that Christ, the Son of God, was truly born of a virgin, suffered, and rose from the dead. Origen also taught that the Holy Spirit is associated in honor and dignity with both the Father and Son, but in his belief, God was before all. He created the Son as the intermediary between him and man and only through Christ can the spirit of man attain that perfect condition which is necessary for him to enter heaven."

"When he was on earth, Christ was still a man."

"Both God and man, according to our belief," Eusebius corrected him. "But when Christ was taken up into heaven after his resurrection, the glory of our Lord's divinity was given him once again by the Father and now he rules with the Father as God. As Origen said: 'From him there began the union of the divine with the human nature, in order that the human, by communion with the divine, might rise to be divine.'"

"I still fail to see what the controversy is all about."

"Arius teaches that Christ was a creation of God who did not exist before his birth as a man and, therefore, is not a part of God himself, but a separate being. The doctrine of the Trinity, which most of the church favors, teaches that God is actually three—Father, Son and Holy Spirit—and has been from the beginning. Christ, the Son, was made human and came to earth to accomplish the salvation of men. Though no longer present on earth, he still sends the Holy Spirit to infuse the souls of men and give them the attribute of his divinity by which they may live forever."

"I must confess that I see little difference between the two concepts," Constantine said. "Where do you stand?"

"Arius is my friend; I sat at his feet while in Egypt. To a Greek like myself, his teachings seem logical, so I would not deny him the right to teach, as Bishop Alexander has done in Egypt. Actually,

I believe the truth lies somewhere between Arius' position and that of Alexander."

"And you wish me to mediate between the two, in order that they may come to an agreement?"

"If that is possible, Dominus."

"To me this whole controversy seems absurd," Constantine said. "But I cannot have priests and bishops denouncing each other like women in a neighborhood quarrel. I will send Hosius to both Arius and Bishop Alexander with a letter asking that they reconcile their opinions."

The letter carried by the Bishop of Córdoba, when he left Nicomedia for Alexandria, left no doubt about Constantine's opinion of the controversy or his desire for it to be ended at once.

But Ah! Glorious and Divine Providence (he wrote). What a wound was inflicted not alone on my ears but on my heart, when I heard that divisions existed among yourselves, even more grievous than those of Africa, so that you, through whose agency I hoped to bring healing to others, need a remedy worse than they. And yet, after making careful inquiry into the origin of these discussions, I find that the cause is quite insignificant and entirely disproportionate to such a quarrel. I gather that the present controversy originated as follows: When you, Alexander, asked each of the presbyters what he thought about a certain passage in the Scriptures, or rather what he thought about a certain aspect of a foolish question, you, Arius, without due consideration laid down propositions which never ought to have been conceived at all or, if conceived, ought to have been buried in silence. Dissensions therefore arose between you; communion was forbidden; and the most holy people, torn in twain, no longer preserved the unity of a common body.

Such conduct is vulgar, childish and petulant, ill befitting priests of God and men of sense. It is a wile and temptation of the devil. Let us have done with it. If we cannot all think alike on all topics, we can at least be united on the great essentials. As far as regards Divine Providence, let there be one faith and one understanding, one united opinion in reference to God.

Had Dacius been there to exercise his old capacity of Constantine's conscience, he might have pointed out that the letter was an example of what was becoming increasingly frequent—the Emperor's tendency to ride roughshod over the opinions of others where his own decisions were concerned and his intolerance of all opinions which did not agree with his own. But no one sought to persuade Constantine to make the tone of the letter less peremptory and arbitrary so it naturally had the predictable effect upon a brilliant and original mind like that of Arius. Meanwhile there were other things to trouble the mind of Rome's ruler.

II

It was a morose and haggard man who greeted his family upon their arrival at Nicomedia. Nor did the storm flags of color in Fausta's cheeks, warning of her resentment at having been torn from her beloved Rome during the height of the winter social season, do anything to alleviate his mood.

"Why did the children and I have to come to this outpost of barbarism, when you haven't even finished conquering the East yet?" she demanded as soon as the ceremonial aspects of their meeting were concluded and they were alone.

"Because I want you with me. Is it nothing that I have conquered half the world and made you its Empress?"

"I could enjoy it better in Rome than in this—this village. Besides, you will soon be off again to the Persian frontier, or across the Danube, leaving us here."

"Then perhaps you can hear your children's lessons," he said shortly.

"I brought a tutor for that, since you seemed to have forgotten it entirely. Senator Marcellinus recommended him—a nephew of his named Lupus, who was educated at Massilia."

Constantine remembered seeing a rather handsome man among the retinue who had debarked with Fausta. He had been wearing a toga, in itself enough to make him stand out here in the East. And now that he thought about it, the newcomer had borne a strong family resemblance to Marcellinus.

"It's time the children had a good tutor," he agreed, thinking that it might be advisable to gain whatever favor he could with Marcellinus and the faction of Senators led by the old patrician. When they had visited Nicomedia a few months before and Marcellinus had let word drop of the triumph celebrated for Crispus at Rome, he'd been rather rude and sent them packing without ceremony. Then a thought struck him. "Is this Lupus a pagan?" he demanded.

"He's a Roman." Fausta tossed her head. "He will teach the children some respect for the customs and prestige of Rome, which is better than having them listen to your sister everlastingly whining her prayers to a Jewish God. I was warned in Rome that she has been doing everything she can to undermine me with my own husband. You know she only wants to make sure that brat of hers you named a Caesar will get part of the Empire one day."

There was enough truth in Fausta's accusation to keep him from flying into a rage at her because of it. Constantia and her children, including the boy Caesar, Licinianus, had taken up residence at Nicomedia after Licinius' death. There, she had become closely allied with the Christian Church, particularly its bishop, called Eusebius of Nicomedia to distinguish him from the Bishop of Caesarea. And Constantine did not doubt that Constantia was working just as hard to gain a place in the Empire for her offspring as Fausta was for hers.

"Let us not quarrel, when we've been separated so long," he said reasonably. "I shall shortly have to visit Antioch and Alexandria. You always liked to travel and it will be good for the children to see something besides Rome and Italy. Besides, in perhaps another year we will go to Rome to celebrate my Vicennalia."

Mercurial as always, she was immediately contrite. "Crispus said you were working too hard and I can see it now." She nestled against him, certain as always of being able to get around even his most difficult moods. "Now that I'm here, I shall see that you take more time for play."

"I can hardly remember what it is like," he confessed.

"Dacius said the Christian bishops are fighting each other again here in the East. Why trouble yourself about them, when you know they are always bickering over something?"

"I sent Hosius to settle that," he assured her. "So you saw Crispus in Rome?"

"Yes. His galley was caught in a storm while crossing the Mare Tyrrhenum on the way to Gaul and had to put into Ostia for new rigging. When I heard that he and Dacius were only a few miles away, I naturally invited them to visit me and the children. You know how much they love Crispus."

Either she was a master dissembler, he decided, or she was telling the truth. Certainly nothing in her voice or manner seemed to indicate otherwise.

"Crispus wanted no fanfare," she added. "But he is a Caesar and your son. When the Senate heard he was in Rome, they begged him to appear before them and describe the campaign, particularly the naval battles at the Hellespont and the Bosporus." She stopped suddenly and gave him a penetrating look. "But you already knew about that, didn't you?"

"Marcellinus told me Crispus was honored with a triumph, but he gave me no details." He didn't add that he had sent the old Senator packing before he had a chance to tell more.

"It was only a small triumph," Fausta assured him. "Nothing like what you will have when we celebrate your Vicennalia. Actually Crispus was rather embarrassed by it."

"Surely you entertained for him." Constantine still kept his voice on a casual note.

"I gave a small gala in his honor. Could I do less for my stepson?" Her eyes suddenly twinkled. "Are you jealous?"

"No. Of course not." But he knew a flush had risen to his cheeks, and that she had seen it.

"You are!" she cried. "I should have known it from the way you greeted me and the stiffness of your embrace. Jealous of your own son!"

She went off into a gale of laughter, embarrassing Constantine and bringing back some of the remembered black anger he'd experienced, when he'd first learned that Rome had honored Crispus as the hero of a battle which had actually been won when he'd risked death from Licinius' troops to swim his horse across the river and bring aid to the hard-pressed archers commanded by his son. Worst of all, he knew now, he'd let the anger that was his greatest weakness make a fool of him and lead him almost to disown his own flesh and blood. Realizing that something was wrong, Fausta stopped laughing and searched his face with her eyes. And seeing the agony there, she was suddenly afraid.

"Constantine," she said, almost in a whisper, "did your jealousy make you do anything foolish?"

"I removed Crispus from his post as Caesar of Gaul."

"You didn't!"

"How was I to know the circumstances, when I heard he was sacrificing to Apollo in Rome and being honored with a triumph? Sons have stolen thrones from their fathers before. Look at your brother Maxentius."

Fausta didn't answer and, in his anger at himself at being such a fool, Constantine failed to notice the thoughtful look that had come over her face. It was just such a look as he'd seen there before, when she'd been planning the next move in his march to the heights of sole rulership of Rome.

III

Almost certain now that he had done Crispus a grave wrong in a moment of ungovernable rage, Constantine questioned Adrian when the latter arrived from Rome to take up his new duties as official guardian of the Emperor's own purse. The plump Greek trader listened carefully, his shrewd eyes penetrating easily the casual air with which Constantine sought to cloak his question.

"It was but a small triumph, Dominus," Adrian said. "Caesar Crispus only allowed it to quiet those in Rome who fear that you are going to move the capital of the Empire."

"Then you don't think it was of my son's seeking?"

"I swear it was not. You know how much Marcellinus and some others want to keep Rome the center of the Empire. They arranged the triumph to keep the people from thinking it odd that you did not celebrate your victory there." Adrian paused momentarily. "Is it true that you have removed your son from the Prefectureship of Gaul?"

Constantine nodded. "I'm afraid I misunderstood the whole affair and acted impulsively. But the act is done now and I cannot undo it."

"There is a way, if you are willing to take it."

"By rescinding the order?"

"No, Dominus."

"What then?"

"You could make Caesar Crispus Prefect of Italy and Africa—if the rumors are true that you plan to build a new capital here in the East."

"They are true. I hope you approve."

"I do, completely," Adrian assured him. "The Persian Empire is one of the richest in the world. Conquer the Sassanid kings for all time and Rome's boundaries can extend eastward without limit, even as far as the Indus."

"What do you think of Byzantium as the eastern Rome?"

"No better place could be chosen, Dominus. But before you build there, the Senate and Rome should be pacified. And what better way than by having a strong man you can trust—your own son who is already a hero—as Prefect in Rome."

"You're very persuasive, Adrian."

"Only because I believe the move would be best for all. The Senate will be mollified and, knowing the western half of the Empire will be capably governed, you can then turn all your attention to the East."

"Since it is your idea, when do you think it should be announced?"

"Why not at the celebration of your Vicennalia? It isn't very far off."

"That will be the time, of course." Constantine's face brightened. "As soon as Hosius returns from Alexandria and I can be sure affairs here in the East will be quiet for a while, I will go to Rome. That way I can make up to Crispus for doubting him and can also make Fausta happy at the same time."

Had he not been so relieved that Adrian had shown him a way out of the difficulty into which his temper had gotten him, Constantine might have noticed an odd look in Adrian's eyes, as if the Greek merchant found it difficult to believe the latter part of the statement. But he was pleased and so, when a glum-faced Crispus appeared at Nicomedia several weeks later and knelt before him, he stepped down from his throne and raised his son to his feet, embracing him happily.

"I hope you will forgive me for requiring this journey of you," he said.

"Your will is my desire, Dominus," Crispus' voice was flat, with no inflection.

"Where is Dacius?" Constantine asked, hoping to dispel some of the chill that remained, in spite of the warmth of his own greeting.

"He chose to stay with the army, Dominus. A matter of discipline."

Constantine gave him a searching look. "Did the army of Gaul think I was demoting you in recalling you to Nicomedia?"

"There was some unrest," Crispus admitted. "Dacius felt that he should stay in Gaul and control it."

"And you, son? What did you think?"

"I do not question your orders, sir. After all, I am a soldier." Crispus' voice still had the same flat tone. "If I have become an offender, it is right that I should receive whatever punishment you deem just."

Constantine longed to take his son in his embrace and confess how much he regretted the impulse that had been the cause of the chill which was now between them. But others were present in the audience chamber and he could not afford to admit publicly that he had yielded to an all too human emotion, with a very human mistake.

"You haven't offended," he assured the young man. "I recalled you because I have a larger task for you."

Seeing the look of relief in Crispus' eyes, Constantine sensed something of the torture the weeks of the long journey eastward must have been for him, not knowing how he had offended or what his fate would be when he reached Nicomedia.

"I cannot tell you what your new task is yet," Constantine added. "But you can be sure it is worthy of your talent and your loyalty."

"Thank you—Father."

"In the meantime," Constantine said, "I am sending you to Jerusalem with a detail of troops guarding a considerable sum of money your grandmother has requested to carry on a search for the sepulcher of the Saviour. She hopes to find the tomb and the remains of the true cross upon which Christ was crucified." He rose to his feet, ending the audience. "Quarters have been prepared for you in the palace. Empress Fausta and I shall expect you to dine with us this evening."

Crispus acknowledged the command with the Roman salute. And seeing him standing there, with a shaft of sunlight pouring through a window turning his hair into a casque of gold, Constantine felt his throat fill in a moment of pride greater than he'd ever experienced before. He must thank Adrian again, he reminded himself, for showing him the way out of the impasse into which he had placed himself by yielding to a fit of anger. What was more, he must learn to control it before he was led to an even graver mistake.

The brief pleasure Constantine had felt at the sight of his son was dissipated when he came into his private cabinet and found Hosius of Córdoba waiting there. The features of the dark-skinned bishop were drawn with weariness and his traveling cloak was powdered with dust.

"You need not tell me." Constantine waved the churchman to a chair. "Your face speaks for itself."

"My mission was a failure, Augustus," Hosius admitted. "I delivered copies of your letter to Bishop Alexander and the priest Arius and tried to reason with them both. But they could not come to an understanding."

"What next then? I refuse to be judge in matters of doctrine such as this."

"Why not let the bishops themselves decide the matter?"

"Another council?" Constantine's face brightened. "That may be the answer. It can be held as soon as I return from the celebration of my Vicennalia in Rome next year."

"If I may be forgiven for presuming, Augustus," Hosius said, "the council should be held as soon as possible. Dissension over Arius and his doctrines spread from Egypt to Syria Palaestina some time ago. Now it has reached Bithynia."

"Who is involved?" Constantine asked, startled by the news.

"Eusebius of Nicomedia—for one."

"Then it is poisoning my own household! Bishop Eusebius is confessor for my sister Constantia." Constantine threw up his hands in a gesture of futility. "How such a thing could spread here from

Egypt so quickly is a mystery to me. Who else is involved? Not you, Hosius."

"No, Augustus. We in the western part of the church long ago settled the question of the Trinity for ourselves. But Bishop Theognis of Nicaea does lean to the Arian doctrine."

"If Theognis has fallen victim, it must have more appeal to reason than I realized," Constantine said thoughtfully. "Eusebius of Caesarea told me when he warned me about the schism developing in the church that much of it came from the desire of the Greeks to apply logic to everything. Theognis would be the first to be involved there." Constantine's shoulders drooped unconsciously, as if the burden of another controversy were already proving too heavy for him. "What do we do then, Hosius?"

"You showed the way, Augustus, when you called the Council of Arles over the Donatist schism."

"And failed to solve it," Constantine reminded him.

"Not failed. The majority of the bishops agreed, as they will in this matter. Only a few had to be sent into exile."

"It still seems wrong somehow for those who worship the same God to quarrel to the point where a majority is forced to cast the others out. But we will try again. I will defer the celebration of the Vicennalia until the council is finished, but my wife will not like it and neither will the Senate at Rome. Prepare an edict as soon as possible for me to sign and place the resources of the Imperial Post at the disposal of both parties, so they will have no excuse not to come."

"Where shall the Council be held, Augustus? Here at Nicomedia?"

"No. There is too much political maneuvering here already. Nicaea is quiet and not far away. I have a palace there that can be used."

"Nicaea will be an ideal site, Augustus."

"Arrange it then, as soon as you can." Constantine managed to smile. "Once we have the bishops there, perhaps we can knock enough heads together to bring about a solution."

31

T HE COUNCIL WAS CALLED to convene at Nicaea in Bithynia in June, almost two years after the defeat of Licinius. Constantine had chosen the lovely town on the Ascanian lake, hoping the beauty of the surroundings would have an ameliorating effect upon the tempers of those participating. Only a few churchmen from the western portion of the Empire attended, for as Hosius had said, they were not so doctrinely minded as the eastern church. The aged Bishop Sylvester, occupant of the prestigious chair of the Bishop of Rome, was unable to make the journey, but sent two of his presbyters, Vito and Vincentius, while Hosius of Córdoba was the only representative of the Spanish church present.

It was a colorful assemblage indeed, with magnificently robed prelates from wealthy cities, such as Ephesus, Corinth, Antioch, Caesarea and Alexandria, sitting beside homespun-clad ascetics and monks from the monastic centers of the Egyptian desert. The most revered among them were Potammon from Heracleopolis and Paphnutius of the Thebaid in Egypt, both of whom had lost an eye during the persecutions. Paphnutius in addition had been subjected to the painful and crippling injury of hamstringing—cutting the tendons back of the ankle—and limped painfully as he took his seat.

The Council also included a group from the farthest eastern boundaries of the Empire: John of Persia, James of Nisibis in far-off Mesopotamia, Aitallaba from Edessa, and Paul of Neo-Caesarea, whose wrist tendons had been burned with hot irons during the persecutions. From Carthage came Caecilianus, over whom the Donatist controversy had flared.

In all, more than three hundred and eighteen leaders of the

Christian Church were present when Constantine opened the meeting on the third day of July.* He brought to the meeting all the panoply and magnificence of his office, but entered the great hall alone, unaccompanied by guards or military escort and, passing along a corridor, ascended the dais at the end. No throne chair stood upon the rostrum, emphasizing his desire that earthly power should play as small a part as possible in this spiritually oriented gathering. Instead, a cushioned stool was brought for him by his servant and he seated himself upon this, while the audience took their seats and the meeting was opened with a prayer for its success by Hosius of Córdoba.

When Constantine rose to address the prelates, he spoke in Latin, with which many of the churchmen were familiar. For those who were not, his address was translated immediately into Greek. He welcomed them warmly, but reminded them somewhat pointedly that there was no place for internal dissension in the Church of God and adjured them to discard the causes of dissension which had arisen and loosen the knots of controversy by the laws of peace.

The address finished, Constantine signaled to a chamberlain and two slaves brought into the hall a brazier filled with glowing coals. Behind them walked a clerk, carrying a basket filled with scrolls and waxed covered tablets, such as were widely used for correspondence.

"The basket borne by my scribe contains petitions addressed to me by many of you and some who were not able to attend this Council," Constantine told the assemblage. "When the first few of them were read and I was informed by my *magister memoriae* that many of you had accused others of heresy, various intrigues, support of my enemies in the recent war and like crimes, I ordered that no more be read."

Now his voice grew stern and none could doubt his displeasure. "Condemnation by anyone of his fellows who labor in the vineyard of the Lord has no place in a council dedicated to bringing peace to the church. I, therefore, choose to burn these documents publicly before all of you assuring you that they have not been read by me nor will the accusations they make even be considered."

* A.D. 325

With the words, he tossed the first of the scrolls upon the brazier and the clerk began to pile them upon the flames.

"Christ bids him who hopes for forgiveness first to forgive an erring brother," Constantine told the gathering in conclusion. "As I forgive all of you now who have sent me these scurrilous documents, so do I charge that you forgive each other."

II

Though designed to bring the warring bishops to their senses, Constantine's dramatic burning of their charges and countercharges against each other was in a way symbolic of the council that followed. In it, he took little part, but reports of its deliberations were given to him nightly by Hosius, and nightly they became more discouraging.

First, Arius presented his thesis that Christ, having been created by God the Father, was therefore a "creature" and not the equal of the Father—the essence of the doctrine which had caused all the trouble. Against the Arian doctrine—already identified as heresy by one synod of the church—now rose one of the most eloquent voices to be heard in the Council. It was that of Athanasius, secretary and spokesman for the aging Bishop Alexander, who had opposed Arius from the first, and he countered the Arian doctrine point by point.

As the deliberations of the Council dragged on—and were reported faithfully to Constantine by Hosius—a great mass of sentiment gradually developed for an intermediate position between the two extremes. One group described the position of the Son in relation to the Father with the Greek word *homoousios*, meaning roughly of the same substance or being—in a word, consubstantial—while the Arians, on the other hand, held out for the lesser position of a created being for the Son.

"Why is all this so important?" Constantine cried out in exasperation one evening, after Hosius had finished his report of the Council's futile wrangling during the day.

"If you had been there to hear Athanasius attack the statements of Arius, you would see why, Augustus," the Greek priest said.

"He is a fighter, that one." Constantine forgot his irritation for a moment in admiration. "He is so slight, though, that I expect one day to see the fire of his indignation consume him, as the flame does a burning splinter."

"If such a man as Athanasius is willing to battle daily in debate, even slight and in poor health as he is, there must be something to what he says," Hosius said.

"Then you agree with him?"

"On all major points, yes. You see, Augustus, if the church admits that Christ is a created and therefore lesser being, other lesser beings could also conceivably be created by the Father, as Athanasius pointed out today. This means that others might later claim to be Sons of God and start churches of their own."

"I can see where such a condition would be as bad for the church as it was for the Empire, when six claimed the title of Augustus," Constantine agreed. "Is there much chance that the theories of Arius might eventually prevail?"

"I think not," Hosius said. "The great danger seems to be that the Council will end without the question of whether Christ is *homoousios*—of the same substance as the Father—or *homoiousios* —a lesser being created by the Father to form a bridge by which men can take on the aspects of divinity and thereby attain eternal life—being decided."

"This Council must write a creed to which all Christians can subscribe," Constantine said firmly. "It is as vital for the Christian Church as it was vital for the Empire to be ruled by one instead of six."

"But they are still far from it, Augustus."

"You spoke once of sentiment for a middle position. Has nothing like this been considered?"

"Not upon the floor of the Council," Hosius said. "But I heard today that a group is considering such a proposal."

"Who is the leader of this faction?"

"Eusebius of Caesarea, among others."

"But he came to me originally in favor of Arius."

"Eusebius and Arius were friends when they were students together," Hosius explained. "But the Bishop of Caesarea is a learned man and has become well versed from his historical studies in the troubles questions of doctrine have caused in the past. I think he realizes now that a compromise is necessary, but that neither the followers of Arius nor those who completely support Athanasius and Alexander will ever be able to reach it."

"Send for Eusebius at once," Constantine directed. "Do you think a majority of the bishops will agree to a compromise?"

"I doubt whether the majority of them even understand what is at stake, Augustus," Hosius admitted wryly. "And I know it will make little difference to the people whether Christ 'sprang from' or is 'consubstantial with' the Father."

"Only a Greek—and a learned one at that—would quibble over such a difference," Constantine agreed. "I must confess that it means little more to me than the *iota* in the word *homoiousios* that seems to mark the difference between the warring parties."

III

"Hosius tells me you have prepared the draft of a creed by which the controversy over Arius may be settled," Constantine greeted Eusebius. "I sent for you so I could hear of it."

"I have no creed, Dominus," Eusebius protested. "Only a confession of faith used in my diocese. I would not offer it as an answ—"

"Would you mind repeating it for me?"

"Of course not. It is this: I believe in one God, the Father A¹ mighty, Maker of all things both visible and invisible, and in one Lord, Jesus Christ, the Word of God, God of God, Light of Light, Life of Life, the only-begotten Son, the First-born of every creature, begotten of the Father before all worlds, by whom also all things were made. Who for our salvation was made flesh and lived amongst men, and suffered and rose again on the third day, and ascended to the Father, and shall come in glory to judge the quick and the dead. And I believe in the Holy Ghost."

"Ghost?" Constantine frowned. "I don't understand the word."

"Spirit is probably a better one," Eusebius admitted. "The Holy Spirit sent by Christ to those who follow him, setting them apart from all others."

"Do you agree with this creed?" Constantine asked Hosius.

"Yes, Augustus," the Spanish prelate said. "But I think some among the Council will want more specific definitions."

"I would be the first to admit that they are indicated," Eusebius agreed.

"For myself, I must confess that I find nothing wrong with it," Constantine said. "Will you present it to the Council tomorrow, Eusebius, as a basis upon which to begin the formulation of a final creed?"

"If that is your wish, Dominus."

"It *is* my wish," Constantine said firmly. "Please tell the Council that."

And so it came about that the Council of Nicaea was presented the next day with the building blocks from which to construct a creed for all Christians. Eusebius presented the proposed creed and Hosius reminded them that Constantine himself had directed the submission of the tentative draft of the creed and that so far they had enjoyed imperial hospitality with little accomplishment in return.

Those bishops who had held out for the simple definition of a Triune God—composed of the Father, Son and Holy Spirit—pointed out at once that the creed was not sufficiently precise in defining the main point of conflict, the relationship between Father and Son. The debate went on for another day but defections were occurring steadily from both of the extreme viewpoints toward the median position in favor of a compromise creed. By the end of another day's discussion, Hosius of Córdoba was able to read the draft finally prepared for approval by the Council:

"We believe in one God, the Father Almighty, Maker of all things both visible and invisible. And in one Lord, Jesus Christ, the Son of God, begotten of the Father, only begotten, that is, from the substance of the Father. God of God, Light of Light, very God of very God, begotten not made, being of one substance with the Father by whom all things were made, both in heaven and earth. Who for us men and for our salvation came down and was made flesh, and was made man, suffered and rose on the third day, ascended into the heavens and will come again to judge the quick and the dead. And we believe in the Holy Ghost."

When the vote was taken, an overwhelming majority of the Council approved the creed. In fact, so pleased were they by having at last discovered a statement of faith to which all but the most intransigent might agree, that the followers of Athanasius and Alexander had little trouble in gaining approval from the Council for a codicil to the main creed, in effect denouncing the Arian doctrine:

> "But those who say, 'once He was not' and before He was begotten, He was not' and 'He came into existence out of what was not,' or those who profess that the Son of God is of a different person or 'substance' or 'He was made' or is 'changeable' or 'mutable'—all these are anathematized."

The codicil had been put forth over objections by the followers of Eusebius of Caesarea, who had been largely instrumental in hammering out the final wording of the creed. Because of grave misgivings over the anathema, Eusebius himself waited a day before signing. Knowing, however, that Constantine was insistent that the bishops work out a statement of belief which could be presented as the concrete work of the Council, he finally signed both the creed and the codicil.

Two of the bishops, Eusebius of Nicomedia and Constantine's old friend, Theognis, refused to sign the anathema although they would have signed the creed. And, since they had defied his will, Constantine had no choice save to deprive them of their sees and send them into exile.

Because of his long friendship with Theognis, Constantine summoned the aging bishop to the palace before signing the decree that would exile him from the beautiful area around Nicaea. Theognis was as straight and tall as he had been more than twenty years before, when he had performed the marriage rites for Constantine and Minervina. In fact, Constantine thought, the years had been kinder to the churchman by far than they had been to him.

"It pains me that we should find ourselves at a place of parting, Theognis," he said.

"You must do what you think is right for the Empire, Augustus."

"And for the church?"

"Who can tell? The Lord moves in mysterious ways."

"But aren't you judging them for yourself in refusing to sign the creed?"

"Not the creed," Theognis corrected him gravely. "I am not entirely in accord with its wording, but I think it is an excellent thing for a man to state in words what he believes. It is the anathema that we have refused to sign."

"But why? If what Arius and his followers teach is wrong, it can only bring further dissension in the church."

"I told you once long ago that most of my difficulties come from being both priest and philosopher," Theognis said. "As priest, I must have faith in the pronouncements of my church decided upon by its councils. But as philosopher, I have a passion for logic, like all Greeks. You will remember that I was once severely criticized by my brother priests for yielding up the Scriptures and staying alive to guide my flock during the persecution."

"And now you are forcing me to deprive them of your presence."

Theognis raised his hands in a gesture of deprecation. "The responsibility can now be shifted to younger shoulders than mine."

Constantine picked up the edict of banishment and held it so that Theognis could see the space at the bottom, where no signature had yet been placed.

"Affix your name to what you call the anathema," he told the old bishop, "and this edict shall remain unsigned."

"I am sorry, Augustus. But it is a matter of principle."

"What principle?"

"Once I was judged by my fellows to be guilty of grave sin in yielding up the Scriptures, but I think time has proved that I served God's purpose best by doing what I did. Yet had men like Donatus been in control of the church then, I would have been anathematized, as Arius and a few others are today."

"Then you believe Arius is right?"

"I don't know, Augustus. But I am sure he should not be cast into the outer darkness for daring to question what many accept as fact. I am priest enough to believe God's purpose will eventually be revealed to us, even through the acts of fallible men. But I hope I shall always be philosopher enough to keep on asking questions until I can be sure, and, what is more important, stand up and be counted on the side of others who ask them too."

"You know you leave me no choice, don't you?"

"I ask for no mercy, Augustus. In fact I shall pray that you are carrying out God's will, when you sign the order before you."

Constantine looked into the wise old eyes for a long moment. Then almost as if he were casting a weapon in battle, he picked up the pen and scribbled his signature across the bottom of the edict of banishment.

"Will you forgive me, if it is proved that I am wrong?" he asked Theognis.

"Forgive, Augustus?" Theognis' smile was like a warm mantle enveloping him. "Why should I forgive, when I do not condemn?"

Once the creed and the anathema were signed, the Council of Nicaea had little more business to transact. A date was set for the simultaneous celebration of Easter throughout the church and an important set of guides, called the Canons of Nicaea, were prepared for the clergy. Before the Council disbanded, Constantine entertained them at a ceremonial dinner at which gifts were given to all. After the meal, he delivered a brief address, begging each not to judge his fellows harshly but to leave all judgment in matters of doctrine to God, to be solved through prayer and tolerance one for another.

"How can you convert the world, if it shall not be through your own example?" he challenged them.

Finally, he stated his firm conviction of the great accomplishments of the Council in words which he repeated later in a specific letter to the churches of Alexandria, in whose congregations most of the dissension had arisen.

"That which has commended itself to the judgment of three hundred bishops cannot be other than the doctrine of God," he wrote in the letter, "seeing that the Holy Spirit, dwelling in the minds of so many honorable men, must have thoroughly enlightened them as to the will of God."

And indeed, the Council of Nicaea was a great success, if for no other reason than that for the first time in history a majority of leaders in the Eastern church—as had been accomplished to a lesser extent by the Council of Arles for the Western church some years earlier—had been brought together to discuss, in the light of reason, their common problems. And even if it were not true, as

Constantine said in his final word to the Council, that "all heresy has been cut out of the church," at least he had made a sincere effort to achieve a unanimity of opinion among them.

Pleased though he was by the action of the Council, Constantine could only be disappointed by the decision of Hosius of Córdoba to return to his homeland. The Spanish prelate had been absent for more than a decade, first as confessor to Empress Theodora and her family and then as religious adviser to Constantine himself. Besides, Hosius was of the West, where the church was coming more and more to look for leadership to the Bishop of Rome, while Constantine's religious leanings, influenced by Eusebius of Caesarea and others, were now more and more to the East —as were his political leanings also.

"What shall I do without the strong rod of your faith and wisdom to lean upon?" Constantine asked the Spanish bishop when the request was made.

"One who led three hundred bishops to a decision is a shepherd beyond compare, Augustus," Hosius said with a smile. "I am an old man, too old for arguments of doctrine such as these Eastern churchmen love. In Spain no one would think of questioning the truth of the Trinity."

"Theognis went into exile defending the right of any man to question anything."

"Were I a Greek, I might do the same," Hosius admitted. "Just now I am thankful to be a Spaniard and satisfied with things as they are."

"Give my love to Empress Theodora and her children. And ask her to forgive me for doing so badly with the marriage of her daughters."

"She knows you sought the good of the Empire and the will of God, Augustus," Hosius assured him, but Constantine shook his head.

"Sometimes I wonder whether it is God's will or my own I obey," he admitted. "Some of the happiest days of my life were spent here in Bithynia, running with my fellow cadets in the morning, riding over the countryside and wrestling together in the afternoon, but I find few pleasures anymore. Dacius once quoted to me a question asked by the Saviour: 'What shall it profit a man, if he gain the whole world, and lose his own soul?'"

He looked up at the dark-skinned bishop, whose jet black hair was now shot through with gray, as was Constantine's own at barely fifty. "I have gained the world, Hosius. But sometimes I wonder whether I haven't lost my soul."

"No man who has done so much for God's church could have lost his soul," Hosius protested. "Keep on as you have done before and one day you will see the Lord again, as he appeared to you with the *labarum* before the battle for Rome."

"I would give all I possess to believe that," Constantine said, and now he was not the most powerful man in the world but only a supplicant. "Pray God it happens before I die."

32

Not long after the Council of Nicaea ended, Empress Helena returned from Syria Palaestina and Jerusalem. In spite of her age, she had stood the journey well, buoyed up by having discovered what appeared to be the authentic site of the tomb in which Jesus of Nazareth had been placed, when his body was brought down from the cross. With the money sent by Constantine, she had already begun plans for building a magnificent shrine, to be called the Church of the Anastasis—or Resurrection—upon the spot. But in spite of Helena's happiness over the visit to Jerusalem, a household containing three strong-willed women of varied natures and ambitions could not long remain peaceful.

Constantia had moved into the palace after the execution of her husband, Licinius. The coming of Fausta from Rome and now the return of Helena from Jerusalem added two quite dissimilar ingredients to the pot, which quickly began to bubble. There were quarrels nearly every day, usually with Helena and Constantia united against Fausta. Still another ingredient was added when Crispus, who had also returned from an inspection tour of the East, fell in love with a younger Helena—oldest daughter of Constantia and the late Augustus Licinius—and asked his father to approve the marriage.

Constantine was fond of Princess Helena and gave his approval. But Fausta naturally saw in the marriage of Crispus and Helena a union between two lines of the imperial family which could only have the effect of diminishing the inheritance left for her own three sons. And being the daughter of one schemer and the sister of another, she began to lay plans to promote the cause of her own offspring at the expense of the others.

With so many volatile ingredients, it was amazing that the troubled pot did not come to a full boil for almost a year. During that time the piling of scheme upon counterscheme gradually built a towering structure whose toppling was certain to cause a crisis, though none of the participants—save perhaps one—could possibly have forseen the tragedy to come.

As a wedding present, Constantine dispatched Crispus and Helena to Rome, where the young Caesar was to supervise preparations for celebrating the Vicennalia, the twentieth year since Constantine had first been proclaimed Augustus by the people of Britain and Gaul. He did not mention to anyone his decision to adopt Adrian's suggestion that he elevate Crispus to the role of Augustus during the Vicennalia and make him ruler of the Empire's western half, preferring to make that announcement in Rome itself.

Constantine's own plan to go to Rome about a month after Crispus' departure was disrupted by a sudden invasion into Scythia and Moesia by the Sarmatians, a half-savage people who lived north of where the Danube emptied into the Pontus Euxinus. Quickly putting an army together, he prepared to march northward and punish the rebels, but Fausta had no intention of waiting patiently in Nicomedia for his return.

"How long will the revolt of the Sarmatians delay the celebration of your Vicennalia?" she asked him the night before his departure.

"Probably several months. I shall have to drive them back across their borders and set an example for the Goths."

"Why not destroy them? I hear they're only barbarians, with few weapons of iron."

"But barbarians clever enough to overcome that lack by making scale armor out of thin slices cut from horses' hooves and sewn on a thick tunic," he told her. "Such a garment can turn spears and arrows almost as effectively as scales of metal. And such people can be valuable to the Empire."

"How will you control them, then?"

"The same way, I hope, that I controlled Bonar, the Pict chieftain, long ago—by convincing them they have more to gain from an alliance with Rome than from fighting. After all, we have many things they lack." He gave her an appraising look, having long ago learned that questions on a subject about which she ordinarily didn't concern herself usually had some purpose behind them. "Why do you ask?"

"I was thinking that with you away for several months, I might as well go to Rome and get the palace ready for the Vicennalia. You will have to give a huge reception and some special dinners while we're there. I can be making preparations for them."

"You still don't like Nicomedia, do you?"

"I was born in Italy and lived there, until my father took me to Arles to marry you. You couldn't expect me to like another part of the world as well, unless your Nova Roma is to be even more magnificent than the old."

"Nova Roma! Where did you hear that?"

Fausta smiled knowingly. "Even in Rome they know you plan to build a new capital on the site of Byzantium."

"How did you learn of it?"

"Lupus hears frequently from friends in Rome and so do I."

Constantine had not paid much attention to the tutor since the latter's arrival in Nicomedia with Fausta, except to determine that he seemed to carry out his duties well, drilling the children in mathematics, philosophy, Latin and Greek—the latter tongue being particularly important to potential rulers of an empire that was looking to the East for its expansion.

Once or twice he'd felt a twinge of resentment when he heard Lupus and Fausta chatting avidly about the theater, the games and social affairs at Rome, subjects about which he confessed to know little and cared less. In another way, however, he'd found that the presence of the other man actually made for domestic harmony, since having someone of similar interests to talk to left Fausta less time to complain about Constantia and his mother, or bewail his having shut her away here in what she still considered a barbarous part of the world.

He'd have to pay more attention to Lupus, Constantine decided. For if the tutor received letters from Rome describing activities there, he no doubt wrote in reply about matters here in the East. And many in Rome would resent very much the establishment of another major capital, even though they were given their own Augustus to rule the western part of the Empire.

"Do Lupus' friends say how they feel about my new Rome?" he asked.

"You couldn't expect them to be very happy about it. Or that your son is married to a daughter of Licinius."

"You didn't object to Crispus' marriage when the question first came up. Why do you speak against it now?"

Her eyes opened wide in a look he knew well by now. "But darling, I didn't say I objected. Helena is a nice girl, though a little too meek to my liking. If Crispus loves her, who am I to object?"

"I once thought he was enamoured of you, and was jealous."

"That was only puppy love. I was flattered." She laughed lightly. "After all, Crispus is very handsome and sweet, and he *is* old for his age."

She stood on tiptoe to kiss him, a caress he'd never been able to resist, though he knew she often used it to persuade him to let her have her way. "May I go to Rome while you're fighting those barbarians who cover themselves with horses' hooves?"

"If that is your wish."

"I wish your Vicennalia to be the greatest triumph Rome has ever celebrated. And with me there to help Crispus with the planning, it will be."

Weeks afterward, huddled under a shelter north of the Danube with a cold rain pouring down outside and his bones aching from the long ride northward, Constantine remembered that Fausta had not denied Crispus' infatuation. And with Fausta and Crispus in Rome, planning together for the celebration, meek little Helena— his son's bride—would not show up very well against the sparkling gaiety and high spirits that the capital always brought out in its Empress. The thought gave him no pleasure but instead increased his vexation at the Sarmatians for their stubborn resistance against placing themselves under the domination of Rome, even to the point of using lances, arrows and daggers, whose points had been dipped in a venomous liquid so powerful in its action that a mere scratch could bring death in a few hours.

Never very great any more, Constantine's patience was almost exhausted before the preliminary details of the treaty with the Sarmatians were finally worked out and he was free to ride to

Nicomedia and take a galley for Rome and the Vicennalia. His mother and Constantia, with her son, Caesar Licinianus, had gone to Rome at the same time as Fausta, so it was a lonely trip, during which he had only his thoughts, and his doubts, with which to occupy himself.

II

Word of Constantine's approach to Rome went ahead of him, when his galley debarked at Brundisium on the eastern coast in order to avoid the often stormy trip around the tip of Italy. By the time the official party reached the outskirts of the capital, a great crowd of people lined the streets and, as he rode through the cheering throng in a golden chariot with Crispus driving the six white horses drawing the vehicle, Constantine felt his spirits lift at the spontaneous enthusiasm of his reception.

In spite of the pomp and panoply which the Senate and the nobles had marshaled in the hope of convincing their ruler that Rome was still the center of the Empire, the triumph was doomed as a spectacle—in comparison with other such affairs—by Constantine's refusal to sacrifice to the old gods, a ceremony which had formed the most colorful part of former triumphant celebrations. Instead, he went alone to the great new church of St. John Lateran —so called from the name of the family, the *Plautii Laterani*, whose palace formerly occupied the site—which he had ordered constructed as the seat of the Bishop of Rome, but which he had not yet seen.

One of the first Christian churches to be built in the form of a basilica, the new sanctuary at Rome had already—though barely completed—become a pattern for others throughout the Empire. Basically, it consisted of a long hall of assembly, divided into a central nave with side aisles flanking, and lighted, except for banks of candles, only by windows in the clerestory above. This type of church was, of course, much larger and better adapted for the colorful and elaborate ritual of worship in which the steadily increasing Christian congregations took part, than older types of buildings or abandoned pagan temples.

Kneeling before the great altar alone, Constantine experienced once again the feeling of kinship with a higher power that had been such a vital part of his life immediately following the miracle of the flaming cross at Saxa Rubra, but which had been too much lacking—he realized now—during the long campaigns against Licinius. Coming from the church to face the crowd that filled the square and the streets opening into it, he could sense the resentment of the people—most of whom were still not Christians—at his having forsaken the old gods. He gave it hardly a thought, however, having long since become convinced that the future of the Empire lay in the East and the new capital, which, according to his plans, would eventually dwarf even Rome in magnificence.

Tired from months of campaigning, Constantine put in only a token appearance at the many gala social events that were part of the Vicennalia. Fausta, however, loved them and so did Crispus, though Constantine noticed that the boy's shy bride of a few months was often left alone with her mother outside the whirl of gaiety that always eddied about Fausta.

Had he been less tired, he might have envied Fausta and Crispus their youth and gaiety, but he was occupied daily with meeting a long queue of ambassadors and subject kings that formed outside the door of the audience chamber every morning, each with his petition to be considered and decided upon. And by nightfall he was always thoroughly worn out and exasperated by the petty bickerings which seemed to characterize almost all relationships, not only between men but also between countries. Fausta, on the other hand, having spent much of the day lying in the steaming scented bath she loved, was always ready for another night of gaiety and merriment.

And so the final day of the Vicennalia approached, marking the climax of the celebration. Constantine still had made no public announcement of his intention to elevate Crispus to the rank of Augustus and did not feel that it was right to do so now without discussing his plans with Dacius, who had been a part of them from the very beginning. The old general had come from Gaul for the Vicennalia, but, occupied with the chores that formed such a burdensome part of his role as Emperor, Constantine had had almost no chance to talk to him. On the day before the climax of the celebration, he refused to hold any more audiences and, accompanied only by Dacius, rode out to the Villa of Livia, where Fausta had sent the children and their tutor so they would not be disturbed by the excitement going on in the city.

The children and the tutor were gathered in a circle on the grassy slope before the villa where Lupus was instructing them in writing. Each student had a wax-covered tablet upon which to copy the lesson Lupus had written out upon a large sheet of parchment in bold flowing strokes. At the approach of Constantine and Dacius the lesson ended abruptly, however, and the children crowded about the visitors, while Lupus watched in the background to see that they did not disturb the Emperor and provoke his formidable temper.

Realizing how long it had been since he'd heard the bright-voiced chatter of his sons and daughters, Constantine let them gather freely about him. With one arm around Constantine II and the other hand rumpling the fair curls of small Constans, youngest of the boys, he walked over to where the lesson stood upon the easel. It was in Latin, he saw, a group of verses from the Aeneid of Vergil. And seeing them, he remembered how much he had loved to read about the adventures of the defeated Trojans after the fall of their city, as they had sailed the raging seas seeking the site of Rome itself, which, according to tradition, they had founded.

"This is General Dacius, Lupus." Constantine introduced the tutor. "Lupus teaches my children," he explained to Dacius. "Though I don't imagine he is getting much done with so many exciting things happening in Rome."

"The Empress Fausta is allowing the children to come into the city this afternoon for tomorrow's parade and the ceremony of thanksgiving by the Senate for your continued success, Dominus," Lupus informed him.

The ceremony was no part of Constantine's desires, but he had agreed to it as a means of placating the Senate and the people by being present when offerings were made to the old gods, though he had refused actually to sponsor the sacrifices, long since forbidden by his order as part of official rites.

"I suppose they will find it interesting," he said. "Where is Licinianus?" The boy Caesar, who was about thirteen, usually had his lessons with Constantine's own children.

"He was allowed to remain in Rome, Dominus, at the request of Caesar Crispus."

"Don't let me interfere with your lessons, Lupus," Constantine said. "General Dacius and I rode out here to get away from the city and discuss some affairs of state."

Leaving the horses tethered to a low branch, so they could crop the lush grass covering the hillside, Constantine and Dacius climbed the slope a short distance to the height from which he had surveyed the surrounding countryside when last he had visited this charming villa built by Augustus to honor his beloved Livia. Was it possible, he wondered, that only fourteen years had passed since he'd descended from this same hill to face one of the blackest moments of his career—the appearance of the shining cross in the heaven which almost everyone, especially Maxentius, who had left the safety of Rome's walls because of it, had considered to be a promise of victory from Apollo?

"It has been a long road." Dacius echoed his thoughts, as had so often happened when they were alone together.

"And with many turnings, the lowest, I think, at the bottom of this very hill, when we met Adrian and Camianus and they told us Maxentius had consulted the Sibylline Books and had been told that the enemy of Rome would die."

"Yet here you are at the top of the world, and ruler of most of it."

"One other man ruled more—Alexander the Great."

"Then it's true that you're going to expand the Empire eastward?"

"I hope to. The Sassanid kings of Persia have been raiding into Armenia and killing Christians."

"And I suppose the bishops have asked you to come to their aid?"

"Why not? Tiridates was my friend when he was alive. I owe that much at least to his people."

"I should have seen, when you first stood before me in Nicomedia, that ambition had already put its curse upon you," Dacius said, a little sadly. "Will you never be satisfied?"

"Don't forget that you have profited considerably from that ambition," Constantine said stiffly. "From centurion to general is quite a step."

"Some have made it to emperor in less time—Diocletian for example."

"And finished his life tending cabbages."

"I dare say he was happier with them than he ever was ruling Rome," Dacius observed. "Look what the purple of an Augustus has brought you: burdens so heavy that you rarely smile any more and everyone goes about in fear and trembling of your anger."

"There's little enough to smile about."

"Unless you seek it. Look at your children back there. Any man could be proud of them—and of Crispus—even though you did hurt him deeply."

"I explained to him what happened, when he came to Nicomedia. And I wrote a letter to you."

"Nevertheless, the wounds a father deals a son are always slow to heal."

"Surely Crispus doesn't still resent what I did."

"I don't know," Dacius admitted. "He's been so busy preparing for the Vicennalia that I haven't been able to talk to him. When your order came removing him as ruler of Gaul, he was more hurt than angry. After all, he did worship you and it's always a blow to find that a god is as human and fallible as the rest of us. And you've given him little of importance to do since—almost as if you still didn't trust him."

"I'm going to make it up to him tomorrow," Constantine said, "by appointing him Augustus of the West, to rule over the territory that was my father's after the abdication of Maximian."

"Have you told him yet?"

"No. And if you reveal it, you will be a centurion this time tomorrow. This is going to be a surprise, to everyone."

"Believe me, it will be!"

"With Crispus as Augustus ruling the West from Rome, perhaps Marcellinus and the rest will stop pestering me about my new capital of Nova Roma."

"What about Licinianus?"

"When he's old enough, I will make him ruler of some small province, perhaps Armenia or Augusta Euphratensia. That should please Constantia, since both are part of the territory his father once ruled."

"Have you told Empress Fausta about your plan for Crispus?"

"No. But she knows I intend one day to divide the Empire among my sons."

"With half going to one—and him not her son?"

"Are you against Crispus?" Constantine turned on Dacius almost savagely. "What kind of loyalty is this?"

"My first loyalty has always been to you. If you don't know that by now, my life has been wasted."

"I do know it." Constantine was instantly contrite for having spoken so sharply to his old friend. "With my Empire expanding eastward, there will be more than enough for all my sons, and Licinianus too. By making Crispus Augustus of the West now, I can placate those who wish to keep more power here in Rome. At the same time, I will be placing someone I trust in control here, leaving me free to take an army into Persia and put that area once again under my rule."

"Don't expect as much of others as you have always demanded of yourself," Dacius warned. "Few of us can be measured by such a standard. Remember Bassianus and Licinius."

"I've learned my lesson." Constantine had recovered his good humor. "From henceforth, I shall trust only my own family—and of course you." He looked up at the sun. "We'd better be riding back. I promised Fausta to put in an appearance at Senator Marcellinus' gala this evening, though what she can see in these affairs, I'll never be able to understand."

As the two men descended the slope to where the horses were tethered they did not see a tall man in the robe of a scholar hiding in the cover of a clump of bushes, from behind which he had obviously been listening to their conversation. It was Lupus, and barely were the two riders out of sight of the villa when the tutor rode furiously away toward Rome by another route, leaving the children to be taken into the city by the servants who had been caring for them at the villa.

III

The entertainment prepared by Senator Marcellinus for his guests was as dull as any Constantine had ever attended. First, a pair of gymnasts performed feats of strength and agility, of which they appeared very proud, although he'd seen better by far elsewhere. And next a poet recited a long epic praising the career of Constantine and attributing his success, rather pointedly, to the favor of the gods of Rome who had watched over her—according to the poet— through all her illustrious history.

To Constantine's surprise, Fausta did not even pout when he told her he was leaving the gala, or object to his going. She seemed less gay than usual tonight and even appeared somewhat distraught, but when he questioned her, she denied that anything was wrong. Leaving her and Crispus to rule over the merrymakers from twin thrones erected by Senator Marcellinus for his royal guests, Constantine made his way to his sedan chair, accompanied only by a half dozen of his guards, at least two of whom never left his side except when he was in his private apartment at the palace.

The nightly activity of Rome was in full sway as he was borne to his palace. Carts loaded with food and goods for the shops and stalls of the city clogged the streets—all vehicles other than military ones being forbidden to use them during the day, when they were thronged with people. In the time of Maxentius, bands of highborn thugs had roamed the streets at night, making them unsafe for honest citizens. But Constantine had put an end to that by lighting the streets with flaming torches and sending fully armed soldiers to patrol them in pairs from dusk to dawn.

At the door of his private apartment, which adjoined Fausta's quarters by a communicating door, Constantine was surprised to see the tutor Lupus waiting. He had never particularly liked the man, perhaps because Lupus and Fausta seemed to have so much in common which he could share. Tonight the tutor's presence irritated him.

"What is it?" he asked sharply. "Is one of the children ill?"

"No, Dominus. I must speak to you privately, upon a matter of considerable urgency."

"Can't it wait until morning?"

"I would not trouble you if the matter could wait, Dominus. You said in the edict that all information concerning danger to you, the Empress or the state should be given you, whatever the hour."

Constantine would have preferred not to be reminded of the unfortunate edict encouraging informers, since it had brought him nothing except trouble. But Lupus was a member of his own household and, as far as he knew, very devoted to both Fausta and the children, so it was hardly right to refuse to hear what the tutor had to say.

"Come inside then," he said resignedly. "You can tell me your story while I prepare for bed." Then his eyes narrowed suddenly as a new thought came to him. "Isn't Senator Marcellinus your kinsman? I would have expected you to be at his house for the gala."

"I was, for a while." Lupus smiled. "But like you, I found an evening listening to a poet recite his own verses less than inspiring."

"We are agreed upon that. What information do you have for me?"

"I hesitate to speak of it, Dominus, but—"

"Speak up, man. In my edict I promised to listen, so get on with what you have to say."

"It concerns Caesar Crispus."

Constantine turned and seized the teacher by the loose front of his robe, shaking him until his teeth chattered. "I'll have no tale-telling—" He stopped and released the grip. "You are right. I did promise to listen and, if the information is true, to act upon it. What do you have against Crispus?"

"Nothing, Dominus. I admire him very much. But I cannot stand by and see him force his intentions upon the Empress and not speak, when I know she remains silent only because she doesn't want to prejudice you against your son."

"Crispus and Fausta! You're mad!" But even as he spoke, Constantine remembered the occasions when he had seen the two together and had been jealous.

"I wish I *were* mad, Dominus." The tone of deep concern in Lupus' voice was convincing. "Time and again she has been forced to fend him off."

"When did all this begin?"

"Soon after we arrived in Rome from Nicomedia. Not long after *they* began to urge him to name himself Augustus in the West."

"They? Who are they?" Constantine shook his head like an animal at bay, trying to control the tidal wave of anger that flooded through him and threatened to seize his senses.

"It's common gossip here in Rome that a strong party in the Senate favors naming your son Crispus Augustus," Lupus said. "The whole city has been talking about it."

"And I suppose the whole city would like to see this change?"

"Rome is fighting for its very life. You can hardly blame—"

"I freed Rome from Maxentius! I restored honor and position to the Senate! Is this the way they thank me, by turning my own son against me? But of course Crispus didn't listen."

"I know little of the affair, Dominus. After all, I'm a member of your household, so the plotters didn't confide in me. But I thought you should know about his infat—, about the other matter, so you could warn him about it."

"This infatuation you speak of—you say Crispus has tried to force himself upon the Empress?"

"Not once but several times, Dominus. At first she laughed it off, but lately he has become more importunate, perhaps because—" He did not finish the sentence, but Constantine finished it for him.

"Because he hopes to enlist her against me? Is that what you were going to say?"

"The Empress would have no part of that," Lupus assured him. "She knows how much you love Caesar Crisp—"

"Leave me," Constantine said hoarsely. "I must think."

"I hope nothing will happen to him, Dominus." Lupus' voice once again was filled with concern. "He is young and his head is easily turned by flattery."

"Leave me, Lupus!"

"I hope I didn't do wrong."

"You were right in coming to me, but say no more of this to anyone."

When the tutor had left, Constantine stepped out upon the balcony adjoining his bedchamber, hoping the night air would cool the heat of his anger so he could think more clearly. The rumble of cartwheels on the cobblestoned pavements was like the distant sound of thunder, presaging the threat of a storm. And from the streets came the dank foul smell of waste dumped into shallow gutters that carried it to the openings of the great *cloacae*, the sewers which had served to carry off Rome's waste for five centuries. His throat already tight with anger, the smell of the streets almost made Constantine retch, and he made a firm resolve to leave the city he had come to hate as soon as possible, taking Fausta and the children with him.

From the street below came the sound of gay laughter, as a party of merrymakers—on the way from one reception or gala to another, for the night was yet young, as Rome's social life went—turned a corner and disappeared down a side street. One of the women had a high-pitched voice that reminded him of Fausta. And when he pictured her and Crispus, easily the handsomest couple on the floor as they led the festivities at Senator Marcellinus' reception, his fingers tightened upon the stone balustrade around the balcony until the rough edges cut into the flesh, bringing blood. He didn't notice the pain, however, so great was his agony from another source.

In his heart Constantine knew that part of what had happened —if Lupus were telling the truth—was his own fault for leaving the two together so much, while he was occupied with the cares of state. But even accepting the blame failed to lessen the pain and anger he felt, for most damning of all was the knowledge that Crispus had listened to the blandishments of those who would divide the Empire in order to assuage the pride of Rome and, more particularly, restore the worship of the old gods and deal a blow to the resurgent force Christianity had come to be under imperial sponsorship.

For a moment he considered waking Dacius and discussing the information Lupus had given him with his old friend, but deep inside himself the knowledge that to do so would be an admission that Dacius was closer to his own son than he was, held him back. Finally he left the balcony and, pouring a cup of wine from the flagon that stood always beside his couch, drank it down, filled the cup again and emptied it a second time. Lying in the darkness, unable to sleep, the black tide of his thoughts still threatened to overwhelm him, and finally he put the flagon itself to his mouth, draining it before he put it back upon the table. Soon thereafter the numbing effects of the drink drew a blanket of oblivion across his turbulent thoughts.

Constantine did not know what time it was when he came suddenly awake, or what had awakened him. Then a scream came from Fausta's room and, leaping from the couch, he crashed against a chest in the semidarkness of the room, illuminated only by the rays of the moon shining through the door leading out to the balcony. Cursing the effects of the wine which made him stagger, he finally managed to find the door to Fausta's room and jerked it open.

The scene that met his eyes was enough to sober him in an instant. Fausta stood beside the couch in a diaphanous nightdress that fully revealed her still virginally lovely body—though she had borne him six children. Hardly a pace away Crispus, obviously very drunk, leaned against a chair for support while he stared at his father with horror and—Constantine thought—guilt written large upon his face.

33

FAUSTA BROKE the silence as she threw herself, sobbing, into Constantine's arms. "I can usually handle him! But tonight he had too much to drink and—" A gale of tears drowned out anything else she might have said, but the scene spoke for itself—except for one thing, the dazed and incredulous look in Crispus' eyes as they stared at his father and at Fausta.

The hubbub in Fausta's bedchamber brought the lady-in-waiting, who slept nearby, and also the guard on duty in the corridor outside. Both stood wide-eyed at the dramatic tabloid in the bedchamber, but Constantine—far from being seized by the paroxysm of anger he would have expected—felt himself almost a dispassionate observer, watching the climactic scene in a play whose ending, he knew now, had been foreordained ever since Lupus had come to him earlier that evening.

"Take Caesar Crispus to his quarters and have a guard maintained there," he ordered the soldier. "He is not to leave except upon my order, and no one is to speak of this—on pain of death."

When the guard touched Crispus' shoulder, he moved for the first time since Constantine had entered the chamber. Before closing the door leading out into the corridor, however, he turned to look back at Fausta and his father and the pain in his eyes was like a naked blade twisted in Constantine's own heart.

"Leave us," Constantine told the lady-in-waiting. When she was gone, he led the still-sobbing Fausta to the bed and cradled her in his arms until her weeping stopped and she was able to talk about what happened.

According to Fausta's account, she and Crispus had stayed to the end of the gala at the home of Senator Marcellinus. When it was over, Crispus had sent his own wife, Helena, home with Constantia, while he escorted Fausta to her palace. He had drunk a good deal of wine during the evening, Fausta said, and had staggered a little as he escorted her to her chamber, but had left her at the door. Then, just as she was about to retire, he had re-entered. She had tried to talk him into leaving the chamber but, influenced by the wine, he had sought to force her to submit. It was then that she had screamed, waking Constantine.

The sorry tale told, Fausta quickly fell asleep, but there would be no more sleep for Constantine that night. Covering her gently, for the flimsy nightdress was no protection against the chill that had settled over the city in the early hours of the morning, he left the room. The chill of the night, however, was not half so penetrating as the one that gripped his heart, and he was thankful that either the wine he had drunk at bedtime or Lupus' news had prepared him for what had happened so he could consider it almost with a detached point of view.

His first act, he decided, must be a conference with Dacius. Nor could it be put off until morning, for, although he had admonished the guard and the lady-in-waiting to say nothing of what had happened in Fausta's bedchamber, he knew the story would be all over Rome before the day was half over—the day that was to have marked the climax of the Vicennalia—and of Constantine's own happiness with the announcement of Crispus' elevation to the rank of Augustus.

Dacius was asleep in his quarters but awakened immediately at a touch upon his shoulder. One look at Constantine's face in the light of the candle the younger man carried brought him bolt upright. While he dressed, Constantine told of the conversation with Lupus earlier that evening and the dramatic scene that had followed Fausta's scream.

"And you did no more than place Crispus under guard?" Dacius asked when he had finished the story.

"Lupus had prepared me, or in my anger I might have struck the boy dead then and there."

"Has it occurred to you that Lupus might have been preparing you on purpose—for a play that was already written?"

Constantine's hands clenched into fists but, with an effort, he kept them by his side. "I know you have never liked Fausta, Dacius, but even you have no right to accuse her of such a thing. To seduce a mere boy, her own stepson, and then cry out so he would be arrested—it's beyond belief."

"Only a very ruthless woman would get rid of a man she hated that way," Dacius admitted.

"Fausta and Crispus have always been friends. She even tried to keep all this from me—until tonight when she was forced to cry out or yield to him. No, Dacius, the least damning explanation I can think of for the whole thing is that the boy was drunk and didn't know what he was doing."

"Did Crispus give any explanation?"

"No. He seemed stunned by it all. Actually, I could forgive him for being infatuated with Fausta. She's beautiful and high-spirited and I know how provocative she can be without really meaning it. But to conspire with those who would divide my kingdom and destroy my church—such a thing is beyond forgiveness."

"If it really happened."

"That's why I came to you. I must be fair to my son, but the welfare of the Empire is involved, too, so I've decided to turn the investigation of this affair over to the Quaestor. It is his duty to pass final judgment on all questions of law, but though his integrity is above question, Rubellius is still a member of my court and looks to me for his position. You love Crispus, so I want you to work with the Quaestor in ferreting out the truth and bringing it to me with your recommendation."

"What if we discover that the situation is not what it appears to be?"

"I promise to abide by your decision. In this matter I am so torn with emotion between my son and my wife, that I can hardly be unbiased one way or the other."

II

The ensuing three days, during which Crispus was under house arrest and Fausta, at Constantine's request, remained in her palace, were the worst he ever remembered experiencing. He was prepared to forgive Crispus the episode with Fausta, though there would have to be some sort of punishment to remind the boy that a ruler of an empire should control his passions. But the rest of the accusation could not be ignored, for it amounted to treason.

When Dacius and the Quaestor Rubellius presented themselves in Constantine's audience chamber three days later, he dismissed everyone except his *magister memoriae,* who would be required to keep a record of the findings, the two officers, and Crispus himself, who had been brought from his quarters for the final hearing. The young Caesar was haggard and his eyes were red from lack of sleep, but he comported himself like a soldier and came to attention before the throne, his clenched right fist held over his left breast in the Roman salute. Constantine returned the salute and motioned all of them to seats before him.

Reading in Crispus' eyes something of the hell the younger man had been through, Constantine's heart went out to his son, but he resolutely steeled himself against feeling even pity, until he could hear the truth of the matter presented by Rubellius and Dacius, as well as Crispus' own defense. For where the welfare of the Empire was concerned, he could not be influenced by emotion, even when his own flesh and blood were involved.

"I have asked the Quaestor Rubellius, as final legal authority, and General Dacius, as a friend to both of us, to investigate certain charges that have been brought against you, Caesar Crispus," Constantine said formally. "Are you satisfied to let them constitute a court for deciding this matter?"

"Your will is my command, Dominus." The voice was strained and its tone hopeless.

"I am inclined to overlook one charge against you," Constantine told him, "since you were known to be intoxicated and not in full possession of your senses."

He saw a look of hope spring into Crispus' eyes, only to die away when he added: "But another and graver charge has been made by an informer, a crime against the state, which I cannot ignore. Have you anything to say before Quaestor Rubellius reports to us on his investigation?"

"No, Dominus."

"Then proceed please, Rubellius."

The *quaestor's* report was made even more damning by Dacius' concurrence. It told of an ambitious and highly capable young man, who had been dazzled when important men among the Senate and nobles of Rome had honored him with a triumph reminiscent of the days when heroes of the Empire had been welcomed to its capital with every honor the state—and the gods of Rome—could bestow. It revealed how a carefully planned campaign of flattery and persuasion had been launched to gain Crispus' confidence and convince him that the cause of the Empire was being poorly served by Constantine's rumored intention to build another capital in the East at Byzantium. And it recounted how, in the past several months since the young Caesar had come to Rome to arrange the celebration of his father's twentieth year as Augustus, argument after argument had been marshaled to convince him that Constantine should be forced to follow the example of Diocletian and Maximian, relinquishing power at the end of the twenty-year period and placing Crispus at the head of a state divided into two parts.

"Who was to rule the eastern half of the Empire?" Constantine asked.

"The young Caesar, Licinianus," Rubellius said. "With regents appointed by the Senate until he attains his majority."

"The son of Licinius!" The familiar red haze of uncontrollable anger exploded before Constantine's eyes and he half-rose in his chair. Every muscle in his body suddenly tightened and the pressure in his chest made it difficult for him to breathe, while his heart hammered against his ribs with a force that threatened to burst it from his body. Only a tremendous effort enabled him to grip the arms of his chair and gain control of himself.

"The boy is thirteen, Dominius." Rubellius' words gave Constantine time to think. "Which means that the East would have been governed by regents for another eight years, or longer."

"Long enough to destroy the church there," Constantine said hoarsely, "as it would be destroyed here in the West, too, if the Senate had its way with a young and pliable Emperor. Then the whole Empire would be pagan once again."

"That seems to have been one of the main purposes of this conspiracy," Dacius agreed.

"How could you repay my trust with such a betrayal?" Constantine demanded hoarsely of Crispus. "Surely you saw what the scoundrels intended?"

"They said it was best for the Empire." The words tumbled out in a confession. "They reminded me that you have given up so much of your power to the Christian bishops that soon Rome will be run by them and all who do not worship their god will be destroyed for what they call heresy."

"What of me? Would you have put me in prison, or executed me?"

"That seems to be the point where the scheme began to fall apart." Dacius spoke before Crispus could answer. "Crispus refused to be part of any plan that did not allow you to abdicate voluntarily after the Vicennalia. He refused to sanction the use of force, in fact, you probably owe your life to him, for many in Rome would welcome your assassination."

"Is this true?" Constantine asked Crispus. "You have my leave to call witnesses to disprove these charges against you, if you can."

Crispus' eyes met his and at the shame and agony showing in them, the last vestige of Constantine's anger melted away. He found himself wondering what would have happened, had he been forced to live in his father's shadow during the years following his escape from Nicomedia. And remembering his own ambitions and his impatience toward anything that blocked his climb to high position and responsibility, he could feel only sympathy now for his son.

"The noble Rubellius has stated the truth," Crispus said. "I did listen at first, especially when they spoke of the bishops controlling the Empire."

"I am equally responsible there," Dacius interrupted. "Crispus knows my views about the meddling of the bishops. I have spoken of them often in his presence."

"But you did not conspire to overthrow your Emperor," Constantine reminded him.

"By the time I realized what the plan would really mean, what you call the conspiracy was already in progress," Crispus admitted.

"Do you give it a better name?" Constantine asked.

"No, Fath— Dominus. I have not denied my guilt."

"Nor offered a defense?"

"No, Dominus."

Constantine turned to Rubellius. "Who gave you this information?"

"Most of it came from Caesar Crispus himself. He has withheld nothing, except the names of those who conspired with him."

Constantine fought back a sudden surge of anger. "Why?" he demanded. "Why are you protecting traitors?"

"The conspiracy would have gone no further than idle talk if I had not listened and been tempted by the dream of power," Crispus said. "But I did listen, which makes me responsible for everything."

"And Licinianus?"

"He is only a boy, with no real idea of what was involved."

"Except that he wished to assume power in his father's former domain—if the regents appointed by the Senate didn't murder him and keep the power for themselves. Do you see now what a fool unscrupulous men can make of an honest man with ambition, Crispus?"

"Yes, Fath— Dominus."

Constantine leaned back in his chair. "You have betrayed my trust, and must suffer because of it. But your punishment will be mitigated if you reveal the names of the other conspirators."

"I cannot do that," Crispus said quietly.

"In the name of God, why not?"

"I alone am the chief culprit. Without me there would have been no conspiracy."

It was the truth and, in spite of his anger and exasperation at the boy's stubbornness, Constantine couldn't help feeling a certain pride in Crispus' stalwart honesty and the strength of character that would let him choose degradation and perhaps death—for treason was involved here—rather than shift the blame for his own yielding to an overweening ambition upon the shoulders of others.

"Is that your final decision?" Constantine asked.

"Yes, Dominus."

Constantine turned to the *quaestor*. "What punishment do you recommend in such a case, Rubellius?"

"It is a clear case of treason, Dominus. The punishment customary in such cases is death."

Constantine heard Crispus catch his breath in what might have been a sob, but the near breakdown was only momentary. Standing stiffly erect, he stared fixedly at the wall—as if awaiting the headsman's axe.

"What do you say, Dacius?" Constantine asked. "Do you agree that the prisoner is guilty?"

"Yes."

"And the punishment?"

"Almost exactly three centuries ago, a wise and good man in Galilee of Judea said, 'Blessed are the merciful, for they shall obtain mercy.' I have no other advice."

Constantine knew well what Dacius implied—that more than once he had not hesitated to remove those who stood in his way, using whatever means came to hand. In fact Crispus had not acted differently in this affair than he had on occasions—save that, when it came to the final act of destroying the only stumbling block barring him from power and glory, he had refused to harm his own father. And that in itself justified leavening punishment with mercy.

"I would not withhold from my own son the mercy recommended by the Son of God," Constantine said. "It is my will that Caesar Crispus and Caesar Licinianus shall be banished from my presence. They will remain under guard at Pola, in the district of Istria and the province of Pannonia, until I shall decree an end to their sentence of banishment. Quaestor Rubellius will order their transfer to Pola immediately, and the *magister memoriae* will record the sentence."

He rose from his chair. "General Dacius, I would speak with you in my cabinet."

As Crispus turned to follow Rubellius from the room, Constantine saw the dazed look in his eyes, like a doomed man reprieved at the last minute and still hardly able to believe his good fortune.

III

"Was I fair to the boy?" Constantine asked as he doffed the purple robe of a judge. "The palace at Pola is small but comfortable, and it overlooks the Mare Adriaticum."

"You were more than generous," Dacius assured him. "I expected—" He did not continue, but the listener understood his meaning: that with Constantine's tendency lately toward blind rages, the sentence was very light indeed compared to what it might have been. Istria was one of the loveliest areas along the Dalmatian coast of the Adriatic Sea and Pola was located at the tip of a peninsula jutting out into the water. No banishment could be pleasant for one who realized how he had let ambition make a fool of him—as Crispus well knew he had done—but if banishment it must be, less punishing circumstances could hardly have been chosen.

"If only the boy hadn't thrown away everything I planned for him." Constantine put his hand to his left breast to lessen the feeling of constriction and pressure he'd felt there ever since Lupus had come to him with the damning story. "I was prepared to give him half the world, with no strings attached save that he consult me about any major change. Yet in one night he destroyed what could have been a glorious career."

"Then you plan to make the banishment permanent?"

"What else can I do—when he refuses to name those who conspired with him? I could hardly return him to a position of power and responsibility, knowing he might yield to them again."

"But if the conspirators are revealed and destroyed?"

"Then I might review his sentence—after a suitable period of punishment by isolation from the rest of the world." Constantine gave Dacius a searching look. "What do you have in mind?"

"The boy trusts me. If I go with him and young Licinianus to Istria, I might persuade him that it is his duty to reveal the details of the conspiracy."

"But you are practically ruler of Gaul in the name of young Constantine."

"Crocus can handle that. He is much younger than I am and better fitted to bear heavy burdens."

"Do you love Crispus enough to bury yourself with him, Dacius?" Constantine's voice was husky with emotion.

"I buried myself with his father at Salonae, when Diocletian went there," Dacius reminded him. "I've never seen the palace at Pola, but I dare say it is fully as luxurious. Perhaps I shall even take up growing cabbages."

"You have my leave to go. And if you can somehow give me a valid reason to admit the boy once again to my favor, I shall always be grateful." Constantine put his arm across the shoulders of the old general in an affectionate gesture. "Thank you, too, for reminding me of Christ's teachings about mercy. In spite of your distrust for bishops, I sometimes think you are a better Christian than any of us."

IV

Many in Rome breathed deep sighs of relief at the news that Crispus had refused to identify his co-conspirators and had been banished with Licinianus to Istria. Not so Empress Helena, to whom Crispus was like a second son. She came to Constantine as soon as the sentence was announced.

"I never thought the day would come when you would spurn your own flesh and blood," she upbraided him bitterly. "Crispus' only crime was letting that woman make a fool of him."

From anyone else, the designation of Rome's Empress as "that woman" would have brought instant retribution, but Constantine had known for a long time how his mother felt about Fausta and, in truth, was inclined to agree. He had not consulted his wife about the banishing of Crispus, since the affair that night had played no part in his decision. He could not believe she had been entirely innocent in the affair, however, for it was just like her to lead a young and impressionable young man on, simply to demonstrate the power her beauty still had over men.

"Crispus was not banished because of Fausta, Mother," he explained patiently. "He conspired with a group of Senators and noblemen to seize the Empire from me."

"I don't believe it!" Helena exclaimed. "She made up a tale to keep everyone from knowing she got him drunk and tried to seduce him."

"Crispus confessed."

"Who else is implicated then?"

"He wouldn't tell."

"Don't you see?" Helena cried in triumph. "He is protecting her!"

THE MIRACLE OF THE FLAMING CROSS

The same idea had come to Constantine, but logic had already refuted it. As fiercely possessive as a lioness where the future of her young sons was concerned, Fausta would never have helped Crispus in his plan to gain control of the Empire, knowing that her sons would probably be left out of the succession entirely—as had been those of Empress Theodora and Constantine's own father following his accession to the position of sole Augustus.

"Dacius and the Quaestor Rubellius investigated the case, Mother," he explained. "Even Dacius agreed that the sentence was mild, where treason was concerned."

"Is it treason for a young boy to become infatuated with an older and unscrupulous woman?"

"I told you that affair had nothing to do with Crispus' being banished," Constantine repeated. "He was drunk and the provocation was possibly considerable—"

"So you admit that she led him on?"

"Let us say I didn't punish him because of it. Believe me, Mother, I let the boy off as lightly as I could. I had planned to make him Augustus over the Prefectures of Gaul and Italy during the Vicennalia. Now I must continue to bear those burdens myself."

Fausta was considerably more violent in her reaction to the news of Crispus' banishment when Constantine went to her quarters to tell her of it. She had just come from the bath and the heat of it—since she liked to lie in hot water for hours—still filled the apartment. Seeing her thus, Constantine was less inclined than ever to blame Crispus for becoming infatuated with her, for, flushed and rosy from the bath, she was fully as desirable as on the day he'd first seen her here in Rome more than twenty years ago.

"You executed my father for a lesser crime," she stormed. "Yet you let one who tried to rape your wife go free. Is that all the respect you have for me—and for your children?"

"Crispus is being punished severely."

"By banishment for a few months to a palace on the Mare Adriaticum. What will the people think of a ruler who has no more regard for his wife's honor—"

"You should have had more regard for it when you deliberately set out to turn Crispus' head. And when you lured him here that night to prove your power over him, then found you'd unleashed a force you couldn't control and had to call for help."

The thrust went home, confirming that he had hit upon the truth about the scene that night, when he had come into this very room to find Fausta almost nude and his son seemingly in a compromising situation. Knowing Fausta, he didn't expect her to be overtaken by guilt and was surprised at the sudden look of fear in her eyes and the blanching of her cheeks. She even swayed a moment as if he had dealt her a blow and put her hand to her dressing table to support herself. But the effect was only momentary and she quickly regained control.

"So you accuse the mother of your children of being a wanton?" She flung at him.

"Not a wanton." Even knowing to what lengths she had gone to prove her power over a younger man, he could not help admiring her fiery beauty, stirred as it was by anger and indignation. "I don't think you would be false to me, if only because you know I would kill you if you did. But I cannot forgive you for letting your pride lead you to destroy Crispus."

"Destroy? When your mother will talk you into forgiving him in a few months and bringing him back from banishment?"

"I meant that you have destroyed his immediate future."

"Then you don't intend to make him Augustus of Gaul and Italy later?"

"Where did you learn that?" Had he been less startled at learning that the secret he'd revealed to no one else except Dacius was now known to others, he might have been warned by the sudden guarded look in her eyes.

"It has been common gossip in Rome for weeks," she said with a shrug.

"Only Dacius knew of my plan. I told him of it the afternoon before all this happened."

"You must have talked in your sleep, then," she said quickly. "Yes, I remember now. You did mention it in your sleep."

"But you and I haven't shared a bed since I came to Rome. You've been out to receptions and dinners every night and never get home before dawn."

"Then one of the servants probably told me."

"You're lying, Fausta. Why?"

To his utter surprise, her eyes filled with tears. He'd forgotten how easily she was able to simulate weeping, so it never occurred to him that, when she threw herself into his arms, the tears were not genuine.

"It hurt me that you would make such a decision—to disinherit your own children—without telling your wife." She began to sob bitterly. "And after I let my beauty be destroyed in bearing you the children you wanted. What have I done to be treated this way?"

Although still half-certain that she was playing a dramatic scene for purposes of her own, as he'd known her to do many times before, Constantine instinctively put his arms about her and held her close. And as he did, he felt a resurgence of the old yearning, a renewal of the rapture which, in the press of the affairs of Empire, he had almost forgotten could be so precious.

It had been a long time, he thought, since they had been so close together. As she nestled against him, no longer sobbing, he felt a great tenderness well up in his heart, washing away, for the moment at least, his suspicion that she was playing a part. And in the excitement of her embrace, he quite forgot that she had not answered his question about how she had learned of his secret plan to name Crispus Augustus of the West on the last day of the Vicennalia.

v

With no deputy upon whom he could depend now—as he had planned to depend upon Crispus—Constantine was forced to remain in Rome for several months to straighten out affairs there. One of these concerned the construction of several new churches, which he had ordered and for which he had provided the funds. Another was a series of conferences with the governors of the two western prefectures and the several provinces, in order to assure himself that the men were capable and worthy enough for him to share some of the authority of his office with them.

Although Pola and Istria were only a few days' journey away by horseback, and even less from the eastern shore of Italy by boat,

Constantine had heard no word from Dacius about any progress he might be making in the attempt to learn from Crispus who his co-conspirators had been. Then one morning, as he was holding his daily audience for ambassadors, officials of the government and others with cases to be heard by the Emperor, he became conscious of a sudden disturbance outside the chamber. Moments later, the captain of the Imperial Guard burst into the room.

"An assassin has tried to kill the Empress, Dominus!" he shouted. "We have him under guard!"

Constantine rushed from the chamber to Fausta's quarters, where he found a state of pandemonium, with women screaming and servants and soldiers running about. Fausta herself was unhurt, he determined quickly, but she was having hysterics and it took him awhile to calm her and persuade her to swallow a mixture of wine and poppy prepared by the court physician. When she was quiet, he left the room and summoned the commander of the guard.

"What happened here?" he demanded.

"The Domina was in her boudoir, preparing for her bath," the officer explained. "The assassin burst in and tried to kill her with a dagger."

"How could any man get into the Empress' apartment?"

"The guards were on duty outside the door, Dominus. But since he is a general and known to be one of your closest friends—"

"A general?"

"It was General Dacius, Dominus."

34

CONSTANTINE EXCLAIMED, "Dacius! But that is impossible. He is in Istria."

"Nevertheless the assassin is General Dacius, Dominus. I served under him in Gaul and know him well."

"Where is he now?"

"In a room down the corridor. The Empress screamed when she saw him draw his dagger and the guard outside the door managed to get into the room in time to wound him mortally with a spear before he could strike her down. The physician is with him now."

It was Dacius, as the officer had said, but for a moment Constantine thought he was already dead. Then he saw the wounded man's chest move slightly and dropped to his knees beside the couch upon which his old friend—and, it appeared, the would-be murderer of his wife—lay. A bulky bandage covered much of Dacius' torso, but from the spreading red circle already staining the cloth, Constantine could see that the wound was still bleeding seriously. He glanced across the couch at the physician, who touched his right side below the ribs.

"A spear thrust, Dominus." The physician shook his head to confirm what Constantine could see for himself from the spreading circle of red upon the bandages, the shallow breathing and the pallor of the wounded man's lips. The wound was indeed mortal, as the commander of the guard had said.

Dacius opened his eyes and, seeing Constantine, tried to push himself up from the couch but fell back. When Constantine reached out to help him, however, the wounded man found the strength to strike his hand away.

"Murderer!" he gasped, but a fit of coughing put an end to

further words, as a trickle of red appeared at the corner of the dying man's mouth and ran down his chin.

"I don't know what you're talking about, Dacius," Constantine said. "Who have I murdered?"

"Crispus and Licinianus," the dying man gasped. "I saw your signature on their death warrants—and mine. But I escaped."

"When was this?"

"The warrants came to Pola by courier from Rome a week ago. The garrison commander carried out two of them, but I managed to escape." His head fell back on the pillow as the effort of speaking brought on unconsciousness once again.

"Is he dead?" Constantine asked the physician, who was keeping his fingers upon the wounded man's wrist.

"No, Dominus. There is still a pulse, but it is almost gone."

"Revive him if you can. I must know the truth of this story."

"There was a paper in the breast of his tunic, Dominus. The guard's spear penetrated it."

"Can it still be read?"

"Most of it." The physician handed over a sheet of parchment bearing the imperial crest. It was signed at the bottom with Constantine's own signature. And even though it was stained with the old general's blood, there was no doubting its meaning. It was an order to the commander of the garrison at Pola for the execution of Dacius; but though it bore Constantine's personal seal and what appeared to be his signature, he had never seen it before.

"This is a forgery!" Constantine looked up to see the physician regarding him oddly. "Surely you can see that. Would I murder my son and a mere boy—as well as the man who taught me all I know?"

"General Dacius seemed to consider it genuine, Dominus," the physician said.

"But why would he try to kill the Empress?"

"I don't know, Dominus. But he would have succeeded, if the guard had not thrown his spear. She was naturally shocked and distraught so I ordered the draught of wine and poppy and asked her ladies to prepare a hot bath for her. You know how much she loves them."

Constantine knew that nothing could be gained by trying to question Fausta. On more than one occasion he had been irritated by her habit of lying in a steaming hot bath for hours, but she was always more tractable after such a session, so he did not suggest any other treatment for her now.

"Awaken him, if you can," he ordered the physician. "I must know more about this document."

From a small case the physician took a vial and, opening it, passed it briefly under Dacius' nostrils. The sharply acrid smell of the bottle's contents made even Constantine cough and the concentrated whiff of it revived Dacius enough for him to open his eyes again.

"This order is a forgery, Dacius." Constantine spoke rapidly, hoping the dying man would not lapse into unconsciousness again before he could learn what he needed to know.

"But how—"

"I don't know, but I intend to find out."

"Do you swear—?" A spasm of coughing interrupted the halting flow of words.

"By my faith in Christ Jesus and my hope of salvation, I swear that I never saw the order for your death until this moment. Did you say Crispus and Licinianus are both dead?"

"Yes. Beheaded—"

"Why did you try to kill Fausta?"

"I was sure she had tricked you into signing the death warrants. Crispus told me how she duped him that night in her chamber. He brought her home, but when he started to leave, she threw herself at him and screamed for you."

"But why?"

"You were going to name Crispus Augustus of the West, over her own sons."

It all fitted so perfectly that he cursed himself for not seeing it before, though in his heart he had really suspected something like this all along but had not been willing to face the truth. And because he had not—he realized now—his son and Licinianus were dead and Dacius was dying, with the burden of guilt for their deaths resting upon his shoulders alone.

"Why didn't Crispus tell what really happened?" he asked.

"The boy was infatuated, and drunk. He wasn't sure what he had done or had not done." The dying man's voice had grown steadily fainter. "Promise me she will be punished—"

"She will; I swear it." Constantine spoke from the depths of the agony gripping his heart at the thought of Crispus, the handsome, the promising, the brave, cut down by the headsman's axe—and all because of a woman's relentless ambition.

"She will be punished," he repeated mechanically, staring at the wall with eyes that were blind now to everything save the pain of a breaking heart. He didn't realize that the sound of Dacius' whispering—and his breathing—had ceased until the physician said quietly, "He is dead, Dominus. Shall I prepare his body for burial?"

A sob broke from Constantine's throat and, heedless of the bloody bandage that stained his tunic, he gathered the dead form of his old comrade to his breast while tears streamed down his cheeks. For only a few moments, however, did he yield to the paroxysm of grief, weeping not only for Dacius but for his son and the young Licinianus. Then, his face set, he got to his feet and started toward the door.

"The document, Dominus," the physician called out to him. "Shall I destroy it?"

Constantine understood the reason for the question. With the death warrant for Dacius destroyed—as the death warrants for Crispus and Licinianus would be destroyed if he gave the order to expunge them from the official records—no one could accuse him of having ordered the death of the three. Then in far-off Istria, the commander of the Pola garrison could be singled out as a scapegoat and duly executed, on the claim that he was a tool of the interests who had sought to put Crispus forward to succeed his father at the end of the Vicennalia.

But Constantine had no intention of glossing over the tragedy, or his part in it. His very real agony for his son and Dacius—and Licinianus, too, for the young Caesar had been only a boy—was far too great for him to let their deaths go unavenged. Besides, he had given Dacius his solemn promise that those responsible would be punished.

"Give me the sheet," he ordered the physician. "But say nothing about it at the moment. This is the only evi—" He was looking at the bloodstained document as he spoke and broke off in the middle of a word, his heart suddenly hammering with excitement. He'd thought when he had first seen it that there was something familiar about the angular strokes with which the words of the warrant had been written. Now he remembered where he had seen that same handwriting before.

It had been when he and Dacius had ridden out to the villa of Livia on the afternoon before the final day of the Vicennalia and he'd revealed to Dacius his plan to make Crispus Augustus of the West. The children had been doing their lessons with Lupus when they arrived, copying verses from a large sheet of parchment upon which the tutor had written a section of the Aeneid. The angular script in which the poem the children had been copying was written and that on the death warrant he held in his hand were the same.

"Find the tutor Lupus," Constantine commanded the officer who stood by the door. "Bring him to my quarters without delay."

II

Lupus' eyes were wary when two guards brought him into the private apartment.

"Did you know General Dacius tried to assassinate the Empress Fausta less than an hour ago?" Constantine demanded.

"I heard the commotion, Dominus. I hope he didn't harm the Empress." The concern in the tutor's voice seemed genuine.

"She is unharmed. A guard thrust him through with a spear before he succeeded in killing her."

"I shall make a sacrifice of thanksgiving for her safety to Apoll—"

"Dacius died a few minutes ago, but not before he warned me of a conspiracy that has already destroyed my son Crispus and Caesar Licinianus. Someone forged death warrants for both of them and also for General Dacius, signing them with my name."

"But surely the commander of the Pola garrison suspected—"

"They were very clever forgeries, Lupus. Whoever made them is closely connected with my household. He used parchment bearing the imperial crest and wrote my signature as well as I can write it myself."

"Such a traitor should be hunted down at once and destroyed," Lupus said piously. "If I can help—"

"You can." Constantine fingered the dagger he had placed on the table before him. "You can help more than anyone else I know."

"You have but to command, Dominus."

Constantine leaned forward, his eyes boring into those of the tutor. "Why did you do it, Lupus?"

"I—I don't know what you mean."

"Then this should refresh your memory." Constantine tossed the bloodstained death warrant across the table, but Lupus drew back as if it were a venomous serpent, ready to strike. His face was livid now with fear.

"Don't mind the blood," Constantine told him. "After all, you murdered Dacius, just as you did Crispus and Licinianus!"

"I deny any part in this affair," Lupus said hoarsely. "And I demand trial before the Sen—" He broke off as Constantine rose to his feet, with the dagger in his hand.

"Seize him!" Constantine ordered and one of the guards, a burly fellow who could have made two of Lupus, quickly drew the tutor's arms behind him, holding the struggling man as easily as he might have held a child. Reaching out with his left hand, Constantine seized Lupus' gown and ripped it from his chest with a single jerk. Then putting the point of the dagger against the pallid skin, he pressed the handle until it just penetrated into the flesh, causing Lupus to scream with pain and fear.

"Whose idea was it to forge death warrants for Crispus, Licinianus and Dacius?" he demanded.

"Empress Fausta's."

"You lie!"

"By the gods—I swear it. She was angry because you did not prosecute Caesar Crispus for attacking her—"

"You know there was never any such attack. When did you and the Empress first plan to trap Crispus?"

"When I heard you telling General Dacius at the Villa of Livia about your plans to make him Augustus of Italy and the West. I rode by another way to the palace and warned the Empress. We decided to get Caesar Crispus drunk that night, so she could accuse him of trying to attack her."

"And you forged the death warrants?"

"Empress Fausta thought of them—"

"When?"

"About a month ago—one night in her quarters." It was a slip of the tongue and the sudden stutter in Lupus' voice betrayed his realization of it. "I—I mean that I—"

The full meaning of the tutor's words struck Constantine like a slap in the face and, unconsciously, he pushed the point of the dagger deeper into Lupus' flesh. Only the breastbone kept it from penetrating the tutor's heart, but the pain was enough to make him scream again.

"How long have you had free access to my wife's quarters?" Constantine demanded.

"Si-since right after I became the children's tutor, Dominus. She made me—"

But Constantine was no longer listening. "Put him under guard until I can arrange his execution," he ordered the guard as he turned to the door leading to Fausta's quarters.

Only a lady-in-waiting was present in the Empress' boudoir; at the sight of his face, and what was written there, she scurried out without waiting for an order. Fausta herself was not in the room, but the heavy miasma of scented steam coming from the adjoining bath told him where he would find her. Giving no warning, he pushed aside the hangings and stepped into the room, whose marbled walls and floor were wet and slippery from condensation of the hot vapor from the bath. Fausta, her body rosy from the heat, lay in the sunken tub, her head resting upon a pillow suspended across the tub by stout cords and her dark hair streaming out upon the surface of the water.

"Lupus," she murmured at the sound of Constantine's footfall upon the floor of the bath. "I had the most exciting experience this morning."

Her eyes opened drowsily, then widened when she saw her husband standing there instead of her lover. And at the caressing note that had been in her voice, an ungovernable rage he could no more have controlled than he could have seized the force of a raging storm with his bare hands, took complete control of Constantine's actions, and his senses.

III

When Constantine became conscious of his surroundings again, he was still standing beside the pool, his right hand gripping the handle of a broad paddle with which Fausta's servants stirred the water in the tub to mix it. The cords holding the pillow upon which her head had rested were broken, and she lay motionless, face down on the bottom of the pool, with her hair strewn out behind her in the water.

The puddle of water which had obviously slopped over the edges of the pool and now stood upon the marble floor around it; the wet hem of Constantine's long robe; the water sloshing in his shoes—all betrayed that a struggle had taken place. Of it, however, he had no memory, all rational thought having been swept away by the caressing note in Fausta's voice when she had spoken her lover's name. Strangely enough, too, he felt no emotion whatsoever, as he looked down at the body on the bottom of the marbled-lined pool, the tide of anger which had seized him having been completely washed away by the violence of the action it had set in motion.

If anyone had ever deserved death, the cold force of logic assured him, it had been Fausta. Already unfaithful as a wife, she had become a murderess, too, when she had forced her lover to forge death warrants for the two who alone had stood in the way of her plans for her own children. And knowing that if Dacius were allowed to live, he would denounce her to Constantine, she had included his own death warrant as well.

Any court in the Empire, Constantine knew, would condemn her to death instantly upon the evidence he himself had gained, but he could see no point in letting the children know that he had taken upon himself—however unconsciously in a fit of anger—the execution of their mother. He therefore shouted for help and when the guard and the lady-in-waiting came hurrying into the room, they found him standing in the marbled-lined bath, lifting the body of Fausta from it.

"Your mistress drowned when the cord holding her pillow broke," he told the lady-in-waiting. "The potion the physician gave her must have been strong enough to render her unconscious."

He felt a moment of anger when he placed Fausta's body upon the bed in the adjoining boudoir and thought how often Lupus must have shared it. But he could punish Fausta no more than she had been punished already, and Lupus too would die before the day was over, so the matter was closed.

The official view of Fausta's death would be the one he had given the lady-in-waiting and the guard, but he knew the city would be abuzz with rumors before two hours had passed. Nor did he make any move to stop them, if indeed he could have done so. Instead he ordered the body of his dead wife prepared for burial and went to break the news to his children.

Dacius was given a quiet military funeral the following day and Fausta the honor, pomp and ceremony of an imperial funeral on the day after that. No honors were given Lupus, felled by the headsman's axe on the order of the *quaestor* after a rapid trial, and Constantine moved forthrightly to write an end to the whole affair in a private audience with Rubellius the same day.

"I want all official records connected with the death of the Empress removed from the archives," he told the chief legal officer of the Empire. "Some day my children might read them and it would only bring them pain to know what really happened."

"It shall be done, Dominus," the *quaestor* said, then dared to add: "But those who hate you will say you ordered the execution of Caesar Crispus and Caesar Licinianus because they stood in the way of your own desire to be sole ruler of the Empire."

"I *am* sole ruler," Constantine said. "Let future generations judge me on what I have been able to accomplish, not on what crimes men may accuse me of committing." He rose to his feet. "Have my galley made ready, Rubellius. We are returning to Nicomedia at once."

35

THE SUN WAS SHINING as brightly on the peninsula of Byzantium as it had when Constantine stood there with Dacius less than a year ago and talked of his plans for Nova Roma, but there was no gladness in the heart of the world's greatest ruler today. Rather, his shoulders were bent, as they had been since that terrible day in Rome, when Dacius had appeared with the news of Crispus' death and the forged warrant which had condemned its author, Lupus.

The burden of mourning for his brilliant son and his old friend had been almost more than Constantine could bear. To it, in time, had been added a certain amount of sorrow over Fausta, for he could not look upon the delicate beauty of his three daughters without seeing once again the girl with whom he had fallen in love long ago, when she was barely as old as the eldest of his daughters was now. And remembering the brief period of rapture they'd shared before the cares of state had begun to erect a barrier between them, he asked himself whether, had he been less concerned with ambition and less eager to enlarge the territory under his rule, they might somehow not have drifted apart.

"What shall it profit a man, if he shall gain the whole world, and lose his own soul?" Dacius had once quoted to him from the words of Christ. As he stood upon one of the seven hills of Byzantium, where he'd already decided that his new great city of Nova Roma would be built, Constantine asked himself the question again, but found no answer to it, or to the black malaise which had seized his spirit that terrible day in Rome and had held it in its grip ever since.

The Senate had accepted without question his story that, dazed from the wine and poppy given her by the physician as a sedative after Dacius' attempt to assassinate her, Fausta had drowned in the steaming tub of which she had been so fond, when the cords supporting a pillow beneath her head had broken. Privately, he knew, however, the city had buzzed with the rumor that, learning of the affair between the Empress and the tutor, of which many in Rome had long been aware, he had simply executed her by drowning her in her bath, an act to which he had every right both as a betrayed husband and as supreme ruler of the Empire.

Upon his arrival in the East from Rome more than a month earlier, Constantine had recalled Bishop Eusebius of Nicomedia from exile and had confessed his destruction of Fausta in a fit of blind rage. The absolution given him by the obliging bishop had not brought peace to his soul, however, nor had the turning over to Empress Helena of a large amount of money to be used in building a great new church on the site of the Tomb of the Saviour, which she had discovered at Jerusalem. Old and already worn out by the journey to Jerusalem, Helena had taken to her bed at the news of Crispus' death. Constantine knew she would never forgive him for trusting Fausta and thus making possible the death of Crispus. Nor, in truth, could he forgive himself.

Seeking to dull somewhat the pain that still gripped his heart at the memory of his first-born son—as he had ridden beside Crocus in his first battle, proudly displaying his bloody sword afterwards; as he had led the archers in the defeat of Licinius at Hadrianopolis; as he had accepted without question the order removing him from Caesarship of Gaul, bowing like the fine soldier he was to the will of his command—Constantine tried to spend as much time as he could with his other children.

The girls were already young ladies, except Helena, the youngest. Constantine II, eldest among the boys, and Constantius II, next to him, were growing into stalwart young men who had already begun their military training, while Constans, the third son, looked forward eagerly to joining them. None of the six, he was sure, held him responsible for their mother's death, but he could not as easily throw off the burden from his own conscience. Nor, as he stood upon an elevation now and looked out over the sparkling waters of the Bosporus and the Pontus Euxinus, was he able to conjure up again the feeling of excitement and anticipation that had gripped him, when he and Dacius had stood upon this very spot and talked of the great expanse of empire still to be conquered in the East.

"The surveyors are waiting, Dominus." Adrian's voice reminded Constantine that they had come to Byzantium to mark out the boundaries of Nova Roma, the first truly Christian capital in the Empire.

"In a moment, Adrian." Constantine's gaze once more swept across the city of Byzantium and the mounds of earth he'd ordered raised during the siege, so the city could be put under attack by his great engines of war. The mounds were covered now with yellow flowering broom and the sea breeze reaching his nostrils brought the pleasant aroma of blossoming flowers, as it passed across the triangular promontory upon which the city stood, surrounded by the lush fields of grain and vegetables, the rich orchards and vineyards that made Byzantium largely self-supporting.

In the horn-shaped waterway that gave the city an ideally protected harbor, barges were already at anchor, loaded with blocks of marble quarried in the Proconnesus, a rocky group of islands in the Sea of Marmara. And on the forest-clad slopes in the distance, great slashes of bare earth showed where timbers that would shortly form the framework for much of the city's buildings had already been felled and hauled down the mountainsides, to be shaped by woodsmen in the valleys.

Though busy and prosperous, Byzantium had been spared the incessant hurry that characterized Rome, whose citizens went from one form of entertainment to another, seeking satisfaction for jaded tastes. In fact, it almost seemed a desecration to turn Byzantium into a great city which must inevitably take on some of the less pleasant attributes of the western capital, but Constantine did not let himself be swayed by any question of sentiment from his decision to build here a new heart for the Roman Empire.

What Rome lacked, Byzantium already possessed, a strategic position, with the opposite shores of Europe and Asia in full sight, and excellent harbors, both upon the Pontus Euxinus and in the creek forming one side of the peninsula. Easy of access, the city could be defended strongly in case of attack, as Constantine al-

ready knew from his own siege, which had ended only when the inhabitants had realized that Licinius was defeated.

From this elevated and highly defendable position he could
protect the districts of the East, under almost constant attack lately
either by the Persians to the south or the Goths to the north, much
better than he had ever been able to before. The new city could
also act as a barrier to invasion of the fertile area of Asia south of
the waterway by the Sarmatians, the warlike tribe dwelling north
of the Euxine Sea. And with the Hellespont—where Crispus had
won his great victory over Licinius' fleet—in Constantine's hands
and both the Sea of Marmara and its eastern mouth, the Bosporus,
under his control, the most important waterway in that part of the
world was now his personal lake, through which ships could ply
in the vast trade that had kept Byzantium prosperous for more
than five hundred years.

From the East would come gems, spices, fine cloth and other
articles of trade, while from the West flowed products manufactured by the skilled artisans of Greece, Italy and even far-off
Gaul, all serving to make the tradesmen prosperous and enrich the
coffers of the Empire through taxes imposed upon articles passing
through the port. Satisfied now that what he could bring to Byzantium outweighed anything he would take away from it, Constantine started down the slope toward where the surveyors waited
patiently upon the shore below.

II

Leaving the walls of Byzantium behind, Constantine strode
briskly along the shore at the head of the surveying party, tracing
a line upon the earth with the point of a spear as he walked. Pant-
ing with the effort of keeping up, Adrian finally reminded him that
he had already indicated the boundaries of a city far greater in
area than any in that part of the world. But he only said, "I shall
advance until the invisible guide who marches before me thinks
it right to stop," and continued on his way.

The walls of Byzantium were well behind him when finally Constantine turned and began to march landward across to the shore

of the creek sometimes called the Golden Horn by the inhabitants, marking out an area that included all of the seven hills. Though the rest of the city was walled, no walls were planned for the shore of the Golden Horn. Instead, the mouth of the waterway was to be secured by placing across it a great chain of iron, supported upon floats, denying passage to any ships except those admitted on the order of the Emperor.

During the four years required for the construction of Nova Roma, the whole world was combed on Constantine's orders for treasures with which to glorify the city. Many magnificent churches were erected. One he selected as his very own and gave orders that upon his death his body was to be buried there in a golden sarcophagus. Dedicated to the twelve apostles, it was to be one of the most magnificent structures erected to the glory of God—and the salving of his own conscience—by the unhappy Emperor of Rome.

In the center of the city, he laid out a grandiose structure called the Augustaeum, a large open area paved in marble and surrounded by stately buildings of similar construction. North of the Augustaeum, he ordered the building of another great church, and on the east, the Senate House. Constantine's personal palace lay to the south, entered by a gate closed by doors of bronze, while nearby was the great Hippodrome for the games, always an important part of any Roman city, and the Baths of Zeuxippus, also considered indispensable by Romans.

In the very center of the Augustaeum stood a single marble column called the Milion, marking the point from which distances would thenceforth be measured throughout the Empire instead of, as had previously been the case, from Rome itself. On either side of the column was placed a group of statues. One represented Constantine and the Empress Helena with a great cross between them, while a second statue of Helena alone stood upon a pedestal.

The Forum, political center of the city, lay to the west of the Augustaeum, a magnificent structure with a spacious portico in the form of an arch of triumph, marking the very spot where Constantine's camp had stood during his siege of the city in the campaign against Licinius. In the center of the Forum area, he erected another magnificent pillar, constructed from drums of porphyry, brought especially from Rome.

Each drum—almost twice the height of a man—was bound with heavy bands of brass engraved in the form of laurel wreaths, the whole resting upon a foundation, or stylobate, of white marble. It was easily the most prominent architectural feature in all the city and at its foot Constantine ordered these words inscribed:

> Oh Christ, Ruler and Master of the world, to Thee have I now consecrated this obedient city and this scepter and the power of Rome. Guard and deliver it from every harm.

From its very beginning, Nova Roma—soon dubbed Constantinopolis by the rank and file of the people—was dedicated to the worship of the God and his Son to whom Constantine had given allegiance for so many years. Yet strangely enough, at the very summit of the porphyry column was placed a huge statue of Apollo taken from Athens, but with the head replaced by a likeness of Constantine himself.

Because Byzantium boasted little in the way of springs, much of the city was excavated to form great cisterns into which water was brought through aqueducts from a considerable distance. One of these reservoirs was so large that its roof was supported by three hundred and thirty-six columns, measuring three hundred and ninety feet in total length and a hundred and seventy-four feet in width.

Not content with constructing many of the most magnificent buildings in the world at Nova Roma, Constantine also sent agents to all parts of the Empire for objects of rare beauty and worth to enhance its glory. In fact, Rome was called upon for so many contributions that the Senate angrily claimed the old city was being gutted to add magnificence to its rival in the East.

From Greece came priceless items like the Serpent Column of Delphi; the Hercules of Lysippus—a statue so great that it measured as much as the height of a man from foot to knee; the Brazen Ass; the Poisoned Bull; the Angry Elephant; and the Horses of Lysippus, seized from Rome and carried to the new city—so many treasures, in fact, that when the entire city was dedicated four years after Constantine's tragic visit to Rome, Nova Roma could rightly claim to equal in magnificence, if not exceed, Rome itself.

Nova Roma was not the only place in the Empire where magnificent structures were being built upon Constantine's orders, however. He erected great churches in all the major cities and, since the whole of the Empire was taxed to provide funds for this construction, the Christians soon came to be hated by the great mass of the population—most of whom did not profess that faith —almost as venomously as they had been hated during the persecution under Diocletian and Galerius.

Actually, Constantine's building of churches was something of an act of penance for the deaths of Crispus, Dacius and Fausta. However much he sought surcease in prayer, he could not rid himself completely from the burden of guilt which had assailed him ever since that terrible day in Rome. And, as if to punish Rome for the part it had played in that tragedy, he did everything he could to lure its nobles and richest inhabitants to his new capital.

One of Constantine's most effective acts in building up Nova Roma was the issuance of a decree that no one could enter the imperial service without maintaining a home at the new capital, causing many officials from Rome to make the journey eastward. To further increase the population, he changed the port of the corn ships of Egypt from Rome to the new city and began a lavish distribution of grain, oil, wine and money to the people of Nova Roma. Thus in his grief and guilt, Constantine did much to turn the new city quickly into a copy of the old, even to the point of transporting Rome's vices eastward.

Inevitably, the burden of taxes required to pay for all the construction, to say nothing of the expense of maintaining two major capitals, caused people to turn against the man who had been their idol and champion. Constantine was too busy ruling the Empire and putting down small rebellions which arose frequently now because of the heavy taxes and his gradual development of despotic habits, to pay much attention to the complaints of the people. And thus a chasm gradually widened between him and the populace he ruled with a hand of iron, whose grip was steadily becoming less yielding.

Nor was Constantine free from distractions abroad, for his old enemies, the Sarmatians and the Goths, chose these years for rebellion, rapine and plunder. Forgotten long ago was his dream of spreading the Empire eastward. So busy was he, in fact, controlling the many uprisings to the north that he was forced to leave the Persian frontier more or less to itself and this area too became turbulent and unsettled, as it had been in the days of Diocletian and Galerius.

As his troubles mounted, Constantine became increasingly morose and his temper more uncertain, beginning a period of gradual degeneration of character and spirit in which his only real source of happiness lay in his children. To reward them for the only pleasure he enjoyed during these years, he divided the Empire in anticipation of the day when he would either abdicate or be taken by death.

Constantine II, who had been made ruler of Gaul following the removal of Crispus, now became his father's most active and trusted lieutenant. To Constantius, the second son, went the *Praefectura Orientis*, with the exception of Pontus, Cappadocia and Armenia Minor, which were given to Constantine's nephew Hannibalianus, grandson of his father, Constantius, and the Empress Theodora. Constans, the third son, was named Prefect of Italy and Africa, while another nephew, Dalmatius, was assigned the Prefecture of Illyricum. The title of Caesar was given to all except Hannibalianus, who was named *Rex*, or king, a title which had not existed in the Roman Empire for more than a hundred years. Constantine himself remained as Senior Emperor, with a final veto over the decisions of the younger rulers, but he gave them as much responsibility as possible, hoping to avoid the sort of contest for power which had taken place in the Empire every time a strong emperor had either died or abdicated, as in the case of Diocletian.

The Empress Helena, who had never recovered from the death of Crispus, died without ever forgiving her son for the tragedy which had left him an embittered, unhappy man. In her honor, the town of Drepanum where she had lived so long was renamed Helenopolis, but a splendid and more enduring monument to her memory was under construction in far-off Jerusalem—the beautiful church being built there over the tomb of the Saviour.

During these years of turbulence and sorrow, Constantine found pleasure in only a few things. One was the way his sons and nephews were proving themselves capable rulers of the districts assigned to them. Another was the rapid growth of Nova Roma, not only into one of the most beautiful cities of the world but also one of the most important.

The lavishness with which he built new churches and the magnificence of his new court steadily increased the burden of taxation, however, and the people groaned ever more loudly against their Emperor, who seemed to have forgotten entirely the concern he had shown for them as a young man and was now quite oblivious to their welfare and their needs. Thus, from a popular and efficient ruler, Constantine became in the space of about ten years little more than a despot in political matters. And, as if he were not troubled enough already, dissension once again broke out in the church so that, to his troubled heart, it almost seemed that the God in whom he had placed his trust had deserted him.

36

Tʜᴇ ᴅᴇʟɪʙᴇʀᴀᴛɪᴏɴꜱ of the Council of Nicaea—and particularly Constantine's firm hand upon the reins during that period —had produced a creed which put into relatively few words the truth of the great mysteries concerning man's relationship to God. In addition it had produced the anathema which resulted in the banishment of Arius and the two recalcitrant bishops, Eusebius of Nicomedia and Theognis of Nicaea, and sowed the seeds of further controversy.

In Egypt the patriarch Alexander had stepped down shortly after the end of the Council and Athanasius, the fiery advocate of the concept of *homoousion*—literally, of the same substance as the Father—had been chosen to succeed him. With the foremost opponent of the Arian heresy, which firmly adhered to the concept of *homoiousion*—acknowledging the Son to be like the Father, but not of the same substance—now Bishop of Alexandria, it would seem that no more controversy would arise from that source.

Much more separated Egypt from Nova Roma, however, than the peninsula of Asia Minor and the eastern coast of the Mediterranean Sea. Before long, the doctrine of Arius began to be preached once again in Asia Minor and Syria Palaestina, providing the tinder needed to kindle the flames of controversy once again. And Constantine himself gave impetus to the movement when, influenced by the brilliant and persuasive Bishop of Caesarea, he allowed Eusebius of Nicomedia and Theognis of Nicaea to return from exile and, a little later, extended imperial clemency to Arius, who had been banished to Galatia.

The recall of the two bishops was without reservation, allowing them to take up their duties once again. Arius, however, was forbidden to go to Alexandria, where a clash between him and Bishop Athanasius, whose position in the church was steadily growing in importance, would have been an immediate result. Nevertheless, having gained their first objective, the recall of Arius, friends of the rebel priest now attacked their second target, Bishop Athanasius himself.

Knowing Athanasius' reputation as a fighter, they first concentrated their efforts upon one of his strongest supporters, Bishop Eustathius of Antioch, and managed to have him banished. This arbitrary act of a highly prejudiced religious court stirred many people to anger and brought on more division, but the unyielding Arians next drove two other bishops from their sees. Only then did they consider themselves strong enough to launch an attack against Athanasius himself.

By the time Constantine dedicated Nova Roma, the controversy was in full swing. And when the Emperor, his mind poisoned against Athanasius by Eusebius of Nicomedia and others, ordered the Bishop of Alexandria to readmit Arius to the communion of that church, Athanasius refused. This was exactly what the followers of Arius had been trying to bring about. But to their considerable dismay Constantine—who by now was disgusted with the infighting that kept the church in the East in such a constant turmoil —refused to punish Athanasius. Further accusations followed and, three years after the dedication of Nova Roma, the Bishop of Alexandria was ordered to appear before a religious court at Caesarea.

Skilled warrior in doctrinal battles that he was, Athanasius refused to defend himself in the territory of his enemies before an already prejudiced tribunal. When he was finally tried two years later at Tyre, old charges, mostly absurd, were brought against him. But as he had done during the Council of Nicaea, he defended himself so skillfully and the trumped-up evidence was so flimsy, that the court did not dare convict him, lest it bring down upon itself the wrath of Constantine. A commission was therefore dispatched instead to Africa seeking further evidence upon which additional charges might be brought.

Meanwhile, Athanasius boldly threw himself upon imperial

mercy by going to Nova Roma. Standing in the middle of the road, he barred Constantine's passage into the city, as the Emperor was returning from a brief journey. But when the Imperial Guards would have thrust the churchman aside, Constantine ordered them back.

"Your face seems familiar," he said. "Have I seen you before?"

"I am Bishop Athanasius of Alexandria."

"I remember now." Constantine's face cleared. "You were very eloquent in the prosecution of Arius."

"I hope I can be equally eloquent in my own defense, Dominus —if you will but allow me an audience."

"I have always admired a bold fighter, even in the wrong cause," Constantine told him.

"But mine is the right cause, Dominus, the cause of Christ."

"Yet you have been condemned by a court of bishops."

"Not condemned, Dominus. They postponed the trial, until they could bring more evidence from Egypt."

"And will they be able to find such evidence, Bishop Athanasius?"

"Only if they manufacture it themselves, Dominus."

Constantine looked into the eyes of the slender bishop and liked what he saw, for no fear or subservience showed there. "You have become a stormy petrel, Bishop Athanasius, and in their desire to be vindicated, such often damage their own cause, even though it is right. Find quarters at my expense in Nova Roma while I send Count Dionysius to Tyre, to learn the truth. Then you shall have a chance to face your enemies in my presence."

"I ask no more than that, Dominus," said Athanasius and stepped aside to let the party pass.

The report of Count Dionysius confirmed Athanasius' claim that the so-called Council of Tyre had been only a travesty of what a religious court should be, and Constantine ordered the bishops who had taken part in it to Nova Roma at once to face Athanasius before him as judge. In the meantime, the commission which had gone to Egypt had already condemned Athanasius on further trumped-up charges, pronounced Arius free from all heresy and recommended his readmission to the church at Alexandria. When they repeated their charges against Athanasius in Constantine's presence, however, the so-called evidence was so patently absurd that Constantine was disgusted with the whole affair.

By now Athanasius had become a storm center of controversy and Constantine was sure that, even though he was in the right, the cause of peace in the church could not possibly be helped by vindicating him and returning him to his see. He therefore placed upon Athanasius the sentence of banishment, but sent him to Treves in Gaul, where Constantine II ruled as his father's deputy. And to make sure that Athanasius would be fairly treated, he wrote to young Constantine, directing that the Alexandrian bishop be free in every way except to leave the country.

Even though the charges against Athanasius had not impressed the Emperor, the banishing of the most eloquent voice raised against the Arian concepts could only strengthen his cause. Arius returned to Alexandria, expecting to be acclaimed, but his victory turned literally to ashes in his mouth, when the Alexandrian Christians largely ignored him and remained faithful to their fiery bishop in exile. As a result, trouble between the two factions flared again and Constantine ordered Arius back to Rome, this time to defend himself.

"Do you hold to the faith of the true church?" he demanded.

The priest gave an affirmative answer.

"Can I trust you? Are you really of the true faith?" Constantine insisted.

Arius again affirmed his adherence to the faith and even recited the creed, but Constantine was not quite satisfied.

"Have you abjured the errors you held in Alexandria?" he asked. "And will you swear to it before God?"

Arius gave the necessary oath, so Constantine had little choice except to draft an order permitting him to return to Alexandria. He did, however, admonish him finally with these words: "Go, and if your faith be not sound, may God punish you for your perjury."

Considering himself vindicated, Arius prepared to leave for Alexandria, but before he could depart he was stricken with a serious illness and died from a violent hemorrhage. People throughout the city naturally took this to be a punishment from God for the sin of perjury, as indeed did Constantine himself. Moreover, the startling death of the rebel priest—seemingly giving dramatic proof that Constantine had obeyed the will of God in handling the affair—had a remarkable effect upon the Emperor.

As he approached the Tricennalia, celebrating thirty years of his reign, Constantine's preoccupation with religious affairs increased considerably, leading him to renewed efforts toward finding peace through building new shrines for the worship of God throughout the Empire. At the same time, Adrian, who was now his most trusty emissary, was despatched to the eastern border to assay conditions there preparatory to a military campaign that would carry Roman rule—and, more important, Christianity—farther eastward than it had ever gone before. Fired by what appeared to be an opportunity to expiate his guilt in promoting the spread of the faith, to whose furthering he now devoted most of his time, Constantine went to Rome for the Tricennalia. But on the way back to Nova Roma, he was stricken with a grave illness.

II

The pain was worse than anything he had ever experienced. Starting deep in the left side of his chest, it spread outward like waves from a pebble dropped in a pool, until that whole side of his body seemed to be in the grip of a vise being tightened steadily by some malignant hand. Along with the feeling of constriction went a radiating pain into his left shoulder and arm, as if spikes were being driven into the flesh itself.

The physicians could do little except prescribe large doses of poppy leaves crushed in honey or wine, a remedy for pain which had been in use for over a thousand years. One had the temerity to recommend that he lie in a hot bath, but the suggestion brought on such a violent attack of anger that the unhappy physician was forced to flee for his life.

All that day and into the next, the pain lasted, dulled but not completely removed by the effect of the poppy. Even after it began to subside, the slightest effort would bring it on again. For one who had known the active life of a soldier during all sorts of campaigning, such a helpless condition was galling. And even when the physicians allowed him to be up several weeks after the beginning of his illness, a short walk brought on such a feeling of difficulty in getting his breath that he hardly dared to stir from his room for another month.

From anger at his own inability to do even the most ordinary things himself, no great step was required to decide that the illness from which he suffered was further punishment for the deaths of Crispus, Fausta and Dacius. By the time Adrian arrived from the inspection of the eastern frontier, Constantine was in a black mood indeed.

"It grieves me to find you ill, Dominus," the Greek merchant said.

"No more than it grieves me. These cursed physicians will hardly let me stir ten paces abroad without twittering around me like a flock of swallows."

"But you are better?"

"The pain has gone, except when I exert myself. But the strain of keeping still is almost as bad as it was. What did you discover in the East, Adrian?"

"Not much to make you feel better, I'm afraid. The kings of Persia grow more daring every day. No longer can we trade through the city of Nisibis on the eastern frontier with the people of India and the yellow men for spices and other rich goods without paying a tribute to the Persians that takes away all the profit."

"They will have to be punished, as soon as I am able to direct the campaign," Constantine said. "First the torment in my soul kept me idle. Then, just when I was beginning to hope I could rid myself of that, my body decided to punish me too."

The shrewd Greek merchant did not miss the significance of the word "punish," though Constantine himself appeared not to be conscious of it. After years of close association, Adrian understood perhaps better even than Constantine himself what had been happening to the Emperor's soul these past ten years. And though not a physician, he had his doubts that the disease could be cured.

"The Persians have dared to push northward as far as the shores of the Pontus Euxinus at Trapezus," he added.

"Have they denied the port to us?"

"Not yet, Dominus."

"Then a swift strike through southern Armenia might still cut them off and leave them to be destroyed by the Armenians?"

"It could be done, with you leading the troops."

Constantine suddenly grimaced and put his hand to his chest, pressing there to relieve the warning stab of pain brought on by his excitement. "Not in my present condition," he confessed. "Once I dreamed of pushing the boundaries of the Empire as far as India. Now I cannot even keep the enemy from seizing territory that has been mine for thirty years."

"I bring *some* cheering news," Adrian told him.

"Then give it to me. God knows I've had little enough to bring me joy these past years."

"We are enjoying more trade every year through Antioch."

"What of the new church there? The one built in an eight-sided figure?"

"The work goes on steadily. You can be sure that when it is finished in another year, it will be one of the most beautiful structures in the world."

"And also the first of its kind," Constantine said. "Until now, most of the churches have been built in the form of the basilica, but I think this new style will give us more beautiful structures."

"By the way, Dominus," Adrian said, "the new church at Jerusalem is finally finished. I saw Bishop Eusebius at Caesarea and he asked about its dedication. You know your mother planned to do that herself."

"And now she, too, is gone." Constantine's face suddenly brightened. "But I can dedicate it, Adrian. I've never been to Jerusalem. The Saviour performed many miracles of healing there and perhaps I too can be healed. Then I could raise an army in Syria Palaestina and Augusta Euphratensia to drive the Persians back across the Tigris again."

"Wouldn't the journey tax your strength too much, Dominus?"

"No harm can come to me if I go to Caesarea by galley. I can rest all the way and the sea air should do me good." Constantine sat up straighter, his pain forgotten. "You've given me a new purpose, Adrian. Order a galley prepared at once. When the dedication of the church at Jerusalem is over, I might even go to Dura."

"Dura?"

"The Lord first appeared to me there in an abandoned church," Constantine explained. "If he does not heal me at Dura then I will know I have lost all right to his forgiveness and am doomed for eternity."

37

I<small>T WAS EARLY SPRING</small> when Constantine and his party debarked at Caesarea and began a leisurely overland journey to Jerusalem. The younger Eusebius, Bishop of Caesarea, accompanied the Emperor at his request, riding beside the horsedrawn litter upon which Constantine rested. Once they left the coastal plain and began to ascend the high ridge of hills among which Jerusalem lay, the country grew rapidly more bleak and forbidden, yet touches of rare beauty could be seen here and there, softening the stark rocky masses.

Grapes grew well upon the lower slopes and every town was surrounded by its own cluster of arbors and olive groves on terraced hillsides. In places, the burnet thorn that covered many of the hills with a blanket of dark shining green was already in bloom, spattering the terrain with patterns of scarlet which, at close range, looked startlingly like drops of blood. Here and there an additional burst of color announced the early blooming of spring flowers such as daffodils, sea-leek, star-shaped "Flowers of Sharon" and "cuckoo flowers," forming a pristine white background for clumps of lilac.

"It's hard to believe yonder bush with the red blossom formed the cruel crown of thorns pressed upon the Saviour's brow before he was crucified," Eusebius said. "But if you were to look closely, Dominus, you would see the spikes behind the green leaves and the scarlet blossoms."

"I've noticed before that outward beauty often hides an inner cruelty," Constantine said and Eusebius understood that he was speaking of Fausta.

"Perhaps that is God's way of keeping us from being so taken with beauty that we forget its sources, Dominus."

"The same God who created the blossoms and the leaves also made the painful thorns, Eusebius. Lately it seems I cannot reach out to touch one without being pricked by the other."

"Wait until you see the Church of the Anastasis you have built on the site of the Holy Sepulcher. Only beauty can be there, never pain."

"Yet it was built at Aelia Capitolina—Jerusalem—where Christ suffered his greatest agony."

"And his Resurrection, Dominus, the climax of his ministry."

"I only wish my mother could have lived to dedicate it," Constantine said wistfully.

"Surely she died happy in the knowledge that the church would soon be finished."

"I would like to think so; she had little else to be happy about during those last days. You know she never forgave me for Crispus' death."

"But you were not to blame."

"I ask no absolution from you, Eusebius. The Bishop of Nicomedia gave me that long ago, but his words brought no peace to my soul. I come to Syria Palaestina now, hoping to find some form of absolution from God himself, though I can hardly believe I could discover it in this bleak and forbidding country."

"You have taken too much of the burden of guilt upon yourself, Dominus," Eusebius protested. "One of Israel's greatest kings saw his rebellious son killed not far from here. His sorrow was as great as yours, yet God forgave him and another son of his went on to build the first temple to the glory of God."

"Dacius told me the story long ago," Constantine said, "but I've forgotten the details."

"The king was David, who established Jerusalem as the Holy City of his people. The son was named Absalom. He was too impatient to wait for his father to yield the throne so he led a rebellion. But in the course of the fighting he was cut down when his long hair became caught in a tree."

"Did David mourn the traitor son who sought to destroy him?"

"Yes, Dominus. In one of the most moving passages in the holy writings of the Jewish people, he cried out: 'O my son Absalom, my son, my son Absalom! Would God I had died for thee, O Absalom, my son, my son!'"

"I too know the pain from which such a cry can come." Constantine's voice broke momentarily. "I knew Crispus was capable of ruling the Empire and, if I had possessed the wisdom of Diocletian, I would have announced earlier that he would succeed me at the end of twenty years. But my selfish desire for power would not let me relinquish it, so I can only hold myself responsible for his death."

"You forget that the Empire quickly went to pieces after the abdication of Emperor Diocletian," Eusebius reminded him. "Had not a man of strength who trusted also in God—yourself—arisen to save it, Rome might now be ruled by its enemies and Christians everywhere would be living in bondage, if indeed the church were not completely destroyed."

"Then you think God will one day forgive me?"

"I know he will, Dominus. God is merciful and no one ever deserved his mercy more than you."

II

The dedication of the beautiful new church on the holiest spot in Christendom, site of the very tomb where Jesus of Nazareth had risen from the dead, was an impressive and moving ceremony. It was conducted by the Bishop of Jerusalem, assisted by Eusebius of Caesarea. But when it was over and the low-voiced chant of the white-robed catechumens—converts receiving instructions in the fundamentals of the Christian faith—had died away, Constantine had still not found the peace and absolution for which he had come to Jerusalem.

Overcome by a great weariness and depression of spirit at the prospect of the long journey to Dura on the banks of the Euphrates, which now seemed his only hope, he returned to the palace of the Bishop of Jerusalem, where he was staying. There, weary and uncomfortable from the pain in his chest, which had returned during the trip from Caesarea, he went early to his couch and fell immediately into the troubled sleep that gave him so little rest. Awakening just before dawn, he rose from his couch and, without disturbing his servant, went out upon the balcony outside his bedroom, hoping his breathing would be easier in the open air.

The building occupied the very crown of the rocky escarpment upon which Jerusalem was built and as he looked to the east, he could see the earliest rays of the sun, painting a line of brightness across the tops of the dark mountain range beyond the Jordan. It seemed eons ago since he and Dacius, with the five hundred cavalry placed under his command at Alexandria by Emperor Diocletian, had ridden northward along the banks of the Jordan at the foot of those very hills, on their way to meet the troops of Galerius in Augusta Euphratensia.

In those same forest-clad slopes east of the Jordan river, lying in the deep rift where it was always summer, King David had mourned a rebellious Absalom more than a thousand years ago, according to the story Eusebius had told him. Going back into the room, he picked up a scroll Eusebius had given him containing the psalms of David and returned to the balcony, where he lifted the scroll and, in the faint morning light, began to read. And as he did, his voice unconsciously took on the impassioned cry which, he was sure, had marked David's own plea to God for mercy:

"My God, my God, why hast thou forsaken me? Why art thou so far from helping me, and from the words of my roaring?

O my God, I cry in the daytime, but thou hearest not; and in the night season, and am not silent. . . .

Be not far from me; for trouble is near; for there is none to help. . . .

Be not far from me, O Lord: O my strength, haste thee to help me."

Dropping the scroll to the stone floor of the balcony, Constantine fell upon his knees with his eyes uplifted in humble entreaty to heaven, confessing his sins once again and begging forgiveness. As his impassioned cry to the God to whose glory he had dedicated an empire was wrested from the depths of his being, a deep stillness seemed to fall upon the balcony where he knelt. And in the midst of it, he heard in his heart and soul a familiar voice saying:

"Come unto me, all ye that labor and are heavy laden, and I will give you rest. Take my yoke upon you, and learn of me; for I am meek and lowly in heart: and ye shall find rest unto your souls."

With those reassuring words from the man who had guided him since that night at Dura so long ago, when he had gone alone with a torch to look at the painting of the Shepherd of Galilee on the crumbling walls of the abandoned church, Constantine felt the burden of guilt and sin he had carried so long lifted from his shoulders. For a little while longer he remained kneeling, with tears of joy streaming down his face. Then rising to his feet, he re-entered the room and lay down to a restful and dreamless sleep for the first time in the many months since that tragic day in Rome.

Constantine's spirit was now at peace, but he recognized, and accepted as God's will, the burden of what he now knew was his final illness. The pain and sense of constriction in his chest grew steadily worse on the journey from Jerusalem to Caesarea and he yielded quite willingly to Eusebius' entreaties that he remain there for a few days and be treated by the bishop's own physician, before going aboard the galley for the return to Nova Roma.

The physician was a Greek and highly skilled. He recommended bleeding in order to decrease some of the plethora that now suffused the sick man's face and body, making even breathing difficult. The effect of the blood-letting was so dramatic that Constantine felt able to embark upon the galley for the journey at once. The physician assured him that it was only temporary, however, and long before the spires of the great new eastern capital came into view, both the pain and swelling had returned with increased severity.

Carried to the magnificent new baths he had built in Nova Roma, the ailing Emperor found no relief. Certain now that the hand of death was upon him, he had himself borne by galley across the straits to Drepanum and his mother's home there—maintained since her death as a shrine. But though prayers were offered up continuously in the Church of Lucian the Martyr at Drepanum for the now desperately ill Emperor, he continued to grow worse and summoned Bishop Eusebius of Nicomedia to his side.

"In Jerusalem, Christ spoke to me while I prayed and took the burden of my sins upon himself," Constantine told the churchman. "It remains only for me to be baptized now, so I can go joyously to meet him."

"I will prepare for it at once, Dominus."

"Not here. I wish to receive final absolution in the Church of St. Lucian. It stands upon ground dear to me from the past."

Through the streets, Constantine's litter was borne by six captains of the household troops, who had been closest to him throughout the years, to the beautiful new church which had replaced the building where he had first heard Theognis of Nicaea preach and where he and Minervina had recited their wedding vows. When the litter was placed before the altar, he put off the purple cloak of an Emperor. Wearing the white robe of a catechumen and humbly begging to know the mysteries of his faith, he knelt to confess his sins publicly and was baptized by Bishop Eusebius at the font in the baptistery of the church.

"Now I know in very truth that I am blessed!" Constantine cried as he rose from his knees. "Now I have confidence that I am a partaker of divine light!"

The effort of the journey to the church and the baptism had exhausted the dying Emperor. At his request, the litter was carried to his chariot, where it was placed for the short drive to his palace at the edge of Nicomedia. That afternoon a stream of people from all levels passed through the room to bid their ruler farewell. Toward evening the pain became more than he could bear and he allowed the Greek physician, who had come with him from Caesarea, to mix a strong draft of an opiate for him.

Shortly he fell into a deep sleep, but roused after about an hour to ask whether any of his sons had arrived. When he was informed that Constantius II, the nearest, was expected hourly, he drifted back into a sleep haunted no longer by the dreams and nightmares that had troubled him for years, until he'd found peace in the dawn's light that morning in Jerusalem.

As he slept he became conscious of a familiar face taking form in the shadowy darkness surrounding him. It was the Shepherd of Dura, but instead of the familiar wooden crook, Jesus now carried the labarum, as he had that night at Saxa Rubra. And when he reached his hand out to Constantine in a beckoning gesture, the dying man suddenly found that his swollen limbs and body were weightless. Joyously, then, he rose from the couch and took the hand that guided him, as they traversed the darkness together toward the light beyond which, he knew now with a surge of joy, there would be no guilt or sorrow to burden a soul freed from all pain and all grief.

"He is smiling!" the physician standing beside the couch cried. "The poppy has taken away the pain."

But neither the physician nor the graying bishop standing beside the couch could know what had really taken away the pain and given Constantine a joy greater than he had ever known, even as Emperor of Rome. It was the gentle voice to which he was listening, the voice that had said so long ago, in a promise sacred to all who would believe and trust in him:

"Let not your heart be troubled: ye believe in God, believe also in me. In my Father's house are many mansions: if it were not so, I would have told you. I go to prepare a place for you. And if I go and prepare a place for you, I will come again, and receive you unto myself; that where I am, there ye may be also."

AUTHOR'S NOTES

Constantine the Great died on May 22, A.D. 337, and was buried in the Church of the Twelve Apostles at Constantinople—now Istanbul. Almost from the day of his death, a controversy raged concerning his true relationship to the Christian faith. Many have labeled him an opportunist, who saw in the highly organized structure of the Christian Church in his day an opportunity to utilize this vital force in gaining power for himself. Others credit him with being sincere in his choice of Christianity over paganism and the weight of historical evidence confirms this latter assumption.

In any event, the facts are unassailable that Constantine was baptized and died a Christian, the first Christian ruler of the Roman Empire. And that he favored Christianity to the point where, during his reign of a little over thirty years, that faith grew to a position of power and influence among the people which it had never enjoyed before. Moreover, since the time of Constantine, Christianity has never ceased to be a major force in the shaping of civilization and in the course of world affairs.

By placing religion in an intimate relationship with secular affairs, Constantine undoubtedly laid the groundwork for the political difficulties that led to turmoil between church and state in later centuries and even to wars between nations. Judged by any standard, however, he was a great emperor and a military genius whose bravery upon the battlefield was proved over and over. And if as an administrator, he was perhaps considerably less than perfect, allowing an intricate and top-heavy bureaucracy to develop in connection with the affairs of the Roman Empire, he may perhaps be forgiven on the grounds that during his lifetime he was troubled by more incidents of treachery, even within his own household, than any man should have to face.

More than sixteen centuries after the tragic events occurred, mystery still surrounds the affair which resulted in the deaths of Crispus, Fausta and Licinianus. Constantine's first biographer, Eusebius of Caesarea, does not even mention the incident. Less sympathetic writers, who lived and wrote during the same period, denounce him as a murderer, while others lay all blame on Fausta and her ambitions, perhaps with equal reason. Whatever Constantine's personal guilt or innocence in the matter may have been, there can be no doubt that the events changed him into a brooding sorrowful man, whose despotic tendencies increased as his reign continued.

As always in dramatizing people and periods of ancient history, I have consulted hundred of references. Of them, four have yielded more information than all others combined and to them I wish to acknowledge my indebtedness. They are: *The Decline and Fall of the Roman Empire*, Volume One, by Edward Gibbon, published as a Modern Library Giant; *Constantine the Great* by J. B. Firth, G. P. Putnam's Sons, London, 1904; *The Life of the Blessed Emperor Constantine* by Eusebius Pamphili, from the same author's *Ecclesiastical History*; and *The Cambridge Medieval History*, Volume One.

Constantine is the first in a series of dramatized biographies of major figures in the history of religion, to be published from time to time under the general title of *The Pathway of Faith*. The choice of the Age of Constantine for the initial volume in this series was dictated by the fact that, as the first Christian Emperor of Rome and one of its greatest rulers, he changed the church from a persecuted minority into a vital world force which—though threatened a few times, as in the abortive attempt of Julian the Apostate to reassert paganism as the Roman religion—has steadily continued to grow and spread across the face of the earth. Future volumes will cover other major crises in the story of faith, told by dramatically re-creating the lives of men and women who played a major part in that story.

FRANK G. SLAUGHTER

November 8, 1964
Jacksonville, Florida

Frank G. Slaughter is one of America's most popular and prolific authors. A member of Phi Beta Kappa at the age of seventeen, he graduated from Johns Hopkins Medical School at twenty-two, and commanded an Army Hospital ship in the Pacific during World War II. His many novels include *Epidemic!*, *The Curse of Jezebel*, *Devil's Harvest*, *The Thorn of Arimathea*, and *A Savage Place*.